Arousing the Legacy

The Colville Mysteries

A.J. Raven

Arousing the Legacy

The Colville Mysteries

The contents of this book constitute a work of fiction. All events, themes, persons, characters, and plots are fictional inventions of the author. Any resemblance and/or reference to actual events, as well as to any persons living, deceased, or yet to be born is purely coincidental and entirely unintentional.

Beau to Beau Publishing
E-mail: info@beautobeau.com
Website: http://www.beautobeau.com
ISBN: 978-1-6184-5245-0
Printed in the United States of America

Arousing the Legacy centers around the small town of Colville which appears to have been chosen by a paranormal power for a very deliberate purpose. It is up to a small group of friends to discover what that purpose is and why their town was chosen, all while encountering vampires, werewolves, and zombies, and barely escaping with their lives. But could one of their own be among the paranormal?

Table of Contents

The Secret page 9

When four friends explore a nearby cave, a transformation begins to occur in one of them. Soon afterward, he leaves town, but while he is away a creature of some type begins killing at random, feeding off of his victims like a werewolf. Determined to find the killer, the group of friends set out on a quest that leads them to an unlikely source and into a well designed trap for which they are not prepared.

The Swamp page 85

A trip to a swamp believed to be haunted is intriguing to the group of friends, and what they find is disturbing, to say the least. The pale, yellow green water looks sickening and there are bodies in the swamp. After this discovery, along with moans in the night, the rumors of a haunted swamp and the zombies within it are a little more believable.

The Cold page 163

When the group of friends come upon a car crashed into a tree, they are surprised to find that the woman inside is alive. She tells the group that she and her co-worker had been filming the abandoned Singleton residence for a news report when it grew cold inside of the house. They left and walked toward the swamp not far from the abandoned abode. The swamp was frozen, with thinner ice in places and frozen footprints emanating from the swamp and going into the forest…human footprints. Thinking that the prints were made by kids as a joke, the two reporters followed them and noticed what appeared to be an animal or a human zoom into the trees. Assuming that the creature was hiding, the man approached it, and the couple found themselves surrounded by bodies staring at them. The news duo turned and ran back to their car where they found another creature preventing them from getting away. The creature grabbed the man's neck as the woman screamed and watched helplessly as the creature dragged her co-worker into the forest… The group of friends are mesmerized by the woman's story and set out to solve the mystery.

The Moon page 269

The man who came to Colville knew there was something unique about the young men he was ordered to observe. They had been able to ward off a curse and survive a vampire attack. The man had spent most of the day observing the town and keeping an eye on the young men. One was ill and the man knew why. The other one had no idea he was being followed, but as far as the man was concerned, he was a below average werewolf at best. Still, there had to be a reason for a vampire to show up in Colville, other than creating two werewolf slaves.

The Secret

One

It was a regular sunny day in the quiet small town of Colville and four teenaged friends were having lunch at their favorite fast food joint, *Fries*.

"Nothing good happens here," complained Anya, a girl with long black hair and bright brown eyes, as she played with her French fries.

"What's your definition of good?" questioned a tall black haired boy in glasses.

"Get a life, Eric," said Carl to his bespectacled friend. He passed his hand through his brown curly hair. "Don't be serious all the time."

"Anya, can I have your burger?" asked Susan. Without waiting for an answer, she picked up Anya's half eaten burger and put it on her empty plate. Susan loved to eat and she never got fat, even though she never exercised.

Anya watched as Susan gobbled up the burger. "Don't you ever get fat?"

"Nope," Susan answered casually, brushing her blonde hair out of the way.

"I'm getting bored," said Carl as he suppressed a yawn. "Let's go out for a walk."

"Nah, can't do that," Eric replied. "I've got some work to do in the garden."

The three of them watched as Eric walked out of the restaurant without saying another word to them.

"We have been together for nine months and still he doesn't feel at ease around us," said Anya in disbelief.

"He's complicated," said Susan with a smile. "With his parents moving from country to country, it must be tough."

Eric lived alone in his house, and his parents were abroad. The three friends felt that he was lonely all by himself in the house at the age of fifteen. They never asked him about his parents, about what they did and why they never came to meet him, and he never mentioned them either. The friends talked about Eric as they walked toward the town's forest. It had its own stories about witches and magical creatures that supposedly lived inside.

As if, thought Anya as the friends reached the forest. *I have been living in this town my entire life and I've never encountered anything out of the ordinary*.

Colville was a quiet town and everyone minded their own business. Wishing for something exciting to happen was like wishing that pigs could fly. But all of that was about to change. Something sinister had already entered Colville and the teenaged friends were oblivious to it as they walked further into the forest.

"What is he doing there?" questioned Anya, pointing at a known figure.

"Eric," said Carl, walking toward him. "You told us that you had work to do in your garden."

"So I did," answered Eric. He was sitting on a rock just a little into the forest, looking at the trees.

"You could have told us," said Susan. "We're your friends, you know."

"And so you are," said Eric. He was still looking at the trees with a strange expression on his face.

Anya gave Susan a look that clearly meant, 'He is impossible.'

"Since we are already here," said Carl, talking to the group at large. "Why don't we explore?"

"I have to clean my room," said Eric, getting onto his feet.

Anya felt that was Eric's kind way of saying, 'I've got better things to do'. And he was right. Anya had explored the forest more times than she bothered to count and she too was not in the mood to add another exploration trip to the total number.

"Lame excuse, my boy," smiled Carl, and he put an arm around Eric's shoulder.

"Come on," urged Susan. She looked at Eric and Anya. "It'll be fun."

"Okay, fine," replied Eric, as he adjusted his glasses and sounded bored. "Let's go."

I would rather go to the mall, thought Anya. She noticed Susan looking at her and sighed. "Fine," she answered, and Susan smiled.

The four friends walked further into the forest with Carl in the lead. The trees, the rocks, everything was just as Anya remembered, old and creepy looking. After a while they reached the caves. Even the caves were rumored to be magical. There were three caves inside the forest and the friends had searched each of them as thoroughly as they could. There were many stories about strange monsters living inside the caves, but that was all they were, stories told by the town's people to scare little children from wandering off alone, or so the friends had thought.

"Want to go inside?" Carl asked with a smile.

"We need a torch, a flashlight," said Susan and looked at the others. "Anyone got one?"

"I have one," Eric replied, and he took out a flashlight from inside his pants pocket.

"Then let's go," said Carl.

They walked into the cave in the middle. The walls looked strong and the roof was quite high. *Just as it always is*, thought Anya as they walked a little farther into the cave and the light began to dim.

"Stay close," said Eric, and he switched on the flashlight.

"We shouldn't be going too far inside," warned Susan. She felt Anya holding her hand. "Getting scared?" she whispered to Anya with a smile.

"Yeah, sure," she replied, rolling her eyes and immediately letting go of Susan's hand.

Anya didn't know why she was getting the feeling that something bad was about to happen. She began to feel uncomfortable walking in the cave with her friends even though she had done it plenty of times before. She looked at her friends. They seemed calm. *Stop it!* Anya scolded herself. *Nothing bad is going to happen*.

"What's that shine?" asked Carl.

"It's all around us," said Eric. He flashed the beam from his flashlight all around himself.

The four of them were looking at a sparkle coming out from the cave walls. It was giving a beautiful shine.

"I've never seen that before," said Anya confused. She looked at the beautiful green shine. It was if the cave walls had turned into green emeralds.

"What is it?" questioned Carl, and he went closer to the walls.

"Don't touch it," said Eric, looking worried.

"It feels kind of funny," said Carl as he placed his finger on the cave wall to his right. "It feels so wonderful."

The friends watched as Carl placed his palm on the wall.

"Are you all right, Carl?" asked Eric.

Carl's face was giving an expression as if he was in a wonderful dream. The girls stood still, silent.

"I can't resist it," replied Carl. "It wants me. I've to go!"

"Stop him!" yelled Eric, and he grabbed Carl by the arm and pulled.

"What are you doing?" he screamed, trying to break free from Eric's grip.

Anya rushed forward, grabbed Carl by the collar and pulled. He was still trying to reach for the cave wall and was yelling a lot, trying to throw the two off of him.

Then everything happened in a flash. There was a loud bang and a lot of green light, the sound of someone screaming, and the four friends found themselves lying on the ground.

"What happened?" questioned Carl as Eric helped him onto his feet.

"You don't remember anything?" asked Susan, worried about him.

"I do remember feeling wonderful and happy," Carl replied. He looked confused.

"What made that loud bang, anyway?" Eric asked, cleaning his glasses.

"I don't know," Susan replied. "But I know one thing, and that is not to come here again."

"I agree," said Anya. She brushed dirt off of her shirt when suddenly her eyes noticed something.

"What's that?" she asked, looking at Carl's hand.

Carl lifted his hand and appeared afraid as well as confused. His palm was giving a faint pink glow and it felt wet and cold.

"We need to show this to a doctor," said Susan.

"There are no doctors here," said Eric, looking at Carl's palm. "He'll have to go out of town."

"Guys, I know this means nothing," said Carl trying to be cool. "Let's just get out of here."

The cave walls were still glowing green and none of the friends felt comfortable staying there after what they had just been through. Eric, Anya and Susan, still worrying about Carl, followed him out of the cave. They walked toward his house and waved him goodbye, and then each of them left for their own home.

***

The next day Anya was applying makeup just for fun when the phone rang.

"Anya, it's for you," came her mother's voice from downstairs.

"Coming!" she yelled back to her mother. *I seriously need a phone in my room.*

She put her nail polish back on her vanity and went downstairs. Her mother was watching some soap on the television.

"Anya speaking," she said, answering the phone in the kitchen.

"Anya," answered a familiar voice. "It's Susan."

"What's up?"

"Nothing, just getting bored," Susan replied. "Want to go out?"

"Where to?"

"Just a walk around town with the others," said Susan. "We're going to meet outside of Carl's."

"Count me in," said Anya. "See you all later."

A few minutes later, after going outside, Anya saw Eric and Susan standing outside of Carl's house and they looked a bit worried. Eric was talking to Carl's mother.

"He said that he was going out with you," said Mrs. Smith.

"He wasn't with us," said Eric. "We haven't seen him all day. We came here to pick him up."

"Well, he is going to be in trouble," said Mrs. Smith sternly. "Find him for me, dears."

"We'll send him home," said Susan. They both waved at Mrs. Smith and walked away.

Anya walked toward her friends. "What happened?"

"Carl isn't home," Susan replied. "He went somewhere on his own without telling his mother."

"You have any idea where he might have gone?" Anya asked. *This was an unusual thing for Carl to do*.

"I'll go and check our common hangouts," said Eric. "You two check the forest as well as the cave."

"We'll meet you in the forest!" yelled Susan as Eric ran away. The girls saw him give a nod and then he ran out of sight.

"He couldn't have gone in there," said Anya, thinking of the cave and what they had faced yesterday. "Am I right?"

"It's Carl we are talking about," said Susan. "Going to creepy caves is his idea of fun. Now, come on."

The two girls made their way through the forest, looking in every direction for any sign of their friend. Finally, they stopped outside of the caves.

"You don't reckon?" asked Anya, watching the cave's mouth, the same cave they had been in a day ago.

Susan nodded and went into the cave holding Anya's hand in hers.

"I don't think he's in here," said Anya in a different voice from hers. There was no need for a flashlight as the cave was emitting a light greenish glow.

"We have to check either way," said Susan. "Stay close."

The two of them walked on a little, hoping to find Carl and get out of the cave as quickly as possible. Suddenly the girls found themselves surrounded by a strong green glow and Anya noticed a figure some feet away from her.

"Oh, my God!" Anya exclaimed in a high voice.

"Carl," said Susan. "Are you okay?" She ran forward and grabbed Carl who was lying on the ground. He was wearing a cloak so Susan couldn't make out the face.

"Blood!" said the figure in a deep voice.

"Carl, get up," said Anya, inching forward with reluctance. She was having the same feelings she had yesterday inside the cave. "What are you doing lying on the ground?"

Susan placed her hand on his shoulder. He turned around to face her and Susan screamed as he yelled, "Blood!"

He stood up. His face was horrifying. His eyes were blood red and had cat-like slits for pupils, and his teeth were two inches long like a vampire's teeth. The creature had claw-like nails on long fingers and looked hungrily at Susan who stood frozen with fear in front of it.

"Carl?" said Susan in a weak whisper, unable to move.

"Blood," said the cloaked figure hungrily. In a second he jumped on Susan and pinned her to the ground.

"Get off!" yelled Susan, fighting him.

It took a long sniff and lowered its head toward Susan's neck, giving a small laugh as it saw the blood running through her veins. Unable to do anything, Susan closed her eyes waiting for the pain, but it never came. She looked up and noticed that Anya had grabbed the creature by the neck. It gave an angry yell and threw Anya four feet away into the air and turned its attention toward her. It got up and slowly walked toward Anya, ready to strike, but suddenly it dropped to the ground.

"Anya!" said Susan, helping her friend back onto her feet. "Are you all right?"

"Just go," Anya answered. She grabbed Susan's hand and ran toward the cave's mouth without looking back.

"Guys?" came Eric's surprised voice as the two reached the exit. "What happened?"

"Carl," Susan replied in a hurry. "Vampire... Tried to bite me...He's a vampire...must get out...NOW!"

"Hold on," said Eric, grabbing Susan's shoulders and shaking her a little.

"But Carl's a vampire!" said Anya out of breath.

"What are you talking about?" asked Eric confused. "I met Carl in the forest awhile ago. He was just roaming around."

"Then where is he?" asked the girls together. They both looked behind Eric, as if to see Carl. "Where is he?"

"He's at home," he replied calmly. Then Anya saw Eric look at Susan in a strange way. "Why do you look worried?" he asked, looking straight at her.

"No…I'm all right," said Susan. "Let's just go home."

They started to walk out of the cave, but Anya stopped Susan.

"What is it?" she asked as Eric continued to walk away.

"I believe what I saw," Anya replied. She was close to tears now. "I'm going to keep an eye on him from now on."

"Are you girls coming or not?" came Eric's voice from ahead of them before Susan could answer Anya.

"Coming," said Susan, and she walked toward Eric, and Anya followed, confused about what she had just encountered. Colville had begun to change for the worse.

Two

That night a woman came out of her house to throw away her trash bags when she heard some movements behind her.

"Mr. Tinkles, it's not very nice to come home this late," she called out to her cat. She put the bags in the trash can near the road and headed toward her house. The woman walked toward her front door when suddenly it closed in her face. She backed away in fear.

"Who's there?" she asked, her voice trembling. The street lamps dimmed and then went out. Both ends of the street were dark. The woman tried to open the door but it wouldn't budge. She began to panic. The icy wind made her look behind her toward the street when she saw it, a person wearing a long cloak walking toward her, or floating, she couldn't tell. The woman tried to scream but no sound came out of her mouth. Her eyes looked around. There was no one who could come to her help even if she screamed. Her neighborhood always went to bed early. That was why she had chosen this place. She liked the peace and quiet.

The cloaked figure came toward the woman. Her mouth was open, even if no sound came out of her. Their eyes met and she knew that it was the end for her. The creature lowered its face toward her neck, its fangs gleaming in the moonlight as they sensed flesh. The woman looked at the creature. She could feel its icy breath upon her neck. She couldn't move or run away from death even though she tried. Then she felt it, a chill, as the fangs went into her neck pressing inward. She felt dizzy as she sensed something sticky coming out. *My blood!* she thought, and her knees gave way, causing her to fall to the ground, the creature still biting into her and draining her of life.

***

Anya woke up the next morning and went into the kitchen to see her parents looking serious. She sat down on a chair in front of the table and looked at them puzzled.

"What is it?" she asked. She had never seen her parents act this way before.

"You know your Aunt Mary?" her mother replied slowly. "She died last night."

"What?" cried Anya, her eyes were wide open. "How? Who?" She could feel her brain trying to make sense of everything.

"She went out to throw away her trash bags," replied her mom. "The police said that it was a maniac who did it."

"Are you two going out of town to her place then?" Anya asked. Her aunt was such a nice person. Who would do such a thing to her?

"Yes," her father replied. "We'll be back in a few hours."

They were already ready, so they hugged her goodbye. Anya really wanted to go but her parents wouldn't let her as they knew she didn't feel comfortable at funerals. She watched her parents drive off and then began reading the newspaper at the kitchen table. The attack was the main headline. She was halfway through when the phone rang.

"Hello?"

"Anya, it's me," came a voice. "Susan."

"Hi," she replied in a weak voice.

"I read about your aunt," said Susan. "I'm really sorry."

"She wasn't my real aunt. She was my father's cousin, but still…."

"You must be really sad," said Susan. "Want to go somewhere and talk? You know, clear your head?"

"Susan, do you think it wasn't a person?"

"What do you mean?" asked Susan.

"You know exactly what I mean," replied Anya as she remembered her visit to the cave.

"You don't mean Carl, do you?"

"I don't know," Anya replied. *I don't know. Maybe.*

"Anya, Carl had a sleepover at Eric's last night," said Susan. "His parents had to go out to some party."

Anya didn't answer.

"And besides," said Susan. "Your aunt lived in another town. How do you suppose Carl went there without Eric noticing?"

"Fine," said Anya, giving it a rest. "Meet you at the park," she added and hung up. She wrote a message to her parents on a piece of paper and left it on the kitchen table. She put on her shoes and locked the front door.

Colville had two parks. One had playing equipment in it and the other had a lot of trees and that was where the group always met. Anya went into the park and sat down on the bench. The park was deserted.

"Anya," cried Susan walking toward her through the rusty gate followed by Eric, and to her disgust, Carl Smith, who was smiling at her.

"Are you all right?" Susan asked, placing her hand on Anya's shoulder with concern in her eyes. "I told the guys about…"

"I'm all right," Anya cut through, her voice dry, so unlike hers.

"You liked her, didn't you?" Carl asked.

Of course I liked her, you oaf, she thought. *How could you even ask such a thing after you…after you…*

"Anya!" cried Susan, shaking her by the shoulders. She seemed to have zoned out. "Are you sure you're fine?"

"I really didn't want to hurt your feelings," said Carl apologetically.

"No, it's nothing," Anya replied. "Let's go for a walk. I want some air."

The four of them headed toward the gate of the park and went down the street, when suddenly Anya stopped in her tracks. Did she just see a red gleam in Carl's eyes as he walked past her?

"Anya, are you coming or not?" Susan yelled. Her friends were six feet ahead of her.

"Coming," she replied, shaking her head and running toward them.

The four friends walked on and reached *Fries* and ordered some food, as Eric said that eating helped with stress release. Anya was about to bite into her sandwich when she looked at Carl sitting in front of her and noticed something. Carl was wearing a glove on his right hand.

"What's that?" she asked.

Carl noticed Anya watching his hand. "It's nothing to worry about."

"We told you to show it to a doctor," said Anya. *What's this?* she thought. *First I was feeling angry at Carl and now I'm feeling worried for him. What is happening to me?*

"And Eric told you that there aren't any doctors here," said Carl defensively.

"Well, give me your hand," said Eric, putting his coke aside.

"I don't know…you know," Carl hesitated.

"He wouldn't even show it to us," said Susan, eating her food. "And we've asked him twice already," she told Anya.

Defeated, Carl looked to see if anyone else was watching them and took the glove by the fingertip and pulled it off of his right hand.

"What is that?" Susan asked, her eyes wide open as she looked at his hand.

The three of them stared at the purple scales that covered Carl's hand. The fingers had brown nails that were sharp at the ends. Carl felt embarrassed and put the glove back on.

"You shouldn't have touched the wall," said Eric slowly.

"Don't you think I know that by now?" Carl replied. He was feeling irritated.

"It looks like a mutation," said Susan to no one in particular.

He's not a mutant, thought Anya. *He's a blood thirsty vampire.*

"We should go back into the cave," Eric suggested, looking seriously at everyone.

"I'm not going back in there," cried Anya at once.

"Well, I'm going," said Eric getting up. "We have to examine that wall."

Susan got up and looked at Anya. Anya looked at Carl who was looking down at his empty plate. "Oh, all right." Anya rolled her eyes at Susan. "But I know I'll regret it later."

Carl looked at Eric who was looking back at him, and got up with a sigh. They paid for the food and walked toward the forest. Strangely, it had begun to get dark early as the friends walked toward the forest.

"Come on," said Eric with a weak smile as he switched on his flashlight in front of the cave. He led the way and the girls followed with Carl behind them. Eric moved the beam of light from side to side. They were in complete darkness, and there wasn't any sign of the strange green light.

"We are surely not in the wrong cave, right?" Anya asked worried.

Eric didn't say anything and kept on walking. Anya began to panic. *What if we just keep on walking and Carl turns into a vampire and kills us all,* she thought as she followed Eric deeper into the cave.

"Oh!" cried Susan as they were suddenly surrounded by green light being emitted by the cave walls around them.

"I don't like this," said Carl. He was holding his right arm tightly as if it was going to run away from him.

"The light's getting brighter," said Anya. She began to feel as if the cave walls were closing in on her and trying to suffocate her. "Let's get out of here," she added, grabbing Susan who was standing very still.

"I just need a sample," said Eric as he started to break out a piece of the wall.

"Eric, hurry!" Carl yelled. He looked as if he was about to throw up. The light began to glow red and Carl began to cough madly. Eric put a small piece of the cave wall into a plastic bag. "Come on," he said, grabbing Carl by the shoulder. Helped by Susan, Eric supported Carl and followed Anya out of the cave.

"Are you all right?" Susan asked as Carl sat down on a rock, exhausted.

He took some deep breaths. "I was suffocating in there," he replied, soothing his neck, looking dreadful.

"I'd better take you home," said Eric, and nodding at the girls, he walked Carl away.

"I still think Carl's a vampire," said Anya, watching the boys disappear. She turned to face Susan. "You believe me, don't you?"

"Of course I believe you, Anya," Susan answered as they walked through the forest. "But if he really was a vampire, he could have killed us anytime he wanted to."

"He's waiting for the right time."

"Anya, I just don't…"

"His hand, Susan! His abnormal hand!" cried Anya. She couldn't believe what her best friend had just said. "You saw what happened in the cave yesterday."

"It didn't really look like Carl," said Susan as the two girls reached Susan's house. "Give it a rest."

Something is really wrong, thought Anya as she waved Susan goodbye and walked toward home. *Why would Susan deny what I just told her about Carl?* She opened the front door of her house. *If Susan needs proof, then I'll give her proof.*

***

Anya sat down on her couch and surfed through the channels. There was supposed to be a movie starring Tom Cruise on tonight. It struck ten and Anya began to worry about her parents. *Surely it doesn't take this long at a funeral,* she thought angrily. She tried their mobiles but they were switched off. She lay down on the sofa to relax when suddenly.

"AAHHHhhh!"

Anya lifted herself up from the floor. The phone ringing had taken her by surprise. "Hello!" No answer. There was only the sound of someone breathing very slowly at the other end. "Hello!" she said again, and again there was no answer. *Weird,* she thought and hung up.

Three

Anya was walking with Susan in her backyard and telling her about the strange call she had gotten last night. "So what do you suppose?" she asked her friend.

But Susan stood still with a strange expression on her face. Anya followed her gaze and noticed a boy, a tall boy with black hair, bright blue eyes, and a body that definitely looked like it went to the gym on a regular basis.

"Who the hell is he?" asked Susan, shocked as the boy went into the house next to Anya's. "He's going to move in," she added jumping in joy. "He's going to live right next to you. You have to ask him out."

Anya couldn't stop herself from jumping as she noticed a 'moving van' stop outside of the house next to hers.

"I'm going to be his girlfriend," she said, all of her worries gone. She couldn't remember when she last had a boyfriend.

"Not if I get him first," Susan told her with a smile.

***

"Eric, do you know the new boy?" asked Anya.

The four friends had gathered in Eric's garden and were drinking lemonade.

"His name is David," he answered casually. He wasn't a bit interested in why Anya was asking him. "David Rodgers."

"What's up with you?" Susan asked, looking at Carl, who had his hand against his forehead.

"Nothing important, just a slight headache," he answered and immediately withdrew his hand and grabbed his glass of lemonade from the ground.

Susan opened her mouth to say something but her watch started to beep. "I need to go to the butcher," she said, looking at her watch. "Need to buy food for Lizzie."

Lizzie, short for Elizabeth, was Susan's dog. She had found her as a puppy living under a cardboard box and had taken her in two years ago. Having nothing better to do, the friends decided to go with Susan to the butcher shop. *What wouldn't I do to have the people build a cinema in this town,* thought Anya as she walked alongside her friends to the shop. Summer vacations in Colville weren't the most exciting of times. In a few minutes, the four had reached the butcher shop and they went inside.

"Good day, George," said Susan as she smiled at the butcher.

"Same to you, miss," the man smiled back.

Everything was going the same way it always did. Anya was looking outside from the shop's windows as people passed by. Eric was examining the scales placed on one of the shelves. Carl should have been with Eric, telling him to get a new socially acceptable hobby, but this time around Carl was looking at a very large piece of meat placed on the counter. He slowly walked toward it. The smell was unbearable. It was attracting him and he watched as his own hands picked up the meat.

"Carl, what the…!" yelled Eric.

Carl looked at him and then at the piece of raw meat into which he was biting. He threw it away in disgust, his mouth full of blood.

"Come on," said Eric, and he walked Carl out of the shop.

Susan paid the shocked butcher. "He hasn't been feeling well," she said as the butcher forced a smile. "Anyway, thank you for the meat, George."

Anya looked at Susan and both of them walked out of the shop without saying a word to each other.

***

The next morning Anya was watering the flowers in her front lawn when something caught her eye. A postman was putting mail into her mailbox. She put down the watering can and went outside to get the mail. She reached inside the mailbox and cried, "Yes!" She left the letters inside the mailbox, grabbed the parcel, and went next door. *This was the best thing that could happen,* she thought with joy as she pressed the doorbell.

'Bzzzz' the doorbell rang.

"What can I do for you?" asked David, smiling at her.

Anya stared at him. He had strange piercing blue eyes and a sexy smile. "The postman made a mistake…" and Anya gave the parcel to David who smiled back and went into the house.

"Aren't you coming in?" he asked from inside.

Anya felt funny but she went inside after him. The house was beautifully decorated. Paintings lined the walls and the rugs looked expensive. Anya sat down on a comfortable looking chair, feeling a bit nervous.

"My name is David," he said, sitting opposite her as he placed the parcel on a glass table between them.

"I'm Anya," she replied, smiling at him. "I live next door."

"Yeah, I know, saw you in the back yard yesterday," he said with a grin.

Their eyes met and then there was silence. Anya wanted to look into David's bright blue eyes all day long.

"Well, I have to go," Anya said getting up. *God! Why did I just do that?* she thought. She didn't want to leave, but at the same time a voice in her head was telling her that she should go back home.

"Already?" David asked. He sounded disappointed to Anya as he walked her to the door.

Anya blushed. David was standing a little too close to her. "Hey, we're neighbors," she said, backing up a little. "We'll meet again," she added, and went outside.

"Yeah, you're right," he replied, closing the door behind her with a smile.

"He's so sweet," said Anya. She was talking to Susan on the phone. "He's such a babe!"

"That's so unfair," answered Susan. "I didn't even get to talk to him and you went into his house. Why did this happen?"

"It happened because I'm gorgeous."

"Get a life," laughed Susan.

The two friends laughed for a while and then Anya changed the subject. "How's Carl doing?"

"Funny you should ask," said Susan. "He went to the hospital with his mom somewhere outside of town."

"Well, let's just hope that the hospital keeps him there."

"Anya, you and your thoughts," Susan rolled her eyes.

***

It was a cold night and an old man was walking down the street that led to the town's pub. "Who's there?" the man asked.

He had heard some sharp steps behind him. Thinking it was his imagination, he walked on.

"HISSsss" came a cold voice from behind him.

The old man spun around and noticed a cloaked figure coming toward him. The man quickened his pace. He had no interest in facing a mugger right now. He had other things to worry about. The man looked back. The figure was catching up with him. The old man made a quick turn and went into an alley. He hid behind a dustbin and held his breath. He wanted to confront the person but he couldn't. The very air seemed to be inflicting fear into his body.

The figure stopped in the parking lot a little ahead of the alley. The old man closed his eyes, wishing that whoever it was would leave him alone. The figure turned and floated toward the old man. The old man's heart began to beat faster. He wanted to yell, to call out for help, but no sound came out of his mouth. With determination, he got up and ran away, but the alley he was in was a dead end. He had nowhere else to run. There was no way he could climb the brick wall in front of him.

"Noooo!" cried the old man as the creature's teeth sank into his neck. The old figure dropped to the ground feeling weakness in his legs, as the creature drank his blood.

Another attack had taken place but this time in *Colville*.

***

"Susan, did you hear it?" Anya asked the following morning. The news of the attack had spread like wildfire.

"Of course I did," answered Susan on the phone.

"What do you reckon?"

"What do you want me to say?"

"That Carl did it."

"Carl is in a hospital, Anya," replied Susan. "He can't be in two places at once."

"He's a vampire," Anya answered. "I've told you this already. You remember the incident in the cave and at the butcher's shop, right? The newspaper is saying that the victim had lost a lot of blood."

"Oh, forget it," said Susan. "Want to go out?"

Why is Susan changing the subject? Anya thought. She had ignored Anya's every attempt to convince her that Carl was responsible for the murders.

"The attack took place near my home," said Anya. "I can't go anywhere."

"Overprotective parent syndrome?"

"You have no idea," Anya laughed. "Bubye, then," she added and hung up. She got up from her bed and applied lipstick. Pink was her favorite color. She went down to the back yard and felt like jumping with excitement when she noticed that David was strolling in his backyard.

"Time for some girl power," she whispered and made her way toward David. He was wearing a white vest and a pair of blue jeans. He couldn't have looked dreamier to Anya.

"Hello," said Anya, getting closer to the fence.

"Hi, how are you?" he asked with a smile.

"I'm fine. Just worried about, you know?"

"Yes, the attacks," said David. He looked a bit sad.

"What do you reckon?" Anya asked. *He looks great when he's sad.*

"Well," he said with a smile. "You might laugh at this, but it looks like a vampire to me."

"You believe in that stuff?" Anya asked laughing. *Who knew?*

"Yeah, kind of," he answered shyly. "My parents are mostly out on business, so I keep myself busy reading about such things."

Now to reel him in, Anya thought. "I like that stuff too," she said leaning forward over the fence. She looked into David's blue eyes. Both of them had moved closer and closer when the phone rang.

"Where's that coming from?" said Anya, looking around for the source of the noise. *The noise that destroyed my chance with David.*

"Sorry," yelled David, as he ran toward his house to answer the phone. "Later!"

"I'll get you next time," she said to herself, going into her house feeling a bit disappointed.

***

"Anya, come eat your dinner," said her mother from downstairs.

"Coming," cried Anya from her bedroom, and she descended the steps, jumping over the last three.

"Have you met that new boy yet – David?" asked her mother as Anya sat down at the table.

"Yes," she said slowly, unsure where the conversation was about to go.

"He's a good boy," said her father as he bit into the beef in front of him.

"Yes, he helped me with the groceries when I was at the shop," said her mother. "He even helped me load them into the car."

Yeah, yeah, I know he's great.

"Mom, Dad, can I go out tonight?" she requested, her fingers crossed. Maybe she could go next door and tell David what her parents thought about him.

"Nope," her father answered casually and returned to his dinner.

"You now have a phone in your room," said Anya's mother. "You can talk to one of your friends instead."

"Joy," Anya said softly, eating her dinner. *I'm trapped here,* she thought desperately as she went to her room after dinner. Her parents were still talking about buying a new carpet for their bedroom. Anya moved toward the window in her room. It was a clear night and the moon was shining brightly in the cloudless sky. She looked at her surroundings. The air was cold and the street lights were on. David was in his lounge. Someone's dog was barking… *Rewind* thought Anya. *David's in his lounge?*

And sure enough, David Rodgers was watching TV and drinking something from a bottle. Anya couldn't make out what it was.

"RINGgggg," went the phone in Anya's room. "Ringgg."

"I've got it!" Anya cried as she picked it up. "Hello?"

"Hi, it's me, Susan."

"Susan, you won't believe it," squealed Anya. "David is right in front of me."

"What did you say?" yelled Susan, not believing what she had just heard.

"Not in front of me actually, but I'm seeing him from my bedroom window."

"You naughty girl," Susan laughed. "What's he doing?"

"Drinking something, I think," Anya answered, looking at David. "Wait. He's getting up. He's picking up the bottle. He's coming upstairs. Now he's on the bed looking at the mirror."

"What's happening?" asked Susan, unable to control herself. "Wait!"

There was silence on the phone.

"Great, Mom wants me downstairs," said Susan after a while. "Fill me in later," she added and then hung up.

Anya kept watching David as he bent down and reached for something under his bed and then.

"You pig!" Anya gave in a low scream.

"You sneak," he yelled, flashing a flashlight directly into Anya's eyes.

"Stop it!" Anya motioned to him smiling from her window.

David stopped and turned the lights off and went out of the room. But Anya just stood there because of what she had just seen. David's reflection was not present in the mirror as he passed it leaving his room.

Four

"Now you are saying that it's Carl and David?" Susan asked, rolling her eyes as the two girls walked to Eric's house. "You're weird, you know that?"

"I'm sure I didn't see David's reflection," Anya answered. "I didn't see…" She stopped. David was walking toward her, his hands in his pockets, walking with a carefree air. "Hi," he said upon seeing Anya, who smiled back.

"Hi," said Susan before Anya could answer and she gave Anya a 'he-is-so-sweet-look.'

"Hi, David," said Anya. *You aren't a vampire and I don't care even if you are one,* she thought.

"Where you going?" he asked Anya.

"We're going to a friend's," she said, having half a mind to go along with David instead.

Susan sensed what Anya was thinking and added, "It's very important."

"Well okay, see you then," and he walked away.

"Still think he's a vampire?" Susan asked, smiling at her friend.

"We're late," Anya changed the topic and they made their way to Eric's.

"Hi girls," he said, opening the door for them.

"You wanted to show us something?" said Anya as the two walked inside.

"Follow me," said Eric, leading them upstairs. The excitement in his voice was evident.

"Geek," whispered Anya as she entered Eric's room. Eric had huge posters of great inventions on the walls. His table had a laptop, some books and a microscope. A solar system hung from the ceiling. More books littered the bed.

"What is it?" Susan asked, trying to ignore how the room looked.

"You know the sample I took from the cave?" answered Eric while searching for something in one of his cabinets. "It turned out to be quite unusual." He turned and handed Anya a glass tube in which the sample from the cave's wall was floating. But now it was giving a blue shine.

"A blue color is unusual?" Anya asked confused.

"It's not that," said Eric waving his arms excitedly. "Look here," he added and pointed at a book with a brown cover lying on the bed. He opened it up and showed a page of it to Anya.

"You read this stuff?" laughed Anya.

Susan rolled her eyes at Anya and began to read. "It says here," she read, "that the area in which a magical creature lives has special properties. The area in which a vampire lives has some glow in its soil or surroundings. A vampire is a blood sucking, blah, blah, blah, the usual things."

"The cave we went to had a green glow," said Eric pushing back his glasses. "I tested the sample with some chemicals but the glow doesn't go away. It doesn't have any materials I know of in it."

Anya looked at the glass tube and to her surprise the sample was now red in color. "You know what this means?" Anya asked her friends. She didn't know where the words she was going to say had come from. "We have to check Carl's house."

"Don't be ridiculous," said Susan. "You want us to break into a house?"

"Susan, we have to do this if we want answers," said Anya, as if it settled the matter completely. Her friends stared at her as if she had gone mad.

***

"I can't believe we are doing this," whispered Susan as she followed Anya through the bushes that covered Carl's backyard.

The moon was completely behind the clouds and the air was cold. The streets were empty because the people of the town had gone home early due to the stories of the attacks. No one was interested in going for late night walks while a murderer roamed the streets.

"We are so late," said Susan worrying as her friends got up on their feet. "We should hurry up, or else face our parents."

They reached the back door and to Anya's surprise it was open. "Weird," she whispered, opening the door further.

"I don't like this," said Eric. "Is someone inside?"

Anya didn't say anything and went inside, a flashlight in her hand. "Come on," she added as they stepped into the kitchen. "Let's go upstairs to Carl's room."

"Maybe we should split up," said Eric, looking at the girls. "We'll be able to cover more ground that way and get out of here early."

"No," said Susan a little loudly. "We must not split up. People always do that in movies and look where it gets them."

"Eric, you look downstairs," said Anya, ignoring Susan as Eric turned on his flashlight and nodded. "Susan and I will check upstairs."

Susan sighed and followed Anya up the stairs. They reached the very first room in front of them and its door was…

"It's open too," said Anya, a little shocked. "Didn't Mrs. Smith lock the house at all?"

The second door was also not locked. The girls went toward the third and last door. It too was unlocked.

"Oh, God!" exclaimed Anya, clapping her hand to her mouth. The room seemed to be Carl's, as there were posters of film actresses pasted on the wall. But Anya wasn't looking at them. She was looking at the room itself. It looked as if the whole room had been torn apart. Everything was a mess. The bed covers were torn. The desk was overturned. Magazine pages were lying on the floor and there was a green sparkle everywhere.

"Eric," Susan called from the top most stairs. There was a thud and Eric entered the room.

"Who did this?" Eric asked shocked, looking at the torn bed sheet, the torn books and open drawers. The green glow was on everything and it dimly lit the room. The three friends stood still, not speaking a word. Someone had been in this house before them.

"Ringgg!" the phone rang and Anya screamed. The three friends went downstairs and looked at the ringing phone on the kitchen table.

"Should I…" said Eric in a terrified voice. The girls stood still as he pushed the speaker button. "He-Hello?"

No answer, only the sound of someone breathing on the other line, the sound Anya remembered so very well when her parents had gone to the funeral.

"Eric, come on," urged Susan, pulling his sleeve. "We have to get out of here."

The three friends made their way quickly out of the house. Even the front door was open. "That was creepy," said Eric as they went out into the street.

"Do you think whoever it was, was watching us?" Susan asked scared.

"Don't know," Anya answered. The breathing sound from the phone was still fresh in her mind.

"We have to be more careful from now on," said Eric seriously as he pushed his glasses up on his nose.

"But you live alone," said Susan, worrying for her friend.

"There are alarms in every room of the house," said Eric with a smile. "I'll be fine," he assured the girls as they walked toward Eric's house.

"The question is what was that culprit doing in Carl's room?" Anya asked.

"I have no idea," said Eric slowly.

The friends remained silent as they walked. They saw no one in the street. Everyone was already in their houses.

"Take care," said the girls as they reached Eric's house. "We'll call you to make sure everything is right," said Susan with a smile.

"Bye," he said locking the door behind him.

"He'll be alright, won't he?" Susan asked Anya.

"We'll give him a call later," Anya answered as the two walked away.

Again the friends remained silent. Never in her life had Anya seen Colville so quiet, so scared.

"Hey, Lizzie," said Anya looking at the dog, waiting for Susan on the doorstep. It barked in answer and wagged its tail.

"Bye then," said Susan, hugging Anya. "Tonight was creepy. I'll watch you on your way home."

"Thanks, Susan," said Anya letting go, and she walked toward her house.

Anya turned around and noticed Susan's dark outline looking at her. Then she turned a corner and Susan was out of sight. The road was dimly lit by the lights coming from the houses. Anya began to feel the hairs on her neck beginning to straighten, and an odd feeling of someone watching her made her quicken her pace. She ran toward her house and began to knock frantically at the door. She didn't dare look behind her to see if someone was following her.

"Anya, you are very late," said her father answering the door. "Come in and have dinner."

Anya felt happy to be back inside her house, and she began to eat her dinner silently. Her parents talked to each other and she felt glad that they didn't add her in their conversation.

"I'm off to bed," she said getting up and putting the plates in the sink.

"Some letters came for you, dear," said her mother. "They are on the mantle piece."

Wondering who they were from, Anya took the letters to her room and sat down on her bed. Picking up the phone, she dialed Eric's number.

"Hello?" came a sleepy voice.

"Hi," said Anya. "Is everything fine?"

"Of course I'm fine," he answered. "Susan just called. I'll call her and let her know that you've reached home as well. She was worried."

"Thanks. Take care," she replied hanging up the phone. She looked at the letters and picked one of them up. There was no return address. Her eyes widened as she read the note inside. It had some strange symbols on the paper but also a message that was the same in every letter that Anya opened.

"You Might Be Next."

Five

The next morning Anya phoned Susan again and talked to her about the letters she had received yesterday.

"He or she knows where you live," said Susan. She had said that last night too.

"I know," said Anya worried. "He or she knows where I live."

"What did Eric say about all of this?" asked Susan.

"He couldn't translate the symbols."

"I wish I could come over," said Susan. She was worried about her friend.

"I feel the same way," Anya answered with a sigh. "But you know my parents. They aren't letting me out."

Saying that she would talk later, Anya hung up the phone and went downstairs to the kitchen to have breakfast.

"Honey, we are going out," said her mother, taking the car keys from the kitchen table as Anya sat down and helped herself to some toast. "Your father's colleague has invited us to eat together."

"We'll be back soon," said Anya's father. "Take care."

Anya nodded to her parents. She wanted to tell them about the letters but thought better of it. She had given the letters to Eric last night with difficulty and it had involved Lizzie as the messenger.

"Take care," said Anya's mother, kissing her forehead. She smiled and walked out of the house with her husband. Anya watched the front door close and then she heard the sound of car tires on the gravel. And then there was silence. She felt lonely in the house, so she went outside to look at the flowers in the garden and maybe bump into David. But David was not in his backyard. Anya looked at his house. He seemed to have gone out. Anya sighed. She wanted to go out and meet with her friends and talk about the letters she had gotten last night.

She made up her mind and leaving a note for her parents, went outside. *I'll deal with them later,* she told herself, and she made her way to Susan's.

Reaching Susan's house, she knocked on the door. There was a bark from inside, and Susan opened the door followed by Lizzie. "What happened?" she asked surprised. "I was just about to try and come to your place," she added, giving Anya a glass of juice and sitting opposite her at the table.

"My parents have gone out to some group lunch thing," said Anya as she took a sip of orange juice. "I had to get out of the house. Where's your Mom?"

"She's at my aunt's," replied Susan as she patted Lizzie. "I thought of that as a chance to come and meet you, as she wasn't letting me go out either."

"Let's go to Eric's," suggested Anya, putting her empty glass on the table.

Susan nodded and left a note for her mother. "Let's go," she said walking with Anya to the front door. She called to Lizzie to come as well and the friends walked toward Eric's house.

"How are things with David?" Susan asked, trying to lighten the mood.

"I don't know," said Anya with a smile. She appreciated that Susan wasn't bringing up the letters she had gotten last night. "I didn't see him at his house today."

"So you think he's interested?" asked Susan as Lizzie circled around the girls.

"Don't know," said Anya. "We were about to kiss the last time we met."

"You what?" asked Susan with excitement. "Tell me more."

Anya told Susan about how she and David were about to kiss but then his phone rang.

"Tough luck," said Susan. "I feel sorry for you."

"Thanks," said Anya with a smile, and she rang Eric's doorbell.

"Nice surprise," he said opening the front door. "Come in."

"Hi, Lizzie," he added, giving her a pat.

"Did you find anything?" Anya asked.

Eric shook his head. "I can't translate the symbols on the letter."

"It could be a prank," Susan suggested hopefully. "Maybe someone from school was trying to scare Anya because of the things happening around town."

"I have no idea," said Eric sitting down on a chair. "I don't think anyone feels that strongly about Anya at school."

Anya nodded. She kept a low profile at school. And then another thing came to her mind. "What about the phone call we got last night?" she asked. "It had to be Carl."

"It couldn't be him," said Eric calmly. "He's out of town. He couldn't have known the exact time to make the call when we were in his house."

"Who knows for sure?" Anya tried to defend her case. She kept having this feeling that Carl wasn't to be trusted.

"Give it a rest," said Susan, brushing her blonde hair away from her face with her hand and looking at Anya. "It's not him."

"How would you know?" asked Anya. She was surprised to hear her loud voice.

"Listen to yourself," said Susan. "You're accusing Carl of being a murderer."

"Both of you calm down," said Eric before Anya could say anything. "I know what happened was creepy, but let's not go at each other." The doorbell rang and Eric got up to see who it was. Anya and Susan didn't look at each other. After a while, Eric returned with David behind him, and Anya beamed.

***

Carl was sitting on a chair looking at the bulb flickering on the wall when his mother entered the room. "You all right, honey?" she asked with concern.

"Yeah," Carl whispered. It was very difficult for him to say something out loud. He was staying at his aunt's house. He felt relaxed there after all of the tests he had gone through at the hospital. The *'disease'*, as the doctors referred to his hand, had now spread toward his neck making a layer of white scaly flesh as it continued spreading farther up. The doctors had never encountered anything like it before.

"Uncle Jack won't be coming to see you today," said his mother. "He's saying that he'll come tomorrow along with his kids."

"Fine," he whispered, still looking at the flickering bulb. *As if he cares!* he thought angrily. He was in no mood to meet anyone and listen to how sorry they were to hear of his illness. His mother left him in the room and went to the kitchen to make her son something to eat. Carl looked at the ceiling. He missed his friends. He thought about Anya. He knew that she wasn't comfortable around him. *But why?* he thought. Did she think he was responsible for those deaths? And then out of nowhere he felt an urge for revenge. He felt angry at Anya and wanted to cause her harm. He wanted to cause everyone around her harm. He got up from the chair. *"Mom, I'm going out!"*

***

"It's getting late," said Anya, looking at her watch. *My parents are probably home by now.*

After Eric had told Anya that he had met David yesterday and had put her curiosity at ease, the teenagers had begun talking about monsters and magic. David was having fun with them.

"We better get going," said Susan getting up as David nodded. "Bye, Eric."

The two girls and David walked toward the door. "Lizzie!" Susan called to her dog. She came running toward Susan. Lizzie had been wandering around the house amusing herself the entire time.

"Take care," said Anya as Eric locked the front door after them. The air was chilly outside.

"Come on," said David, and the three of them walked toward Susan's house. Susan and David talked all of the way together about school and stuff. Anya was losing her temper. She knew that Susan was her friend, but still, she wished it was only David and her walking.

They reached Susan's house. "Good, Mom isn't home yet," she said unlocking the front door. "See you all later," Susan waved them both goodbye and went inside followed by Lizzie.

"So?" said David as he and Anya started to walk.

"Don't you 'so' me," she said, flaring up for no reason.

"Oh, come on. You aren't jealous now, are you?" David asked smiling.

"Jealous?" snorted Anya as they both walked. "Yeah, as if!"

"It was just a friendly chat."

Anya didn't know why she was angry with him but she was enjoying it. "Of course," she said, rolling her eyes. She liked how David was trying to make her like him.

"Hey," said David as they reached Anya's house. He grabbed Anya's shoulder and turned her around. "You know how I feel about you, don't you?"

Anya looked into his beautiful blue eyes and smiled. "Just go," she said backing away and taking the key from under the doormat.

"Your parents don't seem to be home, right?" he said with a sly smile as Anya unlocked the front door and stepped inside. "You must be feeling lonely all by yourself in your house?"

"Nice try, pretty boy," she smiled and locked the door behind her. "Go home," she said from the other side. She listened as he walked away with a sigh.

***

Carl walked out of the house. The breeze was cool and the sky was clear. He sat down on a bench in the park. He just sat there thinking to himself. The feeling of doing harm to Anya had gone away. Cars zoomed past him. People came and walked out of the park, and time went by. Soon enough it was dark, but he just sat there staring at nothing, not even feeling hungry, not realizing that he had been sitting on the bench for some hours.

People passing by did see the teenage boy sitting alone on the bench as they went home, but no one noticed a dark figure flying in the dark sky. The chill in the air didn't seem to bother it as it flew toward its destination: The boy sitting alone in the park.

Carl looked at his wrist watch. It was about to strike nine. He looked around. No one was in the park. *Mom must be worrying,* he thought, but strangely he didn't seem to care. He was about to get up and walk around a little when suddenly a hooded figure landed in front of him from the sky. Carl gasped. The cloaked figure floated toward him stupefying him with its stare.

"What do you want?" Carl asked unable to move. No one was around to help him.

"You," the figure replied in a menacing whisper, making its way toward Carl who was shaking terribly under its stare.

"You are valuable to me," it added, coming closer to Carl. It placed its hand on Carl's cheek where the disease had reached by now. The fingers scraped at the scales. "It's time to shed," it smiled as the skin fell off and thick gray hair appeared in its place.

Carl looked at the moon in the dark sky and dropped to the ground. "What's happening?" he asked gasping for air. "What?" He felt a horrible pain in his stomach and stared at his hands. The nails began to grow and become sharper on long thin fingers. Hair began to appear everywhere on his hand. His feet extended and tore through his shoes. Carl looked in horror as the surroundings began to change for him. He started seeing everything clearly in the dark. He could see a woman going into her house some miles away. He could smell someone cooking chicken. He felt his face extending, changing into a snout. He could hear many voices because of his now pointy ears. He tore away his clothes and howled facing the moon.

"You are mine," said the vampire looking at the werewolf with adoration.

The werewolf looked at the hooded figure and slowly went toward it, sniffing the air.

"Now for a test," the figure whispered and pointed at something far away. The werewolf turned and smelled something. Something delicious! And then it saw him. A beggar was searching for some food in one of the trashcans some distance away. The creature sniffed the air hungrily and smelled blood flowing through the beggar's delicate flesh.

"Go on," said the vampire in a hurry. "Go and enjoy."

Without warning, the werewolf ran toward the beggar. The poor man didn't even have time to yell. The werewolf bit and slashed at his flesh. The beggar gave a moan and then moved no more as the werewolf devoured his flesh.

There had been another attack but Carl didn't know or remember anything as he woke up tired and naked the next day in his room at his aunt's house.

Six

The next day's newspaper was lying on the bed with the same headline:

Another Attack!

The news about yesterday's attack had spread like wildfire. Anya read the paper again and again. The entire first page was devoted to the news about the attack. The writer thought that the attacker was a mad man. *But even mad men can't rip a person into tiny pieces,* thought Anya as she read the story the tenth time.

"Honey, come down for breakfast," called her mother. Anya got up and went downstairs and into the kitchen. "Are you all right?" her mother asked as Anya came downstairs.

"Huh – I'm alright," Anya replied slowly.

Anya's father was out at work and her mother was thinking of making the day into a Mother–Daughter thing. Anya knew about her mother's plan when they were talking last night in the den.

"So, what do you want to do?" her mother asked with a smile.

"I don't know, Mom," Anya replied as she helped herself to some toast. "It's up to you."

"Why don't we go to the mall?" her mother suggested again with a smile.

"My mood isn't…"

"Come on," urged her mother. "It'll be our day."

"Fine," said Anya as she continued eating her breakfast. The news about yesterday's attack hadn't made her mother change her plan about the morning. After finishing and putting her plate into the kitchen sink, Anya went to her bedroom to get ready.

Maybe Susan will come, Anya thought as she brushed her hair. *Being with Mom alone is going to be weird.*

Making up her mind, Anya picked up the phone in her room and dialed Susan's number. "Hello, Susan?" said Anya as someone answered the phone.

"Hi!"

"Do you want to go to the mall with me and Mom right now?" asked Anya, her fingers crossed. *Say yes. Say yes.*

"I would love to go," said Susan. "I'll go and tell Mom right now."

"Fine, see you," said Anya, hanging up and sighing with relief.

***

After fifteen minutes, Anya and her mother walked toward Susan's house and noticed her waiting for them along with her dog, Lizzie.

"Hello, Mrs. Thomson," said Susan, smiling at Anya's mother.

Lizzie gave a joyful bark.

"Good day, Susan," said Anya's mother. "How is your mother doing?"

"She's fine," Susan answered. "She's at work right now and said to greet you on her behalf as…"

"You know we can do without the pleasantries while walking," said Anya before Susan could finish her sentence. Anya wanted to get the trip to the mall with her mom in tow over with as fast as she could. Leaving Lizzie at home, the three began to walk.

Susan and Anya's mom talked with each other as the three of them walked toward the local mall. Anya kept to herself. She looked at the houses they walked past. The news of the attacks had changed the town. They saw no one on their way to the mall. The streets were empty except for a stray cat or two.

"Come on girls," said Anya's mother as the three of them went inside the mall which had very few people in it, all minding their jobs and getting out in a hurry. The females browsed around the shops. Anya hadn't seen the mall that empty. Even some of the shops were closed. In the end, Anya bought a new lipstick while Susan bought a music CD. They ate a burger and decided to go to the park next to the mall. The people present in the mall looked puzzled as they watched the three of them walking out of the mall laughing and talking.

"Where to next?" Susan asked after sitting in the park for a while.

"Let's go home," said Anya faking a yawn. "It's getting late." *And besides, staying out here while the rest of the town is tensed is making me feel guilty.*

"Kill joy," said Anya's mother. "We just got started."

"Mom, even if we did just get started," said Anya. "Where do you propose we go? It's not like we have an amusement park in town."

"Okay fine," said her mother. "Let's go home and I'll make us all something to eat."

Getting up from the bench, the three of them walked out of the park and then Anya saw a familiar figure walking some feet ahead of them. Susan seemed to have noticed too.

"Carl!" yelled Susan walking toward him.

Carl turned around and saw the three familiar faces.

"Hello, Mrs. Thomson," he said, shaking her hand and smiling at the others.

"When did you come back?" she asked.

"Today, Mrs. Thomson," he answered.

"Why didn't you call?" Susan asked.

"I'm going home now," he answered.

"I'll leave you kids then," said Anya's mother with a smile and walked off. "Don't be out late," she added as she walked away.

"Carl…," said Anya. She was going to burst if she didn't say it now. She just had this feeling that she should tell him about it.

"What?"

"Someone trashed your room."

"WHAT?" he asked outraged. "I should've gone home first."

"Where were you then?" Susan asked scared. She had never seen Carl angry.

"I arrived about an hour ago and went to see Eric. He didn't mention anything," he said as the three went toward his house. To the girls' surprise, the front door was locked and they followed Carl inside and up to his room. Carl opened his bedroom door and was shocked to see the mess. And then he turned to the girls standing behind him. "How did you know about this?" he asked.

"I – we…," Anya blurted, looking at Susan for help who herself was trying to come up with an answer. Someone rang the doorbell and after a minute Carl came back upstairs with Eric behind him. "Explain," said Carl, his arms folded looking at the three standing next to the bedroom door.

"We swear we didn't do it," said Susan slowly.

"How did you know about this?" he asked again. The friends could tell that he was trying to keep his voice down.

"We – I…," said Anya. *Think of a story. Heck! Why hasn't Eric come up with a good story by now?*

Carl sat down on his torn bed and looked at the ground. "I need to rest," he said. "This doesn't matter. What's done is done. Leave me."

Anya, Susan, and Eric didn't say anything, as Carl's tone was clear enough, and they went out of the room quietly.

"He has changed," Susan said as they walked out of the house.

"I'll call him later," said Eric, and then looking at Anya, added, "What are you thinking about?"

"His hand is normal again," she said quietly, looking at them both. No one said a thing. Eric went home and Anya hugged Susan goodbye.

What's wrong with me, she thought. She kept thinking that Carl was responsible for all of those murders. *He's a friend,* she kept telling herself. *You have to trust him.*

"Anya," came a familiar voice from behind her.

She turned around and saw David. She slowed her pace so that he could catch up with her. "How are you?" he asked, smiling at her.

"I'm fine," she lied. Could she tell him what she thought about Carl?

"You don't look fine," he said.

"I just…" she looked straight into his face, into his beautiful blue eyes. "Can I trust you with something?" she asked.

"Of course," said David with concern. "Anya, what is it? Is something wrong?"

Anya looked at him for a moment as they both stood outside of her house. *No, I can't trust anybody right now.*

"It's nothing," she said forcing a smile. "I've got to go."

"But?" David asked confused.

Without answering, Anya went inside her house and ran toward her room.

"Honey, is everything alright?" her mother asked as she saw her running to her room.

Anya didn't reply and sat down on her bed. She couldn't make up her mind. Could it be Susan? No, she was with her in the cave. What about Eric? He was the one who didn't go into the cave with them, but then, he also helped with the letters. And Carl and David, they both appear unexpectedly. David and Eric could be the ones who trashed Carl's room, but what about Susan? What if she's the vampire and just can't remember things or is hiding the truth from her and her friends. What if all of her friends were in on it?

This sucks, she thought, lying on the bed and closing her eyes. She felt restless inside, as if there was a part of her that wanted to come out.

Anya didn't realize when she had fallen asleep. It was eleven at night when she woke up again. Surprised that her mother hadn't woken her up, she went downstairs to get something to eat. After helping herself to some biscuits, she went to watch the television. *Better watch something,* she thought, switching it on. The cable was out. She got up and walked toward her room. *What is David up to?* she thought as she reached her room and had nothing better to do. Making up her mind, she looked out the window.

David's house was dark and no lights were on. Anya tried to look harder but she couldn't see anything. She was about to go away when she saw something move in the bushes below, near her house. Anya looked toward them. "What is it?" she whispered to herself.

The thing in the bushes seemed to be in some kind of struggle. "It could be a dog," said the sensible part of Anya's brain, and then the other part kicked in. "Or a vampire waiting to attack!"

"Ahhhh!" Anya screamed as she noticed two gleaming eyes staring at her from inside of the bushes. The lights in her room clicked on and she was embraced by her mother.

"Honey, what happened?" she asked, worrying about her.

Anya pointed at the window and her mother looked outside. After a while she closed the window. "Nothing's out there," said her mother, sitting with Anya on the bed.

"I saw someone or something out there," Anya whispered.

"Nothing's out there," her mother assured her. "You're just stressed out. Lie down for a while." She kissed Anya on the forehead.

Anya lay down on the bed and her mother turned off the lights. "Good night, Anya."

Anya shifted into a more comfortable position. *What was in the bushes? Maybe Carl is on a night stroll. What if I'm next?* These thoughts haunted Anya all night long. She dreamed a strange dream that night, one in which she was surrounded by vampires and she was their queen.

Seven

The next day Susan came over to Anya's house for a sleepover, as her mother was going out to attend a business meeting. "Meaning it knows where you live?" asked Susan as Anya finished telling her about what she saw last night.

"I don't know," answered Anya, looking at her bedroom window. "I don't know."

"Girls, lunch is ready," came Anya's mother's voice from downstairs. The girls went into the kitchen and sat down at the table. Lizzie was eating meat from her bowl.

"Did you talk to Carl?" asked Anya as her mother came over with the food.

"No," Susan answered. "I still think he would be angry over what happened at his house. Let's call Eric after this and see if he talked to him."

The girls ate their food while Anya's mom told them about a new serial she had started watching on television, some show about a woman who was living with three new male roommates and getting over a breakup.

"Lunch was lovely," said Susan finishing her plate. "Thank you."

"It was nothing, dear," said Anya's mom as she got up with the plates.

"Do you need help with the dishes?" asked Susan as Anya rolled her eyes at her.

"No," replied Anya's mother gently. "You girls go and have fun."

Anya led Susan up to her room and then dialed Eric's number.

"Hello?" came a boy's voice.

"Hi, Eric, it's Anya."

"How are you?"

"I'm fine. Did you talk to Carl?"

"Yup."

"What did he say? How is he?"

"Well, he informed his mom about his room," answered Eric. "He's very upset though."

"Did he ask how we knew?" asked Anya as Susan put her ear next to the receiver.

"Nope," Eric answered. "He didn't say anything about that."

"Susan is at my place," said Anya. "Want to go out?"

"I'll call Carl," said Eric. "And you two can come over to my place."

"All right then, we will see you in ten minutes," said Anya and she hung up.

***

"I should have worn something warmer," complained Anya as she stepped out of her house. The chilly air was killing her. *Why does it always have to be cold when I'm out?*

"Aren't we forgetting someone?" asked Susan, closing the front door.

Anya had no idea who she was speaking of. "Who?"

"D-A-V…"

"We aren't taking him with us," Anya laughed. And then she added, "Are we?"

"Why not?" asked Susan with a smile. Anya shrugged and followed her toward David's house. Susan rang the doorbell and David came outside wearing only a pair of blue jeans that caused both of the girls' hearts to miss a beat.

"What a pleasant surprise," he said looking at both of them with a smile.

***

Eric and Carl were sitting in the park just opposite Eric's house and noticed the girls walking toward them with David.

"Hi, David," said Eric shaking his hand and he introduced him to Carl. The five talked about normal stuff for some minutes when the topic about the killings came up.

"I really think it's a vampire," said Anya, looking at the group at large.

"Yeah, the two deaths certainly look like the acts of a vampire, but about the recent attack I just can't say," said Susan. Anya was glad to hear that Susan was siding with her on this.

"Susan has a point," said Eric. "I doubt if a vampire can rip a person into pieces. Don't they suck out the blood and leave their victims be?"

"I agree with Eric," said Carl. "The thing that ripped that man into pieces was something more sinister."

"Perhaps it's a werewolf," Susan suggested, brushing her blonde hair out of her face.

"A vampire and a werewolf," whispered Anya. She looked at Carl who was busy looking at the grass he was sitting on. *Meaning that there is more than one killer out there?*

"What if they come to this place?" asked David. "Except for one of the attacks, the rest happened out of town, didn't they?"

"Yes, they did," answered Eric. "I can't say if it's this one person who has been doing all of the killings."

"You mean there are more?" asked Susan, shocked at the possibility.

"Could be," answered Eric as he adjusted his glasses. "I mean, the attacks look quite random. First out of town, then in town, and then out of town again. Even if there is a pattern, then the next attack will probably again be in Colville."

"They are not getting me," came a voice.

The kids turned around and saw a grown up man in a police suit walking toward them with a smile on his face. "Hi, I'm Barney," he introduced himself. "I'm here to see into these attacks or as you said, these vampires and werewolves." He gave a smile.

"Are you the only one stationed here?" David asked, taking in Barney's appearance.

"Yes, I'm the only one stationed here," said Barney. "And you kids should go home."

"But it's only five," said Susan looking at her watch.

"Best if you go home early," said Barney giving them a look that made the kids get up. He didn't seem to be the type to take no for an answer. "Go straight home," he ordered, watching them walk out of the park and gather outside of Eric's house.

"He's still looking at us," said Anya. Barney was standing in the park with his arms folded in front of his chest, waiting for them to go home.

"What a bossy man," said Eric as he opened the front door. "I'll see you all later," he added and went inside. Without saying a word, Carl walked away toward his house.

"Would he be able to stop these attacks?" Susan asked as the three walked on.

"Don't know," said Anya as David walked beside her. She could still see Barney standing inside the park. "At least it's good to have some security in this place."

***

"This is Officer Barney," said Barney into his walkie talkie. It was dark and the town's people were inside their houses. "Nothing special to report," he added, turning off his walkie talkie. Then he turned around and noticed a man turn a corner. "Not a nice night to be walking alone," he said to himself with a smile.

The man was hurrying home, as he had just closed the book shop. His old legs were tired and the news about the killer was worrying him when suddenly the street lights went off. The only source of light for him was coming from the closed windows of the houses around him. *I must hurry,* he thought as he got the feeling that he was being followed. He could hear someone breathing close behind him. Unable to run any longer, the old man stopped, clutching his heart, unable to say anything as he felt coldness fill him up. He wanted to yell for help but no sound came out of his mouth. Something black went past him and then he felt pain.

***

Anya woke up the next day and went downstairs to see Susan and her mother sitting at the table reading the morning news. "Why so worried?" she asked. No one answered and Susan handed her the paper.

"Another attack, here in Colville," Anya read the headline. "The victim was a man of 50, Mr. Richardson."

Anya stopped reading and sat down on the chair. There was only one Richardson in town and Anya knew his son well. "Mom, I have to go see him," she said. Her mother opened her mouth to speak when the doorbell rang and Lizzie gave a bark.

"Hello," said Eric as Anya opened the door. "Did you read the news?"

Anya nodded and the three teenagers went upstairs to Anya's room to talk. "We should go and meet Tom," Anya said as she sat down on her bed.

"I just came back from his place," said Eric. "He's at the funeral out of town at his grandparents' place. He might be back later today."

"The attack happened here again," said Susan. "And near your house, Eric. Are you all right?"

"I'm fine," answered Eric with a smile. "I told you my house is quite secure."

"Wasn't that Barney character supposed to be stopping these attacks?" Anya asked angrily. "Where was he when the attack happened last night? I don't trust him one bit."

Eight

It was noon and Anya was applying makeup to Susan when her mother called. “Susan, your mother is on the phone.”

Susan picked up the phone in Anya’s room and after talking a few minutes she hung up the receiver. “She’s on her way home,” she told Anya. She knew that Anya was going to be sad if she left, as she didn’t have a sibling, while at least Susan had Lizzie with her.

The girls spent the rest of the day reading magazines which were now full of articles about vampires and the supernatural. “Some people also think these attacks have something to do with the supernatural,” said Susan, skimming through the pages of a magazine. “Hey, look at this,” she said opening a page. “Vampires used an ancient language in which the symbols…Anya. These symbols look a lot like the ones in the letter you got.”

Without wasting time, Anya took out a letter from inside of her cabinet. “So, this letter has been sent to me by a vampire,” she said, “or perhaps a jerk who knew the language.”

“I don’t know,” said Susan. “It says here that this language is very ancient and no one today knows all of the symbols used in it.”

“But a vampire would know,” said Anya excitedly. “If only the letter had an address on it.”

Susan kept reading when suddenly she yelled with excitement. “The translations can be found in a book called “*Magi History*” which has facts about vampires and other magical things.”

“If they know the book, why didn’t they give some translations themselves,” said Anya irritated. She hated reading books.

“Let’s go and get the book,” said Susan excitedly.

“I would if I knew from where,” she answered. *The town doesn’t even have a library.*

“We can go to Tom’s,” said Susan. “That place is full of old stuff.”

The girls got up and went downstairs, only to be surprised by what they saw.

"Hello, kids," said Barney. He was sitting on the sofa and Anya's mother was pouring him tea.

"Hi, Mr. Barney," said Anya, not sure what else to say. *What is he doing here?*

"I didn't know you knew each other," said Anya's mother with a smile.

"Yesterday," said Anya in a hurry. "In the park," she added reaching for the door. "Mom, Susan and I are going out."

"Dear, I don't think it's safe…," went Anya's mother, but Barney cut through.

"Don't worry, I'll go with them," he said.

Anya's mother didn't say anything and closed the door as the three people along with Lizzie walked outside. "So," said Barney. "Where do you want to go?"

"We are going to the bookstore," said Susan as Lizzie walked behind her. "I'll give you a ride," he said, opening his car door. "Come on," he added. "We haven't got all day. It'll be dark soon."

Hesitating, the two friends and Lizzie got inside. They drove to the store in silence. "Bye," said Barney as they reached the shop and the passengers got out.

Anya opened the front glass door and went inside the shop followed by Susan and Lizzie.

"Anya! Susan!" said Tom, a tall black haired boy in his early twenties. He was dusting some books. He cleaned his hand and patted Lizzie on the head. "Long time no see," he added with a smile.

"We so wanted to come," said Susan, giving him a smile. "How are you?"

"I'm living," said Tom sadly. "Just got back from the funeral."

There was an awkward pause. Anya didn't know what to say to him.

"So," said Tom, becoming cheery again. "Anything new at school and stuff?"

"Tom, do you have a book called '*Magi History'?*" asked Anya. "We need it."

Tom frowned a little and then began searching through some titles, whispering them softly as he went along.

"Find anything?" said Susan, stopping Lizzie from biting into a book lying next to her.

"Help yourselves," he said waving his hand. "This place is a mess." And the girls began to search for the book too.

"What do you want the book for?" Tom asked, opening a box that was filled with dusty delicate looking books.

"We are trying to find some translations," sad Susan, rummaging through a cabinet.

"What?" he asked confused.

"We have some symbols to translate," answered Susan casually.

"What kind of symbols?" Tom asked interested.

"Vampire ones," Susan answered before Anya could stop her.

"Well, I have some translations on some pages," he answered, giving them a piece of paper from a shelf. "My fa…," he hesitated a little. The girls could sense his voice tremble a little. "My dad had these translations and books related to them, but he never told me where he kept the rest of it."

"Can't you," Susan tried to ask but Anya hushed her. But Tom seemed to have gotten the message. "I'll check his room," he smiled at them.

"Thank you," said Anya, and she hugged her friend tight. She had known Tom since they were kids. "You let me know if you need anything."

***

"He looked so lonely," said Susan, watching Lizzie run ahead of them.

"Well, he only has his grandparents with him now," Anya said, looking back at the shop. "His mother died when he was ten."

"I didn't know," said Susan silently.

"Anyway, at least we got something," said Anya, taking out the piece of paper Tom had given them. "Where is that letter?" she asked, searching her pockets.

"I've got it," Susan answered, giving it to her, and the girls walked into the park with the playing equipment.

"Why are people so scared?" Anya asked walking through the gate into the park. They had seen no one out on the street.

"That girl isn't," said Susan. Anya looked to where Susan was looking and noticed a pretty girl with long black hair and green eyes swaying in the swing looking up at the sky.

"What's up with her?" Anya whispered, and the two went toward the other side, far from the new girl.

"The symbols in the letter are…," and Anya began drawing them in the dirt with a stick. "And according to Tom's paper we get," she erased some letters and replaced them with English alphabets. "Yup nothing," she added looking at what they got.

"It looks to me that the last words make up the word 'NEIG'," said Susan looking at the writing. "You know, if you considered this loopy thing a G."

"Well, thank you, Professor Susan," said Anya rolling her eyes. "Forget it. This doesn't make sense."

The girls remained in the park for a long time trying to decipher the symbols, trying to concentrate on the task at hand, but their eyes kept wandering toward the girl on the swing.

"Wonder where the boys are?" Anya asked, looking away from the girl.

"Wonder if she's dead?" Susan asked, ignoring Anya's question and looking at the girl who was swinging slowly and not moving. Even Lizzie was keeping her distance from her.

Anya looked up at the sky. "It will be dark soon," she said and the two of them got up. "You think we should?" asked Susan, pointing toward the girls on the swing.

"All right," said Anya looking at the expression Susan was giving her, and she walked toward the girl. "Excuse me?" said Anya.

The girl stopped swinging and slowly looked at Anya with her green eyes. "Yes?" she asked in a sweet voice.

"My friend and I were thinking that no one is in the park and it'll be dark soon," Anya began, hating Susan for making her talk. "So shouldn't you be going home? I know it's not our business, but…"

"Thank you for your concern," said the girl smiling, and she stood up and without a word walked out of the park.

"Weirdo," whispered Susan looking at the girl walk out of the park. She called Lizzie to come to her. The dog barked and grudgingly woke up from her nap.

"Let's go home," said Anya walking toward the road.

"Where did she go, anyway?" Susan asked scanning the street. "I haven't seen her in town. She's definitely new."

"I don't know and I don't care," Anya answered. *Why is the wind so chilly?*

***

The girls walked home and saw Susan's mom having tea with Anya's mother.

"Hello Susan," said her mother hugging her daughter and then Anya. The mothers and daughters sat a little longer and then Susan's mother stood up. "Thank you so much, Ann," said Susan's mother, hugging Anya's mom.

"It was nothing, Mary," she replied and walked them to the door. "Be safe."

"Want to eat, honey?" asked Anya's mom closing the door behind them.

"Yup, some salad," said Anya giving a big yawn.

"You'll have milk and toast," her mother insisted while walking into the kitchen.

Anya didn't say anything and ate what her mother gave her in silence. "When is Dad coming back?"

"He called today. He will come in a week or so," her mother answered. "You know how he is about his work."

"Yeah," she answered. Her dad worked as a consultant for an electronics company out of town. It was normal for him to be out of the house for days.

Anya sat down at the table and thought about her friends. Eric lived alone. Susan lived with her mom after her parents got divorced. David was also alone, though he said that his parents would be arriving in town soon, and Carl's father was abroad, and none of them had a sibling. Susan had a step-sister, though, after her father remarried.

"I'm going to sleep," said Anya. Kissing her mom good night, she walked into her room and changed into her pajamas. Having nothing else to do, she walked toward her bedroom window to get a peek at David when she saw someone outside and jumped away from the window trying to keep calm. She slowly crouched toward the window again and saw him standing outside. His back was to her house and he was smoking a cigarette. *What is Barney doing standing outside my house?*

Nine

From the corner of his eye, Barney watched Anya close the window. "That kid is trouble," he said to himself and he walked toward the other houses feeling hungry.

***

A dark outline walked slowly in the shadows and made its way toward three men. It came closer and noticed that they were having some kind of argument. It could feed on the three of them, but that would be pointless, as it only wanted one. After a while the three men walked away.

"Dealers," murmured a huge man to himself as he lit a cigar and then he heard something behind him. "Who's there?" he asked, his hands trembling. "The killer I read about in the news?" he asked the darkness that was behind him as his hand slowly went toward his gun. And then he saw it, an outline of a person as the street lights went out. A rush of cold air hit his body and he couldn't take out his gun. He was paralyzed, and then he felt pain.

***

"What the hell is it doing?" Eric asked. "How is the vampire still killing people and isn't being caught?"

The five friends were sitting in the old park. "I thought that when a vampire bites someone that person becomes a vampire too?" asked David thoughtfully.

"Not always," Eric answered. "A person becomes a vampire only when the vampire wants him or her to transform into a vampire."

"Then why isn't it turning people?" David asked again.

"Maybe it's waiting for the right moment," said Carl slowly pulling out some grass from the ground.

Anya looked at him. He was looking at the ground. *How can you be so sure?*

"You mean that a vampire can call all of his dead victims to life whenever it wants?" asked Susan, her eyes wide. "Because I haven't seen that happen in movies. The victims turn into vampires right when they are killed."

"I can't be sure," Eric answered, pushing his glasses back up on his nose.

"Hey," Anya asked, remembering someone from yesterday. "Any idea who that black haired, green eyed new girl is?" She looked at the group for an answer.

"Nope," said Carl. "I did see her once about a day ago and she's a babe."

"You'll fall for a dog," Eric smiled at Carl.

"Hey, you're insulting Lizzie!" Susan yelled out, glaring at Eric who averted her gaze.

"Do you think we should spy on her?" Anya asked, not listening to the group.

"WHAT?" the whole group yelled looking at her.

"Don't look at me like that," said Anya. "I think she has a link with the killing, because you don't show up at some place just when there are attacks happening."

"I don't know," said Susan looking at Anya.

"Hey, look," said David, and the others turned. The new girl was walking toward a house and then she went inside.

"Say what?" said Eric as the group watched Barney arrive outside the same house and go inside too. "They are related?"

"She could be his daughter," said Carl to the group.

Or a little teenaged vampire, thought Anya, and then she asked, "Don't vampires burn up in the sun?"

"Can't be sure," said Eric. "Even if vampires do burn up in the sun, we can't just go around town seeing who keeps themselves at home during the day, can we?"

"I suppose you are right," said Anya. The group went back to talking amongst themselves and Anya looked at them. If vampires indeed burned up in the sun, then her friends weren't one of them. *Maybe they don't burn up in the sun*, she thought. *Maybe it's what writers made up.*

***

Anya went into her room and took out some books from her cabinet that she had borrowed from Eric. She searched through them until she found what she was looking for and began to read.

"A person becomes a werewolf on the night of the full moon. This moon transforms the person….yup same stuff."

She closed the book. *The full moon is only three days away,* she thought, lying on her bed and looking at the ceiling. *And if the werewolf is indeed helping this vampire, then it will probably strike when the full moon comes.* She got up from her bed and began to write on a pad:

Susan couldn't be the vampire because she was in the cave with me, but she could be the wolf!

Then there's Eric. He met us in the cave saying that he had sent Carl home, but he could be lying, maybe he knows about Carl.

Then there's Carl himself. He touched the cave wall and his hand mutated. He went away and an attack happened there. He came back and a series of attacks began.

And David just popped up from nowhere living all alone.

Anya stood up, her head buzzing. Who the hell is the vampire and the werewolf? she thought, and then she thought about her parents. *No, my parents are all right or they would've killed me by now. Right?*

And then Barney and the new girl came into her mind. *Who is that girl?*

***

The next morning Anya went downstairs. Her mother was talking with someone on the phone. "Honey, you look worried," she said hanging up. "Missing Dad? I was just talking to him."

"Yes," she answered absentmindedly and then she asked. "Mom, who do you think is killing these people?"

Her mother was taken aback by the question. "Anya, your father and I think it is a mad person. We were just on the phone talking of moving out of town."

Anya didn't seem to hear her mom properly. "Mom, don't you think it is some kind of creature doing this?"

"Anya, speak sense," her mother answered, laughing at her daughter. "Why would you say such a thing?"

I don't know. "Mom, does Barney have a daughter or someone?"

Her mother looked at her. "I have no idea, dear. Why do you ask?"

"No reason. Just curious," said Anya walking toward the door. "I'm going out for a while. I will be back soon."

***

"Anya," said Susan's mother as she opened the door for her. "Come in."

"Thank you," she said walking into the house and noticed Susan watching T.V.

"What is it?" Susan asked concerned, switching off the tube.

"I'm just worried," she answered as Susan's mother went into another room.

"You're worried about what?" Susan asked.

"The full moon is in three days," said Anya. "And a person is supposed to turn into a werewolf on the night of the full moon."

"Go on," said Susan, making sure that her mom wasn't around.

"So I'm sure the werewolf will attack here on that night," Anya continued as Susan sat back down on the sofa. "We have to get ready for it."

"If this means pinning Carl to some wall…"

"Well, we have to keep a close eye on him."

The doorbell rang and Susan got up and answered it. "Where have you been?" asked Carl as he came inside.

"We went to your place and your mother told us that you were here," Eric told Anya as he sat down on a chair. "So what's up?"

"Not here," Susan whispered as Susan's mother came out to meet the boys, after which Susan led the group up to her room.

"Susan and I are trying to make plans to capture these creatures," Anya answered Eric as if they hadn't been disturbed, and then she told the boys about the full moon and the attack that might happen.

"So, thought of anything good yet?" Carl asked, looking at how neatly Susan had organized her study desk.

Yes. I was thinking of nailing you to a wall, Anya thought looking at Carl who was looking at the clock on the wall. *Why can't I trust him?*

"No, but we are trying to make ourselves safe, you know," said Susan sitting on her bed.

Tring. Tring.

“Sorry, girls,” said Carl, looking at his watch.

“Why an alarm?” Susan asked curiously.

“Mom calls me a little after 1:00, so I have a reminder,” he said and went downstairs, closing the bedroom door behind him.

“Why isn’t his mother with him?” Anya asked the others.

“I did ask him,” said Eric. “But he wouldn’t tell. He said she had some work in that town.”

“Eric,” said Anya. “Susan and I think Carl might be linked to these attacks.”

“No, I do not,” said Susan, not believing that Anya could name her.

“Are you serious?” asked Eric looking at them.

“Yes, we are serious with a capital S,” said Anya. “Okay fine, I’m serious,” she added, after the look Susan gave her. They both told Eric everything, about what they saw in the cave, and the occurrence of the attacks wherever Carl went.

“And you’re telling me these assumptions because?” asked Eric.

“Because you are a friend,” said Anya. “And I want you to spy on Carl,” added Anya, smiling as Eric’s eyes widened.

But what the three teenagers didn’t know was that they had been heard by Carl as he stood outside of Susan’s room. He had lied about his mother calling him. He knew that Anya didn’t trust him and so he left them alone to hear what they would talk about. Smiling at himself, he walked downstairs.

Ten

"What is happening to me?" asked Carl as he left Susan's house. "My friends don't trust me." *Of course they don't trust you,* he thought. *You know what you are, what you have done.*

"That Anya, she's trouble," said Carl as he walked toward his house. The streets were empty. Not even a stray animal was in sight. Carl looked up at the sky as he walked. It was a clear day but no bird was flying around. It seemed as if the whole town had gone into hiding.

You want revenge, don't you? asked a voice inside his head as he reached his house. Carl opened the door to his house and went to his bedroom. *I know I'm going to transform and kill,* he thought. It was only some days back that he had begun having dreams about the night he first transformed and he knew those dreams were real. *Don't think about that,* came a voice inside his head. *Enjoy the killing. You want REVENGE! You want to show Anya what it means not to trust you.*

"AAHHaaa!" cried Carl as he smashed his fist into a vase. He felt some pain and he looked down at his hand. His knuckles were bleeding and then the cuts healed.

***

"Come on, Susan," urged Anya.

"I can't go," she said. "Walk with Eric."

"Okay fine," said Anya. "Bye."

Anya and Eric walked out of Susan's house. "Well," said Anya as the two teenagers walked in the street.

"Well what?"

"Don't you get bored living alone?" she asked cautiously. Even if Eric seemed to be hanging out most of the time with them, Anya wasn't sure if he felt comfortable talking about himself yet.

"Nope," he smiled. "I have you guys."

"I just…your parents…," said Anya and she knew she was crossing a line.

"They call sometimes," said Eric adjusting his glasses. "And e-mail me."

"You have any siblings?" Anya asked slowly, a question none of the friends had dared to ask him before.

Eric remained silent and then said, "I have an older sister. She lives in Brazil."

I never knew, Anya thought. They walked in silence to Eric's house. "Bye," Anya hugged Eric to his surprise, and then walked on. The air was chilly even though it was a clear day. She quickened her pace. She wasn't comfortable walking in the street with no one around. She looked at the houses she passed. All of the windows were closed. "Young girl," an elderly man called to Anya from his front door. "You shouldn't be out here walking by yourself. Haven't you been listening to the news?"

Anya nodded at the old man and ran toward her house. She stood outside and looked at David's place. *There's still one thing I haven't checked,* she thought. She went into her house and came back a few minutes later with something in her back pocket and rang David's doorbell.

"Anya," he said smiling at her. "What's up?"

"I just need to check something," she said with a smile.

"What?" he asked curiously.

"Just come here," she whispered and grabbed him by the collar.

"Anya," said David surprised, and then he remained silent as Anya kissed him. She slowly put her hand inside her back pocket and took out a small mirror and extended her hand in such a way that David wouldn't notice.

Nope, he's all right, she thought, looking at David's reflection in the mirror.

"David, get back," she said still feeling his lips on her.

"You started it," he mumbled pressing harder.

Anya gently pushed him away. "Bye," she said and walked toward her house.

"Why so soon?" said David, pain in his voice. "Just a little…"

"Bye," she yelled back and ran to her house.

Reaching her bedroom, she phoned Susan. "What?" Susan asked. "Tell me you found something."

"Yup," said Anya smiling. "That David's a good kisser."

"You what?" Susan asked and Anya told her everything. "So he's safe then?" Susan asked.

"I did see his reflection," Anya replied.

"But what if it's just a myth," said Susan. Anya was thinking the same thing as well. "What if real vampires aren't affected by the mirror thing?"

"Stop complicating things," said Anya rolling her eyes. She said goodbye and hung up. *What if Susan is right?* she thought, taking out her note pad and looking at her. *Well, I am no detective but I do enjoy writing,* and she began to write:

Susan's alright as far as I know, so this leaves the boys and that Barney and his weirdo of a daughter. Work to do – contact Tom and ask for the translations.

Anya picked up the phone and dialed Tom's number. "Hi Tom, it's Anya."

"Oh, hello," he said.

"So, did you find anything yet?"

"Yeah, I found lots of books in his room," he sounded excited. "The cross-like symbol is actually an A and…"

"Not on the phone," Anya laughed. "I'll come by your place tomorrow around 11:00."

"Okay, see you then."

Saying goodbye, Anya hung up the phone. *This letter mystery is about to be solved.*

***

Anya woke up earlier than her usual time in the morning and went down for breakfast. "You look down," said her mother, ruffling her hair as she sat down at the table. "Cheer up, Dad's coming after tomorrow."

Making it three days, Anya's mind buzzed. The words stung her hard. *Dad is coming tomorrow,* she thought. But before she could think more about it, the bell rang and her mother got up to open the door.

If Carl isn't the one, and neither is Eric, she thought. *Then it has to be…*

"Tom," said her mother. Anya turned around. Tom was standing in the doorway smiling at her mother. "Hello, Anya," he added, seeing her in the kitchen.

"Sit down," said Anya pointing at the chair next to hers. "Wasn't I supposed to come?"

Tom sat down on the chair and put the books he was carrying on the table. "Nah, I was free so I thought of coming over myself."

"Nice of you to drop by," said Anya's mother. "Want anything to eat?"

"Nothing, thank you," he answered with a smile.

"Well, I'll leave you two alone then," said Anya's mother, and she went to her room.

"Take a look at this," said Tom, picking up an old book from the table and opening it. He showed a page to Anya which had many translations.

"The ink has worn off, though," he said, pointing at some faded letters. "But something is better than nothing, right?"

Anya took out the letter from her pocket. She never parted from it, and looked at the symbols.

"What's the letter about?" Tom asked curiously, looking at it.

"Nothing," Anya lied. "My cousin sent it to me as a joke. He wants me to decode the hidden message."

"Well, still some letters are missing," said Anya as she read the translations, "because I only have – AM-I--, -EI—B---, and can't make any sense of it."

"I'm sorry, Anya," said Tom.

"Don't be," said Anya hurriedly. "It's just a stupid code anyway," and then remembering something, she added, "Just one more thing left."

"What?" he asked as he watched Anya take out a mirror from her pocket.

"Just checking something," Anya replied seeing Tom's reflection in the mirror and putting it away. *This is pointless if what Susan said about vampires is true.* "Never mind."

"I better get going," said Tom getting up and taking the books from Anya as she handed them to him.

"Bye," said Anya watching him on his way. *His skin did feel cold when I handed him the books,* she thought. *Oh, give it a rest!* she scolded herself. She locked the front door and went back into the kitchen.

"Weren't you supposed to meet Tom?" her mother asked coming into the kitchen.

"Yes, I was," Anya answered still thinking about Tom. *Does this mirror thing really work,* she thought, pocketing the letter after reading the words 'you might be next', *because after tomorrow I might be dead.*

"Mom, I'm going out," she said.

"Again?" asked her mother. "Don't you think you should stay inside with all of those attacks happening?"

"Mom, I'll be just a few minutes," said Anya, her fingers crossed.

"Well," her mother gave in as she cleaned the table. "Don't be late."

Anya left her house. Tomorrow was the last day before the full moon. She looked at the sky. The wind was chilly and even though the sun was out, it didn't seem to have its shine, its warmth. Anya passed Susan's house and didn't stop to take her along with her. She wanted to be alone. She walked toward the park with the playing equipment. The roads were empty as no one liked being outside lately. *At least my mom isn't a scaredy cat,* she thought as she watched a women scolding her children because they were playing in the garden, and she ordered them to go inside.

Anya reached the park and sat down on a bench. *Who the hell is the creature,* she thought angrily. *Is it anyone I know? My friends? My parents?*

Anya looked around and she felt strangely happy as she watched the strange new girl come into the park and walk toward the swings.

"Time for some answers," Anya whispered to herself and walked toward her.

Eleven

"Hello," said Anya, reaching the girl.

The girl stopped swinging and looked at her with a smile.

"Can I sit with you?" Anya asked. She nodded and Anya sat down on the swing next to hers. "My name is Anya," she added sitting down.

"I'm Tabitha," said the girl with a smile.

Strange name, thought Anya.

"People here think my name is strange," the girl said looking at the sky.

How the…? Anya thought. *Did she just read my mind?*

"Yeah, it is a bit strange," said Anya with a nervous laugh.

Tabitha laughed, brushing her black hair back, her green eyes sparkling.

"So, you are new here, right? How long do you plan on staying?" Anya asked.

"I don't know," she replied. "Until my father says otherwise, I'll have to live with Barney."

"Isn't Barney your dad?" Anya asked interested. She was getting somewhere.

"No," she answered. "He's kind of a bodyguard."

"Tabitha, you have a bodyguard?" Anya asked surprised.

"Call me T or Tab," she said casually. "Tabitha is too weird for me too, and yes, he's my guard. Dad works in the army and moves a lot so I get a guard and stay put in places for a while. I've known Barney since I was a child."

"What about your mom?" Anya asked. *Just give me a hint that you are a creature.*

"I never got to meet her," said Tab. "She left when I was born, never contacted her, though," she added eyeing Anya, making her wonder if she had read her mind again. Then her expression changed. "What about you?" she asked smiling.

"I live with my parents," Anya answered, not keen to tell Tabitha more about herself.

"Oh, my, look at the time," said Tab. "It's 12:00, I've got to go," and she stood up.

How did she know about the time? I didn't see any wrist watch. Did she just make it up? Anya thought. *I really want to know what she's up to.*

"You can come if you want to," said Tab looking at her. "And I have a feeling that you want to."

She's playing mind games with me, Anya thought. Without a word, Anya followed her to her house. It was quite near the park and neither said a word to each other. Tabitha took the key out of her pocket and opened the door. "Come on in," she said.

"Don't mind if I do," said Anya as she stepped into the house. "AHHaa!" Anya screamed as something black and hairy brushed against her leg.

"It's only Felix," said Tabitha in a sweet voice, bending down and patting her black colored cat. "It's not used to strangers."

"Make yourself at home," she added, closing the front door and switching on the lights in the living room, "while I get something to eat."

Anya watched Tabitha leave the room. She looked around and was surrounded by book cases. She browsed through them. The books had strange markings on them and looked quite old. Some of them didn't even have a single letter printed on the covers.

"Weird place," Anya whispered to herself, walking a little further until she came to a closed door. She was about to turn away when suddenly she heard a sound of someone knocking from behind the door. *This is so not cool!* Anya thought, backing away from the door. The knocks became louder. *Should I open it?* She looked behind her, no sign of Tabitha. Gulping, her hand inched forward toward the doorknob and with one quick movement she opened the door in front of her. Something black and huge came toward her face and her screams were drowned by the screeching of a large bird.

"Raven!" Tabitha scolded her pet bird. The raven settled down on the sofa and gave Anya a mean look.

"Are you all right, Anya?" asked Tab. "I had to put her in the room, as she and Felix just go at each other. She was asleep when I left her in the bedroom." She patted the bird on its black feathered head. "She's always in a grumpy mood."

"No wonder," said Anya. "She lives with you."

"You said something?"

"Nothing, nothing, I'll just read something," said Anya, watching Tabitha leave the room again. Anya went to the book shelves and read the titles. "Evil most Vile," she read. "Potions, Tribes of Africa, History of Witchcraft."

Why does she read these? she thought, looking at more titles. "The Goblin Scrolls, Queen Mape, Shamrock." Having nothing better to do, Anya took out Shamrock and opened it. It was full of strange symbols.

"You wouldn't understand those," said Tabitha placing a tray full of small cakes on the table. "Those are ancient texts."

"Can you read these?" Anya asked putting the book back. "And why do you even bother?"

"First of all," said Tabitha. "I can't read these symbols, though I do try and my father likes these things so this is all his collection." She looked at the cakes. "Now come on, these cakes won't finish themselves."

Anya sat down on the sofa. Raven flew and went out of the room. Anya looked at the cakes. *What if they're poisoned?*

"Don't worry," said Tab laughing and feeding one to Felix. "It's not like they are poisoned."

Defeated, Anya took one. They tasted nice. "Tabitha… I mean Tab," said Anya. "You said Barney is your bodyguard, right?"

"Yes, I did," she answered, watching Felix go into the kitchen.

"Then why did he tell me that he was an officer?"

"Did he say that?" Tabitha asked with a smile.

"Yes, he said he was here to look into these attacks."

"Don't know why he would say such a thing," said Tabitha.

Anya waited for Tabitha to elaborate but she didn't. "Who do you think is responsible for these attacks?"

"Well, as far as the news is concerned, I think it's a mad person," said Tabitha. "But if you ask me personally, well, I think it's a...don't get me wrong because it's just an assumption. I think it's a vampire."

Anya didn't say anything and Tabitha continued. "You know because of how the victims have no other wound other than two teeth-like marks on their necks and they seem to be drained of all their blood."

"How did you know that?" Anya asked surprised.

"My dad got these files and I kind of looked into them," she smiled.

"Why did you come to this place, anyway?" asked Anya. "You know, with the things that this town's been going through."

"I have no idea," Tabitha replied. "Dad just sent me here and I think Barney is all I need to stay safe," she added with a smile.

Both of the girls heard the phone ring. "Must be Dad," said Tab looking at the ringing phone.

"I must get going," said Anya, getting up as Tabitha got up as well.

"Bye, Anya," said Tabitha picking up the phone, a strange smile on her face.

***

"You went into her house?" Susan yelled. She didn't know if she should be angry or excited.

"She's totally freaky," said Anya. "I felt as if she could read minds," she added pointing at her forehead.

"Can vampires do that?" Susan asked, patting Lizzie as she lay on her lap on the sofa.

"Don't know," Anya shrugged. "Why did Barney lie to us?"

"How should I know," said Susan.

"Well, I better get going," said Anya, getting up from the sofa. She had gone directly to Susan's after she met with Tabitha and told her all about it. "Any word from the boys?" she asked walking toward the front door.

"Nope, no calls, no nothing," replied Susan.

"Well, see you," Anya said, closing the door behind her as she left Susan's house.

That's strange, Anya thought, walking toward her house. *One of the boys normally calls us by this time to see if we can hang out.*

***

"Nice day out?" asked Anya's mother, opening the door to let her daughter inside.

"You can say that," she replied, dropping onto the sofa and turning on the TV. Her mother went on about Mrs. Dimply, the woman who lived down the block and how she wanted to move out of town for safety.

After having lunch, Anya got up feeling strangely tired. "Mom, I feel like going to bed."

"So soon?" her mother asked surprised as she put the dishes in the sink.

Anya smiled and kissed her mother on the forehead. "Love you," she said and walked out of the kitchen.

"Love you too," said her mother, watching Anya go upstairs.

Anya reached her room and dropped down onto the bed. *The boys…where are they?* she thought looking at the ceiling. *Should I call them? Yeah, and say what? They'll just say they were busy with something. Are they all involved? What if Tom…Nah! He wouldn't kill his old man, would he? What about Susan, is she toying with me? Why did Barney lie, or was Tabitha lying? And what was with all those books in her house?*

Anya's mind wandered off and she soon found herself asleep.

Twelve

The last day! Anya thought, waking up the next morning. The sky was gloomy and the air was chilly. She changed her clothes and walked into the kitchen. Her mother was watering plants in the backyard. Anya read the news. *No news of any killings,* she thought. *Why? It has been quite a few days now.* Instead of feeling relieved, her worrying grew stronger. The doorbell rang and Anya answered the door. “Hi,” said Susan with a smile. She walked inside and sat down in the kitchen.

“Last day,” Anya smiled. *Why am I so sure that it will happen?*

“Staying home then?” Susan asked, helping herself to some toast.

“Yup,” she answered, sitting down at the table as well. “What about Eric?”

“I just called him,” said Susan. “He’ll be staying home as well.”

“And what about Carl?”

“Well, if Carl is the culprit,” said Susan smiling nervously at Anya. “Then we shouldn’t be worrying about him, right?”

The doorbell rang again. Susan got up and came back into the kitchen, with the boys behind her.

“You went to sleep early last night,” said David smiling and sitting next to Anya. “I called and your mother answered.”

“Yeah, had a headache,” she lied, watching her friends sit around the table. *Can she trust any one of them?*

“Yeah, I remember that a person suffers from a headache before the full moon,” said David laughing at Anya who rolled her eyes at him.

“Well, according to Anya’s assumption,” said Eric. “Tonight’s the night.”

“What if it’s over?” said Carl, pouring himself a glass of lemonade from the fridge. “What if the weirdoes went to another city or something?”

“Wishful thinking,” Susan smiled. “These things aren’t leaving us that easy.”

The teenagers sat in the kitchen talking amongst each other, but Anya wasn't paying any attention to what they were saying. "I have to check something," she said to the group as she got up.

"What is it?" Eric asked as he watched Anya go toward a cabinet.

Anya opened it and clutching something in her palm, she sat down. Everyone was looking at her. "You should know that these are strange times and I've got to be sure," said Anya to the group.

"Oh, great, she's going to kill us right here," said Carl rolling his eyes and sipping juice.

Anya ignored him and placed a clove of garlic on the table. "Yup, we're all going to die because of that garlic," said David as the group laughed.

"Well, excuse me for taking precautionary measures," said Anya looking at the garlic on the table.

Do any of these things really work? she thought as she watched her friends laugh. *Stupid movies!*

***

"Hey, cheer up," said Anya's mother as the two ate dinner. "Dad is coming tomorrow morning and thank god there haven't been any more killings."

Anya smiled weakly and ate her food. After cleaning the dishes, her mom called her to come and join her in front of the TV. She was watching some movie about sharks. Anya wasn't interested. She knew that tonight was the night of the full moon. She made sure that the back door was locked and went upstairs to her room. *Will I be able to sleep tonight?* she thought lying on the bed. *Will it come for me, or someone else out there tonight? Or maybe it's over now.*

She could still hear her mother watching the movie. Anya got up and looked toward David's house. The windows were closed and the lights were off except for the ones in the den. Anya had made David promise that he would sleep in the den near the phone tonight and call her as soon as he heard something. Assuring herself that he was safe, she dropped back onto her bed.

Anya closed her eyes and went to sleep only to be woken suddenly by the sound of her doorbell ringing. "Who is it?" came her mother's voice from downstairs. She heard her mother open the front door. Dreading the worst, Anya got up and looked at the clock next to her bed. It was nearly midnight. She put on her robe and slowly went out of her room and listened. *Why isn't there anyone saying something downstairs?*

"Mom!" she called…no answer. Slowly she went downstairs, clutching her robe, only to see the front door ajar and the chilly air coming in. Where's my mom? she thought looking at the open front door. The street outside was dark. *Please! God!...Please!*

Anya walked toward the front door and looked outside. It was quite dark. "Mom!" she called again into the night…no answer. The full moon shone brightly above her. "Mom!" she called again. "Please answer me," she whispered and closed the door…locking it, when all of a sudden 'SMASH!' the kitchen window broke and Carl was inside of Anya's house down on all fours.

"Ca..C..Carl?" Anya whispered as she went into the kitchen.

Carl looked as if he was in some kind of pain and he tore his shirt off. His red eyes caught Anya. "Just run!" he yelled as his face elongated.

Not needing to be told twice, Anya closed the kitchen door behind her and heard Carl thrashing around inside. She ran toward the front door and slipped.

"ROAR!"

Anya looked behind her. Carl had broken through the kitchen door. His body was covered in black hair and his red eyes were looking directly at her as she got back onto her feet.

Just reach the front door, she thought, not daring to look behind at the creature again. She raised her arm and reached for the doorknob.

"WHAM!"…"THUD!"

Anya had just managed to close the door in Carl's face as he jumped at her. She ran onto the road, wondering where she should go. *David's,* she thought and ran toward his house. But before she could reach for the bell, a hand caught her shoulder and pulled her backward… She turned around to see to her horror, Barney!

"Let me go!" she screamed. "DAVID!"

"SSsshhh," said Barney, trying to maintain his hold on her. "Listen to me!"

"You're going to kill me! Let me go!"

"I am not going to kill you."

"Sure," she said rolling her eyes. Anya kicked Barney in the knee.

"AAhhh!" he yelled, letting her go. Seizing the chance, Anya ran for it, away from the house. Barney was close behind her. *David will have to wait,* she thought running away from Barney. *Where is Carl?* she thought as she ran past her now silent house. She felt something breathe down her neck and then she screamed as a hairy body pinned her to the ground. *It's the end!* she thought, closing her eyes and waiting for the pain to come.

"WHAM!"

Anya felt someone lift her up. She looked around and saw the werewolf on the ground. It lay motionless and something red was coming out of the side of its head. "Just go!" said Barney, throwing a bloody stick from his hand. The moon hid behind some clouds and Anya watched as the hairy body slowly transformed back into…

"Eric!" Anya screamed in shock as she saw her friend lying on the street where the werewolf had been. The moon came back into sight and Eric transformed back and slowly began to get up.

"Anya," said Barney as he got hold of her hand and made her run with him. "Your mother and your blonde haired friend are at Tabitha's."

"You mean Susan?"

"Yes, and we are to go there too."

Anya ran alongside Barney in the dark street when she heard the werewolf give a howl. "What about David?" she asked, still not daring to look back.

"I don't know," said Barney, running faster. "He's not important."

"He's not what…?" Anya stopped in her tracks.

"Just go!" Barney said, pushing her forward.

"What about you?"

"Just go!" he yelled fiercely and took out his gun.

There was something in his voice that made Anya run. *He's not important?* she thought running toward Tabitha's house. *What did Barney mean by that?* She heard someone yell behind her and heard a gun fire. She turned a corner and bumped into David.

"David!" she exclaimed hugging him. "Where? How?"

"Are you all right?" he asked concerned.

"Yes, I'm fine," Anya replied hurriedly. "David, we shouldn't be here. You have to come with me."

"Where to?" he asked, looking at Anya.

"To Barney's," she answered, pulling his hand. "It's safe there."

"Who told you that?" he asked, holding her shoulders and looking directly at her.

"Barney told me just to…"

"What?" he yelled.

"He said…"

"He's lying!" said David. "Susan saw Barney out on the street around midnight walking toward your house. She knew something was up and she called us. Carl and Eric wouldn't pick up the phone. She called me and I saw Barney talk to your mother tonight and I…"

"You saw my mother? Do you know where she is?" Anya was close to tears now.

"We have to get out of here," said David as they heard howling from somewhere in the dark. "To the forest – Susan is also there!"

Without a word, Anya ran with David toward the forest. The roads were all empty and no one in the neighborhood seemed to be awake. The forest was dark and David lit his flashlight.

"Come on," he urged and led her deeper into the forest toward the cave.

"Anya, stop!" came Barney's voice from behind them. "Come back here!"

"Run!" cried David pulling Anya forward. "Run!"

"David, what about…?"

"Don't worry," he yelled, pushing her forward. "Just go! You'll meet Susan inside."

Anya ran toward the cave. Partially blinded by the darkness, she tripped over a rock and hurt her knee. "Great," she cursed, getting up. Ignoring the pain, she ran into the cave. She couldn't hear anything outside. "God," she whispered, slowly going into the cave. "Susan, are you there?"

"Oh!" she exclaimed as the bright green light blinded her vision. "Oh, no!" she remembered what Eric had said about the places where magical creatures lived, having a glow to them.

"Well, Anya," came a cold voice.

Anya turned around and saw two beautiful blue eyes looking at her.

"David," the words stuck in Anya's throat. "Why?"

"Is that even a question?" he asked, laughing as his blue eyes turned red. He held up his arms and black smoke covered him, slowly turning into a black cloak.

"Where is Barney?" Anya asked, scolding herself for coming here. The entire cave was now giving out a warm green glow.

"You can see him," he said and he clapped his hands. A werewolf came into the cave's green light holding Barney's head in its mouth. It threw the head at Anya's feet. She backed away unable to scream as the lifeless face stared at her. Barney's eyes were blank and his mouth was open.

"No," Anya whimpered, backing against the wall. She felt sick. She couldn't get the image out of her head.

"He was asking for it," said David, looking at the head as if it was trash, and then he looked at Anya, her back against the wall.

I'm dead, Anya thought as she watched another werewolf enter the cave. *That's Eric,* she thought, looking at the red shine on the side of the werewolf's head where Barney had struck it with the stick. She felt like laughing and crying at the same time. *I have to buy myself some time,* she thought, looking around. David was standing in front of her and the two werewolves were at his sides. The exit to the cave was blocked. *Maybe someone might come and look for me?*

"Where is my mother?" she asked. *I need some kind of a weapon.*

"She is not important to me," said David. "Barney took her somewhere."

Important! The word stung Anya. "What's so important about me?" she asked, looking directly at David. He looked the same but his eyes were now different…cold and emotionless.

A second later, she found David right in front of her. "All in due time," he said as he stroked Anya's cheek. "You mortals are born with gifts you don't even know exist."

Anya watched David's face come closer to her neck. She reached into her pants pocket and took out the mirror.

"AAHHAa!" David cried as she dug the mirror's edge deep into his forehead. She pushed him away and tried to run but the werewolves blocked the cave's mouth. One of them jumped and pinned her to the ground.

"Nice thinking," said David, taking out the mirror and letting his forehead heal. The werewolf got off of Anya and she got up onto her feet.

"How about a bite now?" he laughed. Anya saw David's teeth elongate.

He was so fast that Anya didn't even know what happened when she felt his hand around her throat. Anya closed her eyes, defeated. She waited for the pain but it never came. She heard a howl and opened her eyes to see one of the werewolves on the ground. A silver knife was in its chest. The vampire let go of Anya and turned his attention to Tabitha, Susan, and Lizzie.

"More friends," David smiled. The remaining werewolf was waiting to attack and was eyeing the girls hungrily. "Hello, David," said Susan. She had Lizzie by her collar.

David smiled and nodded. The werewolf jumped into the air. "BANG!" and it fell to the ground, motionless.

"Silver bullets," Tabitha smiled. "Thank Dad and his hobbies," she added seeing the question mark on Anya's face.

"That won't work on me," said David calmly. He stared at the gun. Tabitha screamed as the gun fell to the ground, too hot to be held.

David smiled at the girls. He lifted his hand and tore the skin off of his face, revealing a skull with two long teeth and red gleaming eyes. The fingers elongated and the black cloak covered him completely.

Anya ran toward her friends and watched the vampire looking directly at them. "Now what?" he asked smiling. David took a step forward and crushed Barney's skull with ease under his feet. Tabitha looked at the face being squashed, unable to say anything.

"Any ideas?" Anya asked as they watched David come toward them.

Susan pulled a crucifix out of her pocket and stood in front of her friends holding it in front of David's face. David looked at it amused. "First the mirror, then the garlic?" he said smiling. "Now this? Don't you people understand?" He took the crucifix from Susan's hand with ease and crushed it in his hand. The girls stood still. Lizzie was baring her teeth at David. "Now to end this," said David, and with immense speed and strength he grabbed Susan by the neck and threw her away. Lizzie attacked him and 'WHAM!' she hit the cave's wall and moved no more. "Lizzie!" Susan whispered, unable to move.

Tabitha took out a knife and came toward David with it, but she was too slow as the vampire dodged her strike and grabbed her by the neck. The knife dropped from her hand to the ground.

"Pathetic," he said and threw her away as well. Tabitha hit the cave wall and dropped to the ground. "Now you," he said to Anya coming toward her.

"AAGGggg!" screamed Tabitha as she grabbed David's leg trying to make him fall. Seizing the chance, Anya also fell to the ground.

"Get off, you filth!" screamed the vampire and he kicked Tabitha in the stomach. She flew into the air landing next to Susan, unconscious.

"You! Get up!" he ordered Anya. He raised his arm and an invisible force made Anya stand up directly in front of David. She felt the grip relax as the vampire clicked his fingers.

"What do you want from me?" Anya asked.

"Nothing much," he said moving toward her staring into her eyes. Anya didn't look away. She looked directly into the red gleaming eyes inside of the skull. "Just your blood line," he added with a smile.

"My what?" Anya asked confused.

"Your blood seems to have gifts in it," he said stroking her cheek again with his long fingers. "And I want it."

"Why didn't you just take it when you first came here?" she asked, feeling the cold fingers against her face. "Why kill innocent people? Why turn my friends into werewolves?"

"I can only harness your powers if you are willing to give them up yourself," said David, gently kissing her cheek and moving toward her neck, holding her close. "These friends of yours are nothing. I just thought that having werewolves by my side would be helpful," he laughed, looking at the two creatures lying motionless on the floor. "But you, Anya, are far more important. Why live with these mortals when you can live forever?" he said looking into her eyes. "Come with me and leave this pathetic life," and slowly Anya watched his face change back into the one she saw when she met David the very first day. Those piercing blue eyes, the beautiful innocent face, "come on, Anya," he said gently. "You know you want this."

"Yes," she whispered looking into those blue eyes, remembering what she felt for him.

Smiling, David kissed her, his eyes closed. Anya kissed him back but then David's expression changed. He opened his eyes in horror.

"What?" he asked and pushed Anya away who was smiling at him. He looked down and saw a knife half inside of his chest, close to his heart, "Anya you…"

Without warning, Anya grabbed the handle of the knife and drove it deeper into his chest.

David smacked her across her face making her drop to the ground. His knees gave way and he fell. With smoke coming from his wound, he looked at Anya with a smile. "I'll be back," he laughed, and slowly he went up in smoke.

Anya got up and went to her friends. They were breathing slowly. They were alive!

"Check Lizzie!" said Susan as Anya helped her onto her feet. "She's okay," said Anya relieved as the dog licked her face and then closed its eyes exhausted.

"Well, the boys are fine too," said Susan looking at them, back in their normal forms, sleeping. Susan turned around and helped Tabitha up onto her feet.

"What was it all about?" Tab asked clutching her rib, unable to stand straight.

"I don't know," said Anya picking up the knife and giving it back to Tabitha.

"So it worked," Tabitha smiled pocketing it, and then her face fell as she saw the place where Barney's head had been smashed. Anya tried not to look at the blood and the broken skull.

"Let's just get out of here," said Anya, slapping Eric on the face, trying to make him wake up.

"What happened?" he asked confused. "God, my head hurts."

And after a while the friends helped each other out of the cave and not one of them looked back at it as they left the place.

Epilogue

A week later, the five friends were sitting in the park watching children play. Eric was all right. His head had healed quickly, and Carl's ribs had healed remarkably fast as well. Tabitha was more cheerful. Barney's death was sad news but Tabitha made her dad give her permission to stay in town with her new friends. What she told her dad about the way Barney died, the rest of the friends didn't know. She had smiled at them saying that everything was all right and taken care of. Lizzie had recovered as well and was chasing butterflies in the park. Anya's mother was unharmed and so was Susan's. Barney had them in some kind of a semi-conscious state at Tabitha's house. Neither remembered leaving their house that night. Anya's dad was back and so was Carl's mother. Things were normal again in Colville.

"Next week is school," said Carl sadly looking at the clear sky.

"And I'll be starting with you guys," said Tabitha smiling.

"Let's play something," said Susan and she took out a ball from her bag.

"Come on guys," said Eric getting up and stretching. "Isn't it nice to have things back to normal?"

Anya watched her friends get ready to play with the ball. David's talk about her bloodline came rushing into her mind. *Well, he's gone now and he was a freak,* she added to herself, getting up. *And seriously, what more can happen after this, right?* And with that thought in mind she joined her friends in a game of catch.

The Swamp

One

Anya was running in a lush green field, her black hair shining in the sunlight, her long sky blue dress dancing in the wind, when all of a sudden she stopped. She could see a figure in the distance. She felt her heart race watching the figure come closer. She smiled as her prince rode toward her on a magnificent horse. He stopped in front of her. The horse neighed as he dismounted it. The prince smiled at her and his green sparkling eyes met her brown ones. He took her hand and drew her closer. Anya's heart began to beat so fast it hurt. He pulled her closer still, and looking directly in her eyes, he said, "Anya, wake up."

"Ahhha!" Anya yelled as her mother's voice came into her head.

Everything around her changed. She felt her prince let go of her hand and she began to fall down…and down…and down until she opened her eyes and found herself in her bed.

"Great," she said, lying on her bed and looking at the ceiling. "Why now?"

"Get ready," came her mother's voice again from downstairs.

"Okay, okay," Anya answered, finally getting up and going into the bathroom. "School," she mumbled, brushing her teeth. "Why so soon?" She took a quick shower, put on some clothes, applied lipstick, and went downstairs.

"Hi guys," she greeted her parents, walking slowly into the kitchen. Once there, she sat down at the table looking grumpy.

"Oh, come on Anya," said her father. "School can't be that bad," he added, smiling at his only daughter as he took a sip of his coffee.

"You have no idea," Anya mumbled, as her mother served her some toast. *God, I don't even feel like eating,* she thought, poking her breakfast with a fork. *I need to act sick.*

"I know what you are thinking," said her mother, cleaning her hands with her apron and looking at her daughter who was feeling her forehead. "And it isn't going to work," she smiled at her. "You are not sick and you are not going to get sick any time soon. Now eat your breakfast."

"Yay for me," Anya smiled weakly, taking a bite of her breakfast as she rolled her eyes. It didn't take long for her to finish her breakfast. Her family didn't talk much during breakfast.

"Now have a nice day," said her mother, handing Anya her bag. "And hurry back home."

Anya didn't say anything. She just smiled at her parents and left the house, the bright sky blinding her for a moment. She stopped herself from looking at the house next to hers. She didn't want any bad memories ruining her first day back to school. Taking a deep breath, she walked toward Susan's house. Once there, she pressed the doorbell.

"You look gloomy," smiled her blonde friend, opening the front door and stepping outside.

"Good work, detective," Anya smiled back, hating the day already.

The two friends made their way toward the bus stop where they saw the boys waving at them. "Hi girls," said the curly brown haired Carl, smiling as they came closer.

"Already hating today?" Eric asked, smiling as well, as he adjusted his glasses.

"You have no idea," Anya replied, tying her hair into a knot. She wasn't in the mood to even look good.

"Has anyone seen Tab?" asked Carl. "I can't wait to show her around."

"That really won't be necessary," came a sweet voice from behind him. He turned and noticed Tabitha smiling back at him. "I have already planned the day with Anya and Susan," she added, looking at the girls.

"Yeah, that's okay," said Carl, sounding a bit disappointed. "It's cool. No problem."

They didn't have to wait long for the bus to arrive, and the five friends along with some other kids, got on. Anya and Susan made their way toward the back seats where they always sat, saying hello to anyone they knew. Tabitha and Eric followed. Carl, on the other hand, sat down with the basketball team. The bus began moving and made two other stops to pick up more passengers.

Anya wasn't paying any attention to who was entering the bus until it stopped for the third time.

"Who the heck is he?" she asked, eyes wide open.

A boy with brown wavy hair, a well-built body, and dreamy sea green eyes had just entered the bus and was looking around for a seat. *Why did Susan and the rest have to sit with me?* she thought as the boy made his way toward her. He came closer and Anya wished she was sitting alone with him at the back of the bus. But then he stopped, turned to his right, and sat down on a seat in front of Carl and his mates. The rest of the journey passed as Anya scolded herself for sitting with her friends and not near the new boy who was already talking to a girl sitting next to him.

Susan and Tabitha looked at each other and smiled. Eric looked at Anya for a second and then returned to his book. He, too, knew what she was thinking.

***

"God, that new principal is a weird woman," said Tabitha, coming out of the principal's office with her timetable. "Anyway, why are you so into boys?" she added.

"You tell me, Tab," Anya replied as she and Susan got up from the chairs in the waiting area. "Is there anything good in this world except boys?" she added, looking around for the new boy as the three of them walked. Anya hadn't gotten the chance to catch a second glimpse of the new boy as she and her friends got off of the bus earlier. Now she was hoping to bump into him at school.

Tabitha just smiled at Anya's question and Susan rolled her eyes as the three of them headed toward the lockers. "There's your locker," Susan pointed out as they came near it.

"Oh, great, you got this one," said Anya, looking at it closely.

"Why?" asked Tabitha, looking at the locker surprised. "What's wrong with this one?"

"Don't you know?" Anya replied, pretending to be surprised. "Locker number thirteen is supposed to be haunted."

"Well, I'll take my chances," Tabitha laughed, stacking her books into it. "And by the way, how can a locker be haunted?"

"You can only imagine," came a voice from behind them. The three girls turned around and saw another girl in a black hood, which was concealing a lot of her face.

"Cassandra, how are you?" Anya asked, smiling at her.

"Never better," she replied silently.

"Cassie," said Susan, smiling at the girl. "I want you to meet Tabitha. She's a…" she stopped and looked around. Tabitha was nowhere to be seen.

"Where did Tabitha go?" Anya asked surprised, looking at Susan. She turned around to talk to Cassandra. "Have you…?" She too stopped, as there was no one behind her.

"That was weird," said Susan as she followed Anya toward their first class. "Both of them just disappeared," she added, putting her books on her desk.

"Yeah," Anya answered, sitting down. "It's as if…" Anya didn't complete her sentence because her eyes were busy following the new boy as he walked past her classroom door.

***

"I'm telling you," said Anya, putting her books into her bag as the bell rang. "He's the right one."

"You said the same about David," Susan reminded her, copying some things from the board as the teacher got up to erase them.

"You can't hold that against me," Anya replied getting up. She needed to find the new boy and fast.

"You don't even know his name," said Susan, closing her notebook. "Anyway, I have to go," she added, stuffing everything into her bag. "See you later" and she ran toward her next class.

Anya walked around for a while, her next class books in her hands, thinking about the new boy, when all of a sudden she found herself in front of the library. "What am I doing here?" she asked herself surprised, and hoping that no one had seen her there, she turned around and 'THUD!!"

"I'm so sorry," came a boy's voice, as Anya looked at her fallen books.

Oh, my God, Anya thought looking at him.

"Let me help you," he said, bending down and picking up the books. "I am so very sorry."

Anya watched as he got back up. "Here you go," he added, handing Anya her things. "Bye."

Don't go, she thought desperately. *I don't even know your name…hey wait a sec, where's my voice?* but too late, he was already gone and Anya went to her next class feeling happy and sad at the same time.

"Miss Anya" came a ringing voice. Anya opened her eyes slowly. She was sleeping in class again and the teacher, Miss Jane, looked angry. "Now," continued the teacher, "As Miss Anya has finally woken up," she gave her a serious look, "I shall make the announcement…if it is okay with you, Miss Anya?"

Anya didn't reply. *Just get on with it,* she thought, her head bowed, wishing for the class to end already.

"This year we will be going on a trip to the swamp," the teacher continued. "And we may even camp there for a while. The date will be posted on the notice boards."

A boy named Jeremy asked a question. "But Miss, isn't the swamp supposed to be haunted?" and some of the students nodded their heads in agreement.

"Of course it is," Anya laughed, but stopped as the entire class stared at her. *Oh, did I say that out loud?*

"Miss Anya is quite right," said Miss Jane, and the class diverted their attention toward her. "I can assure you it is quite safe. There are only animals and insects there, which we will be observing. So, don't forget to read the notice boards. Class dismissed."

***

After a few more classes, Anya met Susan in the cafeteria sitting with Tabitha. "Where were you earlier?" she asked sitting with them.

"I had to go to the principal again," Tabitha answered, smiling. "Well, anyway, what about the trip? One of our teachers was talking about it in class."

"Sounds boring," Anya replied, eating her chips.

"Not from what I've heard," came a voice. Anya noticed Cassandra coming toward them.

"Excuse me," said Tabitha hurriedly and without looking at Cassandra she got up and walked out of the cafeteria.

"What's up with her?" asked Anya, watching Tabitha walk away.

"Never mind Tab," said Susan, taking a bite of her burger. "Go on, Cassie," she added, as Cassandra took Tabitha's chair.

"Well, the swamp according to my knowledge, is haunted," said Cassandra, adjusting her hood. "It is said that many years ago the people in the forest lived happily, but one day because of a heavy downpour, the lake which is now the swamp, flooded, drowning the people."

"So?" asked Anya, taking a bite of her sandwich. *Is this fattening?* she thought.

"So," Cassandra continued. "It is said that every fifty years the people of the swamp, the ones who drowned, come out as swamp monsters and hunt for living flesh. They capture people and drag them down into the swamp with them, not to wake up again for another fifty years."

"Creepy," said Susan, rolling a strand of her hair around her finger.

"Sounds like a bunch of mumbo jumbo to me," said Anya, putting her sandwich down.

"Well, you believe what you want to believe," said Cassandra getting up.

"I'm getting bored," complained Anya looking around the cafeteria searching for the boy she bumped into earlier.

"How about you check out a new class then?" Cassandra asked smiling.

"I'd rather get fat," Anya replied, pressing her forehead on the table as Susan tried to suppress a laugh.

***

Anya and Susan made their way toward the school gate where they met the boys. "Have you seen Tabitha?" asked Carl as the girls came nearer.

"She's with Miss Jane," answered Anya, glad that high school was finally over for that day.

"What about the trip?" Eric asked his friends. "My class is saying that it's a haunted place. You have any ideas?"

"Whatever," Anya replied, her eyes scanning the sea of kids as she waited for the bus. After a while Tabitha came toward them, just in time for the bus. They all got on and Anya waited for the new boy, but he didn't show up. Soon the bus was filled with talk about the swamp, and Anya waited for the bus to drop her off.

Two

Getting off at the bus stop, the friends parted ways and Anya walked toward her home. Once there, she greeted her mother and went upstairs to freshen up.

The swamp is haunted came a voice in her head and it sounded a lot like Susan's. "Yeah, right," she said to herself. She went into the bathroom and took a shower. She was busy brushing her hair when she got an idea and went downstairs.

"Mom, can I use the laptop?"

"Use the laptop for what, honey? Don't tell me they gave you homework on the very first day?" asked her mother from the kitchen.

"I won't tell you that then," she answered, going into her father's study. She turned on the laptop and looked at some old newspapers on the internet, but she couldn't find anything that could tell her about the swamp, or the forest, or anyone missing in the area near it.

"Anya," came her mother's voice. "Susan is on the line, dear."

Anya turned off the laptop and went to answer the phone in the kitchen, "Hello?"

"You want to go out?"

"Where to?" asked Anya.

"We're meeting in the old park, Carl, Eric, the group."

"Meet you there," said Anya hanging up. She gave her mother a kiss, and telling her that she would hurry home, she rushed out of the house.

Things have changed, she thought, making her way to the park. She was right. Things had changed after the vampire incident that began a few weeks back. People of the town seemed relaxed and were coming out of their homes. It was obvious they didn't know about the supernatural stuff. They all thought that the culprit was caught, because that was what Tabitha had told her father, who in turn had told that to the police as well as the press.

Anya thought about herself as she walked, remembering the days when she considered herself to be a chicken, afraid of trying new things, but now after the vampire attacks and facing her fears she felt stronger and independent. As a whole, Anya was happy to see the streets where she grew up filled up with children and happy parents again.

Reaching the park, she jumped over the fence and looked around. No one was there. She felt as if she was being watched and she started to back away from the benches where the group usually sat, when suddenly a hand caught her ankle and pulled her back. She fell to the ground. She sensed someone on top of her and then she felt her mind go blank and she closed her eyes…

"Carl, get off of her!" Susan yelled, coming out from behind a bush and pushing him away from Anya. She was followed by Eric and Tabitha who were looking worried.

"What have you done?" Susan asked, staring at Anya's expressionless face.

"I…I…" whimpered Carl, eyes wide open in fear.

Eric bent down and took Anya's wrist, checking her for a pulse, when he suddenly threw it down. He looked at the three friends and slowly said, "She's dead."

"It... It can't be," said Carl in a hoarse whisper, looking at the girls who were sitting on the ground. Tabitha was staring at Anya with a weird expression on her face, as if thinking something. Susan was hugging her.

"Anya, wake up," said Carl, his voice cracking. "Wake up!"

"Got yah!" smiled Anya. Carl yelled with Susan, and Eric laughed out loud.

"It was a joke," she said, getting up with a smile. "And Eric was in on it."

"That wasn't a bit funny," said Carl, glaring at Eric.

"Yes, it was," laughed Eric. "I knew she was alright and was only acting when I checked for her pulse, so I just played along."

Eric and Anya laughed at their three friends who after a while, seeing the humor in the situation, joined them.

"So why did you call?" asked Anya, sitting on a bench.

"You know," answered Susan as the group settled down. "We wanted to talk about the trip to the swamp."

"The all so haunted one," Anya smiled.

"Try and be serious," said Eric, pushing back his glasses and looking at Anya.

"The people do say that the swamp is haunted," said Susan, looking at the group at large. "And they could be right, you know."

"I agree with Susan," said Tabitha. "The vampire thing just ended a week ago and that was pretty real for me. So maybe this swamp thing really is haunted."

"I agree with Tab," said Carl looking at her with a smile.

"Sounds like we'll have to do some checking," said Eric looking serious.

"Can't we ask Cassandra?" Anya asked. "She did seem to know a lot on the subject."

"Maybe," said Eric. He seemed pleased about the idea.

"When is the trip anyway?" asked Carl.

"Sometime next week, I guess," answered Tabitha.

"We can't do anything about it now," said Eric looking at the sky and getting up. "It's getting late and I'd better go," he added.

"We better go as well," said Carl getting up and stretching.

Eric went away alone, Tabitha followed Carl and Susan walked with Anya.

"You really aren't serious about the swamp thing, are you?" asked Anya as they walked.

"Yes, I am serious," answered Susan. "I'm going to check some old newspapers when I get back home."

"I've already done that, 1990-2009," said Anya with a smile.

"Anya, the monsters are supposed to come out every fifty years, so I doubt you'll be finding anything even twenty years back, much less on the dates you checked."

"Oh!" Anya exclaimed feeling a bit stupid.

The girls stopped outside of Susan's house and Susan took out the key to open the front door. Her mother was out with their dog Lizzie. "You want to come in?" she asked.

"Nah, I'd better get going," said Anya.

She waved to her friend and walked on toward her home. It only took her a few minutes to arrive at her doorstep. She looked at her ex-boyfriend's house. It looked creepy to her. *Oh well, life goes on,* she thought, looking away. *Life goes on and I've got bigger fish to fry,* she added, thinking of the new boy.

She knocked on the door and her mother opened it for her. "Aren't any of your friends coming?" she asked.

"Nope," answered Anya, entering her house. *Maybe I should tell her about the whole vampire thing,* she thought. *Nah, not yet, she's too soft. And who in their right mind is going to believe the fact that me and my friends took down a vampire last week, who happened to be my boyfriend as well.*

She went upstairs to her room and sat down on the bed. *What if the swamp really is haunted? No, it can't be…but what if?* She lay down on the bed. *I've got to stop talking to myself so much.*

***

Susan watched Anya from the window as she walked toward her house. The vampire incident had really made her paranoid and she kept worrying about her friends. She got some crisps from the kitchen and went to her room. She sat down in front of her computer and turned it on.

"What am I looking for?" she asked herself as she connected to the internet. She had gotten an email from Peter. "I'll open it later," she whispered and began going through some old newspapers that were published in 1962 and came across a heading.

"Five People missing," she read and clicked on the headline and began reading it to herself. "Five people of the Singleton Family disappeared last night. Mr. and Mrs. Jerry Singleton along with their three children went camping near the swamp close to their farm.

I was knitting beside the fire last night when I heard some screams, Mrs. Singleton told the press when asked about her son and his family's disappearance. *I ran toward the door to see our dog, Lucy, running toward me with my son's shirt in her teeth.*

"The police are trying to get to the bottom of this. The area near the swamp was checked earlier but nothing was found except for some broken plates."

Curious, Susan searched for some more newspapers or any article regarding the disappearances. "I don't think I'll be finding any newspapers dating that far," she said to herself, and began to search for anything that was linked to disappearances near the swamp almost fifty years ago. She found one telling about a class of youngsters from a local school that went to the swamp and never returned. The entire class disappeared along with three teachers. She reached the last line and found a link to some records dating back to 1862. She clicked it and found herself reading an article about some disappearances occurring that year near the swamp. Going through some links, she found a site telling about a downpour occurring in the area where the swamp was located.

"September 1855," read Susan. "A heavy rainfall occurred near the quiet town of Colville and flooded a lake, drowning most of the inhabitants living near the forest. No one can tell for certain how many perished. The people were simple and had lived in that area for hundreds of generations…blah…blah…blah."

"Seems interesting," said Susan. The idea of a haunted swamp and the disappearances felt terrifying as well as intriguing to her. She couldn't wait to tell the others and especially Anya about her findings.

Three

"Why do you look weird?" asked Anya as Susan opened the front door and walked outside.

"I checked some newspapers last night."

"And?"

"I'll tell you about it on the bus," answered Susan as they walked toward the bus stop.

"Come on, tell me."

"On the bus," Susan repeated. "In front of the others."

Anya knew Susan all to well and didn't ask again. After a while their friends and the bus arrived and Susan told them to sit with her in the back.

"You won't believe what I found out last night," said Susan with excitement as the bus started and the friends settled down.

"Try us," said Carl with a smile, sitting with Tabitha.

Susan told them what she had seen on the internet, everything about the rain falling, the flood, and the disappearances.

"So it all seems true then," said Anya, amazed at Susan's research capabilities. She would have praised Susan, but the bus made its third stop and her attention went to the door. But the new boy didn't come.

"You are saying that this thing happened a hundred years ago?" asked Carl in disbelief, which made Anya remember that they were talking about the swamp.

"More than a hundred years ago," Susan answered, feeling proud of her work.

"According to my calculations, it happened approximately 154 years ago," said Eric. "I should have thought of that first. But good work, Susan."

"Wait a minute," said Tabitha in her sweet voice, and everyone looked at her. "The first event happened in 1862, didn't it, then in 1912, and then again in 1962? So the next event is going to be in…"

"What happened?" asked Carl, as Tabitha remained quiet.

"Oh, my God," said Tabitha, worried. "1862, 1912, 1962…all have a gap of…"

"Fifty years!" gasped Eric, looking at his friends.

"What are you talking about?" asked Carl.

"All have a gap of fifty years," answered Eric. "And following this sequence, the next one is going to be..."

"This year," said Tabitha, completing his sentence as the friends looked at each other worried.

***

"You surely don't want me to believe this?" asked Anya as the girls made their way toward their lockers.

"Well, I believe," answered Susan. "And after the thing with David, I'm surprised you don't as well."

Anya didn't reply, as even she didn't know why she didn't believe that the swamp was haunted. *Maybe I don't want to believe it*, she thought. *Maybe I just want to live a normal life.*

Tabitha walked toward her locker. The number 13 always gave Anya a weird feeling.

"Why do you hate it so much?" asked Tabitha, referring to her locker, and again Anya got the feeling that Tabitha could read minds.

"I don't know," answered Anya. "It may be because it's supposed to be haunted."

"And?" urged Susan with a smile.

"And nothing!" snapped Anya.

"And what?" asked Tabitha curiously, looking at Susan.

"On the 13th of October she broke her nose which ruined her school picture about three years ago," began Susan.

"Here we go," said Anya rolling her eyes, unable to stop her friend.

"On the 13th of December she tore her frock in school and had to run to the toilet crying."

"I was six, Susan! Six!" yelled Anya.

"And after that," continued Susan, clearly enjoying herself. "Her so called boyfriend, Harry, broke up with her. That too happened on the 13th of some month."

"Why?" asked Tabitha listening closely.

"Well, let's just say he didn't like girls," answered Anya, glaring at Susan who was laughing her heart out.

"What do you mean he didn't like girls? Oh," whispered Tabitha understanding, and she too began to laugh with Susan.

***

"Miss Anya!" came a familiar voice and Anya opened her eyes. The entire class was watching her.

"As you can see," began Miss Jane. "Now that Miss Anya has finally opened her eyes, I will begin speaking, if it is still okay with you, Miss Anya."

Giving her an angry look, Miss Jane returned to the white board. Anya didn't say anything. She liked Miss Jane. She was kind, young and good looking, but her biology classes weren't the ones that could be considered the least bit interesting. Whenever she delivered her lectures, Anya found herself dozing off toward slumber land.

At last the bell rang and Anya got up from her seat. "How many of you are certain that you are going?" asked their teacher.

"Going where?" someone from the class asked.

"How many of you are going on the trip? If you all remember?" answered Miss Jane, taking out a register and a pen. "Your names, please."

Everybody began looking at each other. "Come on now, it'll be fun," said Miss Jane, looking at the class. "I know there has been a lot of talk about the swamp being haunted. But seriously, don't tell me that you believe in these childish tales?"

Listening to Miss Jane, a few hands flew up. "What about you, Anya?" she asked. "Don't tell me that you aren't even interested in going on field trips?"

"I…" Anya tried to answer. She really wanted to tell her teacher about the disappearances that had occurred near the swamp.

"Oh, come on, you'll make five," said Miss Jane, looking disapprovingly at the class.

"Okay," said Anya, not knowing why she had hesitated before.

"Guys, will it help if I tell you that this trip is going to count in your grades?" announced Miss Jane. But still no one volunteered. "Okay, fine," said Miss Jane, defeated. "Five kids from this class it is then."

***

"Tell me you guys are going?" asked Susan smiling as the three girls met each other in the cafeteria.

"I am," said Tabitha, putting her tray on the table.

"Yeah, I gave my name too," said Anya as well.

"That's great," said Susan with a smile. She then looked to her right and saw Carl with his basketball team mates. Eric, on the other hand, always went to the library whenever he was free.

"Have you met Seth yet?" asked Tabitha casually.

"Seth who?" asked Anya, eating her chips. *Aren't chips fattening?* she thought. *But why do they taste so good?*

"Your dream boy," answered Susan, trying not to smile. "The bus boy?"

"His name is Seth?" asked Anya, her eyes wide open.

"Yeah and he's quite nice and kind," said Tabitha, taking a sip of her juice.

You must have hypnotized him, thought Anya, feeling angry at Tabitha for getting the chance to talk to Seth, her bus boy, before she did.

"He's yours," said Tabitha smiling, and again Anya felt a chill. *I have to think carefully from now on,* thought Anya, not making eye contact with Tabitha. *Great! Can she hear this too?*

All of a sudden Tabitha felt tense and began talking with Susan about the new mathematics coursework, and Anya told her not to talk about education in the cafeteria as it was against the social rules. The bell rang and the girls got up. Susan and Tabitha had history, so they waved Anya goodbye. Anya went toward the dust bin with the empty food trays. She wasn't paying attention to what was in front of her and bumped into Seth. She fell down with the trays and Seth bent down to help her up again.

"We've got to stop meeting like this," he grinned, helping her up.

"Bump into me anytime," whispered Anya as Seth bent down again to pick up the trays.

"What did you say?" he asked, getting back up.

"Oh, nothing," Anya blushed as Seth handed her the food trays.

They looked at each other for a moment and neither said a word. "I've got to go," said Seth, suddenly remembering something. He took the trays from Anya and dumped them into the bin for her. "See ya," he added and walked out of the cafeteria.

"WOW!" yelled Anya so loudly that half of the kids sitting in the cafeteria stared at her. Feeling embarrassed, she ran for it, tripping once on her way out.

***

"Anya!" yelled Susan. The friends were riding the bus back home and Susan was looking at Anya who was watching the door of the bus, waiting for Seth to arrive. "Earth to Anya," said Susan, trying to get her attention. "Hellooo, anyone home in there?"

"Maybe she's dead," said Carl, poking her in the ribs.

"Stop that," said Anya, slapping Carl's hand away.

"As I was saying," continued Eric. "Before Anya lost it. I think we should check the swamp out ourselves before the trip."

"No way I'm going there to…"

"Anya, SHhhh."

"Don't you shush me, Carl Smith!" yelled Anya.

"Or what?" asked Carl, an eyebrow raised.

"Or this," said Anya, and she punched Carl right in the ribs. He still hadn't properly healed from the vampire incident and it hurt.

"Both of you need to grow up," said Eric, holding Carl's arms as they reached out for Anya. "I am never sitting between you two ever again."

"As I was saying," Eric continued as Carl and Anya settled down, not looking at each other. "We have to check out this swamp thing. I wouldn't have believed it, but after the thing with David, well, I think it'll be foolish of us not to."

"What if it really is just a story?" said Anya. "What if the vampire incident was a one time deal? God, I just want things to be normal again."

"Maybe they have gotten normal," said Tabitha sympathizing with her friend. "But we still have to check the swamp just to be sure, because if the stories are true, then those monsters from the swamp are going to wake up sometime this year, or maybe on the night we'll be camping there with the other kids. This time it's not just us. We have others to worry about too."

The others looked at Tabitha, nodding their heads. "I couldn't have added that up any better myself," smiled Eric. "So it's done. We will be checking the swamp before the trip."

"Fine," said Anya, admitting defeat. *What's so wrong with hoping that it's just a tale?* she thought. "When is the trip anyway?"

"This Saturday," answered Tabitha. "I checked the notice board and I still can't believe how few kids are going. I mean, the trip's free and it's for everybody in our year."

"I suppose some people don't think of haunted swamps as an ideal place to go on a field trip," said Carl smiling.

The rest of the trip passed with the friends talking about the swamp. Anya was disappointed that Seth didn't show up. The bus reached its destination and the friends got off. Eric went with Carl and the girls walked on. "When are we coming back?" asked Anya. "You know, if we do come back from the trip."

"It's for three days," answered Susan as they reached Tabitha's house and dropped her off. After waving goodbye to Susan outside of her house, Anya made her way toward her house. She found the front door unlocked and went inside. Her mother was talking to someone on the phone. "Yes, and then she…" her mother stopped talking as Anya gave her a hug. "Hold on a second," she said into the receiver and smiled at her daughter. "What is it, Anya?"

"Nothing," said Anya. "Just wanted to do that."

She had never kept anything from her parents and really wanted to tell them about David, the disappearances, and the swamp. All they knew was that the culprit had been caught and David had gone to live with his parents. She let go of her mother and went to her room. "Be strong," she told herself sitting on her bed. "And besides, they'll never believe you. Come to think of it, no one would."

Four

The final bell rang. Cassandra picked up her bag and stood up. The rest of the class was also getting up. "What about the trip?" asked Mrs. Carl, their psychology teacher. "How many of you are going, even though it is meant for the biology students?"

With her arm raised, Cassandra walked out of the classroom. "Freak," whispered one of the boys as she walked out. Cassandra ignored him and went on her way, when suddenly she got a strange feeling inside of her. She stopped. Somehow she knew something bad was about to happen. She shook her head and was just about to take another step when she heard a yell from inside of her classroom. She turned around. The boy who had just called her a freak was sitting down on the floor holding his bloody nose.

"Davison!" cried Mrs. Carl, walking toward the hurt boy. "Would it kill you to watch where you are going instead of tripping all over the place?"

Cassandra lowered her head and walked away. She knew something like this might happen. She reached the school gate and saw Anya and her friends getting into the bus. She liked Anya and the others, but there was something strange about Tabitha as she watched her getting on the school bus with Anya and the others.

***

"Hello, Anya here," said Anya answering the phone in the kitchen.

"It's me, Susan."

"What's up?"

"It's about…"

"Wait a minute," Anya cut through. "There's someone on the other line." Anya pressed a button on the receiver. "Hi, Anya, it's Tabitha," answered a voice.

"Hi, I've got Susan on the other line," said Anya. "Hold on a second."

"Susan, it's Tabitha," she said.

"Good, tell her this too then," said Susan. "I want you to come to my house pronto!"

"Why?" Anya asked surprised. "Everything okay?"

"Just come," said Susan. "I hope to see you in five," and she hung up.

"Just talked to Susan," said Anya, switching to Tabitha. "She wants us at her house in five."

"Did she say why?"

"Nope," answered Anya. "Why did you call?"

"Oh, I…I just needed the history notes," answered Tabitha. "Susan told me you might have them from last semester."

"Yeah, I have their softcopy," said Anya, still unsure if that really was what Tabitha had called her for. "Tell you what, I'll e-mail them to you tonight."

"Fine with me," said Tabitha. "Anyway, see you at Susan's," and she hung up.

Anya got ready and walked to Susan's place. Reaching her house, she rang the doorbell.

"Come inside," smiled Susan, opening the door and letting Anya inside. Anya walked inside and saw Eric, Carl and…

"Tom!" said Anya surprised. "How are you?"

"Fine," he answered, smiling at her.

"We're here too, you know," added Carl, pretending to be upset. Anya ignored him and then her eyes fell onto a stack of books on the table near Tom.

"I asked Tom to come over with them," said Susan noticing Anya looking at the books. There were five of them, all big and heavy looking. "Why isn't Tabitha here yet?" Susan asked no one in particular, tying her blonde hair into a knot.

"There she is," said Anya as she watched Tabitha press the doorbell, from the window. Susan opened the door and let Tabitha inside. She too was carrying some books.

"Oh, I just had this feeling," she answered with a smile as Susan looked at the books, eyebrows raised. Smiling at everyone inside, Tabitha placed the books on the table beside the other stack already there. "Felix," she called, looking at the door. "Please come in."

The friends heard something scratching the front door from outside. Susan opened the door again and let a black cat come inside. Lizzie, who was taking a nap, woke up and looked at the new guest curiously as it jumped onto a sofa, stretched, curled into a ball and went to sleep.

"Well, as we are all here," said Susan, sitting with her friends around the table. "Let's begin."

In a minute Anya understood why Susan had asked Tom to come. All of the books he had brought along with him were about magic. *She really is serious about the swamp,* thought Anya as Tom began opening some books. The last time Anya had seen Susan showing any interest in work was when she helped Peter with some research on a disease that occurred in Africa some months ago.

Tom was a big help. He opened a scrapbook which had clippings of old newspapers in it. Most of the things they found out were the same as the ones Susan had already told them. The new thing they discovered was that the people of the small village near the swamp used to practice magic. The Singleton farm was built after the village was destroyed due to the flood.

"But why is the swamp believed to be haunted?" asked Eric, searching through a book.

"The village practiced magic," answered Tabitha as she opened one of her books.

"Where did you get that?" asked Tom, looking with interest at the book that Tabitha had just opened.

"My father collects them," she smiled and began checking something from the index. "There," she said pointing at a chapter that read, *"Resurrection Spells."*

"Sounds a lot like Harry Potter to me," said Carl, raising an eyebrow.

"This is real," said Tabitha, and she began to read. "The resurrection spells include spells that are able to imitate death, create zombies, bring forth spirits, and even those that give immortality."

"Creating zombies? Sounds fun," smiled Tom.

Tabitha opened a new page, page 513. The number 13 felt like a bad omen to Anya. "The spell to create zombies is very complex," Tabitha began to read. "It is the work of pure evil and requires the heart to have no emotions at the time of its casting.

Done under the light of the full moon, this book shall not say anything more about this deed."

"Great," mumbled Anya, and Tabitha continued reading. "We only tell you this, that the curse can be broken by someone of magical descent, or else the cursed will keep on doing what is required of them throughout the ages."

"Where are we going to find someone of magical descent?" asked Susan, confused.

"No idea," answered Eric, still looking at the page that Tabitha had read from.

"If that's the case," said Carl yawning. "Why don't we all just…"

"No," Eric cut through. "We are still going on the trip, witch or no witch."

"You guys seem pretty interested with the whole swamp thing," said Tom smiling.

Oh, this is bad, Anya thought, thinking of an answer.

"Who wants lemonade?" asked Susan, and she walked toward the kitchen leaving the others to handle the situation.

Typical, thought Anya, watching Susan go toward the kitchen. *Should she tell Tom the truth?*

"It's nothing, Tom, really," answered Eric finally. "Our school is planning a trip to the swamp and I was just interested in writing a paper on it for extra credit."

"Sounds fun," Tom answered, taking a glass from Susan as she handed lemonade to everyone.

"Nice going," Anya whispered to Susan as she walked past her.

"Anyway, I've got to go," said Tom, emptying his glass and getting up. He picked up his books and headed for the door. "You guys have fun at the swamp," he smiled as Susan opened the door for him.

"So, magical descent?" asked Susan sitting down, not looking at her friends.

"Who wants lemonade?" said Carl, looking at her.

"You completely ditched us," smiled Eric.

"Hey, what was I supposed to do?" asked Susan laughing. "I knew you could handle the situation."

After a while the friends got up to leave. Carl went with Tabitha and Eric. Anya waved Susan goodbye and walked toward her own house. Colville seemed a lot happier now since the attacks had stopped. Anya smiled to herself watching other people walk past her. *None of them have the slightest clue what happened*, she thought as she walked toward her house. For her, it was better this way. There was no need for her and her friends to try and tell people what had really happened.

"Are you alright, honey?" her mom asked as she came through the front door.

"Yup, I'm fine," she answered, making her way upstairs to her room. She sat down on her bed and looked around. Her clothes were everywhere. Having nothing better to do, she dumped all of them into one corner. She then began cleaning her desk. *Why is there a first grade book here?* she thought, putting it aside.

"That's better," she said, looking around her room. Even though she tried not to look, her eyes stopped at her window and then looked outside. David's house was dark. Ignoring it all, she dropped onto her bed. After a while her mother came up holding a plate of biscuits and a glass of milk. "Are you sure you are alright?" asked her mother, surprised. "I've never seen your room less messy."

Anya just groaned as her mother placed the food on the desk. She got up to have a biscuit and noticed her mother looking at David's house. "I'm surprised," said her mother.

"Why, what happened?" Anya asked, biting into a cookie.

"Didn't he give you a number or something?" she said, referring to David. "He was such a good boy."

"No, Mom, he went away with his parents," answered Anya. "He does e-mail though," she lied.

"Well, good," her mother smiled. "You always make such good friends."

"You have no idea," whispered Anya.

"By the way," her mother continued. "I almost forgot. This came for you," and she placed an envelope on the bed. "I've got dinner to make," and she went downstairs.

Anya drank her milk, remembering the night she fought David. She had later discovered that Tabitha knew something was wrong and Barney had helped put Susan's mother as well as her mother to sleep. They were at Tabitha's house when all of it was happening. Barney had come to save Anya too, but she was already running away from the werewolf. After the incident their parents had woken up in their beds oblivious to everything that had happened during the night. How Tabitha had put her parents back into their bed without Barney's help, Anya did not know.

Why didn't I ask her that? What really happened? she thought, picking up the envelope. *I was so happy that it all had ended that nothing else mattered to me that night.*

Anya looked at the envelope she was holding. It had no return address. *Should I ask Tabitha what happened?* she thought, opening the envelope. She took out the piece of paper from inside and screamed, throwing the letter to the floor. A single message, not more than two words, was on the piece of paper she had thrown onto the floor, two words that made Anya remember all that she had gone through not so long ago. Written in the handwriting she remembered all too well was:

"I'm back!"

Five

"Anya, you alright up there?" asked her mother concerned, from downstairs.

"I…I'm fine," she lied, picking the piece of paper from the floor. She looked at it closely and noticed weird symbols on it. "I thought I saw a mouse."

"Well, with the condition your room is in," answered her mother laughing from downstairs. "It wouldn't be a surprise if you did see one."

Anya did not reply and looked at the letter again. "I'm back," she whispered to herself. *Should I tell someone?* she asked herself, sitting on her bed. The letter clenched in her fist. *Only Susan and Eric knew about the letter from last time.* She knew her friends too well and was quite certain that they hadn't told Carl or Tabitha about it. *But what if they did tell those two?* she thought. *Carl and Tabitha wouldn't pull a prank like this one, would they?*

"Ahhhaaa!" Anya punched the top of her bed. She remembered all of the things David had told her that night, things about her being special and that he would return. This was her fight and she wasn't going to drag her friends along with her like last time. "I'm ready for you," she said to herself, looking at the letter with hate.

***

Anya woke up the next day. It was Wednesday. "Friday is nearly here," she said to herself. She got ready and was just about to leave her room when she stopped. Her hand was on the doorknob. She turned around and walked to her desk. Once there, she opened the drawer and took out the letter she had gotten yesterday and without thinking, she put it in her pocket.

Anya ate her breakfast silently. "Honey, are you sure Anya is here?" Anya's dad asked her mother with a smile. "Because I haven't heard anyone at the table this morning," he added looking at Anya, who still had her head down. "And frankly speaking," he continued as his wife poured him a cup of coffee. "I'm used to waking up to silence at the breakfast table, especially from my daughter."

"Anya, are you alright, dear?" asked her mother, sitting down as well.

"I'm fine, guys," she forced a smile and got up. "I just have this stupid quiz today."

"Did she say a quiz?" asked her father, faking surprise. "Where did she learn that word?"

"Haha," said Anya, rolling her eyes and putting the dishes into the sink. She waved them goodbye, grabbed her bag and went outside. She had just lied to her parents again. *What am I supposed to do if not lie?* she thought, looking at the sky. *It's not my fault that supernatural beings have started to come here.*

She made her way to Susan's house and walked with her to the bus stop. The others were already there. "Friday is nearly here," said Carl with a smile upon seeing the two girls. The bus arrived and the friends made their way to the back seats. Anya waited for Carl to sit down and take her mind off of the letter. She asked him a question that made him raise his eyebrows in interest.

"Why are you asking me about him?" he asked her with a weird smile on his face. The others leaned in.

"Oh, just asking because he's new and all," answered Anya, not looking at Carl. Susan and Tabitha looked at each other with a smile. Eric, too, understood and continued reading his book.

"So, you want me to hook you two up?" said Carl. "You want me to help you because you can't go talk to him yourself?"

"You couldn't be more wrong," said Anya, giving him a fake smile. Before Carl could answer, the bus stopped and Seth got on. He walked toward an empty seat and before sitting down, he did something that made Anya blush.

"Oh, my God!" exclaimed Anya, watching Carl pretending to be sick. "He smiled at me. There, Carl, I don't need anyone's help!"

"Fine, I give up," said Carl, raising his hands in defeat. "Though I still think he could have done a lot better."

Something crossed Tabitha's mind before Anya could answer Carl back. "Susan, what about you?" she asked, looking in Seth's direction with a smile.

"I do have one," answered Susan. "His name is Peter."

"He's a weird guy if you ask me," Carl added, yawning.

"He isn't in Colville?" Tabitha asked.

"Nope," Anya answered. "He has been in Africa for the past two years now."

"It's a long distance relationship," Susan added with a smile.

"Though I still think she should go out with someone near," Anya joked.

Tabitha's eyes met Carl's. "If you're asking me," he said with a smile, "Let's just say I have my eyes on somebody."

Tabitha averted her gaze with a smile and looked at Eric.

"What?" he asked, noticing the group looking at him. "I have more important things to think about."

"Don't kid yourself," said Carl, punching his shoulder. "Spill it!"

"I…uh…we're here," he said in a hurry as the bus stopped. He got up and without a word ran toward the gate, passing Cassandra as she too was making her way to school.

"Do my eyes deceive me?" asked Anya with surprise.

"I don't think so," added Susan, following her out of the bus.

"I think it's sweet," said Tabitha.

"At least we now know that he likes girls," said Carl, getting out of the bus as well. "Hey! What did I say?" he added as the three girls gave him a horrid look. The four friends had just seen Eric glance twice in Cassandra's direction as he passed through the gate.

***

"This really gives me the chills," said Anya.

"Why don't you close your eyes?" Susan suggested, patting her on the back.

"Be strong," said Tabitha with a smile. "It's just a locker. We've faced worse."

Anya didn't answer as she watched Tabitha open her locker and take out some books. Why was the locker giving her a weird feeling? She couldn't tell. "Well, see you after class," said Susan as she followed Tabitha. Anya made her way to her first class. Once there, she sat down and waited for it to end. Miss Jane was going on about some insect. Anya wasn't paying attention. At the end of the class the teacher gave a list to the students who were going on the trip.

"Water bottles, pan, disposable plates…blah, blah, blah," read Anya, throwing the list into the bin as she walked out of class. After three more classes Anya met Susan and Tabitha in the cafeteria.

"The day's not going well for you?" Susan asked as Anya sat down at the table with her food tray.

"No, not yet," she answered. *Where's Seth?* she thought, looking around.

"Hey, girls," said Carl, taking a seat next to Tabitha.

"Where's Eric?" Susan asked him, sipping her juice.

"Look behind," he answered, his mouth already full with his burger.

The three girls saw Eric coming toward them talking with Cassandra. Anya couldn't help but smile.

"Hi guys," he said, sitting down. Cassandra smiled at them and sat down as well. Tabitha looked a bit annoyed. "I'd better go," she said, getting up and looking at the cafeteria clock.

"Where to?" asked Carl, putting down his carton of milk, ready to go with her.

"I thought your next class didn't begin for another fifteen minutes," said Cassandra.

"I have some business to attend to," Tabitha answered, not looking at Cassandra. She grabbed her bag and walked away followed by Carl.

"I think I'd better go too," said Cassandra, getting up as well, and without another word she walked out of the cafeteria. Eric looked sad.

"What was that all about?" asked Susan looking at her friends.

"I have no idea," answered Anya. "Both of them have been like this since they met."

"Forget about it," said Susan. Her eyes met Eric's and she gave him a weird smile.

"What?" he asked surprised.

"You know what," said Anya, smiling. "What's cooking between you and the hood lady?"

"It's nothing. She's just a friend," he answered, not making eye contact with the girls.

"Ooh, just friends?" laughed Susan.

"You make whatever you want of it," said Eric getting up. "I have nothing to hide."

"Just one question though," said Susan with a smile. "Have you seen her face with her hood down?"

"Haha," Eric replied as he picked up his bag and walked away.

"Run all you want, Romeo," Anya laughed, watching him walk out of the cafeteria.

"Anya," said Susan seriously.

"What is it?" she asked, taking a sip of her orange juice from a bottle.

"Have you seen Cassandra's face without the hood?" she asked.

Anya didn't reply, and both friends remained silent. None of them had seen Cassandra's full face. *I've always seen her with her hood on,* thought Anya, getting up and putting away the food trays. *Weird. What is her face like anyway?*

The final bell rang and Anya literally ran out of Mrs. Carl's class, feeling free. She made her way to the gate when her eyes went to the bicycle stands and …Seth. "It's now or never," she whispered to herself and walked toward Seth, who was unlocking a bicycle.

"Hi," he said as he watched Anya walk toward him as he got up.

"Hi," she smiled back.

"We haven't met properly yet," he said, holding out his hand. "I'm Seth. Seth Majors."

"I'm Anya," she answered, shaking his hand.

"Just plain Anya?" he asked with a smile.

Great, he thinks I'm plain…No wait!...He's asking for my last name.

She noticed Seth still looking at her and instead of telling him her last name she asked, "Haven't seen you on the bus after school."

Good going! she thought, scolding herself. *Now he'll think you're nosy.*

"I take a bicycle home," he answered, looking at the vehicle. "I've got a friend. He goes here as well. He comes to school on his bicycle and because he's on the basketball team, he comes home late. So I take his bike and he gets a ride from his friends."

Anya heard the bus stopping outside. "We better go," said Seth with a smile. He grabbed his bicycle and Anya walked with him toward the gate.

"Where do you live?" he asked.

"In Colville," she answered, reaching the gate. "Bye," she waved as Seth got on the bicycle and rode away.

***

Cassandra grabbed her books and walked out of the classroom toward the school gate. Near the gate a voice stopped her. It was Eric.

"Hi, Eric," she said looking behind.

"Hey, Cassandra," he said hurrying toward her.

"So?" she asked, trying to figure out why he had stopped her.

"So nothing," he answered with a smile. "Is it a crime to walk with someone?"

"No, it isn't," she answered with a smile.

"So…," began Eric.

"Look, Eric," Cassandra cut through. "I'm in a bit of a hurry and…"

"Oh, okay," said Eric, sounding hurt. "No problem," and he walked away, his head down.

Cassandra walked on feeling bad for what she had just done to Eric. She couldn't understand why she hadn't talked to him. She had gotten a strange feeling when he came up to her. She watched Eric as he got on the bus after Carl and Tabitha. *What's up with that girl?* she thought as the bus drove away.

Six

"He talked to me!" said Anya excited, taking her seat in the bus.

"What did he say?" Susan asked interested.

"Nothing much," Anya answered as kids began to fill the bus. "He told me his name. It's Seth Majors," she added as Susan raised her eyebrows. "And he walked me to the bus."

"Big deal," said Carl walking toward the girls with a smile.

Anya ignored him. "Where's Eric?" she asked. "He's always earlier onto the bus than you."

"I saw him with Cassandra," answered Tabitha in a weird tone, sitting down. A moment later Eric came onto the bus and took his seat between Susan and Anya. He looked sad. "Hey, what's wrong?" asked Anya concerned, as the bus started.

"Nothing," he answered with a weak smile. "I'm fine," and he took out a book from his bag and began reading it. His friends knew that he didn't want to talk.

Carl got up and went to sit with a group of other students he knew, and the girls talked about what they were supposed to bring on the trip. Anya grew bored, tuned out, and spent the bus ride thinking about Seth. When the bus stopped, the group got out. Carl walked away with Tabitha, and Eric slowly went his own way.

"Susan," said Anya, watching Eric go. "Think you can walk alone?"

Susan noticed Anya watching Eric and understood. "Fine with me," she answered. "Let's just hope that you can get him to talk."

Anya walked after Eric. "Hey," she said, placing her hand on his shoulder. "You really alright?"

"You really are stubborn, aren't you?" asked Eric with a smile.

"Well, I try," she answered and led him to the park with the playing equipment.

"Come on, sit," she pointed at the bench.

"Very well, Dr. Anya," he smiled, sitting down and dropping his bag onto the ground.

"So," Anya began, sitting down. "What happened? What's bothering you?"

"You know Cassandra?"

"You mean the hood girl, right?" Anya answered laughing.

"Yeah," he answered with a weak smile.

"You like her, don't you?"

"I…Yeah, I do."

"Then what seems to be the problem?" she asked, punching his shoulder. "Let me guess. You like her. You even tried talking to her, but you don't know if she likes you back or not?"

"You're good," said Eric impressed.

"I know," she answered with a smile, tying her black hair into a knot.

"But I really think she doesn't like me."

"Why?" questioned Anya. "You're sweet, in a nerdy kind of way."

"Thanks," Eric answered. "I'll take that as a compliment. Anyway, forget about me. What's up with you and the new boy?"

"Is the news all over school?"

"Yeah, kind of," Eric answered with a smile.

"Really?" said Anya faking surprise, and then she thought of something.

"What's wrong?" Eric asked concerned.

"I got this," she answered, making up her mind and taking out the letter from her pants pocket. Eric took it from her and opened it up. "Anya," said Eric shocked when he finished reading it. "I know," she answered, looking at her feet.

"But how?" he asked, the letter still in his hand. "You said that you defeated him," he added, rubbing his chest. He remembered the vampire incident all too well.

"I don't know," she said, taking the letter from him. "Maybe he is…I just don't know…I haven't told anyone else yet."

"We have to check it out," said Eric seriously.

"But how?" Anya asked, not understanding him.

"You remember the cave, don't you?"

Anya remained silent. She could never forget that night.

***

"I don't believe we're doing this," said Anya. She was walking with Eric in the nearby forest, heading toward the caves. Eric remained silent and led the way.

"Are you sure this is the one?" Anya asked as the two of them stood outside of a cave's mouth.

"I'm positive," Eric answered, looking at it closely. "I just know it."

The two of them walked into the cave. Eric took out a flashlight from inside of his bag and led the way deeper into the cave.

"Where is it?" he asked looking around after walking inside of the cave for a few minutes.

"What?"

"Don't you remember?" asked Eric. "A vampire's place is supposed to have a glow. The last time he was in here the walls had those green crystals growing everywhere."

"Maybe he isn't here," answered Anya, trying to comfort herself. "Maybe he isn't using this cave anymore. And the crystals must have disappeared when he died or something."

"Maybe he's further inside," said Eric, aiming the beam of light forward. "Or he's using another cave."

"I don't think we should be going any farther," said Anya as she saw Eric take a few steps forward.

"We have to make sure," said Eric looking back at her.

Again a weird feeling came over Anya. She felt as if she was going to faint, and as sudden as the feeling came, it went away. "Eric, this is bad," said Anya, not understanding what just happened. "Let's go," she added, grabbing Eric by the arm and pulling. "Let's just go. This was a bad idea."

"Anya, let go!" said Eric, feeling her nails dig into his arm. "Anya, stop!" he yelled, but too late. He tripped and the flashlight went flying into the air. The beam of light fell onto the ceiling and hundreds of bats flew at the two friends.

"Anya, get down!" Eric ordered, pulling her to the ground.

"I do not like this one bit!" screamed Anya over the screeching noise that surrounded them. She tried not to scream as she felt bats fly over her, hitting her head along the way.

After some minutes which felt like forever to Anya, the cave again engulfed the two friends in silence. Anya got up and ran toward the flashlight. She picked it up and it went out. She tried shaking it a few times, but to no avail.

"Eric, where are you?" she yelled in the dark, trying to remain calm. A hand caught her by the shoulder and she screamed.

"It's me," came Eric's voice. "Stop yelling."

"I told you this was a bad idea," said Anya, trying to figure out where his face was.

"Leave it," said Eric.

"How do you suppose we get out of here?" Anya asked, unable to keep herself calm.

"Just follow my lead," Eric answered, taking her hand.

"How? We have no light!"

"Well, the funny thing is that my werewolf powers allow me to see in the dark, but they can't help me get rid of these glasses," he answered with a laugh and began leading Anya forward.

"Eric, shouldn't we be going backward?" she asked as Eric pulled her along.

"No. We are seeing this through," he answered.

Anya could hear Eric sniffing the air as he led her deeper into the cave.

"It feels like a maze down here," said Eric.

This is so not good, thought Anya. *There are tunnels here? A maze of tunnels?* She wanted to run back but without a flashlight she had no choice but to go along with Eric. "Thank goodness," breathed Anya as she noticed a narrow beam of light a few feet away from her.

The two of them reached the narrow beam of light coming from between some rocks that were blocking what seemed to be the exit. "I'll see if I can move these," said Eric as he picked up a massive rock and pushed it out of the way. "These things are heavy," he said exhausted after moving a few more big rocks. The opening was a little wider now. "See if you can squeeze through," said Eric, wiping sweat from his forehead.

"I'll try," said Anya, determined to get out of the dark cave. The opening was a tight fit but she managed to get out and found herself quite high from the ground. The sunlight blinded her for a minute.

"Eric, think you can get out?" she yelled from the other side.

"I'll try," he answered. "These rocks are way too heavy for me to move on my own."

"And here I was thinking that werewolf powers were doing you some good," said Anya, dusting dirt off of her knee.

"Well, maybe I can…"

"Maybe you can what?" asked Anya as Eric stopped in mid sentence. She heard something on the other side and a moment later Eric came through the opening, his body bent in a very weird way.

"There," he said, coming out along with his backpack and standing next to Anya. "At least now I know that I'm quite flexible."

"That was catlike, not wolf-like," said Anya watching Eric brush dirt from his black hair. "Where are we?" she added looking around.

"We're outside of our hometown, that's for sure," he answered, pushing back his glasses and looking around. "Hey!" he cried. "Is that the swamp near those woods?"

Anya looked down to where he was pointing and sure enough, there it was, a long way away from them was the swamp as well as the Singleton farm. "I never thought it would be so close to home," said Anya, still looking at the swamp which was near a deserted farm. It looked scary to Anya but she couldn't avert her eyes from it.

"We better get going," said Eric, making her snap out of it. "It'll be dark soon."

Looking at the swamp one last time, Anya turned to Eric. "So you think we are to go back through the cave?" she asked, hoping he would say no.

"I don't know," he answered, looking at the opening from where they had just gotten out. He then looked up and scratched his head. "You don't think it will take us long if we climb this hill or whatever this is and go down the other side?"

Anya looked up as well. *If this is a hill, then it's a huge one,* she thought. *Because I can't make out the top.*

"What do you think?" Eric asked again. "Because I can see a path we can use."

You must have seen it through your wolf eyes, she thought, looking up again and not feeling any better. *Because I don't see it.*

"Okay, you lead then," she said, making up her mind.

The two friends started climbing upward, and still Anya was unsure if they were climbing a mountain or a big hill or something else, because the top still seemed as if it was kilometers from her. After a long climb, Anya finally reached the path that Eric had seen. It was more of a flat surface and they both stopped. The top still seemed way too high to Anya.

"There's Colville!" yelled Eric, pointing at the houses from above. "We're nearly there."

"I admire your stamina," said Anya exhausted and clutching her ribs. "But I can't walk any farther than this." Resting awhile, Anya got up and followed Eric down and toward the forest. "Yes, flat ground!" Anya yelled with joy as Eric helped her down the last few feet.

"At least we found something useful," he said as the two went through the forest.

"Like what?"

"That David isn't back," answered Eric adjusting his bag.

"Yeah, that," she answered in a weak voice, thinking about the letter.

The two of them walked toward the park where Anya had left her backpack behind some bushes. Waving each other goodbye, Anya walked toward her house feeling exhausted. *Why wasn't there any glow in the cave?* she thought, walking toward her house. She remembered quite well that the cave had some kind of green crystals growing on its walls when David first came to town. *Maybe he isn't back. But that still doesn't explain the letter. Or maybe he's living somewhere else.*

"You're quite late," said Anya's mother as she opened the door. "And dirty!"

"Sorry Mom," replied Anya as she dropped onto the sofa along with her bag, and closed her eyes. "I was out with the gang."

"Anya, what are you doing?" yelled her mother, closing the door. "Get up right now and take a shower this instant!"

"Mom, please," pleaded Anya, unable to move a muscle.

"Come on, get up," said her mother.

Defeated, Anya got up grumpily, and grabbing her bag, she walked into her room. Throwing her bag into a corner, she went to take a shower.

"I am dirty," she said, looking at her reflection in the mirror. Her black hair was sticking out at odd angles and her face was covered in dirt. "Very well," she said, taking off her clothes and turning on the shower. The water seemed to wash away all of her exhaustion. Anya dried herself, and putting on some new clothes she went down to eat her dinner with her mom. Her dad was going to come home late. After listening to her mother talk through the entire dinner about how she had fought with Mrs. Drake over the last bottle of cleaning liquid while shopping, Anya got up and went to her room to sleep.

"Finally, some rest," she said lying on her bed and closing her eyes. In a few minutes she fell asleep and had a strange dream. She couldn't make out the stranger's face but it looked as if he or she was watching her sleep. She felt the stranger come closer and she opened her eyes with a gasp, her heart beating fast. The room was dark as she looked around. She felt a chill in the wind and noticed that the window was open. *Weird,* she thought, getting off of her bed and going to the window. "I'm sure I closed it before I fell asleep," she added to herself. Yawning, she walked to her desk to look at the time when suddenly she thought about the letter. She opened the drawer where she had put it before she had gone to sleep.

"Where is it?" she asked herself, searching for the letter in the drawer. "I'm sure I put it in here." The open window, the missing letter, and her dream all seemed to add up to her. She put her arms around herself, trying to remain calm, "Who took it?" she asked herself, unable to come up with an answer.

Seven

Anya didn't feel the least bit happy when her mother tried to wake her up the next morning. The incident that happened last night had her up for two whole hours.

"Anya, are you ready?" her mother asked, shaking her awake.

"For what?" Anya asked, rubbing her eyes.

"School," her mother answered. "How can you forget?"

"Yeah, that," she answered yawning and getting up.

"Don't fall back to sleep now," said her mother as she went back downstairs.

Anya stretched, took a shower, changed her clothes and headed downstairs. After breakfast she went to Susan's and walked to the bus stop with her. She didn't mention anything to Susan about the dream she had last night as they waited for the others to arrive.

"So, how was it?" asked Carl walking toward Anya.

"What?" she asked, unsure about what he meant.

"Eric told us that you two saw the swamp yesterday," said Tabitha joining them.

"What swamp?" Susan turned to Anya as well, eyebrows raised.

"Eric and Anya saw the swamp yesterday," Tabitha answered before Anya could speak.

"They were out walking in the forest and thought of climbing the hill, you know, the one with the caves," answered Carl.

So that's what Eric told them, she thought. Anya knew he had enough sense not to tell about the letter and their little cave trip.

"Yeah," said Anya, catching up. "Eric had a feeling the swamp might be on the other side, so I went along with him."

"Well actually, I forced her to come along with me," added Eric, showing up behind her. The bus came and the friends along with some other kids got on. Susan gave Anya a strange look and followed her to their seats. Once seated, the group began talking about the trip. Anya didn't pay any attention to what her friends were saying. She was still worried about the missing letter and she felt less happy when Seth didn't show up on the bus that morning.

Reaching the school, Carl went to the gym, Eric to the library, Tabitha had a lab session, but Susan on the other hand cornered Anya as she was opening her locker. "What did you find?" she asked.

"Was I supposed to find something?" Anya asked laughing as she closed her locker.

"You don't fool me, Anya," Susan answered, an eyebrow raised.

"Okay, okay," Anya answered. She knew that Susan wasn't going to give up. "Eric and I searched the cave for the vampire shine, but we didn't find it and ended up going deeper into the cave."

"I knew it," said Susan. "You went to the cave to see if David was back. I too keep remembering what happened. I still have nightmares about that night."

"Yeah, me too," said Anya. "I just had to check."

"Just know that we are all here for you," said Susan hugging her, and she went to her class.

Anya didn't have class for some hours. *Should I tell Susan?* she thought, walking in the corridor. *No,* she made up her mind. *I have to keep it to myself. I don't want my friends to get involved like last time.* Wanting to be alone for a while, she went to the library. "Desperate times call for desperate measures," she whispered as she stepped inside.

"Hi," came a familiar voice, and she saw Seth waving at her. Anya smiled and walked toward him.

"I never pegged you for the library type," she whispered to him as she sat down.

"The same can be said about you," he smiled, feeling the librarian's eyes upon him.

"Didn't see you on the bus today," she said, looking into his eyes.

"I know," he answered. "My friend didn't come to school today so I took his bike."

"So you are going on the trip?"

"Of course," answered Seth. "It'll be fun, because of the whole haunted stuff. What about you?"

"Yes, I am," she answered, smiling. She was feeling so comfortable with him.

"And are the guys you hang out with?"

"Yeah, they are coming too. We're kind of a whole package deal."

"Don't mind me asking," said Seth, trying to sound cool. "You don't have a boyfriend, do you?"

Yes! He's interested, thought Anya, keeping herself from jumping with excitement. *Okay Anya, play it cool.*

"Funny you should ask," she answered, smiling at him.

"No, I was just making conversation," he answered. "Nothing more."

"For your information, I don't have one," she answered with a smile. "Not yet, that is."

"Cool," said Seth sounding happy. "Cool!"

The two of them talked about school and stuff while sitting in the library. They had some books open in front of them to appear as if they were studying. From what he told her, Seth lived near the school and had just moved into town. His parents were doctors and traveled a lot. As a child he used to go along with them, but now he didn't like moving from place to place and leaving his friends behind. Anya felt Seth beginning to grow on her. She really liked him. *And maybe he likes me as well,* she thought.

"Hey, Anya," said Seth as the two of them got up.

"What?" she asked, picking up her books.

"You know her?" he asked, pointing behind her.

Anya turned around and saw a girl in a hood walking toward a bookcase in the fiction section of the library.

"Yeah, her name is Cassandra," she answered, looking at Seth.

"She a friend of yours?" he asked as the two walked out of the library.

"We are on talking terms," said Anya. "She's a nice girl."

"She's weird," said Seth, stretching his arms. "With the hood and all. Have you seen her…?"

"Face?" Anya completed the sentence for him, smiling. "No, maybe I did once. I don't clearly remember though."

"Wonder what she's hiding?" he asked.

Forget about her, thought Anya. *Talk about me.*

"I heard that she has something going on with your friend. What's his name, Erin?" he asked as the school bell rang.

"Eric?" asked Anya. "I don't know. This is high school. You're bound to hear rumors."

As much as Anya liked Seth, she just couldn't tell him about her friend's personal life. Seth walked her to her class and then they waved each other goodbye. Anya took a deep breath and braced herself for an hour of boring Biology.

"As everyone knows about the trip," came Miss. Jane's voice after more than thirty minutes of lecture that Anya wasn't interested in, "How many of you are definitely going?"

The class murmured and looked at each other. The teacher took out a list. "I'll call out the names I've got written here and you are to raise your hands if you are still interested in going."

"Terry Nott," read Miss. Jane, and a boy raised his hand. "Pat Feller, Kirstein Heather, Sue Fletcher, Harvey Singleton, Rita Long, and Anya Thompson."

The students raised their hands as their names were called. Some of the other students that Miss Jane called made her cancel their names from the list.

"Very well then," she said, putting the final list back into her bag. "Seven isn't that bad."

Anya looked at the students who were going. Sue, Rita and Kirstein were talking to each other. Every boy in Anya's year had a crush on them. Well, not Eric, but who counts him in such things? Anya liked referring to the girls as H.F.L. They always walked as a group, so it was better to give them a single name instead of calling them each individually. Terry was a member of the chess club and Pat and Harvey were the boys with a *reputation* in school.

"Listen here," came Miss. Jane's voice. "You too," she added, referring to H.F.L. "I want all of you who are going to wait on Friday morning near the gates with the things written on the list given to you. And please inform your parents that we'll be returning on Sunday morning…"

The rest of the announcement was drowned out by the final bell, and the class got up to leave. "Don't forget about Friday morning!" Miss Jane yelled over the mob.

***

"Didn't see you in the cafeteria," said Susan, getting onto the bus. "And you're late."

"I was with Seth," Anya answered taking her seat. She had gone to the bike stand to see if he was there, but he had already gone home. "We just talked."

"We are finally going," smiled Carl sitting down.

"Yes, tomorrow," said Eric sitting down as well, followed by Tabitha.

"You all want to pack together?" Susan asked the girls.

"Yeah sure," answered Anya, tying her hair into a knot.

"No, I can't," answered Tabitha. "I have some things to take care of."

***

Cassandra hurried out of the library as the final bell rang. She had been busy making her assignment. She was near the gates when she remembered something and ran back to her locker to get her book. "I wouldn't be able to complete my assignment without you," she said to herself as she put the book into her bag. She began walking to the school gates when all of a sudden she felt an immense pain in her head as she reached the principal's office.

"Ahaaa!" she cried as her bag fell to the ground. She felt weak, as if she was going to faint. And then the feeling vanished. Cold sweat popped out of her forehead. Not understanding what had just happened, she picked up her bag and made her way outside. She was half way to her house when she felt as if she was being followed. She quickened her pace. She looked back without making it seem too obvious and noticed a tall well built man in a black suit some feet behind her. She didn't recognize him. She turned a corner, going toward her house, and still the man was behind her.

Why isn't he turning? she asked herself. *Maybe he lives here,* she thought, trying to calm herself. She began walking faster. Was the man behind her still? Yes, he was!

Finally she reached her house and quickly opened the door, locking it as she went inside. She peeked through her window. The man in the black suit looked at the house closely and then slowly walked away, whistling to himself.

Maybe I was imagining things, she thought, as she dropped onto the sofa closing her eyes. *Yeah, I was definitely imagining things,* she smiled to herself.

Eight

"Do we need conditioners?" Anya asked Susan. She was at Susan's house and the two girls were packing things to take on the trip.

"I don't think so," answered Susan, packing some clothes. "Okay. We have tissues, snacks, clothes, bottles, shoes, brushes, blankets. Everything, I guess."

"Susan, aren't you worried?" asked Anya, zipping up her stuff.

"You mean worried about the swamp? No, we've faced creepier stuff," she answered, smiling.

"How many people are going?"

"Let me check," Susan answered, taking out a list from her school bag. "What?" she added as Anya looked at her and then at the list. "I thought it would help if I had a list too."

Anya rolled her eyes and Susan continued. "There are five of us, H.F.L, Seth, and Harvey," she read the list. "Well, about fifteen. The rest chickened out. The story about the swamp being haunted and stuff has spread like wildfire all over school."

"What about sleeping?" asked Anya, brushing her hair in front of a mirror.

"Our teacher told us that we are three to one tent."

"And you get two?" said Anya, feeling excited.

"No, Anya," said Susan. She knew what her friend was thinking. "The boys are in separate tents."

"Dumb," whispered Anya and continued brushing her hair.

After a while Anya got up to leave, as she had to pack her clothes at her house. Susan was some sizes smaller than she. "See you," she said waving Susan goodbye. With her packed bag in one hand, she walked toward her house. She was nearly there when she noticed Tabitha walking on the street all alone as if in a hurry.

What's she up to? thought Anya, watching Tabitha turn toward her house. *It's her life, let her be,* spoke the sensible part of Anya's brain, the one that sometimes sounded like Susan or Eric. *It wouldn't hurt to take a peek,* spoke the other side of her brain as soon as the sensible part had finished its sentence. And so

Anya followed Tabitha. Trying not to be heard as she followed her, Anya watched Tabitha go into her house.

"Now what?" Anya asked herself. *Maybe I should give the back yard a try,* she thought, and went behind the house not sure why she was doing this in the first place.

"I told you not to call," came Tabitha's voice as she opened the back door.

Anya dropped behind the bushes and hid as she heard Tabitha walking in her back yard, talking on her mobile.

"You made a mistake," said Tabitha sounding angry. Anya strained her ears, trying to hear more clearly.

"Yes, I know what I'm supposed to do," said Tabitha. "You just do your work."

There was a sound of a door closing and Anya knew that Tabitha had gone back inside. Anya quietly came out from her hiding place and began walking toward her own house.

"I know what I'm supposed to do," repeated Anya to herself as she walked toward her house. *What was Tabitha talking about? And why was she so angry?*

***

"So you guys are really going tomorrow?" asked Anya's mom as Anya sat down to eat her dinner.

"Yes, we'll be coming back on Sunday," she answered.

"Glad you and your friends aren't afraid of the whole swamp thing I heard about," said her father.

"What?" Anya asked, not sure if she was following.

"He's right," answered her mother. "I heard from Mrs. Denver that she isn't allowing her kids to go. I didn't know people still believed in such stuff."

"It's these movies," said her father. "They are scaring the young generation into believing that vampires, werewolves, and haunted swamps exist."

Anya didn't answer and just smiled. *Yeah, they don't exist, Dad,* she thought.

***

Cassandra opened her eyes. "I must have overslept," she said to herself, getting up with a yawn. She checked the time. It was nearing midnight. "Aunt Sue should have woken me up," she said to herself. She closed the open book she had been reading before she had fallen asleep and put it aside. Feeling hungry, she went downstairs to eat something.

"She still hasn't come home," she said, not seeing anyone downstairs. She poured herself a glass of milk and called her aunt.

"Cassie, where were you?" came her aunt's voice as she answered her mobile.

"I'm sorry, I fell asleep," Cassandra answered, sitting down on the sofa and drinking her milk.

"Yeah, I figured," laughed her aunt. "Honey, I'll be working late tonight. Have some things to check up on in Somerville. Don't wait up for me."

"Okay, see you in the morning," said Cassandra and she hung up.

Her aunt was in the police and sometimes came home late. Cassandra got up and cleaned her empty glass. *Might as well check the doors,* she thought, and she checked the front door. She went toward one of the windows and looked outside.

"Who is he?" she asked herself stepping away from the window. Cassandra had just seen a man in a suit looking at her house from across the road. Trying to remain calm, she slowly peeked outside from the corner of the window. The stranger looked at the front door for a while, and went away whistling to himself.

***

"What is it, Mom?" Anya asked as her mother shook her, trying to wake her up.

"Anya, it's Friday," came her mother's voice. "Your trip, remember?"

"Yeah that," Anya answered yawning.

"Get up and get ready," said her mother and she went downstairs.

Anya got up, took a shower, put on some clothes, and went downstairs.

"You've packed everything?" her mother asked as she served Anya some toast.

"Yeah, I've packed."

"Anyway dear, you and your friends stay safe, okay?" said her mother.

"Mom," answered Anya, her mouth full of toast. "Nothing is going to happen, it's just a trip to some God forsa…"

"Hold your tongue, young lady," her father cut through as he helped himself to a cup of coffee.

"Okay," said Anya, her head down.

"Just be safe," said her mother as she poured her daughter some milk. "If any trouble, just call us."

"On what?" asked Anya confused.

Her father took out a brand new mobile from his pants pocket and handed it to Anya. "On this," he added, seeing Anya open her eyes wide.

"You're giving this to me?" she asked out of breath.

"Well yes," said her mother, giving her a kiss on her forehead. "Our number is on speed dial."

"Thanks," she said, pocketing her mobile. Giving her parents a hug, she walked toward the door. "Mom, my bag!" she yelled from the door.

"I knew you'd forget," said her mother, handing it to her. "I've checked the bag myself and added a few things. Just to be on the safe side."

"Thanks, Mom," said Anya. "See you guys on Sunday."

"Want me to give you a ride?" her dad asked from the kitchen.

"No, I can manage," she answered from the door. "Thanks for the mobile," Anya added and went out of the house.

"You won't be getting anything for your birthday now!" her mother yelled after her with a laugh.

"No fair!" Anya yelled back and walked toward Susan's house where Lizzie and Susan were waiting for her.

"These bags are heavy," said Susan as Anya came toward her.

"Tell me about it," said Anya, patting Lizzie.

"No, you can't come with us, Lizzie," said Susan as her dog looked at her with wide pleading eyes. "You go inside and be a good girl," Susan added, and Lizzie went inside.

"I keep having this feeling that Lizzie's going to follow me," Susan told Anya as the two girls walked toward the bus stop.

"All packed?" Eric asked, coming toward the two girls with a smile.

"Yeah," said Anya. "Can't wait to go."

"Where's Carl?" asked Susan.

"There!" said Anya looking at Carl coming toward the bus stop. "He's with Tabitha. Typical."

"Hi, dude," said Carl, giving Eric a high five as he came toward his friends.

"Nervous?" Tabitha asked the group. There were only the five of them waiting for the bus. The students who weren't going to the swamp had a day off. After five minutes of waiting, a bus stopped in front of them. It was different from their usual school bus and the driver was a very old lady. *At least the previous one had some fashion sense,* thought Anya as she got onto the bus and looked at the driver's hairstyle.

"We're finally going," said Eric sitting down.

"Have we got any weapons?" Tabitha asked looking at the group at large.

"I've got a knife," said Carl lying with his feet up in the back seat.

"We can use fire," said Susan, and Carl nodded in agreement.

"So, you guys really think all the stories are true?" asked Tabitha.

"We would have thought differently if we hadn't gone through that ordeal with David," Anya answered, and the group remained silent.

The bus made some other stops but no one got on, and to Anya's disappointment Seth didn't show up either. The bus stopped in front of the school and the friends filed out and walked toward Miss Jane who was waiting for them near the gates.

"I'm glad you came," said Miss Jane as she counted the teenagers who were assembling in front of her. "Fourteen isn't that bad."

We're dead meat if the swamp creatures are more than our number, thought Anya. She looked around. Carl was with some of his gym friends and Susan was talking to Tabitha. Eric was walking toward Cassandra. The H.F.L. was discussing a new perfume. *Why are those three even going?* Anya thought, looking at the girls. *Do they know that there aren't any malls where we are going?*

Anya felt a hand on her shoulder and she turned around to see Seth.

"You made it," said Anya smiling at him, and he smiled back.

"That makes fifteen," said Miss. Jane as she checked Seth on the list. "Now please pay attention. William, will you stop yelling! Thank you."

The teenagers stopped talking and turned to the teacher. "Let me tell you a few things before departing," said Miss Jane. "As the principal has placed me in charge of this trip, there were three of us, but considering the small number of students going, we settled on only one and I was selected." There was a tone of annoyance in her voice. "Now, I don't want any trouble on the trip," she continued. "And I don't want any of you wandering around after dark and away from the group. And keep in mind that this is primarily a study trip for biology students, so I want them to pay attention to the environment around them. Am I clear?"

"Yes," the crowd murmured.

"Okay then, all of you get on the bus," said Miss Jane smiling.

Here we go, thought Anya as she followed the others onto the bus.

Nine

"Excited?" asked Seth, sitting next to Anya on the bus.

"Yeah," she answered with a smile.

"Hey Seth," came William's voice from in front of them.

"Yeah, what is it?"

"Come here, dude. Dan's telling a good story."

"Be right back," Seth told Anya and went away.

"That was good," breathed Eric.

"Why?" asked Carl, noticing Anya give Eric a nasty look. The school janitor finished putting the bags on the bus and it started.

"Because now we can talk more freely," answered Eric. "Here's the plan."

The rest of the group leaned in to listen. "The first thing," continued Eric, "is that we have to set our tents close together. Miss Jane said there will be three kids in one tent, so Susan, Anya, and Tab will sleep together, while Carl and I will take the other one with…"

"Take Seth," Anya cut through.

"Okay," smiled Eric, understanding why she wanted that, and continued, "We should try and be close to Colville, you know, near the path Anya and I used because that will be our escape route if something happens." The others nodded in agreement.

"It might just happen?" asked Anya, looking out of the window. *First vampires and now swamp monsters?*

"Yes, it just might," answered Eric, pushing back his glasses.

"Take a look at this," said Tabitha as she fished out a large book from her bag. Anya remembered seeing it in Tom's bookstore once. The fact that she had remembered something like that surprised her.

"I took it from Tom," said Tabitha, watching Anya twitch. "He got it from a large library abroad. Take a look at what I found," and Tabitha opened a page and began to read.

"The creatures or zombies created through the resurrection spell are a work of pure evil, as these creatures are neither among the living nor the dead. Destroying such beings other than using spells is impossible, as they will not rest until the curse has been broken."

"That totally cancels the option of fighting these things with knives or fire," smiled Carl, looking at the group.

"Don't worry. Eric will think of something," said Susan, smiling at her bespectacled friend.

"Don't put me under such pressure," he smiled, pushing back his glasses.

After a while the bus stopped on a road a little away from the forest. "We are here," came Miss Jane's voice, and the teenagers got out. The bus driver waited for the boys to take out the bags and then he drove off.

"This is inviting," said Kirstein, rolling a strand of her golden brown hair in her fingers and chewing gum as she watched her surroundings.

"Yeah, tell me about it," said Rita. "I'm already bored."

What were you expecting? thought Anya, *Disney Land?*

"Pick up your belongings and follow me," said Miss Jane putting on her sunglasses.

"Sorry I couldn't be with you on the bus," said Seth as Anya went to pick up her backpack.

"No problem," Anya smiled at him, and the group followed their teacher past the forest and toward a clearing. It already had camping equipment there. "Glad the staff didn't forget these things," said Miss Jane, looking at the teenagers. "What are you waiting for? Start building!"

All of the teenagers began working on setting up their tents.

"Let's do this," said Eric, placing his bag on the ground. "Carl and I will figure this out," he added, unpacking his camping equipment. The H.F.L. was having the other boys make their tent for them, and to Anya's surprise, Seth was one of those boys.

"Typical boys," said Anya, watching Seth unpack the H.F.L.'s tent as Tabitha watched amused.

"Don't worry," Susan told Anya laughing. "Let's go get some water."

"Wait a minute," said Anya.

"What?" asked Tabitha, taking a kettle out of her bag.

"I'll go get the water," Anya answered. "You guys make a fireplace."

"Fine," said Tabitha as Susan took out a box of matchsticks.

Anya took the kettle from Tab and walked toward Miss Jane, who was setting up her tent with the help of William and Daniel.

"Miss Jane, where are we to get water from?" Anya asked.

"From the tap over there," her teacher answered, pointing behind Anya. "Now if you'll excuse me, I've got to figure out how to peg this down correctly."

Anya walked away in the direction Miss Jane had pointed out to her and found the tap near the Singleton farm. She could see the Singleton house a little further away. The whole area looked deserted. Not even a single bird was in sight. The Singleton house itself was boarded up.

"Ouch!"

Anya was paying the house so much attention that she forgot to look in front of her.

"Sorry Cassandra," said Anya, helping the girl up.

"It's nothing," she said, bending down to pick up her large plastic jar.

"Creepy house," said Anya, looking at the Singleton residence and turning on the tap. After a while cold water came rushing out and she began filling up her kettle.

"Yeah," said Cassandra. "The Singletons who used to live there just went away, leaving the farm and everything, after the swamp incident."

"Who are you sharing the tent with?" Anya asked as Cassandra began filling her jar.

"There are sixteen of us including Miss Jane," Cassandra answered, turning off the tap. "In which seven are girls and seven are boys, and there are three to each tent."

Anya and Cassandra began walking toward the campsite with their filled utensils. "But you still haven't…," said Anya.

Cassandra looked at her. "I'm sleeping with the babes who were born with a Prada shoe in their mouths."

"Prada shoes?" asked Anya, trying to figure it out, and then it hit her. "Cassandra, surely not?" she added, trying not to laugh.

Cassandra nodded and three beautiful girls came running toward her. "Hello Anya," they said together, looking at her.

"Hey, girls," said Anya, smiling. *Yup, Cassandra's done for,* she thought.

"Cassie," said Kirstein. "Darling, hurry up. After this we are planning to do a makeover. Surely you know that this hood style of yours is such a downer. And I don't like looking at such things around me."

Cassandra followed the three girls with a last glance at Anya who whispered "Good luck" to her.

"There," said Tabitha finally finishing with the fireplace and taking the kettle from Anya. "Oh, the water is quite cold," she added.

"I watched Cassie with the H.F.L," said Susan, smiling. "Poor soul."

"Where are the boys?" asked Anya.

"Over there," pointed Tabitha.

Anya turned around and saw Carl, Eric, and Seth working on two tents. She looked at the place where the boys were setting up the tents and then she looked toward the hill. *Colville seems quite far,* she thought, walking toward the boys.

"I can't get this right!" yelled Carl, struggling with the tent as Seth laughed. Eric, on the other hand, was halfway through the tent he was working on.

"Eric, give me the manual," said Anya laughing, and Eric threw it at her.

"Why aren't you reading this?" Anya asked, catching the manual.

"We are men," said Carl, setting up the poles. "We were born with…Damn this tent!" yelled Carl, as the poles fell to the ground. Seth burst out laughing.

"Let me see," said Anya, trying to be serious and opening up the manual. "Step one: Adjust the poles as in the figure shown here. Step two: Peg the cloth when the poles are adjusted. Step three: By now the tent should be erect…Oh!" Anya stopped reading and blushed. Carl and Seth grinned at each other.

"The tent will be erect," said Eric, coming toward the three, having finished with his tent. "Not the thing that's on your mind," he added taking the manual from Anya and softly hitting her on the head with it. "Let me do this," he said and took the equipment from Carl and Seth.

Anya called the girls and the three of them went into the tent that Eric had just made and unpacked their stuff. "This is fun," said Anya, taking out some blankets.

"It would have been without our problems," said Tabitha opening up her bag.

"Oh, be quiet," said Susan taking out a lantern. "No talk about any cursed swamp right now, Tabitha."

Anya went outside. The boys were unpacking inside their tents. From the sounds that were coming from inside, it seemed as if Carl and Seth were fighting for a better place to sleep. Anya looked around the campsite. The H.F.L. was having Harvey and his gang make a small fireplace for them. *Lucky girls!* thought Anya, watching Rita and Kirstein apply nail polish onto Sue's toes. Cassandra smiled at Anya and walked toward her.

"Having fun?" asked Anya smiling.

"Those three are the biggest creeps I've ever met," said Cassandra. "They wanted to apply makeup on me."

Anya looked at Cassandra, her blue eyes watching the forest near the campsite. *What does she look like?* Anya thought as she watched Cassandra's gaze fall onto Eric who was walking toward them.

"Cassandra," he said smiling.

"Eric," she answered back.

"Anya, come on. Tab wants us inside the tent," said Eric turning to talk to her.

Anya walked slowly toward the tent and heard Eric invite Cassandra as well.

"No, I'll pass," came Cassandra's voice. "I still have some things to unpack."

"Why so gloomy?" asked Anya as Eric caught up with her.

"Never mind," said Eric.

"Never mind?" asked Anya smiling. "I can tell she likes you too."

"You think?" asked Eric, sounding hopeful.

"It's obvious," answered Anya, smiling at her friend.

"I hope she'll be alright," said Eric.

Anya knew he worried about Cassandra. She felt the same way about Seth. *Would they believe me if I told them the swamp is really haunted?* she thought.

"Don't worry," said Anya. "Come on, into the tent we go."

"What is it that you wanted to talk about?" Eric asked Tabitha as he followed Anya into the girls' tent. The entire group along with Seth was inside and it was a little cramped.

"Don't worry," said Tabitha. "I've told Seth everything," she added, looking at the expression on Anya's face.

"Yeah, Tabitha told me that you guys think the swamp is cursed," said Seth, rolling his eyes. "As I didn't have anything better to do, I thought I would play along."

Anya smiled and sat down next to Seth. Tabitha opened up her book and began to read. "The Resurrection spell is believed to have originated from the African tribes, where the chief of the tribe cast this spell to control the dead of his tribe."

"I always knew African mumbo jumbo was weird," said Carl, cleaning his ear with his finger.

"The rest of the chapter," Tabitha continued, "is all about the undead and why they were controlled. But there is nothing about the spell."

"See if there's any way of defeating them, other than magical means?" asked Eric.

"You guys take your magic stuff way too seriously," said Seth laughing, before Tabitha could answer. He looked around the group for someone to laugh with him and he became quiet when he noticed that everyone was serious. "My bad," he whispered.

"No, we can only completely defeat them through magical means," said Tabitha, sounding as if she hadn't just been interrupted.

Miss Jane's voice came into the tent from outside. "All of you please come outside."

The six friends went outside and joined the others. "As it is still daylight," said Miss Jane, "I want you to go into the forest and bring me back the names of the animals you see in there."

The crowd groaned and Kirstein said, "Miss Jane, I can't go in there!"

"Don't worry, Kirstein," said Miss Jane smiling at her. "There aren't any dangerous animal in there."

"I'm more worried about my hair," she moaned. "I just got them done yesterday."

"As I said," continued Miss Jane, ignoring Kirstein. "You are to go in there and collect information. Don't forget that this is an educational field trip. Now go!"

Kirstein screamed. "We are not touching bugs," said Sue as Rita comforted Kirstein.

"For heaven's sake, just go!" said Miss Jane, losing her patience with them.

The fifteen teenagers went into the forest. Harvey and his friends went with the H.F.L. Terry, having nothing better to do, followed suit. Cassandra, on the other hand, tagged along with Anya and the rest.

"We still have time 'til sunset," said Eric checking his watch. "Let's check out the swamp."

"Let's check out the what?" asked Anya stopping in her tracks.

"The swamp," said Eric. "We have to go see the place."

"Why are we going there?" Cassandra asked confused.

"Don't ask me," answered Seth smiling. "These five are a weird bunch."

The group was about to go to the swamp when all of a sudden they heard a scream.

Ten

"What was that?" asked Anya, clutching Seth's arm.

"It was a scream," said Susan sounding worried. "Come on!"

The group ran toward the source of the sound and then they heard another scream.

"Damn you!" yelled Anya when she saw what was happening. Sue was trying to shake off a caterpillar from her shoulder and the rest of the H.F.L. was dancing around her, completely confused.

"It's just an insect," said Susan, picking it up from Sue's shoulder, trying not to laugh.

"That's no excuse," panted Sue. "It's still disgusting." and her friends nodded in agreement.

"Where are Harvey and the boys?" asked Tabitha looking around.

"I don't know," said Kirstein as Rita brushed Sue's shoulder. "They said something about smoking."

"They what?" asked Carl, sounding interested, and Tabitha punched him in the shoulder.

Kirstein didn't say anything else and went away with her two girlfriends.

"Well, that was interesting," said Cassandra as she watched the girls walk away.

"Anyway, to the swamp!" said Eric, and the seven friends walked through the forest. They went deeper into the forest. Anya looked at the huge trees. She got an eerie feeling.

"It's huge!" said Eric when the friends reached their destination. "And it smells."

The swamp was quite huge and it looked sinister. The pale, yellow green water looked sickening.

"Gross," whispered Susan trying not to breathe too much.

Eric carefully went toward it. "The ground's not that soft," he said and bent down to take a closer look at the swamp.

"Eric, don't touch it," said Cassandra looking worried.

Tying her hair into a knot, Anya also inched closer to the swamp. *Why am I doing this again?* she thought as she got closer. Reaching the swamp, she looked into it. The water seemed still. She strained harder and then screamed. The rest of the group came toward her.

"What happened?" asked Seth looking at her.

"There are bodies in there," she whispered closing her eyes.

Eric got up as well and wiped his glasses, nodding his head. Looking at each other, both Tabitha and Cassandra bent down to take a look.

"She's right," said Tab, getting back up and trying to remain calm. "I just saw a face in there."

"I'll take your word for it," said Carl, not daring to look for himself.

"Same here," added Susan, not looking at the swamp.

Cassandra got up. She didn't say a word, but her silence said a lot.

"Oh, come on," said Seth looking at the group, waiting for someone to laugh and yell, "Gotcha!"

No one spoke a word and he walked toward the swamp water, smiling. He bent down and looked into it. "Oh, shit!" he yelled, backing up. "There's a dead dude in there! This is so not cool!"

"Did someone murder these guys and dump them here?" he asked, stepping away from the swamp, not daring to look at it again.

"We told you," said Tabitha, speaking for the group. "This is a cursed swamp. If these bodies were murder cases, then surely the police would have seen them."

"I thought the police checked the swamp after the disappearances?" asked Cassandra. "Why didn't they see the bodies?" she added, putting her arms around herself.

"Maybe the bodies come to the surface only when it's time for them to come back to life, every fifty years," answered Eric, pushing back his glasses.

No one spoke. Eric's words made sense and Seth leaned against a tree, trying to calm himself down. *Well, I don't blame him,* thought Anya as she watched Seth. *It's not easy to believe everything all at once.*

"Don't mind me saying this," Carl cleaned his throat. "But what the hell are we doing standing here right now?"

"Hey!" said Anya walking toward Seth as he opened his eyes, giving her a smile. "Let's go," she added, and the two of them followed the rest of the group to the campsite. No one spoke a word.

"Cassie," came Sue's singing voice as the friends reached the tents. "We need your help."

"I better go," said Cassandra and she walked away.

Miss Jane was sitting with the boys talking about her ex-boyfriend. *I guess camping does make you open up,* thought Anya as she watched her teacher and then walked toward her tent.

"Why don't we light a fire?" asked Susan, trying to sound cheerful. After five minutes the group was sitting around a crackling fire.

"Got room for me?" asked Cassandra as she squeezed herself between Carl and Susan. Anya had a feeling that Cassandra was trying to be as far away from Tabitha as possible, who herself was doing the same thing.

Susan placed the kettle to boil on the fire. The wind seemed to get chilly and Anya got closer to Seth, who smiled.

"How do we know that the zombies won't come tonight?" asked Carl.

"They won't come tonight," said Tabitha. "Because the book clearly states that the undead only rise when the moon disappears and I don't see that happening tonight."

"You mean that if the moon doesn't disappear in these three days," asked Anya, "then there will be no monsters?"

"Not in these three days," answered Tabitha. "Don't know about the rest of the days."

Susan poured tea for the group. Twenty feet away Miss Jane was laughing with the rest of the teenagers.

"We need a plan," said Eric sipping his tea.

"Don't we already have one?" asked Carl.

"We need a new one as these creatures are only going *bye bye* through magical means," Eric answered. "Which we do not have."

"We can only run back to Colville?" said Susan.

"What about the others?" asked Seth concerned. "They won't believe us and I don't think they'll be willing to look into the swamp."

"Can't I just tell them?" said Seth after a pause. "I don't think staying here any longer is going to do any of us any good."

"I don't think the bus will be back to take us away at a moment's notice," said Eric. "Trust me, Seth, we have been through this before. We need to hold our ground."

"You've seen dead bodies in swamps before?" asked Seth.

Anya took his hand is hers. "Trust us, will you?" she asked with a smile. She looked directly into his eyes. "I know what you just saw wasn't easy for you, but you need to trust us on this, Seth."

Anya felt Seth tighten his grip on her hand and give her a nod. *Good,* Anya looked at the others sitting with her teacher. *How can they all survive?*

"Anya," said Susan.

Anya turned around. "Sorry," she said. "I was just thinking." The air around them grew colder.

Susan got up. "Any of you hungry?"

"What do we have?" asked Seth, patting his stomach. He seemed to be back to his normal self again.

"I'll go check," said Susan, and she went into her tent.

Again Anya's mind strayed. *They can only be completely defeated through magical means,* she thought. *Magical means* and then she remembered about the Singleton farm.

"Guys, I was wondering about the…"

"About the farm?" Eric cut through. "Yeah, I've been thinking the same."

"Are we invited to this little chat of yours?" asked Carl, not knowing what the two were talking about.

"The Singleton residence was built after the incident," answered Eric. "And I feel that we have to check it out as well."

"Why bother?" Carl yawned, lying on the ground.

"We'll go there in the morning," said Tabitha.

"Yeah," whispered Seth. "As if dead men weren't good enough."

"Just trust me," said Anya smiling at him. *This is just the beginning.*

All of the teenagers decided they would have a joint dinner that night. Susan and Anya went into their tents to get the plates. The boys were busy roasting beans on the fire.

"So, how is it going with Seth?" asked Susan, handing Anya the plates.

"It's going quite fine," she answered laughing. "Not looking at the fact that we might be attacked by swamp zombies while we are here."

"Let's go," said Susan, balancing some mugs and leading the way to the campsite. The smell of ham and beans was in the air. "This smells good," said Miss Jane joining the teenagers around the fire. Anya began distributing the plates among the group. "Hey, where are Eric and Cassandra?" she asked looking around.

"Cassandra went inside of her tent to sleep," Tabitha answered, helping herself to dinner. "She doesn't feel well."

"And Eric said something about taking a walk," answered Seth as Anya sat down next to him with her food.

"Where to?" she asked. She had a feeling that she knew the answer.

"Into the for…"

"And you let him go?" Anya cut through. She looked at her friends for an explanation.

"Eric's a big boy," said Carl eating his food. "He can handle himself."

Anya didn't say a thing and got up, leaving her plate on the ground.

"What's wrong, Anya?" asked her teacher.

"Nothing," Anya lied with a smile. "I have to get something from the tent," she added and walked away to her tent.

"Where are you going?" asked Seth as she came back outside, pocketing a flashlight.

"To find Eric," she answered. "Where else?"

"We're going with you," said Susan.

"Don't bother," she answered, looking at Carl.

"Hey, what did I do?" he said, defending himself. "If that dude wanted to go for a walk, why would I stop him?"

Anya didn't say anything. She didn't expect Carl to understand. She had gone through the fear of losing her friends during the vampire incident. She knew how close she was to death and she knew the fear of losing her friends forever, and now they were in a cursed swamp and she was experiencing the same fears again.

"It's nothing," said Anya, calming herself down and looking at her friends. "Tell you what, if I'm not back in fifteen minutes, then you guys can come after me. And besides, Miss Jane won't allow all of us to go."

"We'll give you ten minutes," said Seth sounding worried.

Anya gave her friends a smile and walked toward the forest. *Great, just great,* she thought, switching on her flashlight. She cursed herself for not letting the others come with her. *What's wrong with me?* she thought as she made her way toward the swamp. She knew she would find Eric there. She looked all around as she walked. The shining eyes from behind the trees were giving her the creeps. Anya quickened her pace, hurrying toward the swamp, thinking about kicking Eric between the legs when she found him. After about ten minutes she reached the swamp. A green glow was lightly radiating from its depths. "Now where is that bespectacled son of a bit…," she said, looking around.

"Anya?" came a voice from above her and she gave a blood curling scream.

"Ssshhhh!" said Eric as he jumped down in front of her from a tree. "What are you doing here?"

"What are you doing here?" Anya glared at him. "And what were you doing up in a tree?"

"To answer your first question," said Eric, dodging Anya's slap and laughing. "I came here to collect a sample. I wanted to run some tests on it. Anya, stop trying to hit me. As for the second question, I climbed the tree to get a look at the swamp from above."

"That was still irresponsible."

"I know and I'm sorry," said Eric, pushing back his glasses. "Now come on, let's go, the others must have heard you scream."

The two of them walked away from the swamp toward the campsite. "Anya!" came Seth's voice as he came running toward her with his flashlight, followed by Susan, Carl and Tabitha. "We heard you scream," said Seth looking at Anya. "Are you alright?"

"I'm okay," she answered, smiling at him.

"That was dumb of you, Eric," scolded Susan. "Going into the forest alone!"

Eric didn't say anything and bowed his head. His friends knew he was sorry for his actions. "Let's go back," said Carl. "Miss Jane is probably boiling with anger by now."

"You kids are seriously breaking curfew!" yelled their teacher, her hands on her hips, as the six teenagers came into sight.

"Sorry Miss Jane," said Eric.

"All of you, to your tents!" said Miss Jane. "Anya and Eric, I expected better from you!"

How was I supposed to know that? thought Anya, rolling her eyes and going into her tent.

"You guys want me to turn off the lantern?" asked Susan.

"The campfire is about to go out," yawned Anya. "Just dim it a little."

Susan dimmed the lantern and went under her blanket. Tabitha was already in hers.

'Ring. Ring. Ring.'

"What's that?" asked Susan sitting up straight.

"It's my cell," said Anya, searching for it in her bag. *How could I forget that I have a cell?*

"You had a cell?" Tabitha asked yawning. "I don't think cells are allowed."

"I have a cell," Anya corrected her. "And who cares?" She gestured to her friends to be silent and answered the call, "Hello!"

"Hi dear," came a voice.

"Hey, Mom," said Anya, keeping her voice low. If cells weren't allowed on the trip, then she wasn't keen on making Miss Jane find out that she had one.

"Having fun?"

"You have no idea," Anya smiled.

"I just called to ask if everything was alright."

"It's going fine."

"Okay then, dear," said her mother. "Tell your friends to take care as well," she added and hung up.

"How is she doing?" asked Anya's father watching the television.

"She says she's having fun," said his wife with a smile. She sat down on the couch with her husband. "I sometimes worry about her."

"Why?" asked her husband, giving her a kiss.

"You know about the stories surrounding the swamp and I keep having these dreams that they will take our Anya away from us."

"Stop worrying," said her husband. "No one can take her away from us. She is our daughter regardless of what *they* might think. We've discussed this, now stop worrying."

"Okay," whispered Anya's mother as she came closer to her husband watching TV, trying to remain calm.

Eleven

"Damn you," groaned Anya as Susan shook her awake the next morning. "Wake up sleepy head," said Susan giving Anya another shake. Anya got up and looked outside. The shinning sun blinded her for a moment and she retreated back into the tent. "What time is it?" Anya yawned looking at Susan, who was tying her blonde hair into a ponytail.

"It's nine in the morning," said Tabitha entering the tent, looking as great as ever. "Breakfast is getting ready. I came here to ask what you wanted to eat."

"I'll take bacon," Anya yawned, scratching her head.

"I'll come and help," said Susan as she followed Tabitha outside. "Anya, you'd better get ready and come outside."

"Aren't the boys up yet?" asked Anya as she came out of the tent.

"Eric is trying to wake the two of them up," said Susan as she fried some eggs.

"At least someone is up," said Cassandra coming toward them. Tabitha mentioned something about getting a utensil and went into the tent.

"Miss Jane is also up," said Cassandra. "Let's see how she fares in waking up the H.F.L. Because believe me, I've tried."

Cassandra sat down with Susan and helped her make tea. "The boys should hurry up," said Susan, pouring Anya a cup. "We're all going to the farm today."

"Mornin'," yawned Seth as he came out of his tent followed by Eric and Carl.

"Eggs!" said Carl in delight, watching Susan frying them.

"You better wash," said Susan, slapping his hand away from the plate. "Both of you," she added, and Seth and Carl walked away.

"Where's Tab?" asked Eric as Anya handed him some bacon.

"I'm here," said Tabitha, walking toward them with some cups.

"Good to see that some of you are awake," said Miss Jane coming toward the group.

Susan poured her a cup of tea and she sat down with them. "I don't know why the school even bothered with this field trip?" said Miss Jane sipping her tea. "I mean, what's the point if the students aren't the slightest bit interested?"

The teenagers didn't say a thing. It was obvious to them that their teacher was hoping for the trip to end as well. "We are allowed to go out, right?" Eric asked.

"Yes you are, as long as you come back before dark," answered Miss Jane. "I don't want you to repeat what you did last night."

"Let's go then," said Anya as Miss Jane got up and walked away to wake the other kids.

The seven cleared away their stuff and Eric led the way toward the Singleton residence. "Man, this house is creepy," said Carl as the house came into view. The group walked on and stopped in front of it. The windows were boarded up as well as the front door.

"It won't budge," said Eric giving the door a push.

"Let me try," said Carl. He kicked at the door and it flew open, and Seth was impressed.

Seems like Carl has also got some werewolf powers left, thought Anya as she followed Eric inside.

"This place is quite dark," said Susan switching on her flashlight.

She was right. Because of being boarded up, the interior of the house was quite dark. Anya switched on her flashlight as well. Everything was covered in dust and looked very old and weak.

"Well," said Eric looking at his friends. "Split up into two teams and search the place."

Carl instinctively went closer to Tabitha and the two of them joined Eric and Seth. Susan, Anya, and Cassandra made up the second group.

"If you see anything strange," said Eric. "Call out!"

"Let's go upstairs," suggested Susan, and Cassandra and Anya followed her. The stairs creaked as the girls went upstairs.

"Check inside," said Anya, directing her flashlight's beam on the first door they saw. Susan gave a nod and Anya opened it. The girls found themselves in a bedroom. Dust swirled in the tiny specks of light that were entering through the boarded windows. The girls searched the drawers but found nothing strange.

"Why didn't the Singletons take their things?" Susan asked looking at the old clothes in the drawers.

"I don't know, Susan," said Anya. "Maybe they ran away."

They went into another room, but found nothing. "Let's head downstairs," said Cassandra, dusting some web off of her hood. The three went downstairs and found the others in what seemed to be a kitchen.

"Find anything?" asked Eric.

"No. You?" asked Anya.

"Nothing."

"We'd better go," said Tabitha. Carl was behind her, rummaging through a cabinet.

"Where's Seth?" Anya asked.

"I'm over here," came his voice. The friends walked toward him, outside of the kitchen.

"This door won't budge," he said, giving it a push.

"Let me see," said Carl. Seth moved away and Carl kicked the door. The lock broke and the friends saw a small empty room filled with dust.

"Why is this room empty?" asked Eric, entering the room and looking around. The other teenagers went in as well.

"Why don't we all leave?" said Seth. "People always end up dead if they snoop around too much, at least in the movies."

The rest of the group followed Seth out of the room when Anya noticed something.

"Anya, what is it?" asked Cassandra as she watched Anya stop in her tracks.

"Wait a minute," said Anya, and she bent down to examine the floor. She ran her finger over it. "I think this is a cellar," she added, brushing away some of the dust.

Her friends gathered around her. Carl bent down and pulled on the cellar door. There was a sound of something breaking and then it opened up.

"Great!" Seth faked a smile. "A cursed swamp and a creepy looking house with a dark cellar! Wow!"

Without a word, Eric stepped down the stairs, followed by the others. The seven friends found themselves in a dusty basement. Anya noticed a bulb and tried to switch it on by pulling the string. To her surprise, it worked. "What are these books?" asked Susan, taking a dusty book off of one of the shelves.

"These look like magical books," said Cassandra as she opened a book. "It's full of weird symbols."

The friends looked around. The entire basement was covered in shelves full of books and scrolls.

"These are very old," said Tabitha opening up a scroll. "I can't translate them."

"This means that the Singletons performed magic," said Eric looking at the stacks of dusty old books.

"Not a surprise," said Carl opening up a cabinet. It was full of jars. "Looks like ingredients to me," he added looking at the jars which had strange liquids swirling in them.

"Maybe we can find something that will help us defeat these swamp zombies of yours," said Seth looking around.

Cassandra began looking into some scrolls that were lying on the ground. Tabitha opened another large book. "Hey guys," said Susan. She was examining a large trunk in a corner. "It's locked and looks important."

The boys and Anya went toward the trunk. "Let's see what's inside, shall we?" Seth smiled, pulling at the trunk handle, but it wouldn't open. Anya had a feeling that Seth was trying to outshine Carl in terms of strength.

"If I may," Carl smiled. Seth stepped aside, and Carl gave the trunk a pull. "Eric, it seems to be nailed shut. Give me a hand."

Together the two boys opened the trunk. It was full of jars, dead frogs, bats and scrolls, sealed with wax. Anya was shocked to see a small cauldron in it as well.

"They really did perform magic," said Susan taking out a jar which had a frog in it. "Creepy, if you ask me," she added, putting it back.

"You guys find anything?" Eric asked Cassandra and Tabitha.

"No," answered Tabitha, closing her fifth book. "I can't make out more than half of the symbols in these."

"And these scrolls have recipes for potions," said Cassandra. "And something about identifying werewolves," she added, giving Eric a strange look. "Nothing else."

"These seem interesting," said Tabitha as she walked toward the trunk and picked up a scroll.

"Take what you want," said Carl looking around the basement. "Why don't we all get out of here?"

Everyone agreed. Tabitha picked up a book, and Cassandra picked up some scrolls from the trunk and followed the rest of them up the stairs as Eric turned off the light.

The seven friends made their way to the campsite. The rest of the teenagers were awake and eating breakfast. Tabitha went into her tent and Cassandra went into hers to drop off the stuff they were carrying.

"We will be going home tomorrow," said Miss Jane as the rest of the group sat down around the fireplace.

Good, thought Anya as she drank water from her bottle. *Maybe we won't have to deal with the monsters after all.*

Eric got up and went into his tent. "Find anything?" asked Anya as Tabitha came toward them.

"No," said Tabitha shaking her head. "We have to find someone of magical descent," she added sitting down and taking a sandwich from Susan.

"Where were you guys just now?" asked Harvey as he drank his tea.

"We were out near the Singleton residence," answered Carl yawning.

All of a sudden Anya had a thought. *Harvey's full name is Harvey Singleton, right?*

She turned to Harvey. "Any chance you know about those Singletons or are you related?" Anya asked Harvey.

"No," he answered, cleaning his ear with his finger. "My folks aren't from here."

Well, it was worth a try, thought Anya.

"Hey guys," came Eric's voice from inside of his tent.

"What is it with Eric Banna, now?" asked Terry as everyone turned toward the tent. "Why is he yelling at this time?"

"I guess he thought of something," said Seth, and the friends got up and went toward his tent.

"What did you find?" asked Susan.

Eric was sitting inside of his tent. He looked at them with a smile, a test tube and lighter in his hands. "I think I've figured out a way to defeat them," he smiled, his eyes beaming.

"Fingers crossed that it works," said Anya.

After having a combined dinner, the teenagers retreated to their tents.

"Here's to hoping nothing happens," said Anya.

"Same here," said Susan. She looked around. "Tabitha, what are you making?"

"Oh, nothing," she answered as she poured juice into some cups. "As we'll be going back tomorrow, I thought we might as well end our supplies."

"Tastes funny," said Anya taking a sip.

"Dad sent it from abroad," Tabitha answered, drinking it as well. "I also gave the boys some. It's supposed to calm the mind."

"Cheers!" said Susan and she drank the whole cup.

***

"Cassie, what are you doing with these dirty scrolls?" Sue asked as she came into the tent and watched Cassandra reading them under the lantern's light.

"Yeah, take them out," said Rita tying her hair back, and Katherine nodded.

"Fine," said Cassandra getting up and picking up the scrolls. "Anything else you want me to do?"

Cassandra waited for the three girls to answer. "Guys?" she asked looking at them, but they didn't answer. Suddenly Cassandra felt an immense pain in her forehead and she fell onto her sleeping bag. *What's happening?* she thought. She watched as the three girls fell down onto their faces, as if asleep. And then the pain suddenly stopped. Dreading the worst, Cassandra went out of her tent. No one was outside and the campfire had extinguished. She looked at the sky. The moon had hid behind the clouds.

That's moonless enough for me, she thought, remembering what she had read about the resurrection spell and the moonless sky. She ran towards her friends' tents. "Guys, you better come out here!" she yelled.

The six friends came running out of the tents. The moonless sky and Cassandra's expression told them everything. "What about the others?" asked Seth looking at the other tents.

"I don't know," said Cassandra. "The H.F.L. just dropped down as if they were under a sleeping spell or something. I don't know."

"This is really happening," said Susan wrapping her arms around herself as the friends came closer to each other.

"What's that noise?" asked Carl as he looked toward the hill.

"I hear it, too," said Eric looking in the same direction.

"What is it?" asked Anya. She knew they heard the noise because of their sharper senses, but weren't the monsters supposed to come from the swamp rather than the hill?

"Up there!" Eric pointed, and the group saw a black bird flying toward them.

"Raven!" yelled Tabitha in delight as the bird came down and landed on her shoulder.

"There's one more," smiled Carl as the friends heard a dog barking.

"Lizzie!" Susan yelled with joy, hugging her pet dog. "I knew you would come."

"But how?" asked Seth confused looking at the two pets.

"I have no idea," said Anya confused as well. *How did the animals know they were to come at this time?*

"We have bigger problems to worry about," said Eric as the friends heard a moan come from deep inside the forest. The friends stood still in horror as they heard the noises from the forest get closer.

"Everyone remembers what I told them?" asked Eric as the moaning grew louder.

The group nodded, eyes fixed on the forest, their flashlights on.

Twelve

Slowly the moaning grew louder and then it stopped. None of the teenagers made a sound. And then it appeared in front of them. It was a six foot tall person, but it wasn't really a person. Its skin looked as if it was melting. Its eyes were cold and dead, and its entire body was covered in mud. It was giving off a faint green glow similar to that of the swamp.

"There's only one?" whispered Seth aiming his flashlight at it as the creature looked at the seven teenagers standing close together.

The creature moaned again and five more zombies came limping slowly out of the forest.

"You had to ask," said Anya looking at the new arrivals. "Now what?"

"Let's just see what they can do," said Eric as the friends watched the six zombies in silence. Lizzie was baring her teeth at them, ready to attack and save Susan.

The swamp zombies didn't do anything and stood still watching the teenagers with their cold dead eyes. The zombie who was the tallest of them all and the first one that appeared moaned again, and to their horror the rest of them came running toward the friends.

"They can run!" screamed Susan as she watched the five creatures come toward her and her friends.

"Just run! Towards the hill!" yelled Carl as the teenagers ran.

"I didn't know that zombies could run," said Seth. "I mean, come on, this ain't happening!"

"What about the others?" asked Cassandra looking back at the tents. "We can't just leave them."

"We can't just fight five running swamp zombies!" yelled Carl from the front.

"Split up," said Eric.

"What?" asked Anya trying to run as fast as she could. She was finding it difficult to run in the dark.

"We have to," said Eric. "These things are going to catch us any minute now and the hill is too far. We have to fight. See if the fire trick I told you about works. I'm going back."

"I'm coming with you," said Cassandra out of breath.

"Take Raven," said Tabitha from the front with Carl. "We'll come back as soon as we deal with these guys."

Eric and Cassandra separated from the group. The five zombies looked at them, making up their minds as they saw the two of them run back to the campsite.

"Hey, over here you sons of bitches!" yelled Carl, trying to distract the zombies. It worked and the five of them didn't go after Eric and Cassandra.

"Hope this works," said Carl as he burned a stick with a lighter and faced the zombies.

***

"We're nearly there," said Eric as he ran toward the campsite with Cassandra. "Think you're all right?"

"I'm fine," said Cassandra as she ran along with Eric out of breath.

The two friends reached the campsite. It was deserted. Eric checked the tents and found no one in them. "They must have taken them away," he said walking toward Cassandra. "To the swamp!"

"What are we waiting for?" said Cassandra aiming her flashlight at the forest. "We can't just leave them."

Eric led the way toward the swamp and Cassandra and Raven followed, trying hard to be silent. "Stop," whispered Eric hiding behind a tree. Cassandra walked behind him and Raven flew up and perched on the tree's branch.

The two friends looked at the swamp. Fifteen zombies were standing around the swamp looking at the sleeping bodies of the teenagers and Miss Jane, as they slowly sank into the swamp.

"We can't fight all of them," whispered Cassandra looking at the sight.

"I know," Eric whispered back. "I know."

***

"It was nice knowing you," Seth told Anya, trying to smile as the five zombies surrounded the teenagers, slowly coming closer.

"Don't give up yet," Anya smiled back. "Let's just hope Eric's test works."

One of the zombies came toward Carl and he held the burning stick in front of its face. The zombie looked at the flames, moaned and backed away.

"I think it's working!" yelled Carl as he forced the zombies away from his friends with the fire. Seth picked up a stick as well and lit it. "But how do we defeat them?" he asked.

"Might as well burn them," suggested Susan as she held onto Lizzie.

Carl waved the burning stick at the zombie near him and the right hand caught on fire. The zombie moaned as the mud around the arm hardened and fell to the ground.

"They break when they get burned," said Carl, setting the zombie on fire. "And here I thought you could only get these creeps through magical means."

"That's what was written in the book," said Tabitha watching the creature shatter to the ground.

"We need to end this and get back to Eric and Cassandra," said Seth as he burned another zombie.

***

"Eric, we need to hurry," said Cassandra as the bodies kept sinking deeper into the swamp.

"Cassandra, I think we can…Cassandra are you alright?" asked Eric as he watched Cassandra fall to her knees, pressing her hand to her forehead as if in immense pain.

"I…I…" Cassandra tried to speak but she felt as if she was about to faint and then the feeling went away.

"What happened?" asked Eric helping her onto her feet.

"I don't know," she answered feeling weak. "Eric, look!" she pointed at the swamp.

The zombies started going into the swamp. "They are going in," she said.

"Now's our chance," said Eric as he ran toward the swamp.

"But Eric, those things are still in there," said Cassandra as she watched Eric go into the water and swim toward Terry's body.

"I know!" he yelled back, "But we can't just leave them here!"

Mustering up her courage, Cassandra went into the swamp as well. It was difficult for her to swim in it, but she tried her hardest and swam toward Sue's body. Eric had already saved Terry and was now saving Harvey. Cassandra tried her hardest to block out the swamp's smell and the thought that the zombies were still underneath her as she pulled Sue's body out of the swamp. She watched Eric swim toward Katherine's body and she swam toward Miss Jane's. She pulled at her but she wouldn't move. "Eric!" Cassandra called out. "I think she's stuck!"

"I'm coming!" Eric yelled back as he began to pull Katherine out.

Cassandra tried again but Miss Jane's body was slowly sinking into the swamp. Suddenly, Cassandra felt a cold hand grab her by her ankle. She screamed as the hand pulled her into the swamp.

"CASSANDRA!" yelled Eric in horror.

***

"That's the last of them," said Seth looking at the last zombie as it shattered to the ground in front of him. "It would have been a lot easier if we had guns. You know, like in the movies."

"You're my hero," Anya smiled, giving him a hug.

"Let's go get the others," said Susan as she watched Lizzie smell the mess around them.

"Yeah, come on," said Carl as he led the way. "I hope they are alright."

The friends followed Carl and ran toward the swamp. Anya's heart was beating fast. She was wondering about the zombies that would be present near the swamp. There were so many dead bodies in there. Letting Eric and Cassandra split up seemed like a stupid idea now. They should have stayed together.

"Don't tell me you guys defeated all of them alone?" asked Carl, trying to lighten the mood as he watched Eric pull Katherine out of the swamp.

"Shut up and help me!" yelled Eric as he handed her Katherine's body. "Cassandra just went into the swamp!"

"What?" asked Susan in horror as she looked at the green swamp. There was no sign of Cassandra anywhere.

Without another word, Carl and Seth jumped into the swamp. "You get the others!" yelled Eric as he swam toward Miss Jane's sinking body. "Cassandra, where are you?"

Raven screeched and began circling around Miss Jane's body as it slowly sank. Lizzie jumped into the water as well and began pulling Miss Jane's body out as Eric looked around for Cassandra. He held his breath and dove into the water but couldn't see anything. Anya and the other girls looked around helplessly as Eric dove into the water again, looking for Cassandra. Then miraculously Cassandra came out gasping for air. Eric grabbed her body and helped her out of the swamp as Seth and Carl came out with the rest of the teenagers.

"Thank goodness you are alright," said Anya as she helped Eric pull Cassandra out.

Cassandra didn't say a word and sat down on the ground, breathing hard and coughing out murky water. Eric was silent and was looking at Cassandra, smiling as he cleaned his glasses.

"What do you suppose we do with them?" asked Carl, looking at the sleeping teenagers and Miss Jane.

"I am not putting them in their tents," said Susan as she hugged Lizzie.

"What happened? Where am I?" asked Miss Jane as she got up, opening her eyes. "Why am I here near the swamp? What's going on?"

"You won't believe us," smiled Seth exhausted as he watched the other sleeping teenagers wake up as well. "Let's just say the outdoors makes a person sleep walk to weird places," he added as the H.F.L screamed after seeing themselves in dirty clothes.

Epilogue

It was a beautiful Monday morning in Colville. High school was out for the day and the seven friends were sitting in the park with the playing equipment.

"Fine day," said Seth as he lay back in the grass.

"We really didn't need a witch to defeat those zombies," said Carl smiling.

"I still think it wasn't as spooky as the vampire one," said Anya.

"I still can't get over the fact that your ex-boyfriend was a vampire," smiled Seth. "And that you two", he pointed at Eric and Carl, "were werewolves."

"Well, get over it," Anya smiled back at him.

"And to think," said Seth, "of all the people I could have hung out with at school, I got stuck with the ones who get involved in supernatural situations."

"Let's just hope that this was the last one," smiled Susan as she threw Lizzie a ball to fetch.

"Next month is Halloween though," said Tabitha, smiling at them. "I'm sure something is bound to happen."

"Hey, you know they are going to hold a party next month in school?" asked Anya, excited.

"Yeah," answered Cassandra. She felt the locket around her neck grow cold. She had found the locket when she resurfaced from the swamp a few days ago. She had tried opening it but it was shut tight and she hadn't told the others about it. She had tried getting rid of it, but whenever she was close to doing so, she would change her mind and leave it around her neck.

"Hey, you there?" came Eric's voice.

Cassandra blinked. *I must have wandered off,* she thought as she felt the locket around her neck grow colder.

"Yeah, the party," she said, smiling at the group. "It sounds fun. I can't wait."

The Cold

One

"I hate Mondays," Anya complained as she got onto the school bus.

"You have told us that more than a hundred times now," said Susan, rolling her eyes at her black haired friend as she followed her into the bus.

"Five hundred twenty-five and counting," Eric corrected Susan as he adjusted his glasses. "But then again, who's counting?" he added with a smile, getting on the bus and walking toward his usual seat.

"Well, I'm more concerned about the weather," said Tabitha taking her seat at the back of the bus. "I mean, why is it so cold these days?"

"Nature works in mysterious ways," answered Carl with a smile as he sat down next to Tabitha.

"Let's just hope it doesn't work in *too* mysterious ways," said Tabitha smiling back at him. "I'm already tired of saving this place without telling anyone about it."

"I doubt that this place is ever going to be normal," said Eric calmly as the five friends settled down and the bus began to move.

Anya didn't add anything further to the conversation and she looked around. Susan was sitting beside her and tying her blonde hair into a knot behind her head. Eric was reading a book, sitting alone on a seat next to hers. '*Typical Eric*,' thought Anya and her gaze went toward Carl and Tabitha sitting on the seat in front of her. Carl was talking about something with Tabitha who didn't look slightly interested in what he had to say '*and typical Carl*'. She looked out of the window and watched the bus drive past familiar surroundings.

"Waiting for someone?" asked Susan with a smile.

Anya didn't answer and just rolled her eyes, smiling at herself. Of course she was waiting for someone. She hadn't seen him for two days now. The weekend couldn't have ended any sooner. The school bus stopped again and a few more teenagers climbed into the bus. Anya felt her heart beat faster as she watched the last person get into the bus.

"How's my girl?" asked Seth as he flashed a smile at Anya and walked toward her.

"Yeah, yeah, we all are fine too," said Susan rolling her eyes before Anya could answer. Eric was still busy with the book he was reading.

"I was just about to ask you too," said Seth defensively.

"Of course you were, man," said Carl with a smile as Tabitha giggled. "Of course you were."

***

The bell rang for their next class. Anya watched as Tabitha put her books in her 'so-called' haunted locker. "I still say that it's creepy," said Anya as Tabitha took out some notes and closed the locker behind her. "Whether you believe me or not," continued Anya. "Just look at the weird stuff we have been facing…"

"Anya," said Tabitha with a smile and grabbed her hand. She had heard Anya and her theory about her locker being haunted too many times now. "We're going to be late for class."

"As if we are going to listen to anything useful if we hurry," said Anya as she followed Tabitha to their class.

"It's the start of the week," answered Tabitha as the two girls entered the class. There were students already present. "We are beginning an exciting chapter today."

"We are starting an exciting chapter today," Anya mimicked Tabitha as she took her seat behind her. Anya couldn't understand why anyone could be excited about starting a new chapter in class. A few of her classmates gave out a laugh.

"What?" asked Tabitha oblivious to what was going on inside the classroom.

"Nothing," Anya answered with a smile as the teacher entered holding a pile of fat looking books. "Nothing at all."

The history teacher went on and on about how the ancient people had made up stories of vampires and werewolves and how superstitions arose in the world.

'*Yeah, right!*,' thought Anya, twirling her pen in her fingers. '*I'll give that old bat proof! No such things as vampires? What does she know? She'll know about a werewolf when it bites her bony…*"

"Anya!" came the teacher's voice.

"Yes, Miss Flow?"

"Can you tell us why the early Europeans burned women who looked suspicious to them?"

"They…uh…"

RING. RING. RING.

The school bell rang and the students got up to leave.

"Okay, never mind," said Miss Flow, and Anya began to pack up her things. "We'll continue from here in the next class."

"Saved by the bell," smiled Tabitha as she followed Anya out of the room. "The question was so easy. Why didn't you answer it?"

"The same reason I'm not going to answer this question as well," said Anya with a straight face as the girls walked toward the cafeteria to meet the others. '*And you are not going to read my mind*,' thought Anya. '*Oh, I shouldn't have thought that.*'

Anya looked at Tabitha. She was busy texting someone on her cell phone as the girls made their way to the cafeteria.

'*Safe…Stop thinking, Anya!*'

Anya tried to keep her mind blank as much as possible. She still felt that Tabitha was able to read minds, or maybe at least her mind.

"Over here!" came Susan's voice as the two girls entered the cafeteria.

"I hate the noise in here," said Tabitha. The cafeteria was full of students.

"You'll get used to it," said Anya as she made her way toward the table occupied by Susan, Cassandra, and Seth.

"How are you, Cassandra?" Anya added as she sat down beside her.

"Fine," answered Cassandra with a smile. She took a sip of her orange juice and remained quiet.

"Are you going to eat something?" Susan asked Anya as she took a bite of her chicken sandwich.

"Nope," answered Anya. She had stopped wondering a long time ago why Susan could eat so much and not get fat. "I'm full."

"Where's Carl?" Tabitha asked the group at large.

"There he is," said Seth and he pointed at the cafeteria door.

Tabitha and Anya turned around and noticed Carl coming into the cafeteria laughing with a bunch of cheerleaders.

"See you girls later," he said to the cheerleaders as he reached the table where his friends were sitting. The cheerleaders smiled at him and walked away giggling amongst themselves.

"I had the most wonderful time," he added sitting next to Tabitha and passing his hand through his curly brown hair. "I can score baskets while…wait for it!" he tried to sound dramatic.

"We are waiting," said Susan as she took another bite of her sandwich.

"Blindfolded!" Carl answered with raised arms. He looked at the group, hoping to see impressed faces. Anya rolled her eyes at him, Cassandra was busy checking for something in her bag, Susan was enjoying her sandwich, Seth was reading what was written on his juice pack, and Tabitha managed a weak smile.

"Werewolves' powers are coming in handy," said Eric as he walked toward his friends. He sat down next to Seth and put the books he was carrying onto the table. "What you are doing is called cheating."

"Not my fault that I turned into a werewolf," said Carl. He helped himself to some of Susan's chips. "And besides, it makes me look cool."

"It's a real safe feeling you get," said Seth with a weak smile as he looked at Carl and Eric, "when you discover that your two new friends used to be werewolves."

"Werewolf or not," said Anya smugly. "We girls easily kicked Carl's and Eric's butts back then."

Anya's friends knew she was talking about the time when David, who was actually a vampire, had attacked her. They knew that Anya was still not over the whole David thing, so they avoided mentioning him unless she did. Susan and Tabitha laughed at Carl. They remembered that incident all too well.

"Our powers were not fully developed back then," said Carl defensively. He looked at Eric for support, but the bespectacled boy remained silent.

"Yeah, whatever," said Anya, and the rest of the teenagers joined in the laughter as well.

***

"Why couldn't Seth live nearby?" said Anya as the five friends got off of the bus and stepped onto the bus stop.

Seth didn't live in Colville. He went home on one of his friends' bicycles instead of taking the bus after school.

"You can't have everything in life," said Eric adjusting his glasses as a cold gust of wind hit his face. Anya didn't reply. Her mind began to wonder why the weather kept getting colder.

"I'm off then," said Carl as he suppressed a yawn. "See you later."

"I'll come with you," said Eric.

The boys nodded at the three girls and walked away.

"See you two later," said Anya smiling at Susan and Tabitha.

"Bye," said Tabitha. Her black hair was blowing in the cold wind. "Damn it," she added as she tried to keep it in place.

"See you, Anya," said Susan.

Tabitha had to go to Susan's to get some notes, so Anya waved her friends goodbye and started to walk home. The cold air blew Anya's already disheveled hair and she was not enjoying it one bit. As she walked toward her house, she began to feel weird as the cold air touched her arms. She folded them in front of her chest and quickened her pace. She didn't like the feeling. Something was definitely not right about the weather.

***

Cassandra watched Eric and the rest of his friends get into the bus. She waved at them for the last time and walked back inside the school. She walked toward her locker. She needed to take out a book. She was about to open it and reach for the book, when…

SLAM!

"I'm so sorry," came a girl's voice. "I was in a hurry and I didn't…"

"No problem," said Cassandra. She touched her forehead. Her head was pounding after hitting the locker.

"I'm so sorry," said the girl again in a hurry. She was definitely worried. "Are you sure you are alright?"

"I'm fine," answered Cassandra. She smiled at the girl. Cassandra recognized her. She was in one of her classes. "It's okay," she added with a smile. "I'm fine."

"Okay," said the girl. She smiled again and walked away.

Cassandra adjusted her hood and watched the girl walk down the corridor and turn a corner. And then it happened. All of a sudden sweat popped from Cassandra's forehead. She felt her legs lose strength and she fell to the ground. She tried to get up but her trembling body kept her on all fours. She couldn't move. She felt a heavy presence around her as if something or someone was pushing her down toward the floor. "What's happening to me?" Cassandra tried to speak, but could only manage a whisper. And then, just as it had happened, the pain in her entire body went away.

'*Weird*,' thought Cassandra as she got onto her feet. Her body was back to normal, as if nothing had happened. She picked up her bag from the floor, and taking the book from her locker, she walked toward the school gate. *I should get home as soon as possible.*

Cassandra was about to reach the end of the corridor when she heard a scream behind her. She turned around, and thinking that someone might need help, she ran toward the source of the sound. Someone was in pain and she had to go and see. Once there, she noticed a girl sitting on the floor in front of a staircase. It was the same girl who had accidentally pushed Cassandra against her locker. Cassandra watched as two female teachers came to help the girl up.

"You should be more careful on the stairs, Bethany," said one of the teachers as she looked at her, concern in her voice.

"I just tripped," said Bethany, trying not to cry. "I don't know what happened, Miss Flow."

"It's all right," said Miss Flow with a smile, and she took the girl's hand in hers.

"Now let's get you back up and take you to the nurse," said the other female teacher as she helped Bethany stand up. "And hope you didn't twist your ankle."

Cassandra watched the two teachers take Bethany away. She felt confused. She looked at Bethany and felt happy to see her in pain. '*Stop it!*' Cassandra scolded herself. '*What is happening to me?*'

Two

The next morning Anya joined her friends at the bus stop. The weather had changed drastically overnight. All of her friends were wearing warm coats.

"You should have worn a cap," said Susan as she watched Anya's hair blow in the cold wind. "It's so cold," she added, rubbing her hands together. "I should have worn gloves."

"But it shouldn't be like this," said a concerned Eric. "Don't know what has happened to the weather here."

"I didn't hear anything about being this cold in the weather broadcast yesterday," said Carl.

"Whatever it is," said Tabitha as she looked at some dark clouds forming in the sky. "I don't like the feeling this cold is giving me."

"Join the club," said Anya as she tried to control her flying hair. '*I should have worn a cap!*'

The bus came and the teenagers got in, sitting in their usual seats. The bus was quite empty. A lot of students seemed to have preferred staying at home. After a few more stops, Seth got in as well.

"Cold, isn't it?" he said with a smile as he walked toward his friends.

"Tell us about it," said Anya as the bus started again.

Seth rubbed his hands together and sat down between Anya and Susan. "Now that's better," he added, kissing Anya as Susan rolled her eyes.

***

"Hurry up!" urged Anya as Susan opened her locker.

The corridors were ice cold and Anya wasn't keen on waiting for Susan another minute.

"Judging by the student strength today," said Susan as she finally closed her locker, "I don't think there are going to be any classes."

Susan's prediction came true. The classrooms were half empty because a lot of the students decided not to come. The students who were present were making their teachers give them the day off.

"That went well," said Anya as their teacher finally agreed to end the class.

"I'm more concerned about this cold," said Susan as she got up to leave with the rest of the students.

"Why?" Anya asked as they exited the classroom. She had a feeling that she already knew the answer.

"I can't say," said Susan deep in thought. The girls walked toward the cafeteria. "Taking the previous things that have happened into account, I just feel we need to be careful."

"So you think this cold is somehow connected to the swamp incident?" came Eric's voice from behind.

"I don't know," answered Susan as Eric joined the girls and they continued to walk to the cafeteria. "I'm not sure."

"There might be a possibility," said Eric seriously.

'*These guys have lost it*,' Anya thought to herself.

"We should go check it out," suggested Susan casually.

The words made Anya stop in her tracks. "What did you just say?"

"I merely suggested that we go and check it out," said Susan stopping as well. "You know, just to be on the safe side of things."

"I agree," said Eric before Anya could say anything.

Anya knew that her two friends weren't going to change their minds if she directly contradicted their idea. She decided to take another approach to tackle the matter. "The swamp is too far away," said Anya. "We can't go there in this weather."

"We can go through the cave," said Susan excitedly and turning toward Eric. "You know, see the swamp from above."

'*Damn it!*,' thought Anya as Eric nodded at what Susan had just suggested. '*Aren't blondes supposed to be dumb?*'

***

"Mom," said Anya as she got into a warm coat. "I'm going out."

"But the weather?" said her mother sounding concerned. "You should stay home."

"Don't worry," Anya answered as she wore her gloves. *These will keep me warm.*

"You just got back from school," said her mother. She wanted her daughter to stay home and be warm. "Don't you have homework to do?"

"No homework today," answered Anya as she opened the front door. "I will be back home before dark. I promise."

Anya closed the door behind her as she stepped outside of her house. The air on her face was cold. '*Glad I covered my head,*' she thought. She didn't enjoy her hair flying around her. Ignoring the empty house next to hers, she walked toward Susan's house where the rest of her friends had decided to meet. As she went on her way, Anya looked at the familiar neighborhood. People were walking fast, trying to reach their homes and get away from the cold weather. It wasn't as if the people of Colville didn't enjoy the cold, it was just that nobody was expecting it to become this cold a month after the end of summer break.

"Bark!"

Susan's dog came running toward Anya as she came closer to her friend's house.

"How're you doing, girl?" said Anya with a smile. She bent down and patted the animal.

"We need to go to Eric's," came Susan's voice.

Anya looked up and noticed Susan walking toward her. "Why?"

"I just got his call," Susan answered. Lizzie began to run in circles around her legs, barking happily. "The others are going there as well."

"Let's go then," said Anya. '*Why does Eric have to change things at the last minute!*'

"Sorry girl," said Susan looking at Lizzie. "You are to stay home with Mom."

Lizzie looked hurt and went toward the house, her head down.

"I'll make it up to her later," said Susan. Anya was giving her a disapproving look. "I'm worried that she might catch a cold if she comes along with us."

***

Anya and Susan reached Eric's house and Anya pressed the doorbell.

"Carl and Tabitha are already here," said Eric as he opened the door for the girls.

"What about Seth and Cassandra?" asked Anya as she stepped inside.

"Seth will be here soon," answered Carl lying on a couch. He watched Anya walk toward the heater to warm herself. "Don't know if Cassandra will be coming."

Susan walked inside as well and Eric closed the door behind her. Susan felt the warmth inside the house and smiled. "Finally, someplace warm," she said, taking off her gloves. "Nice coat," she added, looking at Tabitha.

"Thanks," Tabitha answered with a smile as she sat down in a chair and looked at her coat as well. "It's a gift from Dad."

'*Whatever*,' thought Anya as she gave Tabitha's coat a quick look and again faced the heater. '*I couldn't care less even if it were an Anna Liam creation*.'

"It's an Anna Liam creation," said Tabitha as she talked to Susan. Susan looked impressed. Anna Liam was one of the best known designers in the world. "Dad brought it when he came back from France last year."

Before Anya could roll her eyes, the bell rang and Eric walked toward the door to open it. Seth appeared in the doorway. He managed a weak smile as he looked at the gathered teenagers. "Are we really going to go through with this?" he asked, knowing quite well that the decision had been made.

***

The six friends made their way to the local forest. The dark clouds overhead were making Anya uncomfortable. Her eyes looked around the forest. For some strange reason she got the feeling that the trees were cold from the inside. *Stop thinking about that!*

"Whose idea was this again?" asked Seth as he walked with Anya, clearly not enjoying their little adventure.

"The blonde one's," answered Anya. She looked at Susan walking next to Eric at the front of the group.

"We had to do this," said Eric from the front. He had heard them speaking.

'*Damn those werewolf ears*,' thought Anya.

"Why did we *have* to do this?" asked Carl as he walked behind Eric. "For all we know, this cold could just be some normal cold, you know, Mother Nature trying to do her work."

"I don't know, Carl," said Tabitha walking next to him. "I checked the internet this morning. Colville's temperature has never dropped this low."

"So it seems we are well on our way to save the town again," said Carl sarcastically.

"Let's just hope that it doesn't come to that," said Eric as he pushed his glasses up on his nose and they continued walking.

"Which one was it again?" asked Carl as the friends reached the caves.

Eric looked at the caves closely. "This one," he said, pointing at an entrance right in front of the friends.

"Are you sure?" asked Susan as she switched on her flashlight. "We should probably mark these caves, you know."

"We will," said Eric. He switched on his flashlight as well. The beam fell a few feet away from him into the cave's mouth. "Let's go."

As soon as Anya entered the cave with her friends, the temperature changed.

"It's quite warm in here," said Seth. He took off his muffler and rubbed his neck.

"Tell me about it," said Anya in an unpleasant tone. She cursed herself for wearing a coat. *Even if I take if off now, I don't want to carry it around with me.* "We shouldn't have worn all of these warm coats."

"Don't worry about that now," said Eric as he led the group farther into the cave.

"Try thinking of cold places," suggested Susan with a smile. "It helps."

'*Yup! That girl is losing it day by day,*' thought Anya as she walked behind Tabitha and Susan. Carl and Seth were at the rear talking about trying out for the basketball team at school.

"Shouldn't we have reached there by now?" asked Anya remembering the last time she went through the cave with Eric.

"These tunnels are like a maze," said Tabitha as Eric led the friends deeper into the cave, making a turn every now and then. "How do you know where we have to go?" she asked Eric.

"Instincts, I guess," answered Eric without looking at Tabitha.

Anya saw Tabitha give Eric a suspicious look. As far as Anya knew, Susan was the only one she had told about the little trip she and Eric had made to the cave to look for David. The rest of the friends heard the story that she and Eric had went over the hill to look at the swamp rather than going through the cave.

"There's the opening," said Eric. He stopped in front of a small hole. It shone a little because of the rays of light making their way through the gaps.

"Finally," said Seth clearly glad that the cave trip was over. He walked closer to the opening. "How do you suppose we go through it?"

"I don't think we will be able to fit through," said Tabitha with concern in her voice.

"Don't worry," said Eric. He handed his flashlight to Carl. Anya knew that he was going to squeeze through, just like he did the last time they were both there.

Eric walked closer to the opening and began to squeeze through. First his hands went through, then his face, and then his torso. If it hadn't been for his werewolf powers, he would have gotten stuck halfway through.

"Ten bucks if he gets stuck," said Carl as the friends watched Eric.

"Okay," said Anya with a smile. '*You are so going to lose.*'

The friends watched as Eric's legs went out of sight as well. "You owe me ten bucks, Carl," said Anya as Seth and Susan laughed at him. Tabitha rolled her eyes at Carl.

"Carl, give me a hand," Eric's voice came from the outside. "If we both try, we can move these rocks to widen the passage."

"Fine," said Carl. He bent down and began pushing the rocks aside. Eric kept instructing him about the rocks he needed to move in order to not block the opening.

"Great," said Seth sourly. He watched as Carl lifted a heavy rock and tossed it aside as if it were made of cotton.

"Don't worry," said Anya. She grabbed Seth's right hand and gave it a little squeeze. "Werewolf powers don't impress me. *Much!*"

"That's quite comforting to know," said Seth, forcing a smile.

"All done," said Carl. He cleaned his hands on his sweater. "Let's go."

"It has gotten cold again," said Susan as she climbed through the passage.

"How much farther to the swamp?" asked Tabitha as she climbed out as well followed by Anya and Seth.

"Half an hour perhaps," said Eric. He looked at the swamp and then his eyes went toward the Singleton farm.

"This place does bring back memories, doesn't it?" said Carl as he joined his friends.

"Let's just hope that they remain memories," said Tabitha rubbing her hands together.

Very carefully the teenagers climbed down and began walking toward the swamp. On her right Anya could see the Singleton farm. She felt as if it was calling for her. '*Stop it*,' she thought. '*Stop thinking about it, no one is calling you*.'

After walking a few more minutes, the group reached the area where they had camped with their classmates. Just a few days ago they were fighting for their lives at this exact place. "Just a little bit further," said Eric leading the way. "We are almost near the forest."

The group saw the trees. They walked toward them and then suddenly they all stopped at once.

"I don't like this," said Susan rubbing her hands together.

All of them felt it. The temperature seemed to have dropped a few more degrees near the forest.

"Wait here," instructed Eric. The friends watched him walk away from them and the trees, his eyebrows together. "It's better away from the trees. It's a bit warmer."

'*Our lives just get better and better*,' thought Anya sarcastically, not enjoying the cold she was feeling.

Eric walked back to the group. "What are we waiting for?" he asked, looking at the group at large. No one was interested in going into the forest. Eric didn't change his expression. His friends knew he was determined. With their hands in their pockets and moving closer together, the teenagers followed Eric into the forest as he led them toward the swamp. Anya looked at her surroundings as she walked. The grey clouds overhead were not moving, as if bent upon covering the sun. No one spoke a word to each other as they walked. Anya wanted to say something to lighten the mood, but whenever she tried to speak, she decided against it. It was as if the forest had somehow taken away her desire to say anything aloud.

"What the…?"

Eric stood open mouthed as he looked at the swamp. Its surface was covered in a sheet of ice. The trees that surrounded it looked dead, their leaves covered in frost. Anya couldn't understand why Eric would be surprised because of a frozen swamp. '*It's natural for bodies of water to freeze up*.'

"Why are you so surprised?" she asked moving closer to him. "I mean, it's only a frozen swamp, Eric."

"It's not that," answered Carl who seemed to have noticed something. He began to follow Eric to the other side of the swamp. Still not understanding what the two were seeing, the rest of the friends followed him as well.

"Look at that," said Eric. He traced a circle over the frozen sheet of ice with his index finger. "This layer is thinner than the rest."

Anya looked at the area and sure enough, the area in the circle that Eric had just made was thinner than the rest of the sheet of ice.

"It looks as if it broke," said Tabitha thinking hard. She looked at the area again. "And after whatever came out or fell in, it froze up again."

"I like to think that something fell in," said Seth uneasily. "You know, a small animal or something."

"I don't think something fell in, Seth," said Susan as she looked at something. Anya followed Susan's eyes. She was looking at the edge of the swamp. Eric and Carl seemed to have noticed the same thing as well. There were wet footprints coming out of the frozen swamp and disappearing into the forest.

Susan walked toward the footprints for closer examination. "They aren't exactly wet," she said as she touched one of them. "The grass has frozen, leaving the prints on them."

"You mean that whatever came out of the swamp freezes grass with its feet?"

"Not whatever, Carl," answered Eric. He bent down to examine the footprints more closely. "These are human feet, guys."

"You mean a person walked…" Tabitha couldn't complete her sentence. Her eyes followed the footprints toward the nearest tree. "Oh!"

The rest of the gang looked at the tree as well. A handprint made of frost was visible on the trunk of the tree. The friends walked toward the tree silently. Anya felt as if someone or something might come running out from behind the trees and attack them. She still remembered the swamp zombies they had to fight the last time they were there.

"Whatever that is," said Seth looking at the handprint. "It isn't good."

"But it is a human handprint all right," said Eric with a nod.

Anya's eyes followed the footprints. "So whatever that thing is," she said. "It seems to have walked into the forest."

"Should we like…?"

"I wouldn't advise it, Susan," said Carl. "It seems dangerous and we don't even know what we are dealing with here."

"What if it's a person in need of help?" said Susan. Anya had to force herself from rolling her eyes in disbelief. "He could be hurt or something."

"Considering what we have gone through over the past weeks," said Eric. "I doubt that it's a person in need of help that broke out of the frozen swamp and disappeared into the forest."

"Maybe he or she threw something into the swamp and walked away?" asked Seth. Anya knew he wanted to look at the situation normally. She couldn't help but smile at him. She too was hoping for something that didn't involve the paranormal.

"There were no marks indicating that a person walked toward the swamp," said Eric, crushing Seth's hope. He already knew the question his friends were going to ask, so he answered it himself. "The only footprints we saw went away from the swamp." "And besides," Eric added as he pushed his glasses up on his nose. "Who walks into a forest barefoot just to throw something into a swamp in this weather?"

"So, now we are being attacked by something else?" asked Seth. His displeasure was evident. "Great! Just great!"

"What if it comes to town?" asked Tabitha clearly worried.

"We will worry about that when it happens," said Eric with a leveled voice. "For now, I suggest we get out of here as soon as we can."

***

"I am going to mirror Seth and say that we are seriously going to be attacked by something else now," said Anya. She was talking with Susan on her phone in her room. The friends had gone back to their homes as soon as their trip to the swamp was over. Everyone was more interested in cozying up in their beds rather than staying at Eric's and discussing what to do next. "You mark my words. It will happen."

"I'd rather not," said Susan. Even she knew that considering everything they had gone through, another supernatural incident was nothing to be surprised about.

"Damn, this cold is killing me," Anya complained as she put on an extra pair of socks while holding the phone between her ear and shoulder.

"Tell me about it," said Susan. And then Susan's voice changed. "Anya, look…"

"What? Where? Huh!" Anya asked, shocked at Susan's voice.

"Out the window," said Susan. "Look out your window!"

Anya grabbed the phone in her hand and walked toward her window. "What the…?" she stared at what she saw. She put the phone back to her ear. "Susan, how come it is snowing outside?"

"Beats me," said Susan just as surprised as Anya.

Three

"Any ideas on what is happening to this town?" asked Anya as she looked at the snow covered road from the school bus window.

"Nope," said Susan. She was sitting in the seat behind Anya. The bus only had the teenage friends in it, as the rest of the kids had preferred staying at home again because of the weather.

"I still don't like the idea of that thing that came out of the swamp," said Seth as he lay down on a seat in front of Anya.

"Same here," said Carl. Both of his legs were on his seat and he looked at some little kids having a snowball fight in their yard as the bus drove by. "I mean, is that thing so powerful that it has the power to manipulate the weather?"

"I can't say anything about it right now," said Eric. He cleaned his glasses with his shirt. "Let's hope it doesn't turn into something serious."

"I haven't found anything about a human resembling creature that can freeze stuff," said Tabitha. She was sitting near Susan who grabbed her bag as the bus reached the school. "And I went through a lot of books last night, but nothing came up."

The bus stopped outside of the school's gate and the friends got up. "Great," complained Anya as she found herself, shoes wet, in six inches of snow.

With a little work, the six made their way through the school grounds and into the complex. As soon as Anya reached the corridors, she bent down to brush the snow off of her shoes.

"I'm off to class," said Eric adjusting his glasses. "If classes happen today as well," he added.

"Me too," said Carl and he followed Eric to his class.

Seth, Susan, and Tabitha waited for Anya to finish brushing the snow off of her shoes. "Damn, these corridors are cold," said Seth as he rubbed his hands together.

"You guys go," Anya said to the others. She too was feeling cold. "I'll be taking a few minutes with these shoes and the classes are about to start."

"See you in History," said Tabitha.

"I could wait for you now," said Seth. He looked at Anya with a smile.

"You already missed two classes this week," said Susan before Anya could answer and she grabbed Seth's arm. "Come on Romeo, I'd better take you to class."

Anya watched her friends walk away. '*Stupid shoes,*' she thought. She gave them another brush with her hands and stood up. She looked at the empty corridor and began walking toward her first class. On her way she saw some of her English classmates having a snowball fight on the grounds.

"Hey, Anya!" called one of the kids. "You want in?"

"Not yet, Jones," she called back. "I've got History."

She walked into her classroom. Tabitha was already there, ready to take notes as soon as Miss Flow started talking.

'*Why did I say no to Jones?*' thought Anya, feeling bored in her class. Miss Flow was making the five students who had the audacity to attend write a two page paper on British rule, which was her demented idea for fun.

'*Fun,*' thought Anya, looking at the two lines she had written on her piece of paper. She turned toward the rest of the class. Tabitha was busy writing, and the rest of the three students looked as if they wanted to kill something or themselves in order to get out of class, Anya wasn't sure. '*I wish I had a snowball that I could throw at that old bat*,' she thought, looking at Miss Flow who was silently reading a book. '*Now that would be fun!*'

***

"I hate today," Anya yelled. The rest of the students looked at her as she sat with her friends in the cafeteria.

"Tell me about it," replied Susan, not even looking at her friend. She was playing with her chips and feeling bored.

"Where are the rest of the guys?" asked Seth stretching his arms.

"Carl is off shooting hoops," Tabitha replied. "Don't know about Eric."

"Has anybody seen Cassandra?" asked Susan looking up from her food. "I didn't see her in Math class today and knowing her, she never misses a class."

"Nope, haven't seen her myself either," said Anya. She couldn't take sitting idly anymore and she got up from her seat.

"Where are you going?" asked Seth. He watched as Anya put her tray into the bin.

"Outside to play," she answered, looking back at her friends, a huge grin on her face. "Who's with me?"

Her friends looked at each other for a second and then nodded at her. The four of them made their way to the school grounds. The few students who had come today were playing in the snow.

"Hey, Anya," called Susan.

"What?" Anya spun around and…WHAM!

"You…," she cleared the snow off of her numb nose. She bent down and scooped up some snow herself as Susan and Tabitha laughed at her.

"Now girls," said Seth. He tried to control his laughter. "We mustn't fight each…"

WHAM!

"Ouch!" yelled Seth. "I thought you were going to hit Susan."

"Sue me," Anya yelled back at him. Seth threw a snowball at her and she dodged it by a few inches.

"Hey, what are you guys doing here?" asked Carl surprised as he walked onto the grounds. "I came as soon as I saw…"

Four snowballs came zooming at him and he dodged each one of them easily. He stood in front of his friends with his hands on his hips. "You have got to do better than…"

WHAM! A snowball hit Carl from behind.

"Your so called talents won't work with me," said Eric as the rest of the friends laughed at Carl. "Nice try," he added, dodging the snowball that Carl threw at him.

***

"Now that was fun," said Anya as she waited for the bus outside of the school gate. Seth had gone home on his bicycle. All of them were exhausted after their snowball match. The principal had given all of them the day off due to the weather. There was no point in making four or five students sit in class and forcing them to study.

"I must have lost like hundreds of calories," said Susan pink in her face as they waited for the bus to arrive.

"Did anyone see Cassandra today?" asked Eric. He brushed some snow off of his hair. "I didn't see her in the library."

"No, we haven't seen her," answered Anya. She couldn't help but sense a hint of worry in Eric's voice. After a few minutes it began to snow gently. Glad that the bus arrived soon, they all got in.

"Now for the serious stuff," said Eric choosing a seat. "What should we do about that thing from the swamp?"

"I don't know," replied Anya sitting with Susan at the back of the bus.

"Beats me," Carl sighed taking a seat next to the window.

"The only thing that I can think of is that we find out what that thing is," said Tabitha. She could sense Anya's stare at the back of her neck. "And then find a way to tackle it," she finished.

"Should we like go to the swamp again today?"

"Eric…no!" warned Anya before anyone could answer him. "That place was creepy enough as it is. Just leave it. There's no point in looking for trouble."

"We have to go," said Eric trying to fight his case. "We have to find where that thing went and see if it really is some kind of monster. We can't risk not doing anything, not after what we all have gone through."

"He does have a point," said Susan. Anya shot her a dirty look. "Or we could wait this weather out and leave the monster be because it isn't harming anyone," she added quickly, and Anya smiled at her.

"What if it's a witch?" asked Tabitha. Anya knew she was going to side with Eric on this one and she also knew where Carl was going to go as well. "We can't just leave everything and do nothing."

'*Where did the idea of a witch came from?*' thought Anya. '*What's Tabitha getting at?*'

"Carl, you have the swing vote," said Eric. He looked at Carl with a smile. Carl looked at Anya who was waiting for him to say something, and then he looked at Tabitha who gave him a smile and he smiled back.

"Oh, we are so going," said Susan, looking at Carl and then at Tabitha. She tried to control her laughter as Eric stopped Anya who swore and tried to punch Carl.

***

"Honey!" Anya heard her mother's voice from downstairs. "Your dad and I will be going out tonight to Aunt Mary's. You want to come?"

"Nah," she replied as she brushed her black hair in front of the mirror. She had decided to dye it brown again but couldn't find the time to do so.

"Are you sure?"

"Yes, I'm sure."

"Okay, fine," her mother's voice again. "Don't stay out too late if you go with your friends and stay out of trouble."

'*If only you knew what I was up to,*' thought Anya with a smile as she put on her sweater. She was getting ready to go to Eric's house where the rest of the group was going to gather.

She still wasn't into the whole idea of going back to that swamp again. She wanted her life to get back to normal. She wanted to forget about David, the swamp zombies, and the anonymous letter she had gotten before the swamp incident. However, deep inside she knew that things weren't going to return to normal anytime soon.

***

"We still have some hours until sundown," Eric told the group as he checked his watch. They were all gathered inside his house.

"Is Seth coming?" asked Anya as she looked toward the window.

"Missing him already?" asked Susan as she adjusted her muffler with a smile.

"Don't make me strangle you with that," said Anya, her eyes narrowed.

"He can't make it," replied Eric. He placed his hand on Anya's shoulder and signaled Susan not to laugh. "Looks like it's going to be the original group this time around," he added with a smile while looking at his friends.

"Let's go and get this over with," said Carl as he got up from the couch.

***

The group walked the familiar path through the forest and toward the cave. Once there, Eric led them into the cave. Anya wasn't surprised to experience the warmth in the cave. None of them talked much as they followed Eric. They all knew they had to find the truth about the thing or person that came out of the frozen swamp. Anya felt as if she and her friends were the town's personal investigation team when it came to the supernatural, and she wasn't feeling quite happy about the idea.

"Great!" exclaimed Eric as the group reached the familiar area. "The hole is blocked again."

"By someone? Or…"

"Stop it, Susan," said Anya before her friend could finish. "Don't make up things. No one blocked the hole. The rocks must have come down from above and blocked it up. Simple."

"That's strange," said Eric as he gave the rocks a shove.

"What?"

"Don't know, Carl. The rocks won't shove easily."

"You're weak," said Carl with a smile. Eric took a few steps back and let Carl give it a try.

"Any luck?" asked Tabitha as the rest of the group smiled.

"We should stay quiet," said Susan trying not to laugh as Carl tried pushing the rock again. "Mr. Hercules here might lose his concentration."

Carl quietly backed away from the rocks, ignoring his laughing friends. "We'll do it together," advised Eric and he walked with Carl toward the rocks. "On one…two…three!"

"Ufff!" exclaimed Carl as the rocks gave way and he landed face first in the snow.

"Great," said Anya sarcastically as the group looked at the snow covered land. "It's nothing less than great."

"Can't stop now," said Eric, and the five fiends began climbing down toward the swamp. Their progress was slow as the snow was quite thick. "We are nearly there," said Eric as he urged the others on. "Just a few more minutes and we'll be there."

"Just a few more minutes and I'll be pinning him to the ground," whispered Anya as Susan walked next to her.

"He might hear you," Susan whispered as well.

"I really don't care," said Anya rolling her eyes. She didn't like the cold. They passed the Singleton farm and the familiar campsite. Ignoring the further drop in temperature, they walked into the forest and toward the swamp.

"Oh!" said Tabitha horrified as she looked at the swamp. The sheet of ice covering the surface of the swamp was thin in many places.

"More came out?" whispered Susan, her eyes wide open.

The group saw a lot of footprints coming out of the swamp and going into the forest on the other side. Eric looked at the group and then at the footprints. All of them knew what he meant and they followed him as he led them forward.

"This is not cool," said Carl as he tried to count the footsteps.

"Twelve," said Eric.

"What?"

"Twelve people or whatever they are," Eric answered Anya's question. "There are twelve pairs of feet."

"You mean there are twelve things somewhere in the forest that can freeze stuff?" asked Susan. She inched closer to Anya and looked at the trees that surrounded them.

"Yup," said Eric as he pushed up his glasses. "Twelve."

"So, should we?"

"No, Carl," answered Tabitha as she walked next to him. "We are not going into the forest any deeper."

"But what if those things come for us?" asked Eric. Anya knew that he was eager to walk further into the forest. "We decided that we'll find out what we are up against."

"Yes," said Tabitha as she stopped walking. "We did decide. But now there are twelve of those things out there and we can't take the risk."

"Don't worry," said Carl. He smiled at Tabitha. "I'll protect you from…"

Tabitha shot him an angry look and he stopped talking. Susan and Anya also stopped walking as well. It was evident that the girls were feeling uncomfortable, and the cold wasn't helping either. Eric thought about what Tabitha had said about dealing with twelve of those things out there and it made sense to him. Werewolf powers or not, they had no idea what they were up against. Defeated, the boys followed them away from the swamp and back home.

Four

It was a cold night and a figure was walking toward the swamp. It was treading so lightly that it made no footprints. It was if the figure was floating, barely touching the snow covered ground. It went through the trees, its pale face coming in and out of the moonlight as it walked below the branches overhead. The swamp came into view and it stopped an inch away from the frozen layer of murky water. It turned around. No one was following her. She had made sure of that when she froze the rocks outside the hole in the cave. She knew she was alone. Satisfied, she stepped onto the frozen layer of ice covering the surface of the swamp. She knew it would not break. She had made herself light enough to walk on it. She looked up at the dark sky and rested her gaze upon the moon shining above her. She lifted her arms as if she was about to fly and began whispering in a language as old as time. She knew the words well. She had recited the incantations before and now she was whispering them again.

The air became cold and the leaves of the trees began to rustle. She heard a howl from somewhere far away. Why was she doing this? Why was she putting her friends in danger? She did not know. All she knew was that there was some higher power making her do it all and it wanted more. It wanted revenge and it wanted it now. At first she had tried to resist the calling, but she was too weak and she could not fight it. She didn't want to fight it. Her whispering became louder and the ice around her began to crack. She saw something deep inside the swamp begin to break the ice from below. The air around her became heavy, as if someone else was also there with her, a sinister unseen presence. She did not stop and began to whisper her incantations faster. The sheet of ice gave way and a decayed hand broke the surface of water.

"AHhhhh!" Anya screamed as she woke up, her hand on her chest. She could feel her heart beating fast. She looked around and found herself in her bedroom. Moonlight came in from her window, dimly lighting the room in a white glow. "I'm alright," she said to herself. "I'm all right. I wasn't at the swamp…I wasn't calling those things…" She closed her eyes and dropped back onto her pillow. She tried not to think of the cold and decayed hand that had broken through the sheet of ice. Unable to calm down, she got up from her bed and went downstairs.

'*I should have asked Susan to stay the night*,' she thought. Her parents weren't back from her aunt's place and it was getting late. '*But noooo, I wanted to stay alone*,' she thought, switching on the kitchen light. '*No, wait. I did ask Susan to come and stay the night, but she couldn't because she was having some relatives over. Right?*'

"Why can't I remember?" she asked herself. She took out a glass of orange juice from the fridge and sat it on top of the kitchen counter. '*The hole was frozen in my dream*,' she remembered. '*But we saw it frozen today as well when we went back there through the cave.*'

Anya didn't feel like drinking the juice. She continued sitting on top of the kitchen counter. '*And the hand*,' she thought, closing her eyes. She remembered the hand coming out of the frozen swamp clearly. '*I watched the ice crack and the hand coming out just now…but when we went back to the swamp, we saw that the sheet of ice was thin from many places. More had come out? Eric said there were twelve pairs of footprints going into the forest. To me it felt as if I saw the hand come out of the swamp for the first time.*'

"What's happening to me," she talked to herself. "What does the dream mean?"

***

"It means that you saw what had happened the night before we went to the swamp again," said Susan, her feet up in her seat, as the bus was empty as it was yesterday. "You know, for the first time when we saw the ice thinned from only one spot."

All of the friends were in the school bus and Anya had wasted no time in telling the group about the dream she had last night.

"But who was the girl?"

"I don't know, Susan," answered Anya. She felt tired. "But it wasn't me because I was home the night the incident occurred and I woke up in my bed last night."

"No one is implying that it was you," said Tabitha. She looked directly at Anya who looked back at her. "You would have to be a witch with a strong magical aura to perform that resurrection spell or whatever that girl in your dream did."

"And a witch I am not," said Anya trying to defend herself.

"We can't be sure," Seth teased her.

"Don't joke about that," said Susan. She laughed at the expression that Anya was giving Seth.

"Yeah dude," said Carl as he extended his legs onto the seat next to him. "I was about to get mauled by her the last time I said something she didn't like."

"But scientifically speaking," said Eric, before Anya could speak and continue the argument, "it is said that if people keep on thinking about things, those things tend to come up in their dreams. So it is possible that Anya was thinking about the swamp and her dream kind of molded itself around what she was thinking about."

"I wasn't thinking about a hand coming out of the swamp," said Anya, ready to fight with Eric. "And science doesn't come into this."

"I'm not saying that what I just said did indeed happen," said Eric, feeling that Anya was in her fighting mood. "I'm just saying that it could have happened. But in your case I do believe that you saw what happened the night before more of those creatures came out of the swamp."

"Not creatures," said Anya, trying to calm down. "I'm telling you that they were people."

"That's really creepy," said Tabitha. "We have a witch who is casting resurrection spells on the swamp. If you ask me, I think the people who came out are the same as the ones we faced some weeks ago."

"But we defeated those muddy mother fuc…"

"Witches are powerful," said Tabitha before Carl could finish his sentence.

"Then how do we fight a witch?" asked Susan.

"Don't look at me," said Eric as the bus stopped in front of the school.

"They must have some kind of a weakness, right?" asked Seth. "Last time we were able to defend ourselves with fire."

"We'll talk about it later," said Eric as he picked up his school bag, "in the cafeteria at lunch. See you all there."

Anya got up as well. She wasn't feeling well and she knew why. She hadn't told her friends she had seen everything that happened in the dream through the eyes of the girl. It was if she was the one who had whispered those incantations and had brought those people back to life. Her friends already thought it was weird that she had such a dream and she wasn't going to freak them out any further by telling them that the girl in the dream she saw felt like her, as if she had done all of those things.

***

"Where is Eric?" asked Susan as she sat down at the table in the cafeteria.

"I think I saw him with Cassandra," answered Seth. He took a bite of his chicken salad sandwich. "But it's been awhile."

"Then the group has no brains right now," said Carl as he ate his chips.

"We aren't that dumb," said Tabitha with a smile.

"Yeah, we can manage without him," added Susan.

"Are you sure about that, Susan?" asked Eric. He smiled at the group and sat down between Susan and Anya.

"Where is Cassandra?" asked Anya. "I thought she was with you."

Seth watched as Anya offered her potato chips to Eric. Anya noticed Seth watching them. "Don't feel bad," said Anya with a smile. "You can have them too if you want."

"Nah, I'm fine," said Seth and he took a sip of his soda.

"She had an assignment to make," said Eric. He stopped taking more of Anya's chips and addressed the group. "She is taking extra courses, even more than me. Anyway, I filled her in about the whole thing and she's worried about it as well. She said she'll go and look at something concerning *cyrokinesis*."

"Excuse me?" said Carl. "Cyro what?"

"Cyrokinesis," said Tabitha. "It's the ability to freeze things. Maybe she'll find something that I haven't."

"What has cyro…or whatever it is got to do with this?"

"Nothing, Carl," said Tabitha looking at him with a '*How can you be so dumb?*' expression. "It's just research, nothing much."

"Anyway," said Susan. "What about the witch thing?"

"We need to go to the Singleton farm," said Eric casually.

Seth choked on his drink, and Anya looked at Eric as if he had gone mad. "You want us to go there even when you know that those things are still out there?" asked Seth.

Eric did not reply. Anya knew that his mind was made up. "You have been thinking of going back there for some time now, haven't you?" she asked.

"Yes, I have," he said. "I really think that we should face those things and see what we are up against." Eric looked at the teenagers sitting around the table. "So, who's with me?" he asked with a smile.

"You are going to get us killed," said Carl rolling his eyes.

"Of all the people you could have hung out with," said Seth looking at Anya with a smile. "You chose the ones who get themselves involved in supernatural situations."

"And that's what you get for hanging out with us as well," Anya answered with a smile. "Just accept it already."

Five

Eric opened the door for Anya and Susan and they stepped into his house, surprised to see the rest of the group, along with Seth, sitting comfortably in the living room.

"Who or what are we waiting for?" asked Anya. She wanted to end their trip as soon as possible.

"Take your coat off and sit down," said Eric as he closed the door behind them.

"Cassandra is coming over as well," said Tabitha. She took a sip of her hot tea and looked at the girls. "Eric's been nervous ever since Cassandra said that she would be coming."

"I'm not nervous," said Eric. He pushed his glasses up on his nose. "What gave you that idea?"

"Be patient," said Seth as Eric looked through the living room window at the street. "She'll be here in a little while."

"I guess you are right," said Eric and he sat down next to Carl on the sofa when suddenly Carl's ears perked up.

"She's here," said Carl with a smile.

"You can?" asked Susan in surprise.

Carl lifted his cup of tea and gave a nod as Eric got up to open the front door for the new arrival.

"Come in," said Eric. He smiled at Cassandra. "You want some tea?"

"No, thanks," said Cassandra walking into the house and looking at the other teenagers already there. "I would rather get this thing over with before dark."

***

The seven friends walked toward the forest. They saw many children playing in the snow on their way. '*If only they knew what we were up to*,' thought Anya as she moved closer to Seth. The wind was cold on her face.

"How long is the walk through the cave?" asked Cassandra as they went through the forest. She had never been inside the cave before.

"Not long," said Eric as he shone the flashlight in front of him. They had reached the cave. It wasn't as cold as they had expected it to be.

"So, this is where you took out that David person?" asked Cassandra as they continued to follow Eric into the cave.

"Yes," said Susan as she walked next to her. She looked at Anya walking in front of her and she knew Anya wasn't comfortable talking about him.

"I would rather we not talk about that dude," said Seth as he walked with Anya in front of Susan and Cassandra.

Cassandra sensed that they weren't comfortable with the topic so she remained quiet. '*It seems understandable*,' she thought as she looked at Anya and Seth who were talking to each other. '*Who wants to talk about an ex-boyfriend who was actually a vampire and out to kill you and your friends?*'

"Here we are," said Eric as they reached the opening they had been using to get to the swamp.

"It isn't closed up today," said Tabitha.

"Maybe someone or something has already…"

"Oh, stuff it Seth," said Susan before he could finish. Anya gave a smile as she followed Cassandra through the opening.

"Don't tell me that we will all be climbing down and walking all the way toward that farm," said Cassandra as she noticed the Singleton farm in the distance.

"Fine, we won't tell you," said Anya as she began climbing down, smiling at Cassandra. "We'll just do it."

The snow covered area wasn't helping their descent. Once down, they started to walk toward the Singleton residence through a foot of snow. Eric and Carl led the group and they tried to move the snow away as much as possible in order to make things easier for the rest.

"It still looks creepy," said Susan as they reached the place.

"The door is still broken from last time," said Carl. He walked into the house and looked around. "Hey, look!" he added. "It's frozen dust."

The others walked into the residence as well. The furniture was frozen and the entire place looked eerie. Anya couldn't help but feel as if the house didn't want them stepping inside of it.

"Should we check the basement first?" asked Tabitha. Everyone nodded and Eric led the way to the basement. That was where they discovered all of the magic related things the last time they were there.

"And what are we searching for?" asked Seth as they began searching around in the basement. He looked at the covers of some books on an old bookshelf.

"Don't know," said Tabitha. She picked up some old jars. "Anything that looks interesting."

"Be specific," said Anya as she looked at some papers lying on a desk. "We have already gone…"

"Did you hear that?" Carl cut through.

"Hear what?" asked Cassandra. She was about to open an old chest. Everyone was looking at Carl confused, except for Eric who motioned them to remain silent.

'*Yes*, *of course*,' thought Anya rolling her eyes. '*Werewolf super hearing*.'

"It's coming from outside," said Eric. He walked up the basement stairs and the others followed. After awhile the rest of them heard a car pull up somewhere outside of the house.

"This is so not cool," said Seth. "We aren't trespassing, right?"

"That's a car alright," said Susan as she looked carefully outside through the frosted window. "And people."

The rest of them also looked through the window. A man and a woman came out of the car. The car was no joke either. It was huge and capable of moving easily though the snow covered surroundings.

"You sure this is the place?" asked the woman. She was good-looking, tall, with long blonde hair and wearing a warm pink coat.

"Yes," said the man in a voice that gave the feeling that he was hot-tempered. He was shorter than the woman but very wide. He bent down to take something out from inside the car.

"I'll go take a look around here," said the woman. She tied her hair into a knot behind her head. "You go and set up… Hey, what do you kids think you are doing here?"

The teenagers had come out of the house and were standing in front of the woman who didn't look pleased. "Did some agency send you?" she asked looking at the seven teenagers in front of her. "Who do you work for? I've told them already that this is my story. Where is your equipment?"

"Where is our what?" asked Carl confused.

"Your equipment," she replied impatiently. "Where are your cameras and microphones? You are obviously here to document…"

"I don't think they are here for that purpose, Katherine," said the man. He looked at the teenagers one by one, his eyes moving from tall Eric, to brown haired Carl, to blonde Susan, to black haired Anya and Tabitha, to Seth and a hooded Cassandra. "They are just some kids," he added. "They were probably messing around in someone else's residence."

"Very well then, Blake," said Katherine, a grin on her face. "Let's get on with our work."

She turned to the teenagers. "I think you should leave now."

***

"So now we have a blonde pompous reporter in the story too," Anya complained as the group walked toward the opening in the cave. "Unbelievable."

"I know," said Susan. She helped Tabitha climb up a rock. "Why document these happenings?"

"We should have done it ourselves, you know," said Carl. He was jumping from rock to rock. "Then we could have gotten some dough."

"And would have gotten into trouble as well," said Eric. "And that too with people who are fanatics about this kind of stuff."

No one understood what Eric meant and all of them knew better than to tell him to elaborate his point.

"Maybe she'll be abducted or killed by those ice things," said Carl as he waited for the rest of his friends to catch up. "I don't think they will be happy to see her running around with a camera in her hand."

“You think we should have warned those two?” asked Susan, clearly worried as she looked toward the now far away Singleton farm.

“I don’t think they would have believed us,” said Seth as he helped Anya climb.

‘*Who can blame them*?’ Anya thought as she took Seth’s hand. ‘*I don’t think anyone would believe us*.’

***

“Today was just a waste of time,” said Anya. She sat down on a couch next to Seth and removed her muffler.

“I know,” said Eric. He handed out cups of hot chocolate. “And this cold isn’t getting any better.”

“There’s another thing that’s weird about this weather,” said Tabitha as she took a sip from her cup.

“Great!” said Seth as he rolled his eyes. “Here comes more weird stuff.”

“What’s weird?” asked Susan sitting near the heater.

“How many people do you know who have fallen sick?” asked Tabitha.

“What do you mean?” asked Anya. “What has falling sick got to do with any of this?”

Eric seemed to have understood what Tabitha meant. “No one as far as I know,” he said. “Even though kids haven’t been coming to school, they are still healthy. They just aren’t coming because of the weather. I checked with the school nurse.”

‘*Now we have two nerds in the group*,’ thought Anya. She liked Tabitha better when she was shy and weird like when they first met.

“You are right,” said Cassandra. She seemed to have caught up as well. “No one getting sick has been bothering me too. Not even a single little kid in my neighborhood has gotten a cold because of the weather.”

‘*Make that three nerds*,’ thought Anya rolling her eyes. ‘*As if having two of them in the group wasn’t enough already*.’

“Sorry to blow up your geek bubble,” said Anya finally. “But what are you all talking about?”

"The weather, Anya," said Susan. Anya looked at her surprised. "Normally cold of this degree would be making people sick, but no one has gotten even a minor cold, not even Lizzie."

'*Lucky me*,' thought Anya. '*There are four of them now*.'

"So people are healthy," said Carl raising his arms. "Big surprise!"

"It's just weird," said Tabitha. "Nothing more. Just thought I would share what I was thinking."

"Anyway, I'm off," said Seth. He gave a yawn. "See you all at school."

"No school tomorrow," said Anya looking at him. "Didn't you hear the teacher's announcement this morning?"

"You think I hear announcements?" he smiled at her. "I'll miss you," he added sounding sad.

"I'll miss you too," said Anya looking into his eyes.

"Yeah, yeah, we are all going to miss each other," said Carl. "Geez! Just go already."

Seth gave Anya a kiss and walked to the front door with her. "Seth, wait," said Cassandra. She got up from her chair. "I'm coming with you."

"Oh, Eric's sad," said Carl. He moved his finger under his eyes as if washing away tears. Eric ignored him.

"Give it a rest," said Anya as she closed the door. Seth and Cassandra were already walking toward the bus stop.

"Anyway," said Eric. He was keen on changing the subject. "There isn't much we can do now because we got disturbed by that Katherine character."

"We should have kept looking around, you know," said Susan.

"That wouldn't have been possible," said Tabitha. "We were there without permission and she would have had some kind of an authorization note or something."

"So?" asked Carl.

"So," said Tabitha looking at Carl. "We were trespassing and that would have gotten us into trouble."

"We don't know for sure if she had the form or whatever," said Carl.

"What is done is done," said Eric before Tabitha could answer and start a potential fight. "I think we should all call it a night."

"Fine by me," said Susan and she got up from the chair.

All of them put on their coats and got ready to leave. Tabitha and Carl walked together, and Anya could still hear them bickering about something. '*Probably the form*,' she thought. She turned to Eric. "You're going to be fine?"

"I'll be fine," said Eric smiling at Anya. "I know how to be safe, and besides, werewolf powers do help."

"Okay, bye," said Anya. She put her hands in her coat pocket even though she was wearing gloves. '*I hate this weather*.'

"See you later," said Susan. She smiled at Eric. "Bye."

Eric watched the girls walk away together. He locked the front door and thought of going to bed. Little did he know that he would wake up again because of a phone call awhile later.

***

"This is nice," said Seth as he and Cassandra waited for the bus to arrive. The cold seemed to have gotten worse. Cassandra gave Seth a weak smile. It was the first time they were alone together. Before this, they had always met as a group. The bus stop being empty wasn't helping either. Cassandra rubbed her gloved hands together for lack of anything else to say. '*If I had known it was going to be this awkward, I wouldn't have come with him*,' she thought. Seth was thinking the same thing as well.

"The bus is here," he said, pointing at the yellow vehicle. '*Finally*,' he thought to himself as the bus stopped in front of them.

The teenagers got onto the bus and looked around. It had very few passengers, mostly old people and a man who was snoring loudly. "Don't sit near him," said an old woman as Cassandra decided where to sit down. "I think he's drunk."

"Thank you," said Cassandra and she sat down on a seat behind the old woman, away from the snoring man. Seth paid for the tickets and sat down next to her. The bus started and Cassandra looked out of the window. The streets were empty. Both Cassandra and Seth remained silent as the bus drove on.

"You both don't talk much, do you?" asked the old lady sitting in front of them. She turned around to face the teenagers and gave them a smile. "Are you not friends?" she added, looking at them both.

"We…"

Both Seth and Cassandra had spoken at the same time. "We are friends," said Seth as Cassandra let him speak. "We just finished a very tedious school assignment and now we just want to go home and rest."

"What does working on an assignment have to do with talking to your girlfriend?" asked an old man sitting on a seat to Seth's right.

"Harold!" said the old woman before the teenagers could speak. "That was very inappropriate."

"Lily, I was just asking," Harold shrugged.

"She isn't my girlfriend," said Seth with a smile. "We know each other from school. We are just friends."

"Don't tell me that you are one of those boys," said Harold and he looked at Seth closely.

"Harold!" said Lily. "What kind of a question is that?"

"I was just asking," said Harold. "I mean, what boy in his right mind stays just friends with such a pretty girl, though I cannot see much from under her hood, unless he is a…"

"I have a girlfriend," said Seth quickly. He understood what Harold was trying to imply. "As I said, she is a just a friend."

Seth looked at Cassandra. She was laughing, her head down, looking at her feet.

"So, why are you alone on a bus with a girl who isn't your girlfriend?" asked Harold. Lily rolled her eyes. "You are so inappropriate," she said.

Seth could hear Cassandra laughing. Other people were also listening to the conversation. He looked at Harold and was about to answer when suddenly the bus stopped.

"Huh, what happened?" asked the man who had been snoring loudly. "Did we hit something?"

"I think the engine froze," said the driver sitting at the front. He tried changing the gears but the bus wouldn't move. "I'll be right back," he added, and he got off of the bus to check the engine.

"So, you were about to tell us something," said Harold, looking at Seth.

"Leave the kids alone," said Lily.

"But Lily, I was just asking them about…"

"Harold," said Lily, giving him a stern look.

"Fine, fine, have it your way," said Harold. He crossed his arms in front of his chest. "I was just trying to make a conversation."

The bus driver got back onto the bus and everyone's attention turned to him. "It's going to take some time to fix," he said.

"Great!" said the man who had just woken up. "I'm going back to sleep."

"We are practically there," said Seth, looking at Cassandra. He got up. "Might as well walk."

"Fine with me," said Cassandra. She got up as well.

"You kids going to be all right?" asked the driver. "It's getting dark and the streets are empty."

"We'll be fine," said Seth with a smile. "My house is just down the block."

"It was nice talking to you kids," said Lily.

"Same here," said Cassandra as Seth smiled at the old woman. Seth smiled at Harold as well and the old man smiled back. "You kids be careful."

"We will," said Seth and he got off of the bus with Cassandra.

Both of them began walking toward their neighborhood. The shops had closed and there was no one in sight except for two teenagers walking in the dimly lit street.

"Never thought this neighborhood could get creepy," said Seth looking around as they walked on. "I can't even hear mothers yelling at their children tonight."

Cassandra smiled at him and then she began to feel strange, as if something was pressing down at her.

"Cassandra," said Seth worried. "Are you alright?"

Cassandra opened her eyes. Her knees were touching the street. The cold snow was piercing her like little knives. "What happened?" she asked confused. She felt Seth's arm on her shoulder as he helped her up.

"You just kind of went down," said Seth. He looked at her closely. "Are you sure nothing is wrong?"

"I'm fine, Seth," she replied. "I'm fine."

"Wait! Is that a car?" asked Seth.

Cassandra looked in the direction he was pointing. At first she couldn't see anything, but then she saw it. A car was crashed into a tree a little ahead of where they were standing. It would have been easily ignored if Seth hadn't bent down to help Cassandra up and looked straight ahead through the trees by chance.

"It looks as if it crashed into the tree," said Cassandra.

"We should go help," said Seth. He looked at the car again. "Wait!" he added suddenly. "That car looks familiar, doesn't it?"

Cassandra looked at it again, trying to make out its structure in the dim light that was available. It was big and looked as if it could move through snow covered areas with ease.

"That's the reporter's car," said Cassandra. "Why is it crashed into that tree?"

"Let's go find out," said Seth. Both he and Cassandra hurried toward the car. Cassandra thought that a car of such size would have left tire marks as it went off of the road and crashed into the tree, but she couldn't see any. '*Maybe the snow covered them up*,' she thought. '*But that would have been awhile ago. Why didn't anyone call the police to take the car away*?'

They both reached the car. It was badly damaged. "She's still here," said Seth as he looked into the car. Cassandra looked as well. Katherine, the reporter they had met earlier, was in the car. Her eyes were closed, her head resting against the steering wheel.

"Is she dead?" asked Seth looking at the woman.

"Don't know," answered Cassandra. "Why didn't anyone report this?"

"Beats me," said Seth, and he opened the front door of the car. He extended his arm and checked Katherine's pulse. "She's alive," he said sounding relieved.

"Get her out then," said Cassandra. '*None of this makes any sense. Where is everybody?*'

Seth carefully got Katherine out of the car. "She is still unconscious," he said as he set her down on the ground. "We should call…Damn!"

Katherine's sudden screaming took Seth by surprise. "They are here," she said to no one in particular. She then looked at Cassandra and Seth wide eyed. "I ran," she said, unable to talk. "Died…they killed!"

"Miss Katherine," said Cassandra. She put her hand on the woman's shoulder for comfort. "Calm down."

Katherine looked at Cassandra again and then fainted.

Six

Ring. Ring. Ring.

"What now?" Anya groaned. Her face was in her pillow. Her hand searched for her cell phone. She knew it was somewhere beneath her bed sheet. She had seen it when she went to bed.

Ring. Ring. Ring.

Her hand touched something square near her pillow. She grabbed it and opened her eyes to see who the call was from.

"Oh," she said to herself and pressed the button to receive the call. "Eric?" she asked. "What is it? Are you alright?"

"I'm fine," he answered. "Anyway, just listen."

And before Anya could tell him off for disturbing her when he wasn't in danger, he filled her in on how Cassandra and Seth had gotten themselves stuck with Katherine.

"That sounds like fun," Anya answered. She smiled to herself as she pictured her two friends and the stuck up news reporter she had seen earlier together. "So?"

"We are going there tomorrow morning," said Eric. "I've already told the others about this."

"Meaning that you told me last?" asked Anya.

"Meaning that if I had told you first and asked you to spread the message, you would have just gone back to sleep."

"Yeah," said Anya trying to suppress a yawn. "You're probably right."

"See you tomorrow then," said Eric. "At the bus stop around ten sharp, don't forget."

"Yeah, see you guys," said Anya and she hung up.

Anya tried calling Seth to talk to him about the whole situation but strangely the call wouldn't connect.

***

"Have you talked to Eric yet?" asked Cassandra as Seth walked back into the room.

"Yeah," he replied. He pocketed his cell phone. "Did she say anything?" he asked, pointing at Katherine. The woman was sitting on the couch, a large blanket wrapped around her. She was staring at her feet. She looked as if she was about to throw up.

She hadn't said a word since she regained consciousness in Seth's living room.

Cassandra looked at Seth. He looked at her and then at Katherine and then at her again as if trying to tell her something. Cassandra rolled her eyes at him and sat down next to the woman. "You have to tell us what happened to you," she said kindly. "Please try."

Katherine looked at Cassandra and then at Seth who was leaning against the wall to her right. "Drink this," said Cassandra and she handed her a coffee mug that was lying on the table in front of them. Katherine took the mug, her hands shaking slightly, and took a sip. She took a deep breath and began in a weak voice.

"After you guys left," she said looking at the coffee mug. "Blake and I began filming the Singleton residence. We took footage of everything inside. We even found the basement and the books and those weird looking jars. It began to get colder so I told Blake that we should call it a day, you know, come back tomorrow." She paused and took another sip of her coffee. Cassandra and Seth didn't say a word. They let Katherine take her time to speak. "But Blake insisted upon filming the swamp," she continued, looking at the coffee mug in her hands. "He said that he didn't want to come back tomorrow and wanted to end the thing today. We still had time so I agreed and then we reached there and…and…"

Katherine stopped speaking. Seth couldn't stop himself. He wanted to know more. "What happened?" he urged her to continue.

"I can't say it," replied Katherine sounding close to tears. "I just can't…please don't ask me to."

"It's all right," said Cassandra. She placed her hand on the woman's shoulder but she shook it off and continued sipping her coffee. Cassandra looked at Seth. He knew she wanted to talk in private as he watched her walk into the kitchen.

"No point in probing her any further," said Seth as he entered the kitchen as well. Through the kitchen door, he looked at Katherine still on the couch. She had gone back to sleep.

"You are right," answered Cassandra. She leaned against the kitchen counter and closed her eyes. She was exhausted.

"Good thing my parents are out of town," said Seth with a smile. "Katherine has gone through a great deal, right?"

"Yeah," answered Cassandra. Her eyes were still closed. "She and her cameraman…wait!"

"What is it?" asked Seth looking at Cassandra who had opened her eyes and was looking excited.

"The camera," she said. "Seth, get the camera!"

Without another word, Seth ran out of his house. Cassandra watched him on his way through the living room window. The street lights were still dim and no one was in sight. Cassandra didn't like the atmosphere. She wished that Seth would hurry back with the camera. After a few minutes, the front door opened and Seth came back inside.

"It was in the backseat of the car," said Seth as he showed the camera to Cassandra. "The whole neighborhood is looking creepy, by the way."

"Did you see anyone at all?" asked Cassandra as they both walked into the kitchen. "Didn't you call the police to check the crashed car?"

"I tried the local police station but no one was answering," said Seth. He placed the camera on the kitchen counter. "Anyway, let's see what's in this."

Cassandra nodded and Seth switched on the camera and the recording began to play. Neither of them spoke a word as they watched.

"Well, that's the end of the house," said Blake. The camera was aimed at his feet. He seemed to be doing something with the device's buttons. "I saved the whole thing in another folder as not to mix it up with the other footage."

"So, should we call it a day?" asked Katherine. The camera went to her and she rolled her eyes at it. "It is getting pretty cold, you know. We can come tomorrow to shoot the swamp."

"I don't know," said Blake. The camera was still on Katherine. "I don't trust the weather. It could get far worse tomorrow. I say we shoot the swamp right now and then do the editing in the studio, away from this cold."

"Are you sure, Blake?"

"Yes, I'm sure."

The anger in Blake's voice was evident. It was clear that he wanted to get the whole thing over with. "I don't want to come here again, unless it's absolutely necessary."

"Okay, fine," said Katherine. "We can't take the car, so let's walk. And take that camera off of my face, Blake!"

Blake directed the camera toward the trees and they both started to walk toward the swamp. "We are walking to the swamp that is next to the Singleton residence," said Katherine. Her voice was different from before. It sounded professional and kinder than what Seth and Cassandra had heard. "You must have heard about the mysterious incident concerning the swamp that happened fifty years ago."

"And this year too," said Seth.

"SShhhh!"

"Come on Cassandra," said Seth. "There are still some minutes before the two get to the swamp. Just fast forward to that scene because the rest is going to be Katherine talking about what we already know and have experienced firsthand."

Cassandra understood what Seth meant and she pushed the fast forward button on the camera and stopped at the scene where they reached the swamp.

"The swamp is frozen," said Katherine. She looked at the camera and faked excitement. "But the ice seems to be thin in some places. What could it all mean? Let us investigate and see what…My God! Blake!"

The camera zoomed to where Katherine was pointing. "Frozen footprints," she said in a whisper. "Coming from the swamp and going into the forest."

"I think we should go," said Blake. The camera was still aimed at the footprints and he zoomed in a little.

"But this could be our golden ticket," said Katherine excitedly. "We have to follow these footprints. We could become famous because of this."

"Katherine, this is not normal," said Blake. He was worried. The camera trembled a little. "And these look like human footprints…a lot of human footprints."

"Don't tell me you're scared?" Katherine laughed cruelly. "Those kids we saw earlier probably made them."

"Then why follow them at all?"

"Blake!" said Katherine. The camera went toward her. Her displeasure was showing on her face. "Only we know that those kids made these footprints. Not the press. Think of the publicity we can get if we edit this thing properly."

The camera didn't move for a while. It seemed as if Blake was making up his mind about something. "Okay," he said finally. "Let's get this over with."

"Keep the camera on the footprints," ordered Katherine as she began to walk deeper into the forest. "We need every inch of this footage."

The camera's view turned toward the footprints leading into the forest. And then Katherine began to talk in her kind voice. "Here I am, following what look like human footprints that seem to have come out of the swamp. All of the footprints lead deeper into the forest. Where do they lead? I do not know, but I still follow them to uncover the mystery concerning the Singleton disappearances…What was that?"

"I don't know," said Blake. He moved the camera around. "Looked like an animal to me."

"It looked like a person," said Katherine. "Zoom into those trees over there."

The camera zoomed in, shaking slightly.

"Do you see anything?"

"Nope," said Blake. "Maybe it was a hermit."

"Hey, there he is again," said Katherine. Blake moved the camera toward the direction she was pointing. "Hello! Do you live here?" she asked the person, but whoever it was seemed to be hiding from view.

"Katherine," said Blake.

"What? Can't you see that I'm…"

"Look around," he whispered. Katherine turned around and so did the camera.

"Who are they?" she asked surprised. "Do you think they live here?"

The two were surrounded by black bodies that were visible from behind the trees. They were just staring at the two newcomers.

"Just walk away," said Blake, taking a few steps back. "And maybe they will leave us alone."

"But who are they?" asked Katherine excitedly as the bodies moved toward them slowly from behind the trees. "We should interview them or something."

"Damn the interview!" yelled Blake. The camera was moving in every direction. The bodies were slowly coming toward them. "Just get to the car!"

"But why are they doing this?" asked Katherine. She didn't want to go back. "We should talk to them. This is turning into a major story…"

"Katherine, just start walking!" shouted Blake. The camera was fixed upon a single black body that was coming toward them.

And then it came, a blood curdling scream from a woman who had appeared from behind a tree on their right. And one by one, all of them began to scream.

"Run!" yelled Blake. The camera was pointed at the ground as the two ran through the forest toward their car.

"What was that about?" asked Katherine as she ran behind Blake.

"I don't know," said Blake. He didn't want to look back. "Just keep moving."

They finally made their way out of the forest. Running through the snow wasn't easy for them. "There it is!" panted Blake. He seemed to be pointing at the car. "Let's go!"

They both walked toward their car. The camera was still filming the snow covered ground as they came nearer.

"Who is that?" asked Katherine. "Blake, film this!"

Blake groaned and the camera was directed at their car. There was a man standing near it. He was wearing very thin old clothes and was looking at the car. He didn't move. He had white hair that touched his shoulders.

"Excuse me," Katherine said to the man. "It isn't safe here."

The man didn't say a word and slowly turned to face the two. He looked at them with his blue eyes. Blake walked in front of Katherine. He was obviously angry at what was going on.

"Hey, dude," he called out. "Didn't you hear the lady? Move away from the car!"

And still the man didn't move.

"What's wrong with him?" asked Katherine as she moved closer to Blake. "He isn't even wearing a sweater. Maybe he's cold or maybe he's drunk."

Blake walked toward the man. The camera was still aimed at him. "Are you deaf, man?" asked Blake as he came near him. "Move aside…what the hell?"

The man grabbed Blake by the shoulders, and before he could fight back, he bit into Blake's neck and Katherine screamed. The camera fell to the ground. Cassandra and Seth watched in horror as the blood came out of Blake's neck. He pushed the man away and punched him in the face. The man didn't feel a thing and grabbed Blake again, this time by his neck. Blake struggled a little and then there was a cracking sound and Blake moved no more. The man picked up Blake's dead body and without looking at Katherine, walked back into the forest.

After a while, Katherine picked up the camera and sat down inside her car. "Oh, God," she kept saying to herself. She switched on the ignition. Her eyes went toward the camera and she switched it off.

Seth and Cassandra remained silent as the footage from the camera ended. "That man or whatever that thing was broke that guy's neck as if it was nothing," Seth finally spoke.

"And he bit into him," said Cassandra. She turned off the camera. "And did you look at that man's face?"

"Yeah," said Seth. "It was cold and pale. His eyes looked dead like…"

"A zombie," Cassandra finished Seth's sentence for him. The man's blue eyes looked like gems, beautiful but lifeless.

"Why would he kill Blake and leave Katherine alone?" asked Seth. "I thought zombies were supposed to kill anyone in their sight."

"That's what films teach us," said Cassandra. She was trying to make sense of what she just saw. "Who knows what zombies really do?"

"So, now what?" asked Seth. He looked at Katherine. She was still asleep on the couch.

"I have no idea," answered Cassandra. "But as far as I know, zombies need flesh to live and they will get hungry again."

"Meaning they will?" asked Seth in horror even though he knew the answer.

"Our town," said Cassandra. "It's the closest from the swamp."

She turned to Seth, her eyes wide. "If they don't go through the cave first."

***

"Yup, she's running again," said the bus driver as he started the vehicle. "Sorry for the delay people."

"Don't worry," said Lily as she looked out of the bus window. "I just hope that those two kids made their way safely."

"Don't worry about them," said Harold. "Kids these days are smart."

"Don't start yet," said Lily. Her eyes looked out of the window again. "There are people coming toward the bus."

"What are all of them doing on the road in this weather?" asked Harold as he noticed a group of people making their way toward the bus.

"Fine," said the driver as he adjusted his cap. "I'll wait for them."

The six people on the bus waited for the new passengers to get in, except for one man who was sleeping soundly.

"Hey, the door's that way," said the driver as he saw the twelve newcomers surround the bus. Irritated, he opened the bus door for them. "Now, come on," he added impatiently. "I haven't got all night, you know."

Suddenly the entire bus grew colder as a man got into the bus and walked slowly toward the driver. "Are you going to sit?" asked the driver. The man didn't say anything as he looked at the driver. "That does it!" said the driver and he looked back at the new passenger and his eyes widened in fear at what he saw.

"What…?" he tried to say something as he felt his body starting to freeze up. The passengers looked in horror as the newcomers slowly got into the bus and soon the air was filled with screams.

***

"I'll see you tomorrow," said Cassandra as she walked out of the kitchen. She tried not to think of the footage she had just seen with Seth in his kitchen. '*Don't think about it*,' she thought as she walked. '*Just go home and rest*.'

"What? You are leaving?" asked Seth as he came out of the kitchen after her. "You are going to leave me alone with her?" He pointed at Katherine who was snoring on the couch.

"Don't worry," said Cassandra looking at the woman. "She's asleep."

"I can walk you home," he said.

Cassandra knew he was worried. "It's alright," she said with a smile and shook her head. "I can manage. Cassandra walked to the front door. "Just behave yourself," she added, smiling at Seth, and she went outside of the house.

The cold air blew around her face and she bowed her head. She calmed herself and began walking toward her house. After a few minutes the air grew colder. Cassandra looked at the streetlight above her. It flickered and went out. Cassandra quickened her pace. Just a few more minutes and she would reach her home. And then she heard a scream. It sounded nearby. Cassandra stopped in her tracks. She tried to ignore the scream but she heard another one. '*Why now*?' she thought. She made up her mind and walked in the direction the scream had come from, even though she knew it was a bad idea. If movies had taught her something, it was that looking for trouble never ends well. But she couldn't stop herself from walking in the direction the scream came from. She wanted to make sure no one was in trouble. She turned right and froze because of what she saw.

A young girl was crawling on the road some distance away from where Cassandra was standing. The girl's legs seemed to be paralyzed and she was using her arms to crawl forward. She was trying to crawl away from something. The young girl was crying as Cassandra saw a woman slowly walk toward the girl on the ground.

'*Not now*,' thought Cassandra, shaking her head as she slowly backed away from the scene. She knew what was going to happen next. '*Please not now*.'

"Help!" screamed the young girl as the other woman came near her.

Cassandra tried to think of a way to help the young girl, but she knew that she could not do anything. She watched as the woman caught hold of the young girl by her neck and lifted her up as if she was a rag doll. The young girl tried to break free but the grip was too strong for her. "No, *please*," she said through her tears. The woman remained expressionless as she looked at the crying girl. Cassandra heard something break and the girl dropped to the ground, motionless, and then she heard screams fill the air around her.

***

"Cassandra?" Seth was surprised to see her again as he opened the front door for her. "What happened?"

"Out now!" she answered as she came inside.

"Cassandra, have you…"

"They are here," she answered in a hurry. "I just saw a group of them outside."

"No!" cried Katherine. Cassandra and Seth looked at her. She had just woken up and had understood what the teenagers were talking about. "You are lying," she added pointing at Cassandra.

"Do I look as if I'm lying?" Cassandra yelled angrily. "You blonde…" '*Control yourself*,' she thought. She took a deep breath. "We have to get out of here," she said turning to Seth.

"But where are we to go?" he asked.

"I don't know," she answered looking out of the window. "Anywhere but here."

Seth got his cell phone out and tried calling Anya. "No use," he said pocketing his cell phone. "No signal."

"We'll try later," said Cassandra locking the windows. "We need to board up if we are to stay here."

"But Anya and the others are coming here tomorrow," said Seth as he watched Cassandra locking the windows in the room.

"We have to tell them what is going…" He stopped in mid sentence as they heard a scream come from outside.

"This is not happening," said Katherine. She covered herself tightly with a blanket and closed her eyes. "This is not happening."

"You have any weapons?" asked Cassandra.

"I've got a hockey stick," answered Seth. "We could use knives from the kitchen and… What the hell was that?"

They had just heard a knock on the front door. Cassandra and Seth stood still. Katherine stopped reciting her mantra. She couldn't make herself look at the front door. No one moved as they heard another knock, this time harder than the first, and then they heard a moan. Katherine got up from the couch and joined Seth and Cassandra. There was another moan from outside, followed by another one, this time different, as if it belonged to someone else.

The three of them got closer together and kept staring at the front door. "Seth," whispered Cassandra, not taking her eyes off of the door. "Got any ideas?"

Seven

"Why do you look so worried?" asked Anya as she and Susan met Eric at the bus stop.

"I can't seem to get a signal," answered Eric. He put his cell phone to his ear but still there was no answer. "I've been trying Seth's cell phone for ages now."

"It's probably the weather," said Anya trying not to think about it too much. "I tried calling him last night but the call wouldn't go through."

"Where are Carl and Tab?" asked Susan as the cold wind swept away the strands of blonde hair coming out from underneath her hat. "Oh, there they are," she added as she saw two familiar faces walking toward the bus stop.

"Why are we even going?" asked Carl. He sounded displeased as he shook off snow from his boots.

"I told you already," said Eric. "Something weird happened to that reporter and Katherine and I want to check it out. Seth and Cassandra found her last night, her car was crashed into a tree and there was no sign of the man who was with her."

"You could have just called Seth and talked to her instead," answered Carl. He yawned and stretched his arms.

No one answered. They knew that Carl was always cranky when he got up early on an off-day from school.

"Here comes the bus," said Susan with a smile. She looked at the vehicle that stopped in front of them. "It looks different."

"It even smells different," said Carl as the bus door opened for them to climb inside.

"It what?" asked Tabitha as Carl got into the bus.

"I said it smells different," said Carl casually.

The five friends got into the bus. They were the only ones in it along with the driver.

"Must be the werewolf smell thing," Susan whispered to Tabitha as they got inside. "It smells like normal buses to me."

"If you kids are talking about the bus being different," said the female driver as the teenagers sat down. "You are right. The one that takes this route didn't report back last night."

"Why didn't it report back?" asked Eric as he pushed back his glasses up on his nose and the bus started.

"Don't know," answered the driver. "We did find it though last night. But no one was in it."

"What do you mean no one was in it?" asked Tabitha. "Did you tell the police?"

"Yes," answered the driver. "The police went to the town where the bus was supposed to make its last stop. They found it parked near the side of the road. As far as they know, all of the passengers must have gotten a lift from someone else or they might have stayed at a motel last night." "But one thing didn't make sense," added the driver.

Anya and the rest of her friends waited for her to speak. Even Carl, who was acting as if he was bored, turned his attention to what the driver was about to say next.

"Even though the passengers and the driver were missing from the bus, their things were still inside. Weird, isn't it?"

"Yeah, weird," said Eric slowly. He was obviously worried. No one spoke a word for a while. They were all thinking the same thing.

"You don't suppose something happened to Seth and Cassandra?" Anya finally asked.

"I'm sure they are all right," said Susan. She gave Anya a comforting smile. "I mean, come on, they fought off swamp monsters. They know how to handle themselves."

"I guess you're right," said Anya. She just had a feeling that something was terribly wrong.

"How far is the place, anyway?" asked Carl as he looked at the houses they were passing by.

"Not far," answered Tabitha. She turned to Eric. "Eric, try Seth's cell phone again."

"I am," said Eric as he put his cell phone to his ear. Disappointed, he put the cell phone back into his pocket. "There still isn't any signal."

The friends didn't say anything during the bus ride. Anya kept stopping her mind from wandering off. She didn't want to think of all of the bad things that could have happened to Seth and Cassandra. The bus finally came to a stop. "Never seen this place so deserted," said the driver as the five teenagers stood up to leave the vehicle.

"Our town is far better," said Carl, looking at the empty bus stop and streets as he got off of the bus. "Where is everybody?"

The teenagers looked at their surroundings as the bus drove away. Snow covered the empty streets and the sky above was covered in dark clouds.

"Maybe everyone is inside," said Susan trying to lighten the mood. "You know, because there's no school today."

"But even then," said Tabitha as she looked at her surroundings. "There should be someone, a cat, a dog or anything."

"I still can't get through," said Eric as he pocketed his cell phone for the umpteenth time. He then turned to his friends. "Anybody know where Seth lives? I thought I would ask him when we got here but I can't seem to reach him."

"I know where he lives," said Anya and she took out a piece of paper from her jeans pocket. She opened the folds and handed it to Eric. "When did he give you that?" asked Susan with a sly smile. "A long time ago," she answered. '*In case I ever wanted to come over*.'

"According to the directions here," said Eric as he read the piece of paper. "We have to go this way." Eric pointed ahead. "And make a right from there."

"Let's go then," said Carl and he began following Eric with the rest of them.

"It feels as if it has gotten colder," said Anya as she moved closer to Susan. She folded her arms in front of her chest in order to try and ward off the cold.

"Oh, come on," complained Carl as they kept walking. "I wasn't hoping for a welcome wagon, but seriously, where is everybody?"

No one answered him. They knew it would only lead to more complaining. The thought that they were alone in the town was also on Anya's mind, but deep down she felt as if she and her friends were being watched. She looked at the houses as they passed them by. All of the windows were shut and she couldn't hear any sound coming from inside either. There wasn't even a single burning chimney in view.

"Here we are," said Eric. The group reached Seth's house.

"Finally," said Carl impatiently. "Let's go inside."

Anya walked to the front of the group. She couldn't help but smile. In a moment she'll be able to meet Seth and everything will be fine. And then she saw it. The windows on both sides of the door were broken. She stopped and looked at them, her heart racing. '*What happened here?*'

"Oh!" Susan covered her mouth with her hand. Tabitha and Carl remained silent.

Eric walked up to the door and turned the doorknob. It was locked. He pushed at the door. There was a sound of something metallic breaking and the door opened.

"What happened here?" asked Carl as the friends walked into the living room. The table was turned over. The cloth of the sofa was torn apart. Broken glass covered the floor.

"Did Seth and Cassandra get into a fight?" asked Carl, trying to make a joke. No one paid any attention to it.

"I'm worried, guys," said Anya. She moved some broken glass away with her feet. "This is very serious."

"Both of them are not here," said Eric. "Or Carl and I would have heard them."

"Then where are they?" asked Tabitha, her eyes moving from the overturned table to the broken coffee mug on the floor.

Susan walked to the kitchen and looked inside. "Nothing here either."

"If only we could get the cells to work," said Anya. The worry in her voice was evident. Susan walked toward her friend and placed a comforting hand on her shoulder.

"I'm going to check next door," said Eric. "Maybe they heard something?"

Without a word, the others followed him. No one wanted to stay in the house unsure about what had happened. Eric and the others walked to the house next to Seth's on the right. He knocked at the door. No answer. He pressed the bell. No answer. Carl tried another house, but still no one came to answer the doorbell.

"This place is deserted," said Carl as he joined the group.

"There!" said Susan suddenly pointing at something in a distance. "I just saw someone."

"Where?" asked Anya looking to where Susan pointed. The thought of not knowing what had happened to Seth and Cassandra was killing her.

"There," said Susan pointing in the direction. "I think she went…no, look, she's back."

The group watched as a woman slowly came toward them. Her skin was pale and she was wearing torn clothes.

"Finally," said Carl. "We see a human being in this place."

Anya saw Eric looking at the woman with his eyes narrowed as if he was trying to figure out something.

"Hello, Miss," Carl called out as he took some steps toward the woman. "Do you know where the heck everyone else is?"

"Carl, this isn't right," said Tabitha as she walked after him. "She isn't right."

"What do you mean?" asked Carl as he turned toward Tabitha. "She looks as if she needs help."

The woman stopped in front of Carl and looked straight at him.

"Are you all right?" he asked concerned.

The woman moaned and grabbed his right arm. "Hey, let go!" said Carl. He tried to break free, but couldn't. She was too strong for him. "Let me go, you hag!" The woman gave another moan and Carl felt his arm grow cold. "Hey," he cried again as Tabitha moved forward to help him.

"Tab, don't touch her!" yelled Eric, and Tabitha stopped. With great speed, Eric ran toward Carl and then jumped into the air. He extended his right leg and it came down onto the woman's shoulder.

She moaned and let go of Carl's arm. She straightened herself and looked at Eric with expressionless eyes. She did not move toward him but instead she screamed. It was a blood curdling scream that made Anya and Susan cover their ears with their hands. Eric punched the woman right in the face and she fell to the ground. And then Susan screamed. Eric, Carl, and Tabitha looked around. They could see people coming toward them. They seemed to have come out of nowhere.

"This isn't happening," said Anya as the air around them filled with painful moans.

The friends regrouped, looking at the slow moving people who were coming toward them.

"Damn!" said Carl as he tried to move his limb. "I can't move my right arm."

They all looked at it. It had gone blue and looked lifeless.

"We will worry about that later," said Eric as he looked around. "We need an escape!"

The friends were trapped. There were too many for them to fight.

"We are surrounded," said Tabitha looking around. "We can't fight this many."

"Inside any house then," said Anya. Susan was grabbing her arm tightly. "Move, now!"

"The one in front of us," suggested Eric. "I'll clear away the two zombies or whatever they are and you make a run for it."

The friends nodded. Eric ran toward the two zombies blocking their way. He kicked one in the face and punched the other one in the gut as it tried to grab him.

"Run for it!" yelled Susan, and the four friends ran toward the house.

"The door is locked," said Tabitha as she turned the doorknob.

Carl stepped in front of the door and gave it a push. The lock broke and it opened. "Get in, all of you!"

"Eric, hurry!" said Anya as she turned to look at her friend. The other zombies were quite near him.

Eric pushed a zombie away from him with force. It staggered a little but did not fall down. "Damn, they are strong!"

"Just come on," Anya called out from the doorway.

Eric ran toward the house his friends were inside. He closed the door behind him. "The lock's broken. It won't hold."

"Try the sofa," said Carl pointing at the huge piece of furniture.

Eric and Carl pushed the sofa in front of the door while Tabitha and Susan made certain the windows were locked.

"They…They came here," said Anya looking out of the window. "Those zombies came here." The zombies were slowly gathering outside of the house they were inside. "Cassandra and…and Seth?"

"They are probably all right," said Susan. She placed a comforting hand on Anya's shoulder and led her away from the window. "They know how to handle themselves. Remember the whole thing with the swamp monsters?"

Anya smiled at her friend. '*Seth and Cassandra are probably okay. They've handled much worse.*'

"The couch won't keep them from breaking in," said Tabitha looking around the room and ignoring the moaning sounds coming from outside. "We need to get higher or something."

The rest of them nodded their heads in agreement and they began to climb the staircase. Eric opened the first door they all saw. "Oh!" exclaimed Susan looking at what was inside.

A couple was lying in bed. They were asleep but something didn't feel right about them. Anya walked closer to the bed. "She's cold," she said to her friends and she looked at the woman's face. She seemed to be in her early thirties. "She looks as if she's been frozen." The man in bed with her was the same way.

There was a loud noise and Susan screamed. One of the zombies had just tried to break down the front door. "We need to go," said Tabitha in a hurry.

"Where?" asked Carl looking around the room.

"The attic!" said Eric and they all ran out of the room. He found the trapdoor above his head and pulled the ladder down. "Everyone climb up now. Hurry!"

Anya climbed after Susan, followed by Tabitha and Carl. "Eric, come up," she said, looking down at him. There was another sound of something heavy hitting the front door. Eric climbed up the ladder and pulled it up after him.

"We can't fight so many of them," said Carl as Eric locked the trapdoor. "They are too strong."

"We could burn them," suggested Susan. "Like we did with the swamp ones?"

"Nobody has matchsticks on them," said Tabitha.

"We can't just wait," said Carl as he tried moving his numb arm.

"A distraction," said Eric, and everyone looked at him.

"What did you say?" asked Anya. She looked at Eric's expression and she understood what he meant. "Oh, no you don't," said Anya harshly. "There has to be…"

"There isn't," Eric cut through. He looked out of the attic's small circular window. All of the zombies were gathered in front of the front door. One of them was throwing himself at the door, trying to break it down. The teenagers didn't have much time on their hands.

"As soon as I go," said Eric as he turned to face the group. "You guys run. Find the others and get out of here. Get to some place safe."

"Dude, are you sure?" asked Carl. He sounded worried. "I can come with you and…"

"No," said Eric. "You are no good in a fight with the condition your hand is in right now. Stick with the others and get to safety."

"But Eric?"

Eric ignored Carl. "Find a car. And just go. I'll catch up."

Susan and Tabitha remained silent. They knew that once Eric had made up his mind, no one could make him change it. They worried about his safety but they knew they couldn't do anything to make him stay. Anya looked angrily at Eric. He looked back. They started at each other and Anya knew that it was of no use. His mind was made up. "You show off," she said finally.

Eric smiled and opened the circular window. "See you all in a little bit," he said with a smile and jumped out of the attic. He landed on all fours a few feet away from the gathered zombies. "Hey, you freaks!" he yelled out at them. "Over here!"

All of the zombies moaned and began going after him. The four friends watched as Eric ran away, yelling at the zombies to come catch him and making them move away from the house.

Anya turned to her friends. "Now!" she said. "Go. GO!"

Eight

"You think he'll be all right?" asked Susan as the four friends ran out of the house.

"He's fast and clever," said Carl as he took in the surroundings, making sure there were no more of those things near them. "What do you think?"

"We have to find Cassandra and Seth," said Tabitha looking at the empty street.

"I don't think they are…"

"Don't lose hope, Anya," said Susan trying to calm her friend. "We can't lose hope."

"I know," said Anya taking a deep breath. "I know. But I don't think that… What was that?"

"I heard that too," said Carl in a whisper as he looked around. The cold air blew around Carl's ears and he stiffened. "They are still here."

"Aren't zombies supposed to follow each other?" asked Susan, clutching Anya's arm as the friends looked around. At first they could only hear the silent wind, but then they heard moans.

"They follow each other in movies," said Anya. "They knew we would try to escape and some of them stayed behind waiting for us to come out into the open."

"Just run," said Carl. He didn't want to discuss what they had learned from movies any further. "Just don't look back…and run."

The four of them ran as fast as they could on the snow covered street, knowing the zombies were coming after them. "Where should we run to?" asked Tabitha as they turned a corner. "We can't just keep…Oh, NO!"

"We are surrounded," said Susan as they noticed six zombies standing in front of them.

Anya looked for a house they could go into, but the friends were in an alleyway and the only back door that was present had a big lock on it. In a few minutes more, zombies would be coming from behind them.

"Get behind me," said Carl as he got ready to fight. He got in front of the girls. "I'll try and break through them. You guys run as soon as you find an opening."

The zombies were slowly coming toward them. There was no way Carl could fight off six of those things with a numb arm and they all knew it.

"Guys!" a voice came from above them. "Up here!"

The four friends looked up. Cassandra was looking from over the roof of the apartment building, and Seth was lowering down the fire escape for them. The four friends moved away as it hit the ground. "What are you waiting for?" asked Seth with a smile.

Tabitha grabbed hold of the ladder and began to climb, followed by Anya. "There isn't time," said Carl as Susan started to climb up the ladder and the zombies came nearer. "Anya, pull up the ladder."

Reaching the first floor landing, Susan helped Anya pull back the ladder as the zombies gathered around Carl. "Carl!" yelled Tabitha as one of them grabbed Carl by the shoulder.

"Get off!" he growled, and with immense strength he jumped and landed next to Tabitha who was on the second floor landing. "Missed me," he added, winking at her.

***

"So, how did you guys make it this far?" asked Susan as Cassandra helped her up onto the roof of the four floored building. Anya was busy hugging Seth. She was least bothered about how they made it this far. She was just glad that all of them were safe.

"We just ran," Cassandra answered. "Seth broke the back window of his house when they came inside and then we just ran. We figured the higher we got, the safer we would be."

"They wouldn't break into this building, would they?" asked Carl.

"The front door is quite heavy and it's locked," said Cassandra. "So I think we just wait here for a while."

"What good is that going to do?" asked Katherine looking at the new arrivals. "Now those things know we are here and they'll be breaking in to get to us. And it's all thanks to you all!"

"She's been a joy," Cassandra smiled at Susan. "Where's Eric?"

"He…he…" Susan hesitated and then told her everything beginning from what happened when they arrived and how Eric acted as a distraction so they could escape. Cassandra didn't say anything and looked at the zombies below.

"You guys should watch this," said Seth, and he handed Anya the camera while the rest gathered around her.

"So all of this started last night?" asked Anya as the recording ended and she closed the camera.

"Yes," said Seth nodding at her.

"These zombies or whatever these thing are, are weird," said Carl as he tried to move his numb arm. "At least I'm getting some feeling back."

"Did you see what they did to the townspeople?" asked Seth.

"Yes, we did," answered Anya, remembering the man and woman she had seen in bed. "They seem to have frozen them all. Why aren't they eating them or something?"

"I don't know," answered Seth. "They aren't turning them into zombies either. They just killed Blake."

"How many are there?" asked Susan as she looked down from the roof. The zombies were looking up at the kids and moaning.

"Maybe twenty or twenty-five," said Seth as he looked at the zombies as well. Their cold eyes were staring back at him. "To top it all off, they seem to be quite smart."

"We noticed that," said Anya. She looked at Tabitha who was closely watching a silent Katherine. She turned back to Seth. "You got any weapons?"

"No weapons," said Seth, and he sat down looking at the dark sky. "We'll just have to stay put until a helicopter comes and picks us up. Other people must know about this incident already. They'll take action."

"Hey!" cried Susan pointing down. "They are leaving."

"They are what?" asked Anya, and all of them, except Katherine, looked down from the roof. The zombies were walking away from the building.

"Where are they going?" asked Tabitha. "You think it's another trap?"

"I don't know," said Carl as he watched the zombies clear the area. "We can't just sit and wait around here. We have to try and escape, get to a car or something."

'*I really hope they all didn't decide to go after Eric,*' thought Anya. She folded her arms in front of her chest, trying to calm herself.

Carl turned to the group. "I'll go down and find a car. You all stay here and wait for my return."

"Forget it," said Anya. "You aren't pulling an Eric, too." She had already seen one of her friends put himself in danger for all of them and she wasn't going to allow another one to do the same.

"But I have to try," said Carl looking at Anya.

"We'll all go," said Cassandra before Anya could answer.

"I agree," said Seth as Tabitha nodded. "I don't want to sit here and wait to be rescued."

"So we go as a group," Susan smiled.

"Whatever," Carl admitted defeat.

Susan turned to Katherine. "You in?" she asked the woman. She looked at the six teenagers looking back at her. "Fine, fine!" said Katherine rolling her eyes and getting up onto her feet.

***

"I can't hear a thing," said Carl as he led the others down the street. "It's all clear."

The rest of the group followed him – Anya, Susan and Tabitha behind Carl, followed by Cassandra, Seth, and Katherine who wasn't pleased to leave the safety of the building roof.

"There's a car," whispered Tabitha pointing at a red vehicle a few feet away. Carl signaled them to stay and he hurried toward the car, his ears on the lookout for any kind of sound. He tried the car's door. "Locked," he whispered. He broke the window with his elbow and unlocked the door. The rest of the group gathered around him.

"Now what?" he asked confused and he looked at everyone. "Anyone here know how to hotwire a car?"

The group remained silent. '*They need to teach us how to hotwire a car at school,*' thought Anya. She felt stuck and helpless, and then she heard something.

Carl's ears perked up. "Do you hear that?" he asked looking around. "It sounds like a car."

"It's a car!" exclaimed Susan as the group saw a car drive toward them. It came to a stop a few feet away.

"Anyone here need a lift?" came a familiar voice as the group watched the car's window pull down.

"Eric!" Anya tried to keep her voice down as the group hurried toward the car. "Thank goodness you are okay!"

"How did you escape?" asked Tabitha as she opened the car's back door.

"They just walked away," answered Eric as he smiled at Cassandra. "So, are all of you getting into the car or not?"

"It looks like a tight fit," said Seth. "There are seven of us in total."

"We'll manage," said Anya. "Just hurry."

With difficulty, the group settled into the car. Eric was behind the wheel. Katherine and Susan were in the front seat. Anya, Cassandra, Tabitha, and Seth took the back, and Carl was half sitting on Seth's lap.

"Dude! You couldn't have found a bigger car?" groaned Carl. He was clearly not happy with the sitting arrangement. Eric didn't answer and concentrated on driving the car.

Seth smiled at Anya. "Don't let this make you think that I'm not into girls," he said smiling at her.

"Don't make me go wolf on your posterior," said Carl as the girls laughed.

"So, where to?" said Eric before Seth and Carl could start an argument. His eyes were looking for any signs of danger as he drove past the houses.

"Let's just go home," said Anya. She felt tired. "There's a good chance that those things haven't made it that far yet."

"And then what?" asked Eric as he pushed his glasses up on his nose.

No one answered. The friends knew they couldn't keep running away from the situation. They had to come up with a plan. They needed to take some sort of action.

"We can't keep on running," Eric broke the silence. "We need a plan."

"What do you have in mind, Mr. Four Eyes?" asked Katherine. All she wanted was to get out of there. She wanted to run far away. She wanted to forget that all of this ever happened, and it annoyed her that the teenagers were talking about taking action. "We need to notify the authorities. Let them take care of this mess. We need to get away from here."

"The authorities," smiled Eric as he thought of an idea. "Cassandra, there's a police station in town, right?"

"Yes," she answered, wondering why Eric would ask. "It's just a few blocks away. You need to take the next right turn. But why would you ask about them? They would probably be frozen up as well, like the rest of the town."

"I know," Eric answered as he took a right turn and began to drive toward the police station. "At least we'll be able to grab some weapons from there."

"Didn't you hear me?" screamed Katherine, and Susan covered her ears. "We need to get out of here! We need to run!"

"Calm down!" Carl yelled from the back seat. "You are stuck with us. Like it or not."

"But…" Katherine tried to make her case.

"You are free to step out of the car and be on your own whenever you like," Anya stopped her from talking. She felt really tired. She wanted to go to sleep and all the yelling was making her head hurt. Katherine opened her mouth to say something, but she remained silent.

"Some of us should stay outside," said Seth as Eric stopped the car in front of the local police station. Eric got out of the car and looked toward both ends of the street. It was deserted. There were no signs of any zombies.

"Seth and I will go inside," Eric addressed the group. "The rest of you stay outside. Keep your ears open and your eyes peeled."

"Be careful," said Anya, and Seth smiled at her as he got out of the car. The group remained silent as they watched the two boys enter the police station.

"This isn't very welcoming," said Seth as he walked into the police station. All of the officers were present but they were frozen.

"We seem to be in a fight with some very powerful magic," answered Eric as he made his around a female police officer who seemed to be frozen while taking a sip from her coffee mug. "The guns are usually stored in the back," said Eric. "Come on."

The two boys walked toward the storage room. The door was unlocked and Eric pushed it open. "How many should we take?" asked Seth as he looked at the different guns hooked to the walls. "These are a lot of guns for such a small town," he added as he picked up a handgun from a shelf.

"You know how to use one?" asked Eric as he grabbed a bag from a corner.

"How hard can it be?" asked Seth as he watched Eric open a drawer and check for bullets. "Don't you just have to point at what you want to shoot at and pull the trigger?"

"Yes, those are the basics of it," answered Eric as he went through more drawers. "But aiming and shooting isn't as easy as you might think."

"I'll manage."

Seth pointed the gun at the window in the room. He noticed a shadow pass by. "Eric, I think we're in trouble."

***

"I wish the boys would hurry," said Susan as she got out of the car and looked toward both ends of the road.

"They just walked in a few seconds ago," answered Tabitha from inside the car. Susan nodded and looked at Carl standing near the car. He was on the lookout for any sign of trouble. Katherine was sitting as low as she possibly could in the front seat, her eyes closed. Cassandra kept looking at the police station and then at the road. Anya was outside trying to get a signal on her cell phone. '*Damn it!*' she thought pocketing her cell phone. She opened the car's door and sat down next to the other girls in the back seat. She closed her eyes and tried to calm herself down when she heard Susan scream.

"They're here!" yelled Susan. Anya opened her eyes and looked outside. She saw a group of the cold zombies already too near for comfort. '*How did this happen?*'

"Why couldn't I sense them?" asked Carl as he noticed the group of six zombies drag themselves closer to the car.

Tabitha got out of the car and yelled, "Eric! Seth! We've got trouble!"

"Both of you need to come inside," said Cassandra looking at Carl and Susan.

"What are we waiting for?" asked Katherine as she watched the zombies come closer. "Just drive!"

"We can't leave Eric and Seth behind," Carl answered from the driver's seat, and then the friends heard a gunshot from inside the police station.

***

"I know," said Eric keeping his voice calm and loading a shotgun. "Grab what you can and let's go."

Without saying another word, Seth grabbed another handgun and a few bullets and ran out of the storage room. "Dude, let's go," he said impatiently. All he wanted was to get out of the police station as soon as possible, and then he heard a moan. He slowly turned around and noticed that the frozen police officers had begun to move.

"Oh, shit!" whispered Seth as he watched the coffee mug drop from the female officer's hand and break. Her cold eyes settled on the teenager and she slowly walked toward him, arms stretched in front of her.

Seth pointed the handgun at her chest. "Stop or I'll shoot!" he yelled at her. The zombie didn't stop and let out a moan. "Stop!" Seth yelled again, trying to steady his hands. He pulled the trigger. The bullet missed and hit the wall. The zombie was too close to him now. In a second he would be able to feel her cold hands around his neck.

"They won't stop like that," yelled Eric and he pushed the zombie away with force. She flew into the air and crashed onto a desk. The rest of the zombies kept walking toward the two boys.

"Come on!" yelled Eric and he pulled Seth towards the exit. Eric pushed away a zombie blocking the door, and they both ran out of the police station.

"Hurry!" they heard their friends yell from inside the car.

"Oh, hell no!" said Seth as he noticed the group of zombies that was coming closer to the car.

"Just move!" yelled Eric and he gave Seth a slight push toward the car. The zombies in the police station were near the exit now. Seth ran toward the car and pulled the door open. A zombie lifted its arms to grab at him.

'BANG!'

Eric shot at the zombie's leg. Black blood began to ooze from the bullet wound. It stopped for a second and that gave Seth time to get into the car.

"Kill them with your guns!" screamed Katherine. Eric pointed at the forehead of the nearest zombie, hesitated for a bit, and then got into the car as well.

"Drive NOW!" yelled Anya as a zombie tried to break the back window.

Without wasting a second, Carl pressed the accelerator and the car drove away from the zombies.

"That was close," said Tabitha from the back seat as she closed her eyes.

"So, what were you able to get?" asked Carl, his eyes on the road.

"I got two handguns and some ammo," answered Seth, trying to ignore how uncomfortable he was being stuck in the back seat with the others. "Eric got some more weapons in the bag."

"I've got a shotgun and another handgun with ammo," said Eric trying to place the bag in a position that wouldn't be too uncomfortable for his friends. "I wasn't able to grab much. We had to get out of that place as soon as possible."

"Meaning that we've only got four weapons?" asked Katherine in disbelief. "You weren't able to grab more from the station?"

"They didn't have a lot of quality weapons," answered Eric. "I hurriedly picked up what I could."

"How did you know that they weren't quality weapons?" asked Tabitha.

"I have some experience with guns," answered Eric pushing his glasses up on his nose. "I also have a gun at home. So that makes five in total."

"Where are we going now?" asked Susan sitting in the front with Katherine.

"I think we should drive back to Colville," said Eric looking out of the window.

"Sounds like a plan," said Anya happy to have Seth's hand in hers.

"Back to where?" asked Katherine, her voice high. She looked at the teenagers as if they were all mad. "Are you nuts? We need to get out of here as fast as we can and away from all of this."

"Be quiet," said Susan. Her voice was commanding. Anya knew that Susan was serious right now. "You should be happy we allowed you to come along with us for this long. Either you go where we go or you can be by yourself."

"I think we should all go back home," Susan continued looking at Carl. Katherine gave her a mean look but kept silent. Anya sensed a hint of worry in her friend's voice. She knew Susan was worried about her mother and Lizzie. She too was worrying about her own parents. Carl turned left and began driving toward Colville.

"Why didn't we freeze?" Cassandra asked the group at large.

"What?" asked Anya. '*What was Cassandra getting at?*'

"I mean, we saw what happened to all of those people," answered Cassandra as she adjusted her hood. "Why didn't we freeze up as well?"

"No idea," said Seth as he looked out of the window at the deserted street. There were no signs of anyone, living or dead.

"Maybe it's the curse," said Tabitha, and the friends turned their attention to her. "Maybe it didn't lift when he defeated those swamp zombies by burning them. The book specifically said that only magical means were able to lift the curse."

"It still doesn't answer Cassandra's question about us not freezing up as well," said Seth. "Our entire neighborhood froze up except us two."

"It could be out for revenge," answered Tabitha, and Anya felt Seth tense up. "You and Cassandra helped us fight those swamp monsters."

Anya squeezed Seth's hand, trying to make him calm down. She looked at Cassandra. Eric was looking at her as well. Her friend remained silent and kept looking out the window.

"Then what about Katherine?" asked Susan. "She didn't freeze up last night as well."

"Don't put me into this!" yelled Katherine. "I didn't do anything with that swamp place and these monsters you keep talking about. Why would, whatever it is, want revenge from me?"

"I'm just lucky to be alive," she continued. "So keep your revenge theory to yourself."

"We'll talk about this when we get back," said Eric before Susan could speak.

Anya rested her head on Seth's shoulder. All she wanted was to go back home. Whatever it was they were dealing with, she felt that going home would help them all calm down. The rest of the drive went silently. They didn't see any zombies on their way, and the dark clouds in the sky began to get lighter. Anya felt a wave of calmness as she watched the familiar houses. Kids were playing in the snow, oblivious to what the teenagers had just experienced. Carl parked the car in front of Eric's house. "Everything looks normal here," he said, getting out of the car and looking at some kids playing in the snow nearby.

"Too calm," said Eric looking around as they got out of the car. "Doesn't anyone know what just happened?"

"Maybe the police are keeping it under wraps," suggested Cassandra.

"Who knows," answered Susan. Life seemed to have returned to her eyes.

"Whatever it is, we can't just stay here and do nothing," said Tabitha.

"Okay, I'm done with all of you," said Katherine, and the teenagers turned to her. "I don't know what's wrong with you all, handling all this paranormal stuff as if it's a walk in the park."

She looked at Carl. "I don't have anything to do with this, so just give me the keys."

Carl looked at Katherine, then at Eric, and then at the keys in his hand. "You can't keep me here against my will," she added looking at Carl who felt uneasy.

"She does have a point," said Tabitha. "We can't make her stay if she doesn't want to."

"Don't you want to help us?" asked Susan, looking at Katherine. She wondered how anyone could be so selfish.

"Listen here, sweetheart," Katherine answered, turning to the blonde teenager. "I don't know what the hell just happened and I'm not staying around to help you find the answers." She turned to Carl again. "The keys, please!"

Anya and the rest of the group watched as Carl handed her the keys. She smiled and sat back into the car. She got comfortable and addressed the teenagers. "It's better that you all get out of here too. I'll try and contact some people, see if they can help fix this thing, if anyone believes me, that is." She started the ignition and drove off without another word.

"Good riddance," said Carl as he watched the car drive away. "She really got on my nerves with all of that screaming."

"I still don't get why she didn't freeze up as well," said Cassandra. "Something is not right."

"Everything is not right," said Seth as Eric unlocked the front door for them.

Anya felt the warmth of the house as she stepped inside. Eric placed the bag on the floor and began taking out the weapons. Carl dropped onto the couch. Seth sat on the floor. "I haven't slept since last night," he yawned. Cassandra nodded and sat down on a chair. Susan went to the kitchen to make something to eat, and Tabitha joined Eric, helping him load the magazines.

"You should go and rest," said Anya as she looked at Seth lying on the floor. "You too," she added looking at Cassandra.

"Choose any room in the house," said Eric as he looked at the shotgun in his hands. "The beds are made."

"Care to join me," Seth winked at Anya as he got up.

"Now really isn't the time," Anya smiled back at him.

"Are you sure?" he asked again.

"Yes, I'm sure," she smiled back at him. "Now go," she added, giving him a shove.

"Have it your way," Seth yawned again and walked out of the room.

"What about you?" Anya asked Cassandra.

"I'll go and rest as well," she answered and got up. She felt a slight headache. '*Maybe it's just because I'm tired.*'

Cassandra walked out of the room. She could hear Seth in a room to her right. She opened a door to her left. '*Damn!*' she placed a hand on her forehead. She sat down on the bed and tried to calm herself. '*Just try and go to sleep.*'

Nine

"Where are Cassandra and Seth?" asked Susan as she walked back into the room balancing a tray of sandwiches.

"They have gone to sleep," answered Anya. She was sitting with Eric and Tabitha on the floor and reading to herself from a box of handgun bullets.

"Finally, some food!" exclaimed Carl and he got up from the couch. "I'm very hungry."

"Don't eat all of them," said Susan as Carl picked up two sandwiches. She placed the tray next to Eric and sat down on the floor. "How many of us know how to use these?" she asked, looking at a loaded handgun in front of her.

"I don't," answered Anya. She picked up a handgun. It was heavier than she expected.

"Try not to point it at any of us," said Carl as he munched on the sandwiches, and Anya rolled her eyes at him.

"I know how to use one," said Tabitha. "Dad made me practice with them when I was young," she added, feeling Anya's eyes on her.

"I think I can aim and shoot a gun too," said Carl as he looked at the weapons on the floor.

"So, only two of us know how to properly shoot," said Susan looking at Tabitha and Eric.

"It seems so," said Anya picking up a sandwich. She didn't feel hungry. '*It's not my fault, looking at what we all went through today.*'

"What's the plan?" asked Tabitha as Eric loaded the final handgun.

"I do believe this whole thing is connected to the swamp curse," answered Eric as he took a bite from a sandwich. "The book said the curse had to be lifted through magical means, and whatever we did wasn't able to cut it."

"But why are they different?" asked Carl. "Why is it snowing everywhere? The zombies seem to be different too. My arm went numb when that woman grabbed me."

"Probably a change in the curse," said Tabitha. She was thinking, trying to make sense of everything.

"What about the girl in Anya's dream?" suggested Susan. "I'm not saying that the girl was you," she added as Anya gave her an angry look. "I'm just suggesting that the girl, whoever she was, could have changed the curse."

"But who is she?" asked Eric. "You said you weren't able to make out a face."

"I just know that it was a girl," answered Anya. "She didn't look familiar. And besides, it was a dream. For all we know, my mind could have been worked up because of all the things it was going through."

She wasn't enjoying the attention. She hadn't told her friends that she was inside of the girl. It was if she was the one who recited the ancient words in order for the zombies to come out of the swamp. "I'm going to call Mom," said Anya getting up. She could still feel her friends looking at her as she walked out of the room. She heard Seth snoring from inside of the room on her right. The door to her left was half open and she saw Cassandra on the bed, her eyes closed. She took out her cell phone and walked toward the kitchen. '*Finally I get signals here.*'

She dialed her home number. *No answer?* She tried again. '*Come on Mom, pick up!*' she thought. She knew her mother didn't have plans to go anywhere today. Her father was also staying at home because of the weather. Even if they did decide to go somewhere, they would have called her. '*Why aren't you guys picking up?*'

Anya tried to keep calm as she called her parents for the third time. She pocketed her cell phone and walked back to her friends. "Nobody is picking up at home," she said grabbing her coat from a chair. She ignored the fact that Eric, Tabitha, and Carl stopped talking as soon as they saw her enter. "I'm going to go and check."

"Are you sure they aren't out somewhere?" asked Tabitha.

"They would have told me about it," answered Anya as she started to wear her gloves. "Where's Susan?"

"She went into my room to call home," said Eric pushing his glasses up on his nose.

"I can't seem to get an answer either," said Susan as she walked back into the room. "Where are you going?" she added looking at Anya standing near the front door with her coat and gloves on.

"I couldn't get an answer either," she said. "So I'm going to go and check as well."

"I'll come with you," said Susan as she began to get ready as well. "I need to check on Mom and Lizzie."

"But..."

"Don't tell us that it'll be all right," said Anya before Eric could finish. She tried to keep her voice calm. "For all we know, the communication lines could be acting up because of the weather. We'll be back soon. You all sit and think of a way to defeat this curse."

"Yes, we'll be back soon," added Susan. She was ready to leave with Anya. Eric nodded, and the two girls walked out the front door.

"At least the sky doesn't look so bad," Susan smiled at Anya. There were dark clouds overhead but they were much lighter than the ones they experienced in the other town. Anya tried not to think about the zombies they left behind. She didn't want to think that they could make their way to Colville too. All she wanted to do was go home and make sure that her parents weren't in any kind of danger. '*But what will I do if the zombies do come here?*' she asked herself, walking with Susan. Her house was nearby, so they decided to go there first. '*How will I protect them? How will they handle knowing about all of the supernatural stuff I have been through?*'

"Anya, are you okay?"

Susan's voice made her come to her senses. "What?"

"I asked if you were okay?" Susan questioned again, looking at her friend. "You had a strange look on your face."

"I'm fine," Anya answered and she quickened her pace. "I'm fine."

There were no kids playing in the snow and Anya couldn't hear any sounds coming from the houses she and Susan walked past. She could still feel Susan stealing worried glances at her as they reached Susan's home. Susan pressed the doorbell and they heard a bark from inside. "It seems that Lizzie is all right," smiled Susan as she heard her dog scratch at the door from inside. "Mom!" yelled Susan knocking at the door. "It's me. Open up."

There was no answer.

"Mom!" Susan knocked at the door again. Still no answer.

Anya noticed Susan's expression change. She was definitely worried now, and Lizzie kept barking from inside of the house. "Don't you have a key to the front door?" asked Anya.

"No," Susan answered. She began walking toward the back door and Anya followed. "There's always a spare key to the back door," she said. Susan lifted a small flower pot placed on a window ledge to her right and grabbed the key. Without anther word, she unlocked the back door. "Mom?" she asked as she stepped into the kitchen.

Lizzie came running toward her owner, barking excitedly. "Lizzie!" smiled Susan and she bent down to hug her dog who started licking her face. Anya looked around the kitchen. She noticed a peanut butter and jelly sandwich placed on the table along with a mug of coffee. "Mom?" Susan asked again as she got up onto her feet. Lizzie barked and ran toward the living room. Susan looked at Anya who slowly nodded. They both heard static as they walked toward the living room. Anya felt Susan grab her hand.

"Mom!" exclaimed Susan, and Anya's heart began to beat faster.

In front of the TV sat Susan's mother. She was staring at the static on the TV screen, completely frozen. "This can't be happening." Susan was close to tears. "This can't be happening. They can't be here."

"Susan, we'll find a way to fight this thing." Anya tried to calm her friend. She placed a comforting hand on her shoulder. Lizzie whined and came closer to Susan. Anya took out her cell phone and tried calling Eric but there weren't any signals.

"Your parents are probably the same way by now," said Susan. She was still looking at her frozen mother. '*Yeah, I know,*' Anya thought to herself, and she looked at Susan's mother as well. Her eyes were still on the TV. Her skin looked pale blue. '*My parents are probably the same way right now too*.' The static from the TV was making it look eerie and Susan turned it off. "That's better," she whispered to herself and turned to Anya. "Now what do we do?"

Anya knew she was waiting for her to make a decision. She knew that if she wanted to go and check on her parents, Susan would understand and go with her. '*You should go and check on your parents*,' said a voice in Anya's head. '*But what if they are frozen too? What good would it do for me to go and check? The best thing I can do now is go back and regroup*.'

"We should go back," said Anya. Her heart ached. She wanted to go and see her parents but she knew that would be too risky. "We don't know how much time we've got left before those things show up here as well."

"I think this proves that the curse is after us," said Susan as she bent down to pat her dog. "Lizzie hasn't frozen."

"I don't think that animals are freezing," said Anya. *Most of them probably died because of the cold or migrated somewhere else*. She gave the room a last look and began to walk to the front door. "Come on, let's go," she added, looking back at Susan.

"We'll put everything right," Susan said to her mother. She forced a smile and walked toward Anya who was waiting for her at the front door, followed by Lizzie.

"Okay, let's go," said Anya, her hand on the doorknob. She was surprised to hear how calm her voice was. She knew she had to keep a straight face. Susan was dealing with her mother in her own way, and Anya knew she couldn't start worrying about her own parents. For all she knew, the zombies were already here, and breaking down and crying about her parents wasn't going to help anyone.

"Wait!"

Anya stopped and turned around to face Susan. "What is it?"

Susan was looking at Lizzie. The dog was baring its teeth at the front door. Anya backed away from the door and slowly turned to face her friend. "They are here, aren't they?"

Susan nodded, and they began to hear moans coming from outside.

***

"You think they'll be all right?" asked Tabitha as she watched Anya and Susan walk away from the house.

"They will be fine," said Carl as he picked up a handgun from the floor.

"How are we going to end this?" she asked sitting back with the boys. "We can't just sit around here and do nothing."

"I'm thinking about it," answered Eric. "I still can't figure out how we can defeat this curse without magical means."

"I've gone through all of the books at my house," said Tabitha. "Every book keeps talking about the same thing…that we need magic to defeat magic."

"I'll let you two geniuses try and work things out," said Carl as he got up. "I'm going to go to the bathroom."

"My mind keeps wandering to the dream Anya had," said Eric as Carl exited the room. "What if, and I still have my doubts about it, Anya is somehow related to all of this?"

"You mean that she performed this curse?"

"I don't know," Eric answered. "Or maybe she felt the curse happen. Maybe she has a magical aura around her. Maybe there is a reason David went after her."

"It's worth a shot," said Tabitha. "But even if she has some magical aura, how are we going to make her fight this? You think it'll be as simple as reciting a counter curse or something?"

"It wouldn't hurt to try," answered Eric. He got up from the floor. "You know any book that might have a counter curse?"

"Yes," nodded Tabitha as she got up as well. "It's at my place. Do you think Anya will like the idea of possibly being a witch?"

"She won't," Eric smiled. He took out his cell phone and called Anya. "But what else can we do?"

"I'll go with you to my place right now and get…what is it?"

"I can't get any signals," answered Eric. He sounded worried. He ran to the nearest window and looked outside. The streets were deserted.

"What did I miss?" asked Carl as he noticed Eric and Tabitha looking out of a window. "Is something out there?"

"Not yet," answered Eric. He turned around. "Go to Tabitha's house and grab the book with the counter curse," he added looking at Carl. "I'll go and check on Anya and Susan."

"He won't know where to find it," said Tabitha as Carl ran to the front door without question. "He didn't even ask for the name of the book."

"I was going to," said Carl raising his arms.

"I'm going with him," she told Eric, and walked towards Carl. "You go after Anya and Susan."

Eric noticed a handgun in Tabitha's hand. "Just a precaution," she added, placing it in the back pocket of her jeans.

"I'll go wake up Cassandra and Seth and then I'll go," Eric told his two friends. "You guys hurry back."

Tabitha and Carl nodded at Eric and walked out. The bespectacled boy took a deep breath and walked toward where Seth was sleeping. "Seth, wake up!" Eric knocked on the door. "Seth, you need to wake up."

"What is it?" came Seth's voice. He sounded tired.

"As if you don't know what's going on," said Eric. He opened the door. Seth was underneath the covers. "Just get up. We need to take action now."

"They are here?" Seth sat up on the bed, his eyes wide.

"I think so," answered Eric. "Carl is headed to Tabitha's house with her to get a book. I'm going to go and check on Anya and Susan."

"Why?" Seth sounded worried and he quickly got out of bed. "Where's Anya? She isn't here?"

"She went with Susan to check on their parents," said Eric. "Don't worry," he added. "I'm going to go and check on them."

"Why did you let them go?" asked Seth walking toward Eric. He was really worried about Anya.

"As if I could have stopped Anya from checking on her parents," said Eric. He didn't want to fight with Seth. The important thing for him was to make certain that the two girls were all right.

"I'm going with you," said Seth as he pulled on his sweater.

"I'll be faster on my own," Eric stopped him. "You go and wake up Cassandra. Tabitha and Carl will be back here soon."

Seth was making up his mind. "Okay," he finally answered. "You are right. You'll be faster on your own. Hurry back."

"I will," Eric nodded. He was about to walk out the front door when all of a sudden he and Seth heard Cassandra scream.

Ten

"Any ideas?" asked Susan as she and Anya stepped back from the front door. They could still hear moans coming from outside.

Anya shook her head. Lizzie was baring her teeth at the door. Anya's brain tried to think of something. She was trying to decide if they should stay in the house and wait for their friends to save them or get out of there.

"Eric and the others are probably facing the same situation," said Susan.

'*And I'm not going to wait around and be saved,*' thought Anya. She turned to Susan. "We need to get out of here."

"We don't know how many of those things are out there," said Susan. Her eyes were still on the front door.

"It's better than waiting for them to break in," answered Anya. She wanted to lock herself in a room and pray to be rescued, but she knew that wasn't the right thing to do. "The back door Susan, let's go!"

"We left the back door open!" exclaimed Susan, and Anya looked at her, her eyes wide. The two friends didn't break eye contact. The room felt cold and then they both heard a moan coming from inside the house.

***

"I really don't like this," said Tabitha as she ran toward her house with Carl. The streets were deserted. There wasn't a bird or a stray cat in sight. She looked up. The sky had darkened as well. All of the signs were telling her that the zombies had arrived or they were going to be there anytime now.

"I can carry you," said Carl as he watched Tabitha run with her. He wasn't sure if she would be able to run so far and that too in such cold weather, but he was impressed by her stamina.

"You would like that, wouldn't you?" Tabitha smiled back and rolled her eyes. "Carl, you are such a gentleman."

"Well, I try," he winked at her. They were almost near Tabitha's house. Carl tried to take in all of the sounds from their surroundings. He wasn't happy that he was unable to sense the zombies outside of the police station.

"I hope that Anya and Susan are okay," said Tabitha.

"They'll be fine," Carl answered. "Eric will be with them."

"Did you hear that?" he added. He was quite sure that he had heard a moan from behind them.

"Hear what?" asked Tabitha. She looked around her.

"Just keep running," said Carl. "We are nearly there."

***

"Cassandra!" yelled Eric as he and Seth ran into the room that Cassandra was sleeping in.

"Where is she?" he asked looking around. The bed was empty and the window was closed.

"There aren't any signs of a struggle," said Seth as he ran toward the window. It was locked. "Where could she have gone?"

"I don't know, I don't know," Eric tried to remain calm. '*This is really bad*,' he thought. The group was separated. Anya and Susan were probably in either one of the two houses. Carl and Tabitha were getting the book, and Cassandra was missing. '*Think Eric! Think!*'

He tried to pick up on Cassandra's scent, but it was as if she was never in the room. "The girls," said Eric looking at Seth. "I will go and get Anya and Susan."

"What about Cassandra?" he asked.

"I don't know," Eric answered and he walked out of the room. "I can't seem to trace her scent."

"I'm coming with you," said Seth as he followed him. "I am not going to wait around here alone."

"I'll get to them faster by myself," said Eric as he reached the front door.

"I'm not a slow runner," said Seth. He was determined to go with Eric and make sure that Anya and Susan weren't in trouble.

"Okay," Eric nodded at Seth. "Grab a gun just in case."

***

"Susan, get back!" screamed Anya as the zombie came toward them. The woman's eyes were dead and they were fixed upon the girls. Lizzie bared her teeth at the zombie, but Susan was holding her back. '*We need to get out of here*,' thought Anya. Her eyes quickly went around the room, searching for some kind of weapon. '*I should have brought a gun with me.*'

The moans coming from outside grew louder. "I don't think the front door will hold for long," said Susan, as they both heard a loud sound, as if a zombie had tried to break down the door. Anya remembered how a zombie had grabbed Carl's arm and it turned numb. She also remembered the video recording in which a zombie was strong enough to break Blake's neck as if it was a toothpick.

"Just push it away," suggested Anya as the zombie came closer. The temperature of the room began to drop dangerously low, and Anya felt her body start to shiver even though she was wearing a warm coat.

"What?"

"There's only one," said Anya. They were running out of time. The front door could break any minute and even if they ran upstairs, the zombies would easily break through the entire house and find them. "Susan, NOW!"

The two girls ran into the zombie and pushed it back. It was much harder than Anya had expected. The zombie tried to regain its balance, but it dropped to the floor. Lizzie barked as they heard the front door begin to break. "Damn! They are persistent," said Susan as the zombie began to get back onto its feet.

"Just go! Go!" yelled Anya, and she ran out the back door followed by Susan and Lizzie.

"Where are we going to run to?" asked Susan. They could still hear the moans. They knew the zombies would begin following them soon.

"Back to Eric's," answered Anya. "Back to Eric's!"

"Oh my God!" Anya stopped in her tracks. Susan stopped as well. Four zombies were coming from in front of them. The only place they could run to were the houses to their left and right, and Anya knew there were zombies coming from behind them as well. Breaking a window to a house was going to take time and they couldn't just keep going from house to house until they reached Eric's place. They would be caught sooner or later.

"Anya," whispered Susan. She came closer to her friend. Lizzie was barking at the zombies, daring them to come closer. Anya felt Susan grab her hand. Her own heart was racing. There was no way they could evade the zombies coming from in front of them. More moans told them that the zombies that were outside Susan's house were going to arrive there soon.

"I'm not going down without a fight," said Anya. She wanted to believe those words herself. Her entire body was shaking. "I'll try and distract them to a side, you take Lizzie and run," she told Susan, her eyes still on the zombies in front of her.

"You really think I'm going to leave you on your own?" asked Susan. She tried to smile.

"Susan, this really isn't the time," said Anya. She was glad that her friend wasn't going to leave her. But she wasn't going to ignore an opportunity if it allowed Susan to escape. Her friends put their life in danger when they came to save her from David, and she still had to repay the deed.

"I'm going to distract them to the right, you run," said Anya, and without waiting for Susan to answer, she ran toward the zombies, waving her arms. "Over here! Come to me!"

The four zombies looked at Anya. Three of them started to walk toward her and one of them continued walking toward Susan. '*This is bad*,' thought Anya. "Susan, try and evade that one," she yelled at her friend. But before Susan could try and run, they both heard a gunshot, and Lizzie barked. The zombie in front of Susan fell to the ground, but it still tried to crawl toward her.

"Over here!" came a familiar voice. Anya smiled upon seeing Seth. He had shot a zombie in the leg.

"Save Anya!" yelled Susan as she ran toward the boy followed by Lizzie.

"I'm on it!" came Eric's voice. Anya looked at Eric as he ran toward her, jumped into the air and kicked a zombie right in its face. It staggered, and Eric kicked it again, square in the chest. It tried to catch its balance and fell onto a zombie. "Go, Anya!"

Taking the opportunity, Anya ran toward where Seth, Susan, and Lizzie were waiting for her. "Glad to see me?" smiled Seth as Anya hugged him. She didn't answer and continued hugging him.

Eric jumped over a zombie and ran toward his friends. "Hate to break your hugging time," he said. "But the rest of our undead friends are here," he added, pointing at the zombies the girls left at Susan's house.

***

"Open the door already!"

"I'm going as fast as I can," said Tabitha as she inserted the key into the lock. The moans around them had grown louder. "Done," she added and quickly opened the door to her house.

"You think the front door will hold?" asked Carl as they both stepped inside and he locked it behind them. "Those things broke Seth's windows in order to get in."

"Let's hope that the windows of my house are made of stronger material," answered Tabitha. She was already at work going through a bookshelf in front of her. "It has to be somewhere here," she said to herself as she read the titles.

They heard a meow and Felix walked into the room. "I still don't like the way it looks at me," said Carl as the cat stared at him.

"Get over it already," said Tabitha. "Found it!" she added, picking up a heavy black book. She turned to her cat. "Felix, go inside and don't come out until I tell you to."

The cat seemed to have understood her. It stretched itself and then went out of the room. "Where's your bird?" asked Carl.

"Here somewhere," she answered. "We need to go."

They both heard a loud thud and the front door shook. "We won't be able to go out from the front side," said Carl as he backed away from the door. "Back entrance?"

"From the kitchen," said Tabitha, and they both walked towards the kitchen trying to ignore the loud moans that seemed to be coming from all around the house.

"Nope, not this way either," said Carl as they watched zombies gather around the back door as well.

"Upstairs!" said Tabitha. They heard another heavy body hit the front door. The zombies were hitting the windows as well.

Carl and Tabitha ran upstairs. Tabitha led him into a room. It was spacious and only had a writing desk and a chair in it. "Ask questions later," she said before Carl could say something about the room, and she opened the window.

"Your plan is to jump?" asked Carl as he looked out the window. There were no zombies on the ground below and Carl knew that could change in seconds.

"You wanted to carry me, right?" asked Tabitha. They heard another loud noise. The front door wasn't going to last any longer and neither were the windows. "You jump down and then catch me."

Carl nodded, and without wasting a second he jumped out of the window, landing on all fours. He could hear the moans coming closer. He saw Tabitha position herself on the window ledge, book in hand, and then she jumped right into Carl's arms. "That was fun," he smiled at her.

***

"We aren't going back to your place?" asked Anya as the four friends ran.

"Carl and Tabitha went to get a book," said Eric as he led the way. "It makes sense to regroup with them instead."

"What kind of book?" asked Susan as she tried to keep up with her friends. Lizzie was running beside her.

"A book that has the counter curse," answered Eric.

"Does that mean you figured out a loophole when it comes to defeating this curse through magical means?" asked Anya. Eric didn't answer. Anya looked at Seth, but he averted his eyes. "Guys, I want answers here," Anya added trying to keep herself calm.

Eric stopped and began to sniff the air. "Carl and Tabitha are near," he said, turning to the group. The moans were all around them. They couldn't see a zombie right now, but they knew that waiting for them to appear wasn't a good idea.

"Found you," came Carl's voice as he and Tabitha rejoined the group.

Anya noticed Tabitha holding a heavy black book. "That's the book with the counter curse?" asked Anya.

"Yes," she answered. She looked at Eric who shook his head.

"What are you keep from us?" asked Anya as she stood next to Susan and looked at her friends.

"We aren't keeping anything from you," answered Tabitha. "Wait, where's Cassandra?"

"She's at Eric's and we need to…" Anya stopped answering. Eric looked worried and so did Seth. "Don't tell me that something happened to Cassandra?"

"After Carl and Tabitha went to get the book, we heard her scream," answered Eric. "Seth and I ran into the room, but it was empty. There were no signs of a struggle. The window was locked. It was as if she disappeared."

"How can someone just disappear?" asked Susan.

"I don't know," answered Eric. He was trying to keep his voice calm. Anya wanted to place a comforting hand on his shoulder, to tell him that they will find her.

"I don't think that waiting around here and talking is a very good idea," said Carl as the moans grew louder.

"We need to find Cassandra," said Anya. She tried not to think of all the horrible things that could have happened to her.

"We need to end this curse," said Tabitha looking at Eric. "It will end this whole mess and maybe save Cassandra as well."

"How are we going to end the curse without magical means?" asked Anya.

Eric looked at Anya and then at Tabitha. He was trying to make the right decision. "We end the curse first," he said.

"And leave Cassandra?" asked Susan. Anya couldn't believe what she had just heard.

"We are not…we are not leaving anyone," Eric answered, not making eye contact with any of his friends. "This curse might spread and we need to end it as soon as we can. There's a high probability that Cassandra was taken by the curse and by ending it we'll be able to save her as well."

"We don't even know where to begin to look for her," said Tabitha as Anya tried to speak. Anya looked back at her. "We need to set our priorities straight."

"And saving Cassandra isn't on your list of priorities?" asked Anya in disbelief.

"Listen to me," said Eric looking directly at Anya. "If I knew of another way to save her, I would have done it. But right now the only thing we are sure about is that ending this curse will save us all."

Anya nodded. She wanted to argue more but decided not to. What Eric said did make sense. It was hard for her and the rest of the group to admit it, but right now the only thing they were sure about was that ending the curse was their safest bet for survival.

"So, what's the plan?" asked Anya.

Eleven

"I still can't believe you think I'll be able to recite the counter curse and put an end to all of this," said Anya as she followed Eric and Tabitha into the forest. She was trying not to remember the dream she had in which she was the girl who resurrected the zombies from the frozen lake.

"We have to try," said Eric as he led the way, his eyes taking in the surroundings, looking for any zombies that might be lurking behind the frozen trees.

The friends had decided to split the group, which Susan said was a bad idea. They knew that every zombie would follow them if they all went to the swamp. By splitting up, they were hoping that at least some of the zombies would split up as well. Susan, Seth, and Carl decided to go to Eric's place and try to hold off the zombies there. Eric and Tabitha decided to go to the swamp with Anya and perform the counter curse. Splitting up was always a bad idea in Anya's book too, but this time it was more of a necessity. Seth had wanted to go with her, but that would have resulted in Carl and Susan ending up together. It was better to be in threes, and Eric, Tabitha, and Anya seemed like the obvious three-man cell because Tabitha knew about the book, Anya was to perform the counter curse, and having Eric with his werewolf powers and brains would be beneficial.

"Can you hear anything?" asked Tabitha, the heavy black book in her hands. Anya looked at it. The book felt evil to her. '*Stop that!*' she thought, shaking her head.

"Nope," answered Eric. They were nearing the caves. "But that's the trouble with these zombies. No matter how much I concentrate, I can't seem to sense them. They just appear. It's as if they are cloaked somehow. They have no scent."

"Cold dead people are supposed to have scents?" asked Anya.

"I don't know," answered Eric. "They should at least smell of decay or ice. They don't smell. Their scents don't exist."

Anya tried not to worry. She couldn't even hear the moans. If Eric wasn't able to sense the zombies, they could be walking right into a big group of them.

The three friends didn't talk much as they reached the cave that would lead them to the swamp. Tabitha took out a flashlight from her coat pocket and switched it on. The cave was dark and Anya had a weird feeling they were being watched. Eric stood still in front of the cave's mouth, his eyes looking inside. He was making certain that it was empty. "I can't sense anything in there," he said turning to face the girls. "Not even bats."

"We still need to go," said Tabitha as she stepped into the cave, aiming the flashlight right in front of her, and then they heard the moans.

"They are here," whispered Anya as the moans grew louder.

***

"You really think we will be able to hold them off?" asked Susan as she ran with Lizzie, Carl, and Seth toward Eric's house.

"We can try," answered Carl. They could still hear the moans. The plan seemed to have worked. A lot of zombies were chasing them. "I just hope the zombies we are going to be dealing with are far more than what Tabitha and the others might go up against."

"I really don't like this plan," said Seth. He had wanted to go with Anya to make sure she was safe. But the group had decided on three-man cells. "Yes, the weapons are still at his house, but I don't know if bullets work on those things."

"You did shoot one of them in the leg," answered Susan. "It did fall to the ground."

"We need to try and take a headshot," said Carl. Eric's house was just a few blocks away. "See if that works."

"I'm not good at aiming," said Seth, glad that he was active in school sports as he followed Carl. All of the running he had to do since yesterday required a lot of stamina.

"Neither am I," panted Susan. She was trying hard to keep up with the boys.

"We are nearly there," said Carl as he looked worryingly at Susan. "Don't give up."

"I'm trying the best I can," Susan shot back at him. "I have been running for quite a while you know, and last time I checked, I wasn't half werewolf or whatever."

"I think we can slow down," suggested Carl looking back. They could still hear the moans, but the zombies weren't in sight. He was glad that they didn't know how to run.

"You sure?" asked Susan as she felt herself slow down.

"You need to take a break," said Seth, gun still in hand.

Susan nodded and touched her knees as she tried to catch her breath. Lizzie stopped as well and whined at her. "It's okay," she added, smiling at her dog. "Just give me a few minutes."

"I don't think we even have a minute," said Seth as he heard the moans grow louder and saw zombies begin to slowly gather on the road behind them.

"Into the house," said Carl as he looked at a house on his left. Seth nodded and helped Susan get back on her feet. Carl pushed open the front door and motioned his friends to hurry inside. "This will give us a few minutes to catch our breath," he added, closing the door behind Seth, Susan, and Lizzie.

"They can easily break in," said Susan out of breath as she watched Carl drag a couch in front of the door.

"If we go through the houses, we'll reach Eric's faster," said Carl as he looked at the zombies. In a few minutes they would all be gathered around the house.

"You want us to break into houses?" asked Susan.

"It's better than running," answered Carl as he started to walk toward the back door, ignoring the two frozen kids sitting at the kitchen table. "It looks clear from here," he added, looking at the backyard. "Let's move… What the?"

Carl heard Susan scream, and he ran back to the room. A woman was slowly making her way down the stairs to where Susan, Seth, and Lizzie were.

"Move! Move!" Seth yelled at Susan as he aimed the gun at the woman. "It's the same as at the police station. The frozen people are coming back to life."

Carl heard movement in the kitchen as well. *The kids?*

"Oh my God! They are just kids!" exclaimed Susan as she saw what looked like seven and six year old boys looking at them.

"No time to worry about that now," said Carl as he ran past Susan and pushed both of the kids away. They didn't make a sound and hit the counter. The woman was nearly at the end of the stairs and the moans outside of the house grew louder. "Run!" yelled Carl pointing at the back door.

***

"This is the worst," complained Anya as she followed Tabitha and Eric through the cave. They hadn't heard moans for some time now. '*I hope I don't ever have to hear them again*,' she thought as they continued walking.

"We are nearly there," said Eric and he quickened his pace. The three friends finally reached the entrance they had used to get to the swamp. Eric moved away the snow and climbed through the hole. "Glad to see that it wasn't blocked," said Tabitha as Eric helped her out. Anya didn't say anything as she grabbed Eric's hand and he pulled her out as well.

"And now begins the long walk to the swamp," said Anya as she noticed the Singleton farm in the distance and then the forest they had to cross to get to the swamp.

"We should hurry," said Eric as he began to climb down. "Be careful, the rocks look slippery."

"Are you sure the counter curse plan will work?" Anya asked again.

"I don't know," answered Tabitha. Anya had asked the same question more than enough for her liking. "But we have to try. It's the only plan we have right now."

Anya sensed the displeasure in Tabitha's voice but she didn't feel sorry for her as Eric helped her down a few steps. As far as she was concerned, she felt a little betrayed by her friends. She kept wondering why all of them thought that she would be able to perform the counter curse. She knew that the dream she told them about had played a major part in the unanimous decision. She tried not to think of how worse the situation would have gotten if she had told them the truth about the dream. '*I mean, if you really look at it all*, *Tabitha's the one who is the weirdest in the group*,' she thought. Tabitha quickly looked at her and then resumed climbing down. '*See what I mean?*'

'But what if I really am able to perform the counter curse?' Anya thought. They were going to reach leveled ground soon. She remembered how David went after her when he came to town, how he said that she was important. And then she remembered the dream. It had felt so real to her. Anya shook her head. In a few minutes they would all find out how special she really was. *'I'm not getting my hopes up*,' she thought as they reached leveled ground and began to walk toward the forest.

"What language is the counter curse in anyway?" asked Anya.

"It's actually quite old," answered Tabitha as she clutched the book closer to her. "It has similarities with Latin. Don't worry, you will be able to read it."

"And I'm supposed to read it without any understanding of it?" Anya asked.

"Even I can't translate the entirety of it," Tabitha answered. Eric remained silent and kept walking towards the forest. "The book doesn't talk about the resurrection curse. It only talks about the counter curse. The words are supposed to send the resurrected away and seal the area."

"Seal the area?"

"It says that no one will ever be able to perform the resurrection curse again wherever the counter curse is performed," Tabitha answered Anya as they quickened their pace behind Eric. "If everything works, I think it will be safe to assume that those swamp monsters won't be coming out after another fifty years as well."

They were near the Singleton farm and Anya remembered the video recording of Katherine and Blake running way from the zombies and then Blake dying and being carried away.

The girls saw Eric stop. "What is it?" Anya asked walking toward him.

"I can smell her," Eric answered. He was looking at the Singleton farm and then at the forest.

"Who?" asked Anya as she looked around.

"Cassandra," answered Eric as he sniffed the air once more. "She was here."

"I don't see any footprints," said Cassandra as she looked at the ground. "And it isn't snowing."

"But she was here," Eric answered looking at the forest again. "Her scent trail leads into the forest, and I'm guessing to the swamp."

"You mean whoever kidnapped her took her to the swamp?" asked Anya. '*What if the kidnapper is still there?*'

"We need to hurry," said Eric and he started to run toward the forest.

Anya and Tabitha tried to catch up with him. "How can someone get kidnapped from a room without there being any signs of trouble?" asked Anya as she ran. The snow was making it difficult. "I don't like this at all. What if the person or thing is waiting for us?"

"I have no idea why someone took Cassandra," answered Tabitha. "But if Eric says she's at the swamp, then we need to get there as fast as we can."

***

"I hate this," complained Seth as Carl unlocked the front door to Eric's house. "I hate this."

"None of us is enjoying running for our lives," said Susan as she and Lizzie ran into the house and Carl closed the door behind them. They had run as fast as they could to Eric's house. The moans had gotten louder, as if the zombies were only a few feet from them. They had seen frozen people in the houses begin to move as well as they ran past them, and they knew that it was only a matter of time before they all joined with the zombie group that came out of the swamp.

"How many of those things are we facing?" asked Seth as he looked out of the window. The street was deserted for now.

"I don't know," answered Carl as he looked at the weapons placed on the floor. "A whole lot, if we count the frozen residents of Colville."

"We can't shoot those people," said Susan sounding worried.

"Why not?" asked Seth, gun in his hand, eyes scanning the street for any signs of movement.

"Because," answered Susan looking straight at Seth. "Those are people, people who were living their lives before all of this happened, people we know!"

"Well, they don't seem to remember knowing you," said Seth. He felt Susan still looking at him. "What do you think we should do?" he asked looking at her. "How are we supposed to defend ourselves? We can't just keep running."

"We can make a fire," said Susan looking at the boys. "Like the last time we faced them when they came out of the swamp?"

"You think fire will work on them?" asked Carl as he heard the moans grow louder. "Didn't Eric and Tabitha mention something about defeating this curse with magic?"

"It worked last time," answered Susan as she patted Lizzie. "What do you propose we do? Shoot at all of them? Do we have enough ammunition?"

Seth and Carl looked at each other. "It's worth a try," said Carl, and he went into Eric's kitchen to find a matchbox.

"What are we supposed to burn?" asked Seth.

"Branches or…"

"Wait!" came Carl's voice before Susan could complete her answer. He walked into the room, a matchbox in his hand. He took out a matchstick and tried lighting it. It lit up for a second and then vanished without leaving a trail of smoke.

Susan noticed a piece of paper lying on the coffee table. She handed it to Carl who tried lighting the piece of paper. A fire appeared for a second and then went out. "There goes that plan," whispered Carl as he looked at the piece of paper in his hands.

"And we have a big problem," said Seth as he looked out of the window. Susan and Carl ran toward him and looked outside. The entire street in front of the house was full of zombies. They were all standing still, looking at the house as they moaned.

Twelve

"Eric, slow down a bit," said Anya as she and Tabitha ran after him through the snow. Eric didn't look back, but he slowed down a little as he reached the forest. "Good," said Anya. She really needed to exercise more. "We all want to make sure she's okay, but you can't just run in there without a plan," she added as the girls reached the forest. The temperature dropped lower as the three friends stepped inside. Anya looked around as they began to half-run, half-walk toward the swamp. She felt weird about the fact that they hadn't seen any zombies on their way there. She hoped that not all of them had decided to go after Seth and the others. They heard no sound as they walked deeper into the forest. It was as if the entire forest was dead. Eric remained silent as he led the way. Tabitha was clutching the book close to her. Anya tried to make out the title, but it was in a language she couldn't understand. In a few minutes they would reach the swamp, and Anya was worried about what they would find. She tried not to think about it too much. But whenever she tried not to think about something, that was the only thing she kept thinking about. '*Stop it, Anya*,' she shook her head. '*Stop it!*'

"Where is she?" Eric sounded worried. The swamp was deserted, a layer of ice on its surface. "Her trail ends right here."

Anya stepped forward and placed a comforting hand on her friend's shoulder. "We'll find her," she said looking at Eric. The boy nodded and then turned to Tabitha. "Let's get this over with."

Tabitha nodded at him and opened the book. She motioned Anya to come near her and she showed her a page. Anya looked at it. By the markings, she guessed that she was looking at chapter thirteen. There were weird symbols on the sides of the page. "You need to start reading this," Tabitha pointed at the middle of the page.

"I just begin reading?" asked Anya as she looked at the text. "La maiora premunt…"

"I think it's better you come near the swamp," Tabitha stopped her.

Anya nodded and walked toward the swamp.

"Didn't you say that the girl in your dream was standing on top of the ice?" said Eric as he examined the surface.

"You want me to stand on top of the ice?" asked Anya, her eyes wide.

"It looks strong enough," he answered, not looking at Anya. "If you fall, I'll get you out."

Anya looked at Tabitha for support. "I think he has a point," said Tabitha as she walked toward Anya. "We are running out of time," she added before Anya could say anything. "You need to hurry."

"Fine," said Anya, and she rolled her eyes. "Hand me the damn book."

Tabitha gave her the book, and Anya stepped onto the ice. She tried not to think of the dead bodies that might be present below.

"Try and imagine that you are canceling everything the curse has done," said Tabitha as Anya looked at the page she had to read.

Anya nodded. "La maiora premunt mala fide," she began to read again. She imagined things getting back to normal as she read from the text. She thought of the sunny days that Colville had this time of the year. She wished that Seth, Susan, and Carl were safe and that the zombies would just disappear. She thought of all the frozen people turning back to normal. "Miserere nobies," Anya read the last line of the page and looked at her friends. "Anything?" she asked. She didn't feel different, and the sky was still covered with dark clouds.

"I don't think it worked," said Tabitha. She looked disappointed. "Now what do we do?" she asked Eric, but before he could answer, they all heard a scream.

***

"Why aren't they doing anything?" asked Seth as he looked at the zombies standing motionless outside the house. "What are they waiting for?"

"I don't know," answered Susan as she sat on the floor with Lizzie, a handgun near her. "I don't know."

The zombies had been standing still in front of the house for quite a while now and the tension was unnerving. Carl was pacing around the room. "They are definitely thinking something," he said. "Or whoever is controlling them is thinking something."

"I think they want us to crack," said Seth. "Put pressure on us or something."

"I hope that Anya and the others are able to perform the task," said Susan as she patted Lizzie. Her dog was feeling uneasy and she was trying to calm her down.

"Wait!" said Seth as he looked out of the window. "They are moving."

Susan didn't get up from the floor, and she grabbed the handgun near her. Carl ran toward the window and looked outside. The zombies had begun to move.

"They are retreating?" Carl was confused as he watched the zombies and the rest of the frozen people walk slowly away from the house.

"It could be a trap," said Seth looking at Carl. "Or they could be going back to where Anya and the others are," he added sounding worried.

***

Anya turned toward the source of the scream. It came from inside of the forest in front of her and it sounded familiar. "It's Cassandra!" yelled Eric as he tried to decide the direction he should run in.

"Anya, get off of the ice!" yelled Tabitha as she watched a figure emerge from behind the tress a few feet away from them. Anya turned toward the new arrival. It was the same zombie that had broken Blake's neck. The zombie's cold dead blue eyes looked at the teenagers.

"That thing took Cassandra," said Eric as he began to step toward him.

"Don't do anything yet," said Tabitha as she grabbed his sleeve and looked at the zombie. The friends heard more movement and then they saw Blake come into view carrying a tied up girl.

"Cassandra," whispered Anya as she saw the hooded girl. Her hands were tied behind her back. She tried to free herself, but

Blake was too strong for her. Blake's head tilted to his left and his neck was still broken.

"Let her go!" Eric yelled at the zombie. It kept looking at the teenagers, and then they began to hear moans coming from all around the forest.

Blake took the struggling Cassandra toward the swamp and then jumped into it along with her. The ice broke and they disappeared.

"No!" yelled Eric and he ran to save her. The blue-eyed zombie came in front of him, and before Eric could react, it lifted its arm and Eric flew ten feet away, hitting a tree.

Eric tried to move but the zombie lifted his arm again. Eric was picked up by an invisible force and thrown into another tree, and then he moved no more. The moans grew louder, and Anya knew that the rest of the zombies were just a few feet away from her, behind the trees. She looked at the zombie who had beaten Eric and then she looked at the broken ice where Cassandra and Blake had fallen in. She knew that Cassandra was running out of time. She felt the ice beneath her begin to crack. She felt her body move, she heard Tabitha scream her name, and then she felt water around her. '*Open your eyes, Anya!*' her mind forced her.

She opened her eyes. The water was warm around her. She looked up and tried to see where the ice broke, but she couldn't. She looked around and saw Cassandra a few feet from her. Blake was nowhere to be seen. Making up her mind, Anya began to swim toward her. The warm clothes she was wearing didn't feel heavy as she swam. '*I'll figure that out later*,' she thought as she grabbed Cassandra's arm. Hoping that Cassandra was still alive, she tried to swim toward the surface. She could still see a layer of ice on the surface and then she saw an opening. She was about to reach the surface when she felt something pull Cassandra down.

'*Is that a locket?*' Anya looked at Cassandra. A golden locket hung around her neck and it seemed to be weighing the girls down.

Anya reached for the locket and tried to take it off of her, but she couldn't. She tried to pull the chain, but it wouldn't break. Anya's body was screaming for air. Cassandra wasn't moving, her eyes were closed, and her arms were tied behind her back. The locket began to glow. Anya felt an invisible force pull her away from Cassandra. She felt something punch her in the stomach and then she was in darkness.

***

"Anya!"

The young girl heard a voice. She couldn't see anything. Darkness was all around her and she felt her body turn cold. '*Am I dead?*'

"Anya!" she heard the voice again. It was a woman's voice. It sounded kind and somehow familiar. Anya saw a golden orb of light in front of her. The orb was emitting a warm glow and Anya held out her hand to touch it. The orb of light grew in size, and Anya saw an image of a woman in light robes standing in front of her. She was the most beautiful woman Anya had ever seen. Her entire body was emitting a golden warm glow. Her long golden hair seemed to be floating in the air.

"Who are you?" asked Anya.

"You know who I am," the woman smiled back at her. Anya tried to remember the woman. "You know in your heart," the woman added. "Evil things are coming for you," she said, and Anya looked at her. "You need to be strong."

"Wait, what? More evil things?" Anya asked.

"Things have been set in motion," continued the woman. "More shall cross your path. A war isn't far away. You will decide the fate of this world when the time comes."

"What are you talking about?" asked Anya. "What war?"

"Evil never ends," the woman answered. "It remains patient, waiting for the right opportunity. We can only keep it at bay and hope that it never recovers its full strength."

"Can you be any more vague?" Anya rolled her eyes.

The woman smiled at her. "You have a lot to learn, young Anya," she said. "Evil is closer to you than you might think. Be strong."

She placed her hand on Anya's forehead. There was a flash of golden light and then darkness.

***

"Anya!"

Anya felt a familiar voice call her name. She tried to open her eyes but they felt heavy.

"Anya!" Eric called her name again as he gently slapped her face, trying to wake her up.

"What? Where am I?" Anya tried to make sense of everything as she opened her eyes. Her hands felt the moist ground. '*No snow? Eww! Am I touching the disgusting forest ground?*'

"Thank Heavens she woke up!" exclaimed Tabitha. She was sitting on the ground to Anya's right. Anya tried to move her body. She felt Eric's strong hands help her up. "The zombies?" she asked looking around. "Cassandra?"

"I'm fine," answered Cassandra with a smile. "It's over," she added. "The curse thing is over."

"How?" asked Anya. The dark clouds had disappeared. The snow had vanished, and the swamp was back to its murky greenish yellow color.

"We'll explain on the way," said Eric as he helped Anya maintain balance. "Let's go back to Colville."

Epilogue

"Those zombies were awful," said Susan as she patted Lizzie on the floor. The friends were at Eric's place. Anya was sitting on the couch, her head resting on Seth shoulder. Carl was sitting on the floor near Tabitha who was in a chair. Cassandra was sitting next to Susan, and Eric was on another chair in front of Tabitha.

"They stood out there for I don't know how long," said Carl. "It really got on our nerves."

Carl and Susan had just finished telling the rest of the group what they had been though. Seth had given Anya a big hug as soon as she walked into the house, and he wasn't leaving her side. "But it wasn't as creepy as what you all had to go through," said Carl. Tabitha had told them what happened…how Blake jumped into the swamp with Cassandra, how a zombie was able to pick up Eric without putting a hand on him, and how Anya fell into the swamp as well.

"So the counter curse worked?" asked Susan as she continued patting Lizzie.

"I don't know," answered Tabitha. "It didn't feel like it. After Cassandra and Anya fell into the swamp, I ran to help Eric. The zombies came toward us and they all began to moan. The snow began to disappear and they started going back into the swamp."

Tabitha had already told them what happened. But the friends were trying to make sense of it all. "So Eric got up and dived into the swamp. He came back with Cassandra and Anya a few seconds later. By then, the weather, the forest, everything had returned to normal."

The friends remained silent. Anya knew that almost all of them were thinking that the counter curse had worked, that somehow she had been able to fix all of this. But deep down Anya knew that she wasn't the one who had ended it. She just felt that if she was able to perform the counter curse she would have realized it. She could hear sounds coming from outside.

Eric got up and looked outside. "It seems Colville is back to normal," he said looking at people walking in the streets. "And none of them seem to have any idea what just happened."

"You can be sure to hear about broken front doors and crazy weather conditions for about a week," he added with a smile as he rejoined the group.

There were a lot of questions in Anya's mind as she watched Eric and Tabitha decide what to do about the 'stolen guns'. The police station will be searching for them, as everything is back to normal now. Anya wondered why Cassandra was kidnapped and how the curse seemed to have ended. She also had a lot of questions about the woman she saw. The woman felt very familiar to her. She just couldn't understand why.

"You okay?" asked Seth smiling at her.

"I'm fine," she smiled back. She tried not to think about all of that…yet!

The Moon

One

A woman walked hurriedly through a well lit corridor. She was trying to remain calm. She had never been to the current level before. Her superior had ordered her to take some files there. She held them tightly to her chest. She dared not open them. Her stilettos echoed in the corridor as she remembered what happened just a few minutes ago. She had been typing away on her computer, making a report about a woman who had gone missing in Somerville, when she received an e-mail from her superior. Not wasting a moment, she got up, and as the e-mail specified, she grabbed the files placed outside of her room and made her way to the corridor…the corridor she was walking along now.

She had heard stories about things happening on the level, things that were kept secret from some of the higher-ups. *'I wish I knew why I was here,'* she thought as she continued walking. She saw no one else as she walked. There were no rooms in sight either. She walked a few more steps and reached a fork in her path. *'Now what do I do?'* She tried to make up her mind. She looked to her left and then to her right. There was nothing mentioned in the e-mail about a fork in the corridor or choosing the direction to go. She stood silently, files still in hand. *'If there was supposed to be a deadline for delivering these files, I am so fired.'*

"Please turn right and continue walking."

The woman stopped herself from screaming out loud. The robotic voice had taken her by surprise. She tried to find a speaker in the ceiling but all she could see were white lights. "I don't have time to figure out where the voice came from," she whispered to herself, and as the voice had instructed, she turned right and continued walking.

Finally she saw a single door right in front of her. She stopped, her hand resting upon the doorknob. There was no name or any number on it. It was a plain white door. She took a deep breath, exhaled, and opened the door, ready to meet anyone who was inside.

"Hello?" she called uncertainly as she entered the empty room. The walls were white and in the center was a wooden table. Not sure what to do next, she placed the files on the white table and slowly backed away from it. *'I guess that's the end of it.'*

She was about to leave when the same robotic voice spoke again. "Miss Jewels."

The woman stopped and looked at the table. She wasn't sure where to look. There were no cameras in sight. *'None that I can see.'*

"Yes?" she asked no one. She felt weird standing alone in the room talking to a disembodied robotic voice.

"How long have you been working here?"

"About a year," she answered, trying to sound confident. Just a year ago she had been working at a local police station. She was there for only a few weeks and then she was mysteriously sent to this place…a place where she worked on cases that didn't make much sense to her. There were a lot of files about missing people. She didn't have the authority to look further into them. All she did was read the case files and organize things. She didn't mind it. Working in the field wasn't one of her strong points.

"What do you know about the Colville and Somerville cases?" asked the robotic voices.

"What do you want to know?" she asked confidently. She was getting used to the environment she was in. "I know there have been a lot of cases about missing people."

"And?"

She understood what the voice was asking her. There were some things in the cases that didn't make sense. It was as if a lot of things had been covered up, things that didn't make sense to her when she tried to look closely.

"There are a lot of things that seem as if they have been covered up," she continued. "Things I can't really make sense of. To me they seem like covered up murders and…"

"Do you believe in the paranormal?"

"What?"

The question had taken her by surprise. *'Do I believe in what?'*

"Do you believe in the paranormal? Do you believe in the supernatural?"

"I…I…," she tried to come up with an answer. *'Paranormal as in vampires, werewolves, and all of that stuff?'*

It wasn't as if she didn't believe in the supernatural. Just last year she had dressed up as a witch at a Halloween party.

"No," she answered firmly. Yes, a lot of things about the cases didn't make sense, especially the things that happened in Colville, but that didn't mean the supernatural was involved. Right?

"Well, Miss Jewels," came a voice. This time it was different. It was human. "You are about to," said a man.

***

"So, we finally got to know about the Halloween party," smiled Anya as she and her friends got into the bus to head back home. The black haired girl walked past familiar faces and sat down at the back.

"Yes," answered Susan as she followed Anya to the back. "The teacher announced it in my last class," she added pushing a strand of her blonde hair away from her face and sitting down.

"It's still about a week away though," said a black haired girl as she walked to her seat followed by a brown curly haired boy. "Enough time for me to come up with ideas for the party."

"Don't tell me you are planning it?" Anya asked Tabitha. *'I'm not really surprised.'* Tabitha had been talking about doing extra co-curricular work in school for a few days now. She said something about wanting to worry about other things and not the next paranormal threat they might have to face.

"Yes, she is," the brown curly haired boy answered as he sat down next to Tabitha. "She talked to Miss Flow about it this morning and I'm helping her."

'Again, not surprised,' thought Anya as she tried not to roll her eyes. *'Trust Carl to find ways to spend more time with Tabitha.'* She noticed Tabitha give her a weird look and avert her gaze outside of the bus.

"What have you got planned?" asked Susan, and Tabitha turned to look at her.

"I've got a few things in mind," she answered with a smile. "The high school is having a party after ten years. That's why I need to make it something that people will remember."

"Our school hasn't had a Halloween party for that long?" asked Susan surprised. "I thought they hadn't had one since we came here. I didn't know it had been ten years."

"That's what Miss Flow told me," said Tabitha as the bus began to move. "She said something about the school not having the proper resources when she took the job here five years ago."

"So why the change?" asked Anya. The bus was filled with chatter, friends talking about what they had done over the weekend and how boring it was to return to school on Monday.

"I don't know," answered Tabitha. "I'm quite okay with having a party this week."

"Same here," Carl said happily. "About time something fun happened around here."

Anya nodded and went back to looking out of the window. People were going about business as usual, oblivious to the fact that about a week ago a group of teenagers had to fight for their lives against zombies in order to end an ancient curse. Halloween was approaching and Anya couldn't help but smile to herself. Again the people of Colville will dress up as vampires, werewolves, and even zombies, not knowing that all of those things existed in real life.

"Anya, are you okay?" asked Susan. Anya stopped looking out of the window. "You had a strange smile on your face."

"I'm fine," she answered. "I'm fine. I was just thinking about what Carl said about something fun finally happening."

"I hope Eric is feeling well," said Susan.

Anya nodded. Eric hadn't been feeling well. He was never the kind to skip school. He had called Anya and told her he wasn't coming, saying that it wasn't anything serious and they shouldn't worry themselves. The friends had decided to check up on him as soon as they reached home.

"He did say that it wasn't anything serious," said Anya. "But knowing him, it had to be quite serious to make him miss the first day of a new school week."

"I thought werewolf powers prevented you guys from falling sick and stuff?" Susan asked Carl.

"I thought so too," said Carl. "It's not as if I have a degree in lycantherapy."

"Lycanthropy," Tabitha corrected him with a smile and she turned to the girls. "I'm kind of worried about him too. As far as I know, werewolf healing powers should at least prevent him from getting diseases that humans are vulnerable to."

"He is human," said Anya. She didn't want to sound defensive but that's how the words came out of her mouth.

"I didn't mean that," said Tabitha before Carl could say something and start an argument with Anya in order to defend her. "I just meant that he should not be getting ill from things that can make us ill."

"That's the thing that worries me too," said Susan. Anya and Carl were glaring at each other. "He was fine after the swamp incident. We hung out over the weekend and he looked fine then as well."

"Whatever it is, it probably happened Sunday night," said Carl as Anya returned to looking out of the window. She had had enough of Carl standing up for Tabitha.

"Or it could have been lying dormant for months," said Tabitha. She sounded worried. Anya looked at her. Tabitha seemed to be thinking. *'If it has to do with something that's related to the supernatural, I guess she's the one who'll figure it out,'* Anya thought as she turned back to looking out of the window. Tabitha had been a great help when it came to figuring out and dealing with the supernatural incidents the friends had to deal with since David came to town. *'Why do I have to think of him right now?'*

"You are making me worried," said Susan as she looked at Tabitha. "What do you mean by 'it' being dormant for months?"

"That's what I'm trying to figure out," answered Tabitha as the bus stopped and a few students walked out. "It's just something I read about a long time ago. I'll have to go and check it out again."

"It's going to be fine," added Tabitha as she gave a comforting smile to Susan.

'That's the problem,' thought Anya as she kept looking out of the window and the bus began to move again. *'When it comes to Colville, nothing is completely fine.'*

Two

"You don't think we are disturbing him?" asked Susan as the friends stood outside of Eric's house. They had all walked to Eric's as soon as the bus dropped them off. Anya had tried calling him from her cellphone but got no answer.

"I think he probably knew we would be coming," answered Anya as she searched her backpack for the key to the front door. It was Eric's idea that the friends should have keys to each other's houses in case of emergencies.

"Can you hear anything from inside?" asked Tabitha as she readjusted her backpack. She was looking at the window above her.

"Nope," Carl shook his head looking at the window as well. "I can't hear anything."

"Can't you listen to his heartbeat or anything?" asked Susan. Anya rolled her eyes. *'Leave it to Susan to be worried about nothing.'* She searched the pocket of her bag for a few more seconds and found the key.

"Let's just go inside," said Anya before Carl could give an answer, and she opened the front door. The house was dimly lit by the sunlight coming from between the curtains. *'Now I'm worried,'* thought Anya as they walked inside and dropped their bags on the floor. No one said a word as they walked up the stairs to Eric's room.

Anya knocked but there was no answer. "He's probably sleeping," said Susan.

Anya knocked again. "Eric?"

The friends still got no answer from inside. Anya slowly opened the door, praying that Eric had slept in his clothes. "Eric?" she called worried. Her friend was lying in bed, his eyes closed and not looking well.

"Eric? Dude?" asked Carl as he walked toward the sleeping teenager.

Tabitha placed her hand on his forehead. "He's burning."

"I…I'll go get water," said Susan and she ran out of the room. Anya went closer to the bed. "Shouldn't we call the doctor?" she asked as she looked at Eric. "Or at least his family?"

"We should definitely call a doctor," said Tabitha. "Where's the phone?" she asked looking around the room.

"It's downstairs," answered Carl. Tabitha nodded and walked out of the room.

"He really is burning," said Anya as she sat down next to Eric and placed her hand on his forehead. She couldn't help but feel angry at him. "He should have told us sooner," she said to no one. Carl didn't say anything but just stood there looking at Eric. Anya knew that Carl and Eric were quite close. Carl was the first to talk to Eric when he moved to town. He had introduced him to her and Susan.

"Here," said Susan as she walked into the room carrying a bowl of cold water and some towels. She placed them on the bedside table. Anya dipped a towel into the water and placed it on Eric's forehead. He didn't move and continued to sleep. "I saw Tabitha downstairs talking on the phone," said Susan as she pushed the curtains away from the window and the light swept into the room.

"She's talking to a doctor," said Carl. "I think we should contact his family as well."

"Do you know how?" asked Anya as she placed a new towel on Eric's forehead.

The three friends looked at each other. Eric didn't mention his family much. All they knew was that they moved from country to country because of their business.

"We can check his e-mails," said Carl as he walked toward the laptop on the desk. "But of course it is password protected," he added and closed the laptop with a sigh.

"I don't know why he doesn't clean his room," said Susan as she looked at the books scattered all around.

"It's cleaner than my room," said Anya with a smile.

"And mine," added Carl with a smile as well.

"If this is cleaner than both of your rooms, then I have no words for you," said Susan as she picked up a book from the floor.

Anya and Carl laughed. Susan's room was spotless. Everything was placed properly. Of course Eric's room looked untidy to her.

"I talked to a doctor I know," said Tabitha as she walked into the room and noticed the friends smiling. "What?" she asked.

"We were just talking about clean rooms," said Carl with a smile. He pointed at Susan. "Apparently Miss Susan over here thinks that Eric's room shouldn't be on the list."

"I didn't say that," said Susan looking at Carl as he laughed.

Eric groaned and the friends looked at him. The teenager slowly opened his eyes. "What are you guys doing here?" he asked looking at them.

"What do you think?" asked Anya as she rolled her eyes.

Eric touched the wet towel on his forehead. He lifted it off and began to get up from the bed.

"I don't think you should be getting up right now," said Susan while Carl nodded in agreement.

"Hey, I'm fine," said Eric as he put on his glasses. He got up from the bed and stood in front of his friends. "Look, I'm fine."

"You weren't fine a few seconds ago," said Anya as she got up as well. "You were burning up."

"The werewolf healing powers must have kicked in," said Eric as Susan placed her hand on his forehead. "See?" he added as Susan finished checking his temperature. "I'm okay and I will be okay. Whatever happened to me last night seems to have ended."

"Either way, I think you should call your parents," said Anya. "I think they should…" she stopped before she could finish her sentence. Eric was giving her a very serious look.

"I don't want to worry them over nothing," he said.

Anya nodded. It wasn't her place to force Eric into something he didn't want to do, especially when it involved his parents. "I really appreciate all of you coming over to see how I was doing," Eric smiled at his friends. "So, tell me. What did I miss today?"

***

"Are you sure he's going to be okay?" asked Susan as the friends walked away from Eric's house. They had spent most of their time showing him notes from the classes he missed and making sure he would call if he didn't feel well.

"He'll be all right," answered Carl as he moved his hand through his curly hair. "Didn't you look at him? He looked completely fine writing down those notes from class. Like he said, his healing powers must have started late."

"Whatever the case, I'm still going to check out what made him ill in the first place," said Tabitha as the four walked with their backpacks. "I still can't believe he canceled the appointment with the doctor."

Anya didn't say anything as the friends walked. Eric had looked fine while they were at his house, but deep down Anya couldn't stop worrying. And who could blame her? Things hadn't been normal in Colville lately.

***

"I can't believe we have to take care of this," said a woman. She was displeased with the situation she was about to encounter. She looked into the mirror and admired herself. *'Leather is the best thing that ever happened to humankind,'* she thought, looking at her skin-tight leather clothes.

"We have to do it," said a tall black haired man sitting on a chair. He looked at the woman as she tried to decide if pulling her blonde hair into a knot would be a good choice. "Orders are orders."

The woman didn't say anything as she continued looking at herself in the mirror and playing with her long hair. The man sighed and went back to shuffling the deck of cards he had put on the table in front of him. His eyes went to the text he had received on his cell phone telling him that they both should head immediately to Colville and deal with the situation. He had been in the business long enough to know that dealing with the situation meant that someone had to die. "Poor kids," he said to himself as the woman hummed a tune.

Three

"So, how's he doing?" asked Seth. He was talking to Anya on the phone.

"I don't think he's well," she answered walking around in her room. "We went to check up on him and he was burning hot. Then he woke up and said he felt fine. His temperature went back to normal."

Anya couldn't stop herself from worrying about her friend. "And he cancelled his appointment with the doctor, and I don't think he wants his family to know."

"Any idea what's wrong?"

"Tabitha has some theories, something to do with his werewolf powers."

"I still can't get over the fact that two of my friends are werewolves or have werewolf-like powers," laughed Seth.

"Yes," smiled Anya as she looked at her reflection in the mirror. "And you're just a human being with no supernatural abilities."

"Hey, not fair," Seth faked disappointment. "I survived swamp monsters and cursed zombies. That's got to count for something."

"It does," laughed Anya. "It does. You are my unsung hero."

Anya walked to her window as she listened to Seth laugh. She looked outside. It was getting dark. She heard some cars drive by. She looked at the house next to hers and stopped her mind from thinking about David. Things got crazy after he came to town. Her eyes went to the bushes outside of her house.

"Anya...Anya! Are you still there?"

"Uh!" Anya didn't know when she had stopped listening to Seth's voice. She shook her head. There was no way she had just seen yellow eyes looking back at her from inside of the bushes. "Yes, yes, I'm still there."

"You didn't answer my question," said Seth.

"What?" she asked looking at the bushes again. There was nothing there. *'Did I just see eyes looking back at me?'*

"I was asking about your Halloween costume."

"Yes, that," she shook her head again. It felt heavy. "I haven't decided yet. I will let you know soon and you can decide how to match me."

"Do I have any other choice?" laughed Seth. "That's what boyfriends do."

***

"How's Eric doing?" asked Susan's mom as she placed the dishes into the dishwasher.

"He felt fine when we left him," answered Susan. She was working on her history assignment on the laptop in the kitchen. Her dog, Lizzie, was lying near her feet.

"Does his family know about him?" asked her mom as she poured orange juice into two glasses.

"I don't think so," Susan answered as she began to read an article about Queen Elizabeth. She tried not to think much about Eric. She wanted him to tell his parents but it wasn't her place to force him. She wondered how he was doing all by himself right now.

"Teenagers," Susan's mom smiled as she placed a glass of orange juice near her daughter. She sat down on a chair and drank from her own glass. "Dear, would you mind taking out the trash right now? I've got to go and start a report for work."

"I'll do it right now," smiled Susan as she got up. She wasn't able to concentrate on her assignment anyway. Lizzie watched Susan take out the trash bag and walk outside. It was dark and the air felt a bit cold on her face. She walked toward the trashcans on the side of the road and put the trash bag inside. She was about to close the lid when she felt as if someone was watching her from across the road. She looked again and saw the neighbor's house in front of her and a couple of trees on the left, but there was no one there. *'Stop being paranoid,'* she scolded herself and walked back into her house.

***

"For the last time, Carl, I haven't decided what I'm going to be for Halloween yet," Tabitha said into the phone as she sat down on her couch. *'I should never have picked it up.'*

"But I was just wondering that if you tell me who or what you're going to be, I can decide on something similar and we could look good and…"

"Like I said, I haven't decided yet," she said again, closing a huge textbook on her lap. Her cat, Felix, was lying near her feet and she knew he wasn't pleased with the person on the phone either.

"But you will soon, right?"

"Yes, Carl, I will soon," she rolled her eyes and smiled at her cat. "Now if you will excuse me, I have to get back to planning the party and figuring out what's wrong with Eric."

"You want any help with that?" Carl asked sweetly.

"Not now," she answered. *'Sometimes he's just too much for me.'* "I will call you if I need anything."

"Okay, see you," he said and hung up.

Tabitha gave a sigh of relief. It wasn't that she didn't like Carl. They both had been through a lot. But she preferred not to be disturbed, especially when she had things to figure out, and finding out what was wrong with Eric was a priority right now. There was no room for distractions. She felt thirsty and got up from the couch, much to Felix's disappointment. "I'll be right back," she smiled at him and walked into the kitchen.

She poured herself a glass of water from the refrigerator and looked outside of the kitchen window. She had been going through books for hours after her visit to Eric's and it had gotten dark. There were still a lot of books she had to read. She was hoping to find something that would tell her what was wrong with Eric. From all of the things she knew, werewolves never got ill. She was about to put the empty glass into the sink when she noticed movement in the row of hedges in front of her. She didn't take her eyes away from them. She knew she was safe from whatever it was from behind the kitchen window, but instinctively her hand put the glass down and reached for the knife on the counter. She waited a minute. The hedges didn't move again. She loosened her grip on the knife, looked outside of the window one more time, and returned to her books.

***

"Who do you think that is?" asked a brown haired teenaged boy as he saw a beautiful blonde haired woman walking down the street. She was wearing high heels and a leather outfit, and appeared eager to get to her destination. It was dark and most of the residents were inside their homes.

"I don't know," answered another teenaged boy. They were sitting on their bikes, smoking cigarettes and watching the woman pass them by. "But whoever she is, she's hot!"

The woman could hear the two boys perfectly and she was trying hard not to turn around and beat them up. *'Mere mortals,'* she thought as she walked. Her heels made sharp clicking sounds on the road. This was the most boring town she had been to. *'Why couldn't we have been sent to some place nice? To a beach? To Spain? Or maybe even a beautiful forest?'*

One of the teenagers wolf whistled and the woman stopped walking.

"Damn, Cory!" laughed one of the teenagers. "I think that bombshell heard you."

"You think she will come back to spank me?" Cory asked in a flirty voice as he passed his hand through his brown hair. "I'm all for it, if she does. Do you think she will come back, Dave?"

The woman clenched her fists. "I don't know, Cory," laughed the boy. The two of them smiled as they watched the woman walk toward them.

"I got this," said Cory and he got off of his bike. He threw his cigarette on the ground and stood up straight. Dave nodded and stood beside his friend.

The woman stopped in front of the two boys and they smiled at her. "So," began Cory. He took a step toward the woman. He could smell the leather and her perfume. "You looking for something exciting to…"

Cory yelled as he felt the pain. The woman had grabbed his right arm. She smiled at the pain in Cory's face. She could break his fragile arm in a second. She should break his arm and teach him a lesson.

"Hey you psycho!" yelled Dave as he took hold of her arm. He tried to pull her away but couldn't.

The woman turned her head and looked at Dave. She gave a smile and her eyes turned from blue to red and Dave stood still in fear. "What…what are you?"

"Don't tell me you guys won't play with me now?" asked the woman sweetly. She could feel Cory struggling with her but she didn't care. There was no chance that he could break free. She grabbed hold of Dave's arm as well. The pain was too much for the teenagers to scream for help.

"Now what to do with you both?" she asked. She loved playing with her food. She could kill them both right there and no one would notice. She was about to kill the boys when she smelled something…her partner. He would never allow her to have fun on the job. She knew he was close even if she couldn't see him. He was an expert in hiding and if he had allowed her to catch his scent, it meant that he wanted her to notice him.

"You are no fun," she said. She knew he could hear him. She let go of the boys and they fell to the ground, still in pain. She rolled her eyes at them and walked away. She heard the boys help each other up and run to their bikes.

The woman kept walking. She could still smell him. A few seconds later she heard a car come near her. She stopped and watched as the black car came to a halt.

"Get in," said a tall black haired man from inside of the car. The woman rolled her eyes and sat down in the passenger's seat. The man began to drive again. He didn't say a word and it annoyed her. She knew he was giving her the silent treatment, as if she were some kid.

"Why did you stop me?" she asked as she looked at the houses they drove past.

"You know very well why I stopped you," he answered. He didn't take his eyes off of the road and his voice was calm. It wasn't the first time she had tried to do something like that. "What have you got about the kids?"

"Those girls?" she asked with a laugh. "It's a surprise they have been able to survive this long." She had been watching the three teenaged girls who were mentioned in her report the entire day. To her, they looked unimportant. "Not one of them was able to sense they were being watched," she told the man. "I had to rustle the bushes or show them glowing eyes for a second to make them realize. They wouldn't survive a second in the field. I don't know what's so special about them. Why don't we just kill them now and take care of the boys?"

"They were able to ward off a curse and survive a vampire attack," said the man. "Give them some credit. As for us not killing them right now, I'm not the one who gives orders. We were told to look at them and gather information."

"The only information I got is that those three girls are lame and ordinary. They have nothing about them that needs to be recorded."

The man didn't answer. The car reached the house they were staying in and he pulled into the driveway.

"What did you find out about the boys?" asked the woman as they got out of the car. She was curious about them. *'There must have been a reason we were sent to this godforsaken place for two boys,'* she thought as the man unlocked the front door.

"Didn't you read the files we received?" asked the man, shaking his head. He already knew she wasn't the kind to read files, but she was one of the best in the field and that's why he was happy to be her partner. They had been taking care of cases for five years now and hadn't failed.

The woman laughed and took off her leather jacket as they entered the house. She looked at herself in a mirror. "I smell like human," she said in disgust. "I'm going to take a shower and go to bed."

The man nodded and watched her walk upstairs to the bathroom. He sighed and took out a pack of cards from his pocket. He shuffled them and placed them on a table with a stack of files. He sat down and looked at the files on the teenagers. There were two teenagers they hadn't seen yet. A boy named Seth and a girl named Cassandra. They weren't a high priority, but as far as he was concerned, it was better to look at everything when working on a case.

He had spent most of the day observing the town and keeping an eye on Eric and Carl. Eric had stayed inside his house most of the day. He was ill and the man knew why. Carl had left his house once to get groceries and that was it. He had hoped to test Carl's skills, but the teenager had no idea he was being followed. As far as the man was concerned, Carl was a below-average werewolf at best.

From what he had gathered from his partner, the girls weren't anything special either. But he still felt that there was something he was missing. There had to be a reason for a vampire to show up in Colville, other than creating two werewolf slaves. "These kids are something," the man said to himself as he opened two files. He was told to take care of business and he was dead set upon doing just that. "I guess I will see you both tomorrow," he smiled looking at the pictures of Cassandra and Seth.

Four

"Glad to see you looking better," said Anya as she saw Eric walking toward the bus stop with Carl and Tabitha. She had been waiting with Susan for the rest of her friends.

"I'm glad that I feel well," Eric answered as Susan gave him a hug and looked at him worried. "I'm fine," he answered smiling at her. "I promise."

Susan nodded and turned to greet Carl. Anya's eyes went to Tabitha who shook her head. Anya understood that she hadn't been able to find anything relating to why Eric had become ill.

"So, we are meeting today for the Halloween party thing?" Susan asked Tabitha with a smile.

"Yes," she answered. "I have also asked other kids to come as well. I'm really excited about the whole thing. I hope we can manage it before the weekend."

"You will," answered Carl, and before Susan could say her words of encouragement, Anya tuned out. She wasn't interested in any part of the conversation. *'Why isn't the bus here yet?'* She looked at Eric. He looked fine talking to the rest of their friends about the party.

A minute later the bus arrived and the teenagers got inside. Anya made her way to her usual seat and so did the rest of her friends.

"I had a creepy feeling last night. It was as if someone was watching me and…"

Susan's words caught Anya's attention as the bus began to move. "You what?" she asked.

"I was just telling Tabitha about last night," said Susan. "Mom told me to take the trash out and I had this strange feeling that someone was watching me from across the road."

"The same thing happened to me as well," said Tabitha, and all of the friends listened. "I went to the kitchen to get a glass of water and noticed some movement in the row of hedges outside of the kitchen window."

"Maybe you were imagining stuff," said Carl. "We've been through a lot lately."

"I don't know," said Anya. "I was talking to Seth on the phone last night when I noticed yellow eyes looking back at me from underneath the bushes outside of my window. It was just for a split second and I thought I was imagining things."

"This is troubling," said Eric seriously as the bus stopped and more students got inside. "Anya said she saw yellow eyes looking at her," he continued. "What about you?" he asked Tabitha and Susan.

"I didn't see anything," answered Susan. "I just had a feeling. I could feel some sort of presence from across the road."

"I saw the hedges move a little," said Tabitha. "No yellow eyes for me or anything. I kept watching them but they remained still after that."

"If we hadn't gone through all of those things, I would have said that we should ignore this," said Eric as he pushed his glasses up on his nose. "But knowing what we know now about this town, we need to be careful."

"I can stay over at your place," said Carl as he smiled at Tabitha. "Be your bodyguard for the night."

"That's so sweet of you," said Tabitha as she rolled her eyes at him with a smile. "But I think I can manage myself."

Anya rolled her eyes at both of them and was glad when the bus stopped and Seth climbed in. He smiled at her and walked toward his friends. "How are you feeling, Eric?" he asked as he sat down putting an arm around Anya. "Sorry I couldn't come by your place yesterday."

"I'm well," answered Eric. "No problem."

"So, what have you all been talking about?" Seth asked with a smile. "Anything creepy happening in Colville?" He moved his fingers in front of Anya's face and made a wailing sound like a ghost.

"And I'm going to regret asking the question," he added quickly as the friends began to tell him what the girls had experienced last night.

***

"You think we can do all of the stuff before the weekend?" asked Tabitha as she looked around the basketball court which she had to make ready for the Halloween party.

"I think we can," Susan said joyfully as she took out some water paint bottles from the bag she had borrowed from their art teacher, Miss Willow. "We just have to start."

Anya rolled her eyes as she sat down on the bleachers. *'Things I have to do for my friends,'* she thought, watching Tabitha and Susan taking out things from some bags. She hoped Cassandra would join them soon, or else she would have to get up and lend a helping hand.

"I think we should do a graveyard theme," said Susan as she placed black cardboards on the floor. "That way we can do gravestones, cobwebs, and stuff like that."

"Sounds nice," Tabitha smiled. "I was thinking of a haunted house kind of thing, but a graveyard sounds nicer. We can do a scary sky with a full moon."

"What do you think?" Susan asked Anya.

"Do whatever you guys are comfortable with," she answered. "You only have four days to do it."

"We can manage," said Tabitha. "I've asked some kids from the arts department to come over as well. They will help speed things up when they arrive in a few minutes."

"That settles it," Anya stretched her arms and yawned as she got up. "My work is done," she added walking down the bleachers and toward the exit.

"You are leaving early," said Cassandra as she walked in front of Anya who was about to leave.

"You're here!" came Susan's excited voice. "Come over here and we can talk about the theme we are going with."

Anya smiled at Cassandra. "I guess you should go and help them. I'm not good with art and stuff."

Cassandra smiled back and adjusted her hood. She knew Anya wasn't one to stick around and help with such things. "See you later," Cassandra added, but before Anya could walk away, they both felt something strange. Anya and Cassandra couldn't explain what they were feeling. It was as if everything around them had stopped, but then the feeling disappeared. Anya didn't say anything and walked out of the court while Cassandra went to help her friends.

"That was strange," Anya said to herself as she continued to walk. She shook her head. It was if she was forgetting something about Cassandra…something important. Ever since she had saved Cassandra from the swamp, she had felt strange. The only thing she remembered was that she fell into the swamp, had tried to save Cassandra, blacked out, and Eric saved them both.

'But there's something missing,' she thought. She felt as if she had met someone…but who? And how was such an encounter possible?

"Earth to Anya," said Seth for the second time and placed his arms on her shoulders. "Are you feeling okay?"

"Huh!" Anya shook her head and smiled at Seth. *'I need to stop blanking out like this.'*

"I'm fine," she added. "I was just thinking about stuff. What are you up to?"

"I was going to go and check on the girls in the court," answered Seth. "See if they needed any help."

"You're so thoughtful," Anya smiled at him. "You can go if you want. Cassandra is already there and Tabitha asked some kids from art class to come and help as well."

"I guess they'll manage," said Seth as he gently caressed Anya's shoulders. "I might as well hang out with my girl, if she's not too busy?"

He leaned forward to kiss Anya when she noticed something. "Wait!" she said looking behind Seth.

"What?" he asked. "Are you sure you are okay?"

Anya didn't say anything. She walked past Seth and ran toward Eric on the stairs. He was near the end of the stairs but he seemed to have stopped and his entire body was swaying. The rest of the students didn't seem to notice anything. It didn't surprise Anya. When it came to Eric, he was quite undetectable in school. "Eric?" she asked worried as Seth ran with her.

Eric didn't say anything. The book he was holding fell to the ground and then his body went limp.

"I've got you, dude," said Seth as he caught hold of Eric's body. "Damn, he's heavy and he's burning!"

The rest of the students stopped to look at Seth who was trying to keep hold of Eric's limp body and Anya who was feeling his forehead.

"Nothing to see here, people," came Carl's voice as he ran to help his friends at the bottom of the stairs. "Get a move on!"

"How is he?" he added giving Seth a helping hand. "How did it happen?"

"I don't know," answered Anya as she picked up the book Eric had dropped. "I saw him walking down the stairs and then his body went limp and he fell. We need to take him to the school's nurse."

"I…I'm fine," said Eric. He had regained consciousness and didn't like the fact that he was being dragged toward the nurse's office by Carl and Seth under his arms.

"No, you are not fine," said Anya, trying to keep her voice calm as Eric made Carl and Seth let him go. "You almost fell down the stairs."

"You should go and see the nurse," said Carl.

"And what will she say?" asked Eric as he adjusted his glasses. "Is she an expert on werewolves all of a sudden?"

"We just want to make sure," said Anya. "It's the same thing that happened yesterday when we were at your house. You were unconscious and then you got up and felt okay."

"I appreciate all of you trying to help me," said Eric looking at his friends. Anya recognized the tone. She knew he wasn't going to listen to them now. "But whatever's wrong with me, I don't think any school nurse has the answer."

He took back his mathematics book from Anya. "I have a class to get to," he said and walked away.

"He sounded annoyed," said Seth.

"He was kind of like that yesterday as well," answered Carl. "He even cancelled a doctor's appointment that Tabitha had set up."

"But he does have a point," said Seth. "If he's feeling this way because of his werewolf side, then I doubt a conventional doctor will be of any help."

"Tabitha has been trying to figure out what's wrong with him," said Anya. She was still worrying about Eric.

“Speaking of Tab,” said Carl. “Is she still on the basketball court?”

“Yes,” answered Anya, rolling her eyes at him. “She’s with Susan and Cassandra and probably some art kids by now.”

“See you later then,” said Carl, and he walked toward where the girls were planning for the Halloween party.

“So?” asked Seth, and he turned to Anya with a smile. “Where were we?”

***

“Carl told us about Eric,” said Susan as the girls exited the high school which was almost empty by now.

The friends had stayed late in order to make sure everything would be done before the weekend. Anya had gone to look at the progress and was quite impressed. Tabitha knew what she wanted the students to do. The five students from art class had already cut out and painted the gravestones they would be placing all around the court. Susan and Tabitha had been working on cutting out cardboard bats and attaching strings to them. Cassandra was halfway through creating a huge cobweb out of white rope. Anya didn’t know Cassandra was good at arts and crafts. She stayed there for a few minutes and then Tabitha decided to call it a day.

“Yes,” answered Anya. “Seth caught him when he fell from the stairs. He didn’t let us take him to the nurse, and he walked away to class. Have any of you seen him?”

“No,” answered Tabitha. “I met Carl a few minutes ago and he said something about Eric going home early.”

“So maybe he did,” said Cassandra as she walked with them. “Tabitha told me why Eric might not be feeling well. I met him this morning and he looked okay. He didn’t want to talk about it, though.”

Anya could sense the worry in Cassandra’s voice as they reached the bus waiting for them outside. Carl was standing there talking to Seth who was leaning against his friend’s bicycle.

“See you tomorrow,” said Seth as he kissed Anya. She nodded and smiled at him as the rest of the friends got on the bus.

“Bye everyone,” Susan waved at Cassandra and Seth as the bus drove away.

There was a moment of silence as the two teenagers watched the bus disappear around the corner. "So?" Seth asked getting on his bicycle. "You want me to drop you off?"

Cassandra looked at the bicycle, trying to make up her mind. "Nope," she answered finally. "I'll pass. Thanks anyway."

"You sure?" Seth asked again. "It won't be any trouble for me."

"I'm sure," Cassandra smiled at him and adjusted her hood. "You go on. I'll take the bus."

"Okay," said Seth with a nod, and he peddled away from the girl.

Cassandra felt the cold air around her face. *'Not with the cold air again,'* she thought as she waited for the bus to come. She was glad that Seth didn't wait with her until the bus came. She wasn't in the mood for more awkward silences. She sat down on a bench and watched some cars pass by her. Her eyes went from the road to a row of bushes across the street. The wind was making the leaves rustle but something didn't feel right to her. The way that one of the bushes was moving made it appear as if something was inside of it.

Cassandra didn't get up from the bench, but her hands formed into fists and her body tensed. Her eyes kept looking at the bush, and before she could be certain that she saw red glowing eyes looking back at her, the bus stopped in front of her.

***

"Okay, that does it!" complained the blonde haired woman as she dropped onto the couch pretending to be exhausted. She never became exhausted but sometimes she felt like faking it. However, she wasn't pretending to not be annoyed. "Looking at those damn kids is such a waste of time!"

The tall man didn't say anything and kept shuffling his deck of cards. It wasn't the first time he had seen his partner in such a mood. He knew she was the one who wanted to do things and not sit around waiting for orders.

"Are you even listening to me?" she yelled from across the room. "It's not like I'm talking to myself, you know?"

"I know," the man answered calmly.

"That weird hooded girl didn't notice me either," she continued. "I had to move the bush again and show her the eyes, and even then she couldn't figure out what was happening. Tell me you made some progress. Tell me that at least one of them has some sort of skill."

The man didn't answer. He had been following a boy with brown hair and sea green eyes since he left for his home on his bicycle. The teenager didn't notice a black car following him. Either the man's skills were too good or the boy was *'too normal'*. He knew there was a reason a vampire had come to Colville and the teenagers found themselves experiencing the supernatural events that recently occurred, but what?

"If you ask me, I say that these kids survived due to dumb luck," said the woman. "Not one of them is anything special. And those two boys give a bad name to werewolves everywhere."

She got up from the couch and walked toward the man. She sat down in front of him at the table. "Tell me that we can go on to the fun stuff?" she asked, making pleading eyes at him. "Tell me that I get to kill."

Before the man could answer, his cellphone rang. He took it out from his pocket and read the text he received. He looked at the woman and gave her a smile. "You'll be very happy to hear this."

Five

"Good to see that people are getting into the Halloween spirit," smiled Tabitha as the friends stepped out of the bus. The teenager looked at the jack-o-lanterns that were placed outside of nearby houses.

"The town always gets into the spirit," Carl said with a smile as he looked at her. "Get ready for your first Halloween here, Tab."

Anya rolled her eyes at the two teenagers. They had more important things to deal with than talk about Halloween. The residents of Colville always enjoyed the scary holiday. To Anya it felt ironic that the town that was so enthusiastic about the night ghosts and demons roamed the realm of the living had no idea what she and her friends had gone through.

"Weren't we all supposed to be going somewhere?" asked Susan. She sounded impatient to Anya. She knew that Susan wanted to go and check up on Eric.

The friends nodded and began walking toward his house. "You don't think he'll be angry at us?" asked Susan as they walked.

'There she goes again,' thought Anya. Susan had been hurting her ears the entire way in the bus, talking about how they should definitely go and make sure Eric was well and then wondering if that would be the right thing to do.

"It'll be okay," said Tabitha. "He's our friend and we should see how he is, whether he likes it or not."

"He isn't answering his phone," said Carl as he tried calling Eric for the hundredth time.

"Why haven't we been able to figure out what's wrong with him?" asked Susan.

"I have been going through a lot of books," said Tabitha. "I've been trying, but there isn't anything that can tell me how a werewolf can get ill or be the way that Eric is right now."

"We'll figure something out," said Carl as he placed a comforting hand on Tabitha's shoulder.

Tabitha gave a nod and the friends remained silent as they walked. There were a lot of things that were going through Anya's mind. She wanted to know what was wrong with Eric and how she could help him. She was also wondering about the encounters the girls had last night. *'Is someone following us?'* she thought.

"Well, the door's open," said Susan as she pushed the handle. "Wait! It won't budge!"

Susan pushed against the door but it wouldn't open all the way. It was as if something was blocking it. Anya looked inside of the house from behind Susan. It was dark. "Eric?" she asked worried.

"Let me try," said Carl, and the girls stepped back. He grabbed the handle and gave the door a push. "Yes, something is in front of it. Maybe it's a couch."

"Why would he put something against the door?" asked Tabitha.

"What if someone tried to hurt him?" asked Susan. "What if he or she put the table in front of the door?"

"Stop worrying," Carl said seriously. "He's going to be fine," he added and pushed against the door. They heard the table being pushed away and the door opened for the friends to step inside.

"I'm so done with him and keeping the lights off!" said Anya as she stepped into the house. She tried turning on the lights but they wouldn't work. "Is the power out?"

Carl stepped in front of Anya and told the girls to keep quiet. Tabitha took out a flashlight from her bag as Susan took a step closer to Anya.

"What is it?" whispered Anya as she noticed Carl looking around the room. Tabitha walked toward the group and aimed her flashlight in front of them. The room was a mess. Broken plates were on the floor, the furniture was overturned, and the couch cushions were ripped. *'Claws?'* thought Anya as she noticed the ripped cushions.

"Someone broke in?" asked Anya as she took in the condition of the room. Her heart began to beat faster. "Carl, can you sense him?"

Carl nodded at her but remained silent. She felt his body tense up. "Carl what's wrong?" she whispered. She felt Susan grab her arm.

"I can smell someone," he answered, keeping his voice low. "The entire room smells of them."

"Them?" asked Tabitha.

"Yes, them," Carl answered. "I don't know. The scent kind of feels the same but also not. It feels like it's from the same person, but it's also as if it's different people who smell the same."

"I don't think it was a person who did this," said Anya as she noticed Carl walking toward the stairs.

Anya took a deep breath and began to follow him. Tabitha and Susan were behind her. Tabitha was aiming the flashlight in front of Anya so she could see where to step.

"Do you think they are still here?" asked Susan, keeping her voice low.

Carl stopped and the girls stopped as well. He turned to face them and Anya could see his eyes glowing. Anya was surprised to see that his eye color hadn't changed. She was expecting glowing red or yellow werewolf eyes. "I feel that they are still here," he told the girls. "I don't think you should follow me up the stairs."

"What do you propose we do?" asked Anya. She was trying hard to keep her voice down. She knew she didn't have werewolf powers like Carl or Eric but if he thought she wasn't going to do anything to help her friend, he could think again.

"I don't know who or what is also in this house right now," said Carl as he looked directly at Anya. "But I don't want any of you getting hurt." He looked at Tabitha for support.

"None of us will get hurt," said Anya before Tabitha could answer. She knew that Tabitha would side with Carl and suggest they all stay back while he checked upstairs. "If there was anyone in the house, they would have attacked us by now."

Carl looked at her for a second and Anya looked back. She wasn't going to back down for any reason. Carl sighed and began walking up the stairs. *'I hope I'm right about us being the only ones here,'* she thought as she started walking up the stairs as well.

She felt that Susan and Tabitha were hesitant to follow, but a second later she could hear them behind her.

The friends reached Eric's room and stopped. Carl gave them a reassuring nod and opened the door. Eric's room was a mess. His bed sheet was torn and all of his books were scattered around the room. In the corner the friends saw a huge blanket and it seemed to be moving. Without waiting, Carl ran toward the blanket and pulled it way.

"Eric!" exclaimed Anya as she saw the whimpering boy in the corner and hurried toward him.

Carl didn't know what to say as he saw his friend cowering in fear. His eyes were closed and tears were running down his face.

"Eric?" asked Anya as she sat down and placed her hand on his shoulder. "Eric, what happened to you?"

The boy didn't answer and kept whimpering. Anya looked up at her friends. Carl was standing near her, the blanket still in his hand. Tabitha looked worried and Susan was grabbing her arm.

"He's burning up too," said Anya as she felt the heat from his body, and before the friends could do anything, the power came back. The lights in the room turned on and they could all see the real damage around them.

"I'll…I'll go and get some cold water," said Susan and she ran out of the room.

"I'll go and help her," said Tabitha, and she ran behind her.

Carl dropped the blanket on the ground and sat down to look at his friend. Eric's eyes were still closed. "I don't know what to do," said Anya as she tried to comfort her friend. "Eric, it's going to okay. You are safe now."

"Who's doing all of this?" Anya asked Carl.

"I don't know, Anya," he answered as he placed a hand on Eric's shoulder. "I don't know."

He came closer to Eric. "Dude, you need to open your eyes."

"I don't think he's listening to us," said Anya. "Can you help me put him on the bed?"

Carl nodded and stood up with Anya. She walked toward the bed and pushed away the torn books and the ripped sheet. Carl helped Eric onto his feet and placed him on the bed. Eric was still crying silently. Anya took off his glasses and placed them on the side table. Eric seemed to have fallen asleep.

"He needs a doctor," said Susan as she came back into the room holding a bowl of cold water and some towels. "The kitchen is a mess too."

Anya nodded as she took the bowl from Susan and dipped a towel into it. She was in the same position yesterday and she wasn't happy about it.

"It could have been Eric who did all of this damage himself," said Tabitha as she walked into the room. "But Carl saying that he can smell people in here doesn't make that an option anymore."

Anya didn't say anything. *'Only Tabitha could think that Eric could do this to himself.'*

"It's not as if I'm suspicious of him," said Tabitha. "It's just that I've read that werewolves go into a rampage from time to time. It could be triggered by stress or something similar. Everything looks as if it has been ripped apart by claws."

"I could go into a rampage because of stress?" asked Carl. He seemed to be more relaxed now that Eric was sleeping and his friends were out of the danger he was expecting.

"There's a possibility," answered Tabitha as she watched Anya place a wet towel on Eric's forehead.

"But Eric didn't go on a rampage," said Susan as she stood near the bed. "Someone else was here."

"But who?" asked Tabitha. "Who would come into his house, turn things upside down, and make him this scared? And why would it have claws?"

"Maybe it's the same thing that was looking at us last night," said Anya as she changed the towel on Eric's forehead.

"Could be a possibility," said Tabitha as she sat down near Susan on the side of the bed.

Carl was leaning against a wall but he still felt a bit tensed. He knew they weren't in danger anymore but the scent was still in the room. He could still sense the presence of whoever had broken into Eric's house. He couldn't make up his mind. He knew the scent was from one person but it still felt as if there had been at least four people, or whatever they were, inside of the house.

"What do we do about Eric?" asked Susan as she looked at his sleeping face. "Can't we get a doctor to look at him?"

"Werewolves can't get sick from anything that can make a human or even a wolf ill," answered Tabitha. "I don't think a traditional doctor can help him."

"What about the doctor you wanted him to meet yesterday before he cancelled the appointment?" asked Anya. She didn't look at Tabitha. Even she wasn't sure why the thought had come into her mind.

"That was before I was certain that Eric couldn't be suffering from any human related ailment," answered Tabitha matter-of-factly.

"Can we please not start an argument," said Susan before Anya could answer back. "We need to be thinking of Eric right now."

Anya turned her attention back to Eric. Tabitha didn't say anything and there was an awkward silence in the room.

***

"Carl and Tabitha are staying with him," said Anya as she talked to Seth on the phone. She was in her room telling him what had happened.

"And no clue who tore up his house?" asked Seth.

"There's a possibility they are the same people who were watching us last night," answered Anya. "But even if it was them, it doesn't take us any closer to knowing who they are or *what* they are."

"You need to be careful."

"I know," smiled Anya. She liked it when Seth worried about her. She walked toward the window in her room. "What about you?" she asked as she looked outside and toward the bushes. There were no eyes looking back at her this time.

"If you are asking if I was followed," said Seth. "Then the answer is no. I don't seem to have a secret admirer after me."

"Do you want a secret admirer?" asked Anya as she walked away from the window and sat down on her bed.

"It wouldn't hurt to have one," he answered with a smile. "Just in case things don't work out with the girl I'm already with."

"Do you want me to hurt you?" Anya laughed.

"Now that would be something I can look forward to," Seth said in a seductive voice.

"You're too much," said Anya. "Anyway, I've got to go before Mom takes the phone away from me. She doesn't want me to be around bad company."

"And I'm bad company?" asked Seth with a laugh. "My life was quite normal before I met you."

"And you're saying that as if it's a bad thing," said Anya.

"You know what I mean," said Seth. "Keep me updated. See you tomorrow."

The two said their goodbyes and Anya hung up. She placed the phone onto her bed and stretched her arms over her head. Carl and Tabitha hadn't called her yet. "Which means that Eric is still sleeping," she said to herself. She wondered how she could help her friend. She didn't have a ton of books like Tabitha about the supernatural and from what Tabitha had told her, Tom didn't have any book that could help either.

"It seems that you're helpless this time," Anya said to herself as she got off of the bed. *'And then there's the matter of who or what broke into Eric's house,'* she thought to herself. The friends had spent some time to make sure nothing had been stolen. But they couldn't be sure because they had no idea what was and wasn't supposed to be in Eric's house.

"We can't seem to catch a break," she said as she looked out of her window. Deep down she couldn't help but feel responsible for what was happening to her friend. She could still remember what David had said about her being special and having a *gift*.

Her eyes went toward the house next to hers, the house in which David had lived when he came to town. She tried to look inside of the house but everything was dark. She remembered looking at David when he used to be there. It didn't feel quite that long ago to her when she was talking to Susan on the phone and spied on David as he walked into his room and shined a flashlight right in her eyes.

'That's because it hasn't been that long,' she thought and shook her head. It was weird to realize what she and her friends had experienced in such a short amount of time. Whenever she thought it was the last supernatural thing they would face, a new threat would emerge. First David, then the cursed swamp thing that just wouldn't end, and now something was wrong with Eric and none of them had any idea what to do.

'Not to mention all of the things which haven't been answered yet,' she continued her trail of thought. The letter that told her David might be back, how they were able to end the curse of the swamp, and the weird encounter she had when she fell into the swamp and tried to help Cassandra. There was something she wasn't remembering but deep down she could feel that it was something important…something she should remember and soon.

She wanted to stop her mind from thinking. There was just too much going on inside her head. Her attention went back to David's house. No one had moved in after him, and all of his belongings were still inside, things that could have a connection with him being a vampire…with the supernatural.

'Wait!' Anya's mind came to a halt and she kept looking at David's house. She knew that what she was thinking right now was probably crazy but most of the things she had gone through had been crazy. So a little more crazy won't hurt anyone, right?

Six

"You want to do what?" asked Susan, eyes wide, as Anya finished telling her friends about her plan. She had been waiting for all of them to be on the bus.

Before that, they had been talking about Eric while they waited with him at the bus stop. Carl and Tabitha hadn't experienced anything unusual during the night. Eric woke up early in the morning and was surprised to know what had happened. He didn't remember anything and his friends didn't force him to remember, either. They had tried to persuade him to take a day off but he didn't listen. One thing that did come out of the whole incident was that Eric let his guard down around his friends. He realized something was wrong with him and that his friends were just trying to help.

"Why am I not surprised," said Seth as he looked at Anya.

"It's worth a try," said Anya as she tried to persuade the people around her. It made perfect sense in her mind. She would have done it herself but she knew it was better to always have backup when getting ready to face the supernatural or anything related to it. "Tabitha hasn't been able to come up with anything," she added looking at her. Tabitha just nodded. "And Eric isn't feeling any better."

"Are you sure you want to do this?" asked Eric, looking at her. Anya knew he was concerned about her. He understood what she was going through in order to find the willpower to complete the plan.

"I'm sure," answered Anya with determination. *'I don't know why, but I think it will work,'* she thought to herself. She saw Tabitha look at her.

"She does have a point," said Tabitha as she addressed the teenagers. "It was because of David that Carl and Eric got these werewolf powers, so it wouldn't hurt if we went in there and looked around."

"Who knew that looking at my girlfriend's ex-boyfriend's house was going to be on my to-do list today," sighed Seth.

Anya rolled her eyes and smiled at him. "Just get over it already."

She was happy to have thought of a plan to help Eric. They might not find anything, but at least they were doing something. Something was wrong with Eric, and judging by the state that his house was in last night, there seemed to be a new threat in town.

***

"How are you?" asked Cassandra as she sat down beside Eric in the library.

"I'm feeling okay," he answered with a smile and turned the page of the physics book he was reading. He had sensed the hooded girl when she entered the library. He was glad she was talking to him.

"Susan told me what happened last night," she said, giving him a concerned look as she opened a chemistry book in front of her.

Eric didn't answer. He didn't know what to say. He couldn't remember a single thing from last night. All he knew was that he went home early, did some homework, woke up in his bed, and Carl and Tabitha told him what had happened. From what he knew, someone had come in and all but destroyed his house. As for the damages, Eric wasn't worried about them. He could call his parents and everything would be put right. The thing he was worried about the most was the state his friends had found him in. He didn't want to feel so scared ever again.

"Eric?" came Cassandra's voice.

The teenager seemed to have wandered off. "Huh? I'm fine, I'm fine," he answered her with a smile.

"I don't want to ask you anything you might not feel comfortable answering," said Cassandra.

"I understand," said Eric. "Thank you."

There was a silence between the two friends, but it wasn't anything uncomfortable. They just sat there reading their books.

"Have you heard what Anya wants to do?" asked Eric as he finished reading a chapter from his book and readjusted his glasses.

"Yes," she answered with a smile. "I got to know about it a few hours ago when I met Carl and Seth going to the gym."

"What do you think about it?"

"She does have a point," said Cassandra. "It might not be the best idea, but I can understand where she's coming from. Tabitha hasn't been able to find anything, and David was the reason you and Carl turned into werewolves. Who knows, you might find something of importance."

***

"So, who's going and when are we going?" asked Carl as he sat down on one of the bleachers with his friends.

Tabitha, Susan, and some students from art class were busy making things for the Halloween party. The basketball court had begun to look ready for the part. They had already lined the walls with the gravestone cutouts and a teenager was carving out pumpkins to fill in some of the gaps. Tomorrow they would begin hanging the cardboard and rubber bats from the ceiling. Cassandra was supposed to be there in a few minutes and continue making her giant rope cobweb.

"Tabitha and Susan look as if they have a lot of work to do," answered Anya as she watched her friends working.

"It's better to not go late at night," said Seth as he sat down beside her.

"Why?" smiled Anya. "Afraid that it'll be a haunted house?"

Seth smiled back at her. "You know what I mean. It's Colville. It's better to not do anything late at night."

"Not anything?" asked Anya, and she winked at him. Seth smiled and leaned forward to kiss her.

"Can we get back to Carl's question?" asked Eric as he rolled his eyes at the two teenagers.

"Like Seth said," answered Anya, still smiling. "It's better not to go there late at night. The sooner we get it over with the better."

"But I don't think we can keep the group intact if we do that," said Eric. "I have a feeling that Tabitha, Susan, and Cassandra might have to stay late at school to finish things over here."

"From my experiences, breaking up the group is never a good idea," said Seth.

"Without Tab we won't know what to look for inside the house," said Carl as he watched her make a cardboard bat.

"So we wait for her to finish?" asked Anya. "That'll make us quite late." She didn't want to waste any more time. She wanted to go into David's house and search for anything that could help Eric as soon as possible. *'I should have done it myself last night,'* she thought. *'Now we have to wait for Tabitha to be free and...'*

"I guess I can go with you guys now." Tabitha's voice took Anya by surprise. The black haired girl was walking toward her friends sitting on the bleachers, followed by Susan.

"What about your work over here?" asked Carl. The teenagers from art class were still working.

"I think those guys can handle it," answered Tabitha looking back at the working teenagers. "It's not much. We just need to carve out the pumpkins and we'll hang the bats tomorrow."

"And the menu has been decided," said Susan with a smile. "The whole thing is coming together quite well."

"Where's Cassandra, by the way?" she asked. "She was supposed to be here awhile ago."

"She'll be here," said Eric. It wasn't like Cassandra to be late.

Before the friends could continue their talk, a brown haired girl ran onto the basketball court toward them. Anya knew the girl. Her name was Cecelia Sanchez. She was a timid girl and never got into any trouble at school.

"What's wrong, Cecelia?" asked Tabitha looking at the worried girl.

"I just had a conversation with the caterers," she said trying to sound calm. "The order for the menu didn't go through. I called them to make sure everything would be ready in time, but they never got the order."

"How can that happen?" asked Susan, wide-eyed. "I personally made the call. I even have the entire transaction when the payment went through."

"Something must have gone wrong," said Tabitha in a calm voice. "We can make the call again, talk to the right people, and get this sorted out."

"Thank you, Cecelia," she added, smiling at the girl, and she walked away to help her friends from art class.

'Wouldn't that take time?' thought Anya as she rolled her eyes. They were wasting time just because a stupid call to the caterer didn't go through correctly.

"But what about helping Eric?" Susan asked in a worried voice. "I don't want any of us to stay here more than necessary. There's no point in all of us staying here."

"You're right," said Tabitha. "I can stay here with you and make sure…"

"We need you with us," said Carl before she could finish. "We wouldn't know what to look for once we are there."

"He's right," said Susan looking at Tabitha. "You should go with them. I'll stay here and make sure this misunderstanding is solved."

"Someone should stay with you," Anya told Susan. She didn't want any member of the group to be alone, especially after what happened at Eric's. It was better if they at least moved in pairs.

"I'll stay with her," said Carl and he stood up from the bleachers. "After things are over here, we'll both come back to Colville."

Anya was surprised to hear him say that. For her, Carl not going with Tabitha and staying back to make sure that Susan was safe meant a lot.

"That's kind of you, Carl," Susan smiled at the teenaged boy.

"So it's settled then," said Anya, standing up as well. "We're going to David's house."

"But what about Cassie?" asked Susan. "She knows about the supernatural stuff as well. She might be of some help."

"If she shows up," answered Anya. "I've never seen her be late to anything."

"She's here," said Eric as he sniffed the air. "I mean she's on her way here."

Anya never felt comfortable about the fact that Eric and Carl could catch scents. She knew every person smelled different but she never asked them what she smelled like. *'And I'm never going to ask them,'* she thought. *'Seriously, who wants to know what their natural body odor is like?'*

***

"What do you think we'll find there?" Seth asked Anya as the friends rode the bus back to Colville. They had been talking about who could be responsible for the state that Eric's house was in. Now Eric, Cassandra, and Tabitha were talking about what they knew about werewolves.

"I don't know," she answered. "I've only been there once."

"Good thing you are very subtle when it comes to talking about your ex," Seth said in a hurt voice.

"Get over yourself," she said with a laugh. She knew Seth was just joking with her. *'I just hope we do find something in there that can help figure out what's wrong with Eric,'* she thought looking out of the bus. She didn't like Carl and Susan staying away from the group. *'I should have waited for Susan.'*

"I just got a text from Susan," said Tabitha as she addressed the group at large. "She says she'll be free in about an hour. Carl is with her so there's no need to worry about anything."

'I've got to stop thinking.' Anya closed her eyes and rested her head on Seth's shoulder. Her suspicion that Tabitha could read minds was still there. She didn't want it to be. She wanted to trust all of her friends.

"Are you tired?" asked Seth as Anya breathed slowly while resting her head on his shoulder.

"I'm fine," she said. Her head felt heavy. Ever since the swamp incident, she hadn't been feeling well. It wasn't anything serious like Eric. It was more of a feeling, a feeling she couldn't make sense of.

"You guys sure seem to like your Halloween," said Seth as the bus passed the houses.

"It's kind of ironic," said Cassandra looking out of the window as well. Kids were running around having fun. A lot of people were putting the finishing touches to their Halloween preparations. Some of the houses they saw were quite impressive. One of them had a model of scary Santa Claus in the lawn and the owners were trying to figure out the wiring.

The friends got off of the bus and began to walk toward David's house. "Are you doing anything outside of your house?" Cassandra asked Tabitha as they walked.

"I want to," she answered. "But with all of the work I'm doing for the party, I can't make time to decorate my house."

"I don't think it'll matter much," said Seth. "All of us will be spending Halloween at the party anyway."

"Even then you don't have to worry," Anya told Tabitha. "You're new in town. Soon you will find out that people over here like taking things into their own hands."

"What do you mean?" Eric and Tabitha asked together.

"You'll find that out when you go home," Anya smiled. "Let's just say that when people are trying to make the surroundings creepy, they prefer that every house plays a part."

"Are they going to decorate my house for me?" asked Tabitha, her eyes wide.

Anya nodded at her and Eric. It only made sense to know about the town they were in. As far as Anya could remember, the houses that didn't look to be into the Halloween spirit had their decorations done by the neighbors. The memories of people trying to convince her parents to increase the scare factor of the house were still fresh in her mind. She knew it wouldn't be different this time around either. In a few minutes she and her friends would be near her house and they will see what her parents had done to it. Her mother was very excited about the little ghost cut-outs she bought from the mall and she had saved a lot of things in the attic as well.

'Mom!' the thought came into Anya's mind. Her dad would be at work at this time, but her mother would be home and she might be outside decorating the house. *'She would never allow us to break into David's house.'*

"Eric," she said and stopped. They were just a few feet away from her house. "Can you sense where my mom is?"

"What do you mean?" he asked confused as he readjusted his glasses.

"I want you to sense if she'll be coming out anytime soon or if she's near any of the windows," said Anya. "I don't know if you can do that but I want to make sure she doesn't come out and sees us breaking in."

Eric nodded. The friends stood still as they saw Eric concentrate, his eyes were closed and he was taking deep breaths. He tried to ignore the laughing kids and the talking adults around him and he focused on Anya's mother. "She seems to be in the kitchen," he said, not opening his eyes. "She's cooking chicken and talking to someone on the phone."

"That's good enough for me," said Anya as she hurried toward David's house. "Let's go!"

The friends followed Anya as she all but ran toward the house next to hers. "Looks to me that preparations are underway," Seth smiled as he saw pumpkin shaped buckets placed outside of Anya's doorstep.

"That's just the beginning," said Anya. *'But we don't have time for that now.'*

The teenaged girl stood outside on the lawn of the house next to hers, the house that belonged to David, the person who had tried to kill her friends.

"Are you all right?" asked Eric as he stood next to her.

Anya nodded, still looking at the empty house. She took a deep breath and stepped onto the lawn. *'That wasn't bad,'* she thought and didn't stop walking until she stood in front the door, with her friends behind her.

"It's probably locked," said Cassandra.

Eric stepped in front of Anya. He placed his hand on the doorknob and gave it a push. There was a clicking sound and the door creaked open.

"Let's do this," said Anya as she looked at the darkness in front of her.

Seven

"I have no idea why the call didn't go through," said Susan as she walked out of the student affairs office.

Carl shrugged at his blonde friend. He had been waiting outside of the office while she talked on the phone. Susan locked the door behind her and pocketed the key. "Let's go and see what progress has been made," she said with a smile, and the two began walking toward the basketball court.

The school was empty except for them, the teenagers working in the court, and the janitor. Carl couldn't help but feel uneasy. Ever since the incident with Eric's house and the girls saying that they were being watched, Carl had been extra sensitive regarding the protection of his friends.

"I never liked being in school this late," said Susan as the sound of their footsteps echoed in the corridor.

"Who does?" asked Carl. He could hear the other teenagers busy inside of the basketball court and talking amongst themselves.

"It's just creepy," Susan continued. "The empty classrooms, the echoing corridors, the dimmed lights…"

"Susan, you need to stop," smiled Carl. "Don't let things get to your head."

Susan nodded and entered the court. The teenagers had finished making all of the bats that would be hung from the ceiling the next day.

"Did you fix the problem?" asked Cecelia as she saw Susan.

Susan nodded. "It's all right now. Don't know where the misunderstanding came from. The good news is that everything will be prepared on time."

Cecelia let out a sigh of relief. "Good to know, good to know."

"I think we should all call it a day," Susan addressed the teenagers at large. "We'll get to this tomorrow as soon as we can and if everything goes fine, this place will look amazing for the party."

The teenagers said their goodbyes to Susan and started to walk out of the court. Carl knew some of them by face. He hadn't properly met any of them, but he was quite certain that all of them knew him.

"We should go too," said Susan. She and Carl were the only ones there.

"How are Tab and the others doing?" asked Carl as Susan turned off some of the lights.

"I messaged her before I began talking to the catering manager," she answered. "They were in the bus at that time."

"Don't worry," she added with a smile as the two walked out of the court. "All of them can take care of each other if they can't take care of themselves."

"I just hope they find something helpful," said Carl.

Susan smiled at him. "They will." She knew that Carl was worried about Eric. She was worried about him too. They hadn't known him for long but when you stick together through life-threatening experiences, you become quite close.

"I wasn't really surprised that Anya came up with such a plan," said Susan as they walked toward the school's exit. "Come to think of it, she did have a point. It was because of David that you and Eric got your powers…"

Carl wasn't paying attention to her. He could hear the teenagers he had seen on in the basketball court walking toward the cycle stands. If he guessed correctly, there were five of them. He could smell them as well. He could also make out the scent of the janitor who was on the floor above them, along with something strong. *'Probably cleaning the floor.'*

But there was something else in the school, a scent he would catch for a few seconds and then it would disappear. It reminded him of the night they were all at Eric's.

Susan looked at Carl. She knew he hadn't been listening to her. His face looked as if he was concentrating. "Are you all right?" she asked, placing a hand on his shoulder. His entire body tensed up. "Carl?"

"We need to go," he answered, grabbing Susan by the arm and hurrying toward the high school's exit.

"Why?" she asked, trying to maintain her balance as he pulled her. "What's wrong? Are we in danger?"

***

"Let me try the lights," said Tabitha. Her hands felt the wall on her left. She found the switchboard and turned the lights on.

David's house was the same as Anya had remembered, or was it? She had been there once when she delivered a package the mailman accidently put in her mailbox. At that time she didn't look around the room much. She was busy looking into David's blue eyes.

"He seems rich," said Seth, impressed by the furniture in the room they were in. Anya looked around as well. The couches, tables, and carpet looked quite expensive. *'So, vampires have a lot of money, good for them,'* she thought.

"What are we looking for?" asked Cassandra as she closed the front door behind her.

"Anything that might look helpful," answered Tabitha as she walked toward some books placed on a counter. "It can be a book, a note, anything."

Anya noticed Eric looking at some bottles placed in a cupboard toward the right side of the room, and she walked closer to him. *'I once saw him drink those.'*

"What is that?" she asked Eric who was looking at them closely.

"I'm not sure," he answered, pushing his glasses up on his nose. "They smell as if they're full of blood and something else."

"Orange juice?" asked Seth as he joined the two.

"Who knows," Anya rolled her eyes at him. "Come on, we have to work to do," she added as she grabbed him by the arm and pulled him away from the bottles.

"Nothing in these," said Tabitha as she finished looking through the books in front of her. "These are English novels."

"So, he liked to read," Seth teased Anya.

She gave him a gentle push. "I don't think we'll find anything here," she said. "We need to check his bedroom."

"And now we're going into his bedroom?"

"Give it a rest," Anya smiled at Seth. "It's getting tiresome now."

"There are still two more rooms to check down here," said Cassandra. "I'll check those with Eric, along with the kitchen."

"I'll go upstairs with Anya and Seth," said Tabitha and she walked toward the stairs.

"The house looks very nice considering it belonged to a vampire," said Seth as the three of them climbed the stairs.

"What were you expecting?" asked Anya. "Haven't you seen how fancy all of those vampires are in films?"

Seth nodded at her. "Do you think we'll find a coffin?"

"I doubt it," said Tabitha before Anya could answer. "I don't think he lived here much."

"What do you mean?" asked Seth as Tabitha opened the first door. The room had beautiful chairs and a table in it. There was also a huge painting of mountains hanging from the wall.

"I think Anya would remember," said Tabitha as she turned to look at her.

"Uh…" Anya tried to come up with an answer. *'What am I supposed to remember?'*

Tabitha turned to Seth. "The places where magical creatures lives have a specific glow."

"What kind of glow?" asked Seth.

Anya remembered what Tabitha was talking about. The cave they were in when everything started had a green glow. The house they were in wasn't glowing. "So he lived in the cave?" asked Anya as Tabitha walked toward the next room.

"Your ex-boyfriend was a caveman?" asked Seth as he laughed.

"A rich caveman, mind you," answered Anya seriously.

"Yes," said Tabitha as she addressed Anya's question. "There's a high possibility that he spent most of his time in the cave. This house was more of a cover."

Tabitha opened the door of the next room. It was David's bedroom. Anya recognized the mirror in the corner, the mirror that didn't show David's reflection when he passed it. *'But when I took out the mirror to see his reflection, I saw it,'* thought Anya. The teenaged girl walked into David's room and toward the mirror. It had a beautiful golden frame with little gold leaves engraved on it. Anya walked in front of it and was surprised to see no reflection. It didn't make sense to her. She could clearly see the reflection of the bed and the rest of room, but she couldn't see herself or her friends inside of it.

"That's a weird mirror," said Seth as he looked at it. "If you can call it a mirror."

"It's a mirror," answered Tabitha as she joined her friends. All three of them were standing in front of it but there was no reflection. The room appeared person-less in the mirror.

"I've read about these," Tabitha continued as she looked at it closely with a smile on her face.

"What does it do?" asked Anya. Her eyes went to Tabitha who was looking too interested in the mirror than normal.

"People used it for communication," answered Tabitha, still not looking away from the mirror. "If used correctly, one can transcend the physical plane into the spiritual world."

"Oookkaayy," said Anya. She wasn't interested in communicating with any spirits, and the way Tabitha was looking at the mirror was making her feel uncomfortable. "We should get back to finding something that can help Eric."

"Yes," coughed Tabitha, standing upright and shaking her head. "Yes, Eric," she added and walked out of the room.

"What was that all about?" asked Seth as he watched her leave the room.

"I'm not sure," answered Anya as she grabbed his hand and walked out of the room as well. She looked at the mirror one more time and closed the door behind her.

"I think I might have found something," came Tabitha's voice from the third and last room on the floor.

Anya and Seth hurried toward her and saw her standing in front of a huge chest. The room had two cupboards full of books as well.

Seth whistled as he looked around. "His own personal library."

"Most of the books are related to the supernatural," said Tabitha. "I already have some of the ones that are. However, I'm interested in this huge chest over here."

Anya looked at it. It was a black chest with a big metallic lock shaped into a skull with two long fangs. Anya rolled her eyes at it. *'Of course it had to be a skull.'*

The friends heard footsteps outside. Cassandra and Eric were on their way to the room. "Eric heard you," said Cassandra as she entered the room. "We didn't find anything of use downstairs."

"This chest looks interesting," Tabitha pointed at the black chest. "But it's locked."

Eric bent down and looked closely at the chest. He tried pulling it open but was unsuccessful. "I can't get it to open."

"I don't think anyone can," said Tabitha as she and Cassandra looked at the lock closely.

"It's probably locked by magic," said Cassandra.

'Oh great, more magic,' thought Anya as she rolled her eyes. *'Didn't we have enough of that with the swamp zombies?'*

Seth raised his arm and pointed at the chest. "Open sesame!" he bellowed. "There," he added, trying not to laugh at the look his friends were giving him. "It's not locked by magic. I tried."

"Thank you, sorcerer supreme," said Anya. "This isn't the time to play around. That chest could have something that can help Eric."

"I was just trying to lighten the mood," said Seth as he lifted his arms in front of him in defense.

"He might be right," said Cassandra before Anya could go into attack mode. Anya turned to look at her. She was looking at the lock. "Here," said Cassandra, pointing at the metallic fangs. "Below the fangs are two little holes that seem to disappear into the chest."

The friends looked at what she was pointing at. "What does it mean?" asked Seth.

"We might have to give it blood," answered Tabitha in a calm voice. "Such a chest would open for the owner but for someone else it needs a payment, an offering."

"I'll do it," said Eric as he pulled up his sleeve.

"It won't work," said Anya, and the teenagers looked at her with questioning looks. She didn't know where the thought had come from. She didn't answer and walked toward the chest. She bent down and extended her arm.

"Are you sure about this?" asked Seth sounding worried.

Anya nodded. She just knew her blood would do the trick. She extended her arm and placed her wrist under the metallic fangs. Suddenly the fangs extended and pricked Anya. "Ouch!" she said, pulling her arm away. The blood from the fangs dripped and fell into the holes below. There was a clicking sound and the chest opened.

"Are you all right?" asked Seth as he looked at Anya's wrist in his hand. The place where the fangs had pricked her had healed.

"I'm fine," she nodded and smiled at him.

Tabitha and Cassandra were already looking inside of the chest. "These are some very old books," said Tabitha as she took two of them out. "I haven't seen them before in my life."

"Let's just hope they have something that can help Eric," said Anya. She looked at Eric. He was looking toward the window in the room. "Eric?" she asked.

"Something's wrong," he answered, and before Anya could ask anything further, he fainted.

Eight

"Carl, why aren't you saying anything?" asked Susan. She could feel her heart racing. "You need to tell me what's wrong."

"I'm not sure," he answered, still pulling her toward the school's exit. And then they both heard it...a howl...a real wolf howl!

"What the hell was that?" asked Susan. She could feel the strength slip away from her legs. The wolf howl made her entire body shiver.

Carl stopped and pulled Susan behind him as he looked back toward the corridor they came from. *'Concentrate, Carl, Concentrate!'* he said to himself. The rest of the teenagers from art class seemed to have gone away. The janitor was still cleaning the top floors and he seemed oblivious to the howl. *'Maybe he's listening to music.'*

"Maybe it was just some stray wolf," said Susan as she tightly grabbed Carl's arm and looked behind her. She didn't know when the bus would arrive but she hoped it would come soon. "Or maybe it was a dog. Dogs howl, right?"

"That wasn't a dog," answered Carl. His eyes were moving in all directions ready to focus on anything that looked suspicious. He didn't know what he was up against but the wolf inside of him was warning him that whatever it was, it was powerful and dangerous. If he had been alone he would have made a run for it, but he had to make sure that Susan was safe. *'Where is that damned bus when you need it!'*

They both heard movement come from behind some nearby trees. Susan held her breath as they both looked at the trees some feet away from them. She felt Carl's body tense and his hands formed into fists ready for a fight. They saw red glowing eyes look at them from behind the trees. It was a wolf, but it wasn't like the one the teenagers had seen on TV or read about in books. It was at least two times bigger and it bared its teeth at them. Susan could clearly see the sharp white fangs and the long claws. The rest of its body was covered in dark black fur. *'That's the thing that destroyed Eric's house and made him scared?'* she thought, not taking her eyes off of the animal. Its eyes were cutting into Susan's soul. She tried to remain calm but she couldn't keep her body from shaking. There was no one she could call for help.

"When I give the word, you need to run," Carl told her, not taking his eyes off of the black wolf. The animal was looking back at him as if daring him to make a move.

"What…what about you?" she asked with a shaking voice. She couldn't even call the rest of her friends. They were all in Colville going through David's house. None of them were aware of the danger she and Carl were in.

"I'll catch up," he said. Susan knew he was trying to remain calm because of her.

The wolf took a step toward the teenagers. Drool dropped from its fangs and onto the ground. It was aching for a fight…a chance to bite into delicate human flesh and break fragile bones. The blonde human girl looked tasty, but the wolf's primary target was the boy. Before it could do anything, it heard the bus come toward the school.

"Is it going back?" asked Susan as she watched the wolf take a step back toward the trees.

Carl nodded. He knew the wolf must have heard the bus coming. The wolf gave another howl and ran back into the trees.

"Thank goodness," Susan felt the tension escape her body. Carl didn't take his eyes away from the trees. The wolf was still there, looking at them as the bus stopped outside of the high school.

***

"Things are bad," said Anya as she moved the curtains a bit to look outside of the window.

They were all in David's bedroom. Eric was lying on the bed with his eyes closed. Seth and Anya had carried him there when he fainted. Cassandra and Tabitha were looking through some books they had taken from the black chest. Seth was leaning against the wall. Susan was sitting on the bed still trying to calm down after what she and Carl had seen in school.

"Things are very bad," said Carl, letting out a sigh as he moved his hand through his brown curly hair while sitting near the door. He and Susan ran to their friends when they reached Colville and had told them everything.

"There's no sign of any big wolf outside," said Anya as she looked out of the window. People were busy decorating their houses and kids were playing. Her mother was placing plastic pumpkins on the lawn. She told her mother that she was at Susan's making plans for the Halloween party.

"Don't remind me," said Susan as she sat down on the bed and brought her knees toward her chest.

"I'm sorry," Anya turned to face her friend. Susan was a mess when she came here. She would be too if she had a staring contest with a big scary wolf and had nowhere to run.

"Was it really that big?" asked Seth. "You said it was as big as a small car."

"I know what I saw," said Susan, sounding serious. "It was as big as a car and it just stood there looking at me and Carl."

"I believe you," said Seth as Anya walked toward her friend to comfort her. "I just want to know what it means."

"It means that we have a werewolf to deal with," said Cassandra, and the teenagers looked at her. She was sitting on the floor and reading from a piece of parchment.

'Wait! What?' Anya couldn't bring herself to say it out loud. She remembered the night that Carl and Eric had turned into werewolves and attacked her. She remembered how scared she was for her life and how feral and vicious the two boys were…the red eyes, the claws, the fangs…half man, half wolf.

"It's here," said Cassandra, and she flattened the parchment and began reading. Tabitha put down the book she was reading and turned her attention toward the hooded girl.

"Werewolves are known to have packs," Cassandra read. "These packs aren't exclusive to just werewolves. The packs that have power also bring in real wolves. They take care of them and they grow up bigger and more powerful than any common wolf. They have a strong bond with the pack leader but their strongest bond is with the one who rears them."

Cassandra picked up the parchment and showed the drawing to them. Anya saw a black wolf that was far bigger than the human it was attacking. Its eyes were red and it had long claws. Under the drawing she could read the words 'Hell hound'.

"That looks bigger than a car," she said as she finished looking at the drawing from the bed. "That's a proper monster."

She turned to look at Susan. Her friend was looking away from the parchment that Cassandra was holding up. "It's all right now," said Anya as she caressed her shoulder. "You're safe here."

Susan nodded but remained silent. The last thing she wanted was to remember that monster.

"You mean to say that we're facing a werewolf pack?" asked Carl still sitting near the door.

"It does look like it," answered Cassandra as she rolled up the piece of parchment. "What else can explain the wolf you saw?"

"But why?" asked Seth. "What did we do?"

"I don't think things these days need any reason," answered Tabitha as she picked up another book. "I don't think all of the things we went through were because we were at fault."

"We just seem to have the worst luck," said Seth as he sat down next to Anya on the bed. Eric was still sleeping soundly.

"Why would the pack attack Eric?" asked Carl, trying to keep his voice down. "Why would they trash his place, follow the girls, and send their pet wolf after us?"

"I don't know, Carl," Tabitha answered him. She looked directly into his eyes. She wanted him to calm down. "I don't know. They must be here because of some reason. From the things I've read, packs don't go looking for trouble. They are highly territorial and secretive."

"But why us?" asked Carl.

'None of this would have happened if David hadn't come to town and messed with my friends,' thought Anya as she looked at Eric, and then she understood.

"It's because of you," she said, getting up from the bed and looking at Carl.

The teenaged boy looked at her surprised. "I'm not saying that he did something wrong," Anya continued. She felt the rest of them giving her surprised looks as well. "David was the reason that Carl and Eric became werewolves. He did something to that cave wall and it infected Carl, and then it happened to Eric. Then he used them both. We defeated him, but Carl and Eric still had those powers."

"I still remember when they both turned into proper hairy werewolves on the night of the full moon when we fought David, but after that I've never watched them transform, even when there has been a full moon," said Anya as she looked at her friends. "They are here for Carl and Eric."

"Nice to know you're presenting us on a platter," snorted Carl. He rolled his eyes at her. *'How can she say his friends were in trouble because of him and Eric?'*

"She does have a point," said Tabitha as she looked at Carl. "Anya isn't trying to blame you for all of the trouble. Werewolves only live in packs and everything that has anything to do with them is highly controlled. It would make sense for them to come for you and Eric."

"To make us a part of their pack?" asked Carl. "There is no way I'm going to go and live my life in some cave up in the mountains."

"I'm not sure what they want," answered Tabitha. "They don't just take people into their pack, but the fact remains that they are here for you and I don't think they are going to go away easily."

"We'll fight them," said Anya in a determined voice, and Seth was impressed. "We'll fight them and force them to tell us what they want from Carl and what's wrong with Eric."

"Fighting a pack isn't easy," said Tabitha. "We don't even know how many of them there are."

"We do know that there's at least one big black wolf," said Seth. He looked at his friends. "How hard can it be to bring down a wolf?"

"You didn't see what we saw," said Susan. "Its eyes were looking into my soul. I couldn't breathe, much less stand there and fight it."

"She's right," said Carl, trying not to remember the wolf too clearly. "Even I wasn't sure if I could beat that thing. My mind kept telling me to run away as fast as I could."

"Then what do you propose we do?" asked Anya, sounding impatient. "We can't just sit here and hope that Eric feels better by himself and the pack will leave us alone."

"Nobody is saying that we shouldn't do anything," said Tabitha. She knew that Anya wanted to do something, but facing a pack of werewolves head on didn't feel like the right thing to do.

"We need to come up with a plan," said Cassandra. She turned to Tabitha. "You had a gun with silver bullets that you used to fight David, right?"

Tabitha nodded at her. "I still have it at home along with the silver dagger we used. You aren't saying that we should go on the attack?"

Cassandra shook her head. "No, but it's good to have something to fight with just in case."

"How are we going to contact them?" asked Anya. She looked at Carl who shook his head. The rest of her friends didn't have an answer either. Before she could say anything else they heard Eric waking up. The boy stretched his body and opened his eyes.

"Don't tell me I fainted again," he smiled weakly.

"It's not your fault," Anya smiled at him.

"Am I lying in David's bed?" he asked picking up his glasses from the side table.

"Yeah you are, dude," Seth laughed. "Congratulations!"

"Stop it." Anya lightly punched his shoulder. They had serious things to address.

Eric sat up on his bed and smelled something. The scent was similar to the one in his house the night someone broke in and messed up the place. But what was the scent doing in the room? It seemed to be coming from Carl and Susan. He could still sense their individual scents, but there was something else mixed in it. He knew something was wrong.

"So, what did I miss?" he asked his friends, knowing quite well the answer wouldn't be pleasant.

Nine

Anya wasn't sure what to do as she walked around in her room. With the swamp zombies she had felt more in control. She knew what she had to do and there was an end in sight. She knew about the curse and how it could be broken, but now she didn't know anything. She didn't know why the pack was after Carl and Eric. She didn't know what their agenda was. She felt helpless and didn't like it at all.

Susan had gone home to her mother and Lizzie. It wasn't easy. It took a lot of persuasion. She wanted to stay with Eric and Carl to make sure they remained safe. In the end she understood. She needed rest and she needed to calm down after the wolf incident. Cassandra and Seth were going to stay at Tabitha's along with Eric and Carl. All of the friends had decided that it wouldn't be safe to send them home. They could be used against them. Cassandra was also the one who had been followed. It was better for the friends to remain as close as possible, and two of them going out of town didn't feel safe.

"At least all of them are here," Anya said to herself as she sat down on her bed. Her parents were downstairs watching some film on TV. She had excused herself after dinner, saying that she had homework to do. Tabitha and Cassandra had said they would call her as soon as they found something from the books they had taken from David's house. "I just hope they find something," said Anya. She felt tired and found herself lying on her bed. She didn't know when she had closed her eyes and fallen sleep.

***

"It's good that Mom's out of town," said Carl as he sat down in Tabitha's living room. He picked up the mug of milk he had been drinking. "That way those werewolves can't get to her."

"Yes, that's good," said Eric as he looked out of the window. He was feeling fine. His eyes scanned the part of the street in front of him. He wasn't sure what they should do about the pack. His friends had told him everything when he woke up in David's house. Carl and Susan standing face-to-face with the black wolf was not a laughing matter. It meant that things were serious, that something was definitely wrong and they had to figure it out as soon as possible. He didn't want to remember what he had felt the night his house was ripped apart and his friends found him in a corner scared out of his mind.

He looked around the room. Carl was looking at the ceiling mug in hand, lost in thought. Cassandra and Tabitha were busy going through the books they had taken from David's house. They still hadn't found anything. Eric began to lose hope. He wondered if there was anything to be found. Seth was in the kitchen making some sandwiches for all of them.

Eric let out a sigh and turned to look outside of the window again. The only thing he could think of was what Anya had suggested. They would have to face the werewolf pack. They had to take action. Who knew how long it would take for the pack to attack them again? They had already been in his house and their wolf had threatened two of his friends already, not to mention they had their eyes on the girls.

"I'm no chef," said Seth as he came into the room holding a tray of chicken sandwiches. "But I don't think they are that bad."

He placed the tray on the table Cassandra and Tabitha had spread the books and notes on. He looked at the teenagers. "Isn't anyone hungry?" he asked, picking up a sandwich and sitting down at the table himself. He took a bite when no one answered.

"I think I found something," said Tabitha. She stood up and walked toward one of her bookshelves. The teenagers watched as she took out a book and walked back to the table. Carl got up from the couch and followed Eric toward her.

Tabitha opened her book and placed it on the table. It was in ancient Latin. "This adds into what's written in my book," she said pointing at a paragraph in one of the books she had taken from David.

"What?" asked Carl as he sat down at the table along with Eric. All of the teenagers were giving Tabitha their undivided attention.

"Carl was the first one David turned into a werewolf," said Tabitha as she addressed everyone around the table. "Then Eric was turned as well."

"We all know that," said Carl. He sounded impatient.

"Let her explain," said Eric as he placed a hand on his friend's shoulder.

Carl relaxed and looked apologetically at Tabitha. "I'm sorry."

Tabitha nodded. "The manner in which Carl and Eric were turned into werewolves was quite different from what's common. Usually werewolves are either born as such or they are bitten. However, Carl and Eric were made. David put the mark on them and that's why he was able to control them as well. But when Anya defeated him, his control over the two vanished. His control diminished. Only residual power remains in the boys and that's why," she looked at Carl and Eric. "You don't go full werewolf when it's the full moon."

"That's all good, for the lack of a better word," said Seth. "How is all of that connected to the big bad pack that's out to get them?"

"Again with the word 'them'!" said Carl. He was surprised to hear the anger in his voice. He didn't like the word. He didn't like the word *'Them'*. To him it sounded as if it was his and Eric's fault that they were all in trouble. "Would you rather Eric and I just go outside and call the pack to come and get us?" he added loudly while glaring at Seth.

"Whoa, Dude!" Seth exclaimed, raising his arms in surrender. He was clearly surprised at Carl's reaction.

"Nobody is blaming you or anyone else," said Tabitha as she looked at Carl. "You need to calm down."

Carl looked at her, but Tabitha didn't back down. The rest of the friends remained silent as the two teenagers kept looking at each other. Carl took a deep breath and relaxed. Tabitha smiled at him and addressed Seth's question. "The connection is that I'm sure the pack that has shown up here isn't very happy about what David did to Carl and Eric. Werewolves are very secretive, and two teenaged werewolves or whatever you guys are, probably doesn't look nice to them."

"So what do they want?" asked Eric. The question was still there. Yes, he and Carl weren't really werewolves, but was that their fault?

"I think they want to end the mistake," said Cassandra, and the friends looked at her. "It says here," she continued as she read a page from a book. "Those that aren't of natural birth are not of pure blood and thus, they need to be expelled."

"Expelled from where?" asked Eric as he pushed his glasses up on his nose. His eyes went to the page that Cassandra had read from. The text was in strange symbols. It was a very small paragraph. The rest of the page had drawings of werewolves on the borders.

"It can't be werewolf school," whispered Seth, and he looked down at his sandwiches when he realized that Eric and Carl had definitely heard him.

"I'm not sure," said Cassandra. "That's the only thing that's written here. I can't find anything else in the books I've read."

"I think what we do know does confirm that the werewolf pack is here because of what David did," said Tabitha as she closed the book in front of her.

"I don't like the whole 'not of pure blood' and 'need to be expelled' part of what Cassandra said," Eric told Tabitha. Carl sat silently next to him but Eric could sense that he was feeling uneasy.

"If they are looking for a fight, then I say we give them one," said Carl, his arms crossed in front of him. *'How I'm supposed to fight that huge wolf, I'm not sure.'*

"Can't we just talk to them?" asked Seth.

"Werewolf packs aren't known for their negotiation skills," answered Tabitha. "There are no instances where I've read about a pack agreeing to something that humans wanted or any other supernatural being. All I've read is about territorial wars. You stay away from them and they'll stay away from you."

"So we fight?" asked Seth. "We are going to face off against a werewolf pack this time?"

"I…I don't know," said Tabitha as she shook her head. "I don't know."

***

Anya felt the cold ground beneath her. *'What is that? Where am I?'* She opened her eyes and saw the night sky above her. She couldn't figure out what was happening. Just a few seconds ago she was in her bed. She got up onto her feet. She recognized her surroundings and her eyes rested upon Eric's house.

"What am I doing here?" she asked herself and then she saw herself standing on her right. "What the hell is happening?"

The other Anya didn't look at her. She just stood there looking at Eric's house. Anya looked to her left and saw herself standing there as well. *'There are two of me?'*

No, there was another one. Anya saw another *'clone'* of herself walking toward Eric's front door. She didn't wait to ring the doorbell. She took out a key from her pocket and opened the front door. The clones that were standing on her sides also walked toward the front door. A force seemed to push her forward too. The four of them were standing in Eric's house.

"Eric!" Anya called out. She had to warn her friend. But Eric didn't answer. The teenaged boy walked into the room. He just noticed the new arrivals and confusion spread across his face but it only took a second for it to be replaced by anger. "What are you doing here?" he growled. "Who are you?"

Anya heard herself laugh out loud. She didn't want to but she couldn't help herself. She laughed hard at the teenaged boy. "You have no right to ask me anything, you pathetic little being." Anya didn't know where the words had come from. She tried to shake her head at Eric to try and tell him that she had no control over what she was saying.

"You see these," Anya spoke again and the rest of her clones took a step toward Eric. "They are far better than you'll ever be."

Eric didn't wait for anything else. He gave a growl and jumped toward her. Anya yelled but no sound came out of her mouth. Instead, her clone tackled Eric and the teenaged boy hit the wall. "See?" said Anya, a smile spreading across her face as she watched the teenaged boy trying to get up onto his feet. He was hurt badly. "You can't even fight!"

Eric growled again and with extreme force he stood back up. "I give you points for trying," said Anya. "Aren't you supposed to be smart one? Can't you see that you have already lost?"

"Are you the one who followed my friends?" said Eric.

"Didn't I tell you already, dear boy," laughed Anya. "You don't have the right to ask me anything. You shouldn't even exist in my presence."

"Get off of your high horse, lady!" growled Eric.

"I would have ended you sooner but I want something from you," said Anya as she walked toward Eric. She could sense the anger coming from him. The boy had guts, but that wasn't enough to fight her.

Two of her clones stood beside Eric and grabbed his arms. The teenager tried to fight but fell to his knees. Anya grabbed him by the chin and made him look directly into her eyes. "I need to know what that vampire did to you and how."

"Get away from me!"

"Now, now, there's no need to be feisty." Anya tightened her grip on Eric and the teenager screamed in pain.

Anya heard herself scream. She opened her eyes. She was back in her bed. The lights were out. She tried to bring her breathing back to normal. She heard footsteps and her parents ran into the room.

"Honey, what's wrong?" asked her mother. Anya felt the woman embrace her tightly. Her father turned on the lights of the room.

"I'm…I don't know," answered Anya. Everything was still blurry to her. Why was she at Eric's? Why were there three of her? How did she get back in her bed?

"Anya, sweetie," said her mother kindly as she brushed the hair away from her forehead. Her dad sat on the bed next to her mother, giving her a worried look.

"I'm fine, guys," Anya smiled. "It was a nightmare. I'm sorry."

"It's all right, dear," her mom gave her another tight hug and stood up with her father.

"Goodnight," said her dad. He bent down and kissed her on the forehead.

"I'm fine, guys," said Anya as she rolled her eyes and smiled. "There's no point in being all lovey-dovey."

"I'll keep the door open just a little bit," her mom smiled at her as she turned off the lights.

"Thanks," said Anya and she got comfortable in her bed. She smiled again at her parents and watched them walk away. She heard them talking to each other as they went to their room.

"What's wrong with you?" she asked herself looking at the ceiling. It wasn't the first time she had such an experience. She still remembered when she had walked to the frozen swamp and brought the zombies back to life.

'But that was a dream,' she thought to herself. *'Or was it?'*

She touched her forehead. Nothing made sense to her. What did she just see? Why would she attack Eric like that? It felt so real to her. She could still feel the sense of power inside of her when she stood in front of Eric. She knew that he would never be able to fight her. She had the upper hand. She was far more powerful than anything he had ever faced.

"But it wasn't me," said Anya. "That wasn't me!"

She would never hurt any of her friends like that. She would never feel so proud and feel that all humans were insects and that there was no point in their existence.

Ten

"So they want to kill Eric and Carl?" asked Susan as the friends got onto the school bus. The teenagers had just finished telling her and Anya about what they read from the books last night.

"I guess that's what the paragraph was hinting at," said Anya as they sat down in their usual seats inside of the bus. "No offense," she added looking at Carl.

"None taken," he answered. He was calmer than last night. He had accepted that staying angry wasn't going to help anyone.

Anya didn't look at Eric. She couldn't after the dream she had last night. She hadn't told her friends about it. She wasn't sure how she could even begin to tell them. She remembered the suspicious looks they had given her when she told them about the dream she had in which she had gone to the frozen swamp and brought the zombies to life. She didn't want to go through the experience again.

"It's weird how our normal lives go on," said Seth as he put his arm around Anya.

"I know what you mean," said Eric. "We have all of these supernatural things to deal with but still have to make time for high school."

"I vote that we leave high school," laughed Seth. He then turned to Anya. "I missed you last night."

"You miss me almost every time," Anya rolled her eyes at him.

"Not that much," he faked sounding hurt. "I have a life, you know."

"This time around we have to deal with an angry werewolf pack and make sure the Halloween party doesn't face any trouble," said Susan as she brushed a strand of her blonde hair away from her face.

"Yes, the Halloween party," said Tabitha as she looked at Susan. "It's this weekend. We have to make sure we have everything ready by Friday."

"What about our costumes?" asked Susan. "What are you going to be, Cassie?"

Anya tuned out of the conversation before Cassandra could answer. Only Susan could talk about something as normal as a Halloween party when there was a threat of a werewolf pack. Anya liked that about her. When the circumstances demanded it, Susan always found a bright side. She was also quite good at changing a conversation's topic to something more light-hearted. Ever since they were young, Susan would be the one who didn't like the head-on approach. Anya, on the other hand, liked dealing with things directly, evident by the suggestion she had given last night about fighting the pack. But now she felt differently. It was better to look at all of their options. *'If there are any options,'* she thought as she looked out of the bus.

***

"Yes, I think it looks lovely," said Tabitha, her hands on her hips. She looked proudly at the basketball court. Everything was almost ready. The caterer would bring the food Saturday morning and they just had to figure out where to hang the cobweb that Cassandra had made.

Anya was impressed. The court had never looked so good. Gravestones and plastic pumpkin heads lined the walls which were now covered in black cloth with cut-outs of small ghosts on them. The bats were hung from the ceiling, and Carl and Eric were following Susan's directions as she told them where to put the tables.

"The center will be the dancing table," said Susan. "It's better if you place the table a little more to the right over there."

"Yes, boss," Carl rolled his eyes at her as the two boys put the table where she wanted.

Susan smiled at them. "There are still four more that you have to bring inside."

Anya looked at Seth. He was helping some art students place cardboard bats on the back of the chairs. Most of the teenagers had gone home in order to prepare their costumes for the party. Seth looked at her and smiled. Anya waved at him from the bleachers. There was no way she would be getting up and lending a hand. Creative stuff wasn't her strong suit. She looked at

Cassandra who was putting glitter on the cobweb she had made. It was quite big and looked amazing. Anya was impressed by the work her friend had done. All of the ropes were tied perfectly together and it actually looked like a cobweb.

She felt comfortable watching her friends work. For just a few minutes they could get away from all of the paranormal stuff and pay attention to being normal high school teenagers. But deep down Anya knew it was all an illusion, a distraction. Sooner or later they would have to go back to the world they couldn't tell anyone else about.

Anya watched Cecelia walk toward Tabitha. "Everything looks ready."

Tabitha smiled at the girl. "Yes, thank you for helping out."

"No, no, there's no need to say thanks," Cecelia answered, feeling embarrassed. "Anyway, I have to go home now."

"Of course," said Tabitha. She looked at the other teenagers as well. "I don't want to keep anyone here longer than necessary. Those who have to go home or somewhere else can go."

"Finally, freedom!" said Seth as he dusted some glitter off of his hands.

"Not you two," said Susan as she looked at Carl and Eric. "You still need to place the tables."

The two boys mumbled to each other and walked out of the court to get the tables that were outside. The rest of the teenagers said their goodbyes and walked out as well.

"Anya, any idea where we should put this?" Tabitha asked as she held up the cobweb with Cassandra.

Anya shrugged. *'How am I supposed to know?'*

"We should put it where everyone can see it," said Susan as she walked toward the girls.

"How about over there?" Tabitha pointed at the ceiling above the dancing area. "Dancing under the cobweb would look nice."

Anya saw the three girls nod at each other, and Seth walked toward them with a ladder. Anya took out her cell phone to know the time when she heard it. Her heart felt as if it had stopped beating and her vision became blurry. She tried to focus on her friends. They weren't moving either. Cassandra and Tabitha were still holding the cobweb with Susan, and Seth was holding the ladder. None of them said a word or moved a muscle as they looked at each other. The wolf howl seemed to have paralyzed them all.

'Move, Anya,' she told herself as she tried to muster all of her willpower. *'Move! Now!'*

She heard the doors of the basketball court open and Carl and Eric ran inside. Eric ran toward Anya while Carl ran toward the rest of their friends. Anya felt the warm touch of Eric's hand on her shoulder and then she felt him help her onto her feet. "Come on," he said in a calm voice and led her down the bleachers.

"They are here?" asked Tabitha, her eyes wide.

"Seems so," answered Carl not taking his eyes off of the entrance.

"This…this can't be happening," said Susan as she wrapped her arms around herself. Anya walked toward her and put her hand on her shoulder. "What are we going to do?" Anya asked looking at Eric and Tabitha.

"We need to get you all out of here," he answered.

"What?" asked Anya loudly. "Are you being serious? You want us to leave you alone with them?"

"They want me and Carl," said Eric. He didn't have time to argue with Anya. "You don't have anything to do with any of this."

"How are you going to deal with them?" she asked. Seth walked over and stood next to her, ready to come between them if she hit Eric.

Before Eric could answer, there was another wolf howl, and Susan grabbed Anya's arm. Cassandra and Tabitha came closer and Eric followed Carl toward the entrance.

"They can't be serious!" said Anya as she looked at the two teenagers walking away. She turned to Seth. "We have to do something!"

"My locker!" said Tabitha and the teenagers looked at her with questioning looks. Tabitha opened her mouth to say something but stopped. She took out a piece of paper from her pocket along with a pen. She wrote something down and showed it to her friends.

Anya read her note. *They can hear us talking. Gun in my locker.*

'She brought a gun to school!' thought Anya. *'Isn't there any kind of security here?'*

Eric wanted to say something and Susan bent down to get a notepad from her bag. She handed it to Eric along with a pen. *I'll go get it*, Eric wrote. *You get out.*

Anya shook her head at the boy. He didn't need her to write down anything to understand what she meant. Carl didn't wait any longer and started to walk toward the entrance, but then he stopped. Anya saw him take a step back from the door. Eric growled and motioned for his friends to stay behind him. The lights dimmed and Susan screamed.

"Sshhhh," said Anya as she felt her tighten the grip on her arm. She could hear her heart beating through her chest. *'Are they playing with us?'*

The door opened and Anya saw something big and furry come inside. She knew it was the same wolf that Susan and Carl had seen yesterday. She could hear the growls coming from the animal. She dared not look at its eyes. She saw Seth walk in front of her. Tabitha and Cassandra were standing on her right. Eric and Carl were snarling at the wolf. There was no way they were going to let the wolf hurt their friends.

"Seth!" said Eric, not taking his eyes off of the wolf as it paced in front of them, waiting for an opportunity to strike. "Take them and go! Just go!"

"But…" Anya tried to say something, but Seth and Susan grabbed her arms and led her toward the exit. "We need to go!" said Seth as he led the girls out of the basketball court.

Anya looked back at Eric and Carl standing in front of the wolf and then she found herself in the corridor away from the boys. "Seth, we can't just leave them," she said as Seth pulled her down the corridor. Susan, Tabitha and Cassandra were behind them.

"I know," said Seth. He turned to look at Tabitha. The girl understood. Anya and the rest of them followed her down the corridor. The lights were dimmed. Anya never would have guessed high school could be so scary at night. All that Anya could hear were their hurried footsteps as they went down the corridor toward Tabitha's locker. She couldn't hear anything from the basketball court. She didn't know how Carl and Eric were doing and it was killing her inside.

"We should call the police," said Cassandra. "Calling someone to the school will make them leave us alone."

"If the pack doesn't kill them all," said Seth as they ran. "Didn't we just watch something on TV where the kids call the police and say they were awaiting a prank call?"

"That was a show," said Cassandra. "We have to try. We have to make a call…" She stopped in mid sentence. "Did you hear that?"

The teenagers stopped. Seth was in the front and he pushed Anya behind him with the rest of the girls. They all heard it. It was a growl. "Is it here?" whispered Susan.

"Does it mean Eric and Carl are?" Anya couldn't say the word. *'They are all right! They are all right!'*

They heard another growl. It was closer than the last one. Tabitha's locker was just around the corner. "Run! Now!" yelled Seth, and they all ran down the corridor. All they had to do was turn right, open Tabitha's locker, and get the gun.

And then it happened. Anya didn't have time to completely comprehend what was happening to them. It all happened so fast. The wolf came out of a classroom on their left. It pushed Seth backward and he fell to the ground. Susan screamed. Cassandra and Tabitha yelled, and Anya felt something heavy hit her hard right in the chest.

"Anya!" a voice was calling her from far away. "Anya!"

Her vision became clear and she felt someone pulling her to her feet. Then everything came back to her in a rush. Seth, Cassandra, and Susan were in front of her but between them was the big black wolf. It was snarling at her three friends and snapping its teeth.

"Anya, come on!" Tabitha's voice pierced her ears. Without wasting another minute, Anya got up and came back to her senses.

Her friends were separated. Carl and Eric were on the basketball court probably wounded because the same wolf was now standing between her and three of her friends.

"GO!" Seth yelled at her. "GO!"

Tabitha pushed her away from her friends and they ran down the corridor. "We need that gun, Tabitha! We need that gun now," said Anya as she ran behind her.

If Eric and Carl weren't able to defeat the wolf, then Seth, Susan, and Cassandra didn't have a chance.

Tabitha stopped in front of her locker and started to unlock it. Anya kept looking behind her back. The wolf could be on them any second now. Tabitha opened the locker and took out her gun. Anya recognized it. It was the same gun she had brought to fight David in the cave.

"Here," said Tabitha, and she handed Anya the silver dagger. It felt warm in her grip. It was as if it recognized her touch.

"Let's go," said Tabitha as she tightly gripped the gun. Anya nodded and they both ran back to where they had left Seth and the others.

"Where are they?" asked Anya. There was no one in the corridor. "Where are they?"

"Stay calm," said Tabitha. "They couldn't have just left."

And then they heard a girl scream. "Where?" asked Anya.

"Upstairs," Tabitha answered.

Without saying anything else, Anya ran toward the stairs. It could be someone calling for help, or worse, it could be one of her friends in grave danger. She had to do something. She felt helpless in the situation. "Tabitha, come on," she said as she reached the stairs, but there was no answer. "Tabitha?" She turned around. Tabitha wasn't there. She was alone. *'Oh, Great!'*

Eleven

Anya tried to calm herself as she began to climb up the stairs. *'Stay calm,'* she kept telling herself. *'Stay calm.'*

She gripped the dagger tightly, ready to strike at any given moment. The scream she had heard didn't sound familiar, but she had to go and check it out. The scream told her there was someone she could help. The upstairs floor held the science labs. She tried to step as lightly as possible but even then she could hear her footsteps, and her heartbeat sounded like a marching band's drum.

She reached the door of the first lab. She took a deep breath, brought the dagger in front of her, and opened the door. The sound of the door opening seemed to resonate along the corridor. "He…Hello?" she asked. She dared not step inside. If someone needed her help, they would surely run toward her, right? She closed the door and walked toward the next lab. She tried opening the door but it was locked.

"Is someone inside?" she asked knocking on the door. "I'm here to help…"

"Oh, thank God!" A woman ran toward the door and unlocked it. "Thank God!"

"Keep your voice down," said Anya as the woman hugged her.

"You…you don't look like the police," said the woman, and Anya sensed a hint of disappointment.

"That's because I'm not the police," said Anya as she looked at the woman. She had a beautiful face and blonde hair. She was wearing a leather outfit and heels. "Who are you? What are you doing here?"

"Henry," answered the woman. "I was with Henry."

Henry was the name of the janitor. "Is he here?" asked Anya as she looked inside the lab.

"No," the woman shook her head. "He told me to lock myself in while he called for help when that…that wolf appeared. Have you seen it?"

Anya nodded. She felt confident now. The realization that she had someone helpless to protect allowed her to ignore her own fear. "We have to get you out of here…uh?"

"Luna," the woman answered. "Luna Salvaje."

"My name is Anya," the teenager told the woman. *'Henry seems to have hit the jackpot.'*

"Okay, Luna," Anya looked to make sure the corridor was clear. "You have to do everything I tell you."

Luna nodded and followed Anya back toward the stairs. She had to get the woman out of there and then return for her friends. Luna took off her heels as not to make noise, and Anya led her down the stairs. She hoped that Henry was able to call for help.

"What is a wolf doing here anyway?" asked Luna. "It was so big!"

"I don't know," Anya answered as the two walked down the stairs.

"Why haven't you called the police yet?" Luna asked. "You have a cell phone, right?"

Anya nodded. How could she tell her why she hadn't called the police? Come to think of it, not calling the police because of a TV show they had watched didn't make sense now.

They reached the bottom of the stairs. "I'll call them now," said Anya and she took out her cell phone. She was about to dial the police when Luna screamed. Anya saw the wolf run toward them and before any of them could react, it jumped and pinned Luna to the ground. The woman screamed as she looked into its red eyes. It tried to hit Anya with its claws but she backed away. She hit the wall and the cell phone dropped from her hand. The wolf grabbed Luna by the leg and dragged her away.

"Stop!" Anya yelled over the terrified screams of the woman, and then she was alone in the corridor again. The teenager tried to breathe. *'This is all wrong! This is all wrong!'*

She looked around for her cell phone. She bent down to pick it up when she heard footsteps…human footsteps. She got up and looked in front of her. A tall man was walking toward her. He was wearing a long coat and sunglasses. "Stay back!" said Anya as she pointed the dagger at the man. "I mean it!"

The man didn't stop. Anya lifted her arm to strike at him but he was too fast. She felt his hand slap her across the face and she fell to the ground.

***

"So these are our little observation subjects." Anya could hear a woman talking, but the voice seemed to be coming from far away. Her entire body hurt and she tasted something in her mouth. *'Blood?'*

"Where are the rest?" asked a man's voice. He seemed unhappy. "I thought you said you had everything under control. You wanted to act sooner."

"Give it a rest," said the woman. "I wanted to act sooner because I was getting bored with all of the waiting around. And who cares if we didn't get all of them."

"They could bring someone here," said the man.

"Oh, please," said the woman. "As if anyone would believe teenagers these days, and besides, I've already alerted the authorities about Halloween prank callers."

Anya opened her eyes. She was inside of the basketball court. She tried to move her arms but they were tied up. She tried to move her body but couldn't. She was tied to a chair.

"She's waking up," the woman said sweetly.

"Leave her alone." Anya heard Eric voice. *'He's alive!'* Anya felt some life come into her body.

"Oh, shut up!" The woman was clearly irritated. She grabbed Anya by the chin and lifted her head up.

"Luna!" exclaimed Anya as she saw the smiling woman.

The woman gave out a mad laugh. "Took you long enough!"

Anya didn't say anything. Of course the woman she had helped was one of the bad guys. She was stupid to have fallen for such a cheap trick.

"Don't stress yourself," said the woman. "You were only trying to help a defenseless woman."

"Where are the rest of my friends?" asked Anya.

The woman rolled her eyes. "What is with you teenagers and asking questions? You don't have the right to ask me anything, you pathetic excuse for a human being."

The words and the attitude struck Anya. She remembered it from her dream. She was the woman who had tortured Eric in his home and made him scared. Anya tried to look around her. Eric was tied to a chair on her right. Carl was on her left but he was unconscious. The tall man Anya had just seen was looking at him with mild interest.

She didn't see the rest of her friends. She didn't see the wolf either. She hoped they all made it out alive. She needed to buy some time for her friends to call the police and send help.

"What do you want from us?" asked Anya.

"From you?" Luna asked her. "Are you serious? Why would I want anything from you?"

"Then why are you here?" Anya asked another question. She didn't like Luna's attitude. She didn't like how proud she was being.

"Damn, these kids don't listen," she said turning to address the man. He didn't answer. He stopped looking at Carl and stood up. He walked toward Anya and she could hear her heart beat faster. He bent down and looked directly into her eyes. Anya wished he had his sunglasses on.

"You remember encountering a male vampire, yes?" he asked. There was calmness in his voice but Anya knew he would hurt her if she didn't answer.

"Get away from her," said Eric, and Luna slapped him across the face.

"Yes," answered Anya, trying to sound as brave as she could. "What's it got to do with you?"

"I take it you already know who we are," said the man as he stood up straight.

"You are a pack of werewolves," said Anya. "Though I thought there would be more of you. Where's your pet wolf?"

"Hold your tongue!" Luna said with a snap.

The man held up his hand to stop her from hitting Anya. "It's all right," he said looking at the teenager.

"We werewolves are very possessive when it comes to our kind," said the man. "We don't take too kindly to those who like to treat our gifts as a science experiment."

"So he made Carl and Eric his pet werewolves," said Anya. She wasn't going to give away his name. "What's their fault in all of this? The vampire is gone and they don't have their full powers anymore."

"But they still have some of it," said the man. "And the pack isn't happy about two new experiments running around unobserved."

Anya still wasn't sure about what they wanted to do with Carl and Eric. Were they going to kill them?

"So observe them," said Anya. "You've been following us for a few days now and you even broke into Eric's house. What more do you want to do?"

"I'm very interested in knowing why a vampire came to this place," said the man as he took out a deck of cards and began to shuffle them. "Do you have any idea?"

"No," answered Anya confidently. "No, I don't."

"I think you are lying," said the man as he continued to shuffle his cards. "Your heartbeat is giving you away."

The man walked closer to Anya. "We've already asked Eric. He didn't know anything. In the end, all we discovered was that a vampire named David turned him into a werewolf after Carl and Eric was left with a nightmare alone in his house."

"You see?" continued the man as he pocketed the cards and extended his arm. Anya could see the nails grow in front of her eyes. They were sharp. "It's easy for you to tell us the truth instead of us extracting it from you with fear."

"But it's more fun that way," laughed Luna. Anya looked at her angrily. She hated her very existence.

"They are still here," said the man and he smelled the air. He looked angrily at Luna.

'Seth and the others are still here?' thought Anya and her heart sank. They should have run when they had the chance.

"Fine," she said rolling her eyes. "Fine!"

She began to unzip her leather jacket. *'What's that got to do with getting her friends?'* Anya thought as she looked at Luna dropping the jacket onto the floor, and she turned around. Anya noticed a tattoo of three intertwined wolves on Luna's back. Luna bent down and the tattoos began to move. Anya watched wide-eyed as the tattoos began to protrude from her back, and in a few seconds three large black wolves stood around Luna, snapping their jaws at each other.

"Now, now," said Luna as she petted the wolves. "We have some work to do."

She turned to face the man. He nodded at her. Luna put on her jacket and gave a laugh. "I'll see you soon," she winked at Anya and ran out of the basketball court with her three wolves.

Anya turned to look at the man but he was gone. Not wasting any more time, she turned to Eric. "We need to get out of here!" she said.

"I know," he answered back. "But the ropes are too tight," he added trying to break free. "How's Carl?"

"He's out cold," said Anya as she looked at the boy. "Carl! Carl!"

The teenager stirred a bit. "Someone is coming," said Anya as she heard footsteps. The doors of the court opened and Anya stopped herself from screaming Seth's name. He had his finger in front of his mouth, telling her to keep quiet. He kissed Anya and began to cut the ropes with a silver dagger.

"How?" Anya asked. She was so happy to see him.

"No time for that now," he answered. Anya felt the ropes around her loosen, and Seth began to untie Eric.

"Where did you get the dagger?" asked Anya as she threw the ropes away from her. "I thought they had it."

"It was lying on the ground in the corridor," answered Seth as he hurriedly worked on cutting Eric loose. "They must not have been able to touch it."

Anya ran toward Carl and tried to wake him up. "Carl," she said. He didn't answer. She slapped him hard across his face and he opened his eyes. "What? Anya? Where?"

Seth ran toward him and began to cut the ropes. Anya gave Eric a tight hug. "I'm so glad you are all right."

Eric smiled at her and then they heard a gunshot. Anya's heart skipped a beat.

"Tabitha and the others are okay, right?" she asked Seth.

"They should be," he answered as he cut the last of Carl's ropes. "But I'm not happy to hear that gunshot."

Eric helped Carl onto his feet. "I can manage," said Carl, but he was too weak to stand on his own.

"What did they do to him?" Anya asked.

"They tried to make him talk," answered Eric as he helped Carl. "They were asking about David and why he had come to this place."

"Sorry to break the little David talk, but we need to go now," said Seth. The others nodded and ran toward the exit. They were almost there when a figure suddenly came in front of them.

The tall man looked at the teenagers and gave a small laugh. "You seriously think I will let you go away?"

Anya grabbed hold of Carl as Eric and Seth stood in front of them.

"Seeing your little display of heroism really warmed my heart," he said as he looked at Seth. "Humans are capable of wonderful things when the lives of their friends are in danger."

'He was watching us the entire time,' thought Anya as she tried to keep Carl on his feet.

"But you won't be able to leave here until I say so," said the man, and his eyes turned red.

Eric growled at him, and Seth aimed his silver dagger.

The man spoke with a voice that sent chills through Anya's body. She felt the air around her become heavy. The man's presence was enough to strike fear in her heart. "You have no idea what you are up against, do you?" he growled.

Twelve

"Come out, come out, from wherever you are!" Luna laughed as she walked along the second floor. She didn't like the smell of chemicals. It messed up her senses. The teenagers had been able to evade her before. A black haired girl had thrown some kind of vile smelling chemical at one of her wolves when it had three of her friends trapped in a classroom. She wanted to get her hands on that black haired girl. She wanted to rip her limb from limb. She saw what her wolves saw, she felt what they felt, and she smelled what they smelled, and she wanted her revenge for having to smell such a disgusting liquid.

Her wolves were following her as her heels made clicking sounds on the floor. She liked the sound of her heels filling out the silence around her. Through experience she realized that the clicking noise struck fear in the heart of her prey. The teenagers were reeking of fear and she found it quite delicious. She didn't like being scolded by her partner. She will have those pathetic teenagers bowing for mercy in front of her. But she won't show mercy. It would be a waste to show mercy to such insignificant souls. No, she will allow her wolves to play with them. She liked watching her three wolves play. They liked to bite the prey, make it bleed, and see how long it would survive. She enjoyed their yells, asking her to kill them.

She caught a scent. It was one of the girls, the one who was wearing a hood. She was alone in the janitor's closet, but what was she doing there alone? Of course it was a trap! She couldn't even hear a heartbeat come from behind the door. "Do you think I'm stupid?" Luna yelled.

"Truth be told? Yes," said Tabitha.

Luna turned around and saw the black haired girl standing behind her. She was holding a flask full of some type of chemical. Before her wolves could attack, the girl dropped the flask. There was a blinding light and a strong unpleasant smell. Luna heard her wolves whine. She could sense their anger. "You little bitch!" Luna yelled. She tried to get the vision back in her eyes. She swiped in the direction the girl was standing, but all she felt was air beneath her claws. She sensed the blonde standing behind her. She turned around. Her wolves were confused and angry. She saw the blonde girl drop a flask onto the floor as well. It broke open and again she was hit by blinding light. Her wolves started to whimper. They didn't like it. She took off her jacket.

"Get back inside!" she ordered, and the wolves began to go into her body until only a tattoo was left. "I don't need my wolves to bring down you insects."

'WHAM!'

She felt something heavy hit the back of her head and she fell to the floor. She was disoriented. She could see, but she couldn't hear or smell properly.

"That went well," said Cassandra as she dropped the iron stool she had used to hit Luna.

"Good thing you both know your chemistry," said Susan. She smiled and ran to join her friends.

"You're the one who came up with the idea of exploding silver nitrate," said Tabitha as she looked at Susan. "It totally worked!"

"Let's go back to the others," said Cassandra.

"Yes, Seth would have freed them by now…AAAHHHHH!" Susan screamed as Luna grabbed her by the ankle, and she dropped onto the ground. Before she could react, Luna was on top of her, her eyes glowing red, her fangs out. "Such a shame to kill a blonde," she said and she raised her arm to strike Susan.

'BANG!'

Luna dropped on top of Susan. Cassandra bent down and helped her friend get away from the woman. They both looked at Tabitha who still had her gun aimed at Luna's motionless body.

***

"Seth!" Anya screamed as she saw him being hit by the man. Seth flew into the air and hit the ground five feet away.

Carl pushed himself away from Anya and joined Eric. "See to Seth," he growled. Anya nodded and ran toward him.

Eric jumped into the air and his leg came down on the man, but before it could make contact he grabbed the leg and spun Eric into Carl. Both of them hit the wall. "You two are weak," said the man. "You aren't even real werewolves. You are mistakes that need to end."

"We won't give up!" yelled Carl as he stood on his feet.

"But one of you already has," laughed the man. Carl and Anya looked at Eric. He was finding it difficult to breathe.

"What have you done to him?" demanded Carl.

"Me?" asked the man. "It's his own body that's rejecting your David's gift. You defeated the vampire and his control was lost. Both of you were his creations and now one of you is expiring."

Anya bent down to look at Seth. *'Yes, he's breathing.'*

"It's only natural for this to happen," said the man as he took a step toward Carl and Eric. "Nature likes things to be in balance. David messed with the balance and now nature is setting itself right."

"I won't forgive you for this," said Carl. He could sense the life ebbing away from Eric as he coughed on the floor, unable to get up.

"You aren't in the position to forgive anyone," the man laughed, and with incredible speed he grabbed Carl by the throat and lifted him into the air. "You see? You can't even put up a proper fight. I still can't believe a vampire would have come to this town for a useless lot like you."

"Leave him alone!" yelled Anya as she stood next to Seth. The boy was unconscious on the floor. Anya looked at the man, the silver dagger in her hand.

"Not you again," the man smiled at her. "Luna was right. I should stop being nice to your species. It doesn't suit you."

"I said let him go!" said Anya and she took a step toward the man. She didn't know where her power was coming from but the man seemed to have sensed something.

"Anya…No…" Carl tried to speak.

The man ignored him. There was a sound of a bone breaking and the man threw Carl onto the ground. Anya didn't break eye contact with him as she walked toward him. She tightened the grip on the dagger.

"What do we have here?" the man was interested in Anya. He seemed to be looking at her differently now. It was as if he had found a puzzle he wanted to complete as soon as possible. "Who would have thought?" he said to himself amused as they both stood a few inches away from each other.

"He came here for me," said Anya as she looked into the man's red eyes. She wasn't afraid of him anymore. She couldn't be, not when her friends were in danger.

The man touched Anya's face with his right hand and took in her scent. "Extraordinary!" he exclaimed as he looked at her as a scientist would his favorite test subject. But then his expression changed. He seemed to have realized something.

"Such a waste," he said, and before Anya could lift the dagger to strike him, he grabbed her by the throat. She felt the dagger slip from her hand and fall to the floor.

"Tsk, tsk," he said, looking at the struggling teenager. "In the end it doesn't matter."

Anya felt his grip tighten around her neck. In a few seconds her windpipe would break and she would be dead. She tried to pull his hand away but it was no use. He was too strong. Her vision blurred. Darkness was calling her.

"RRAAAWWRRR!!!"

The man gave a roar that seemed to shake the building they were in. Anya felt the grip loosen and she fell to the ground. She coughed trying to breathe.

She looked up. The man was in pain. He was in tremendous pain. She saw Eric standing behind the man. The silver dagger in his hand was covered in black blood.

"How?" he asked looking at him.

"I guess the gift took," Eric answered with a smile. He brought the dagger down onto the man again, but he was too quick. The man dodged and started to back off toward the exit.

His eyes went from Anya to Eric in quick succession. Anya saw him smile at them. "Come back here!" yelled Eric as he ran toward the man but he was already gone.

"Eric, leave him," said Anya as life started to come into her body. "Leave him!"

"Are you all right?" Eric asked, helping her onto her feet.

"I'm fine," answered Anya. "Carl," she pointed at him. "I heard something break."

Eric nodded and ran toward his friend. The doors of the basketball court opened. *'Not again,'* thought Anya but, then her face lit up as she was tightly embraced by Susan.

Epilogue

"Let me take a picture, let me take a picture!"

"Moooommmm!" Anya felt embarrassed as her mother aimed the camera at her. Her father was standing behind her, ready to drive Anya and her friends to the Halloween party.

Anya smiled at the camera and posed in her witch costume. She knew it wasn't very original, but she didn't have time for a proper costume. She was just glad that she and her friends were safe and sound after the werewolf pack incident. Carl was alive. He was still healing from his broken back, but other than that he was in the Halloween mood. Somehow he had found the time to dress up as a pirate. All of them suspected it had something to do with his mother being involved in the preparations, but no one said a word.

Eric hadn't felt ill since the incident. He felt more energetic. He was dressing up as an undead nerd for the party. Of course, it was evident that he had given up on the whole thing. All he had to do was wear his normal clothes and make his face look white like a zombie's. The furniture of his house had been replaced. He didn't share with the group what he told his parents.

Seth had a slight back pain after his fight with a werewolf but he was feeling quite good about it. He kept boasting about how he had been able to stand up to two werewolves in one night. Anya was impressed to see how much he was willing to sacrifice to make sure his friends were safe…that she was safe.

"We're taking pictures?" asked Susan as she walked down the stairs into the living room wearing her fairy costume.

"Yes we are," smiled Anya's mother as she aimed the camera at her.

"Okay," Susan smiled and posed in her green fairy suit complete with wings and a wand. Her mom had been saving it for her ever since she heard they were having a party.

Cassandra and Tabitha came down the stairs as well. Cassandra was dressed as an assassin. It meant that she was able to keep her face covered while walking around with a plastic dagger in her hand. Tabitha was dressed as a business woman who was also a vampire. She too didn't have much time to think of a costume. She had been busy fixing the damage that had been done during their little fight in the basketball court and making sure that everything went well at the party.

"All of you come here so I can take a group picture," said Anya's mother, and the girls gathered around Anya. They smiled as the camera clicked and took the picture.

"Let's go, ladies," said Anya's father as the girls thanked Anya's mother, who blushed, and they all walked out of the house.

"Stay on the lookout for wolves," said her mother as she walked out of the house as well.

"We will," Anya smiled at her. None of her friends had told anyone about any wolf attack. It was Henry who reported to the police about seeing a wolf and then fainting and some people had heard howling from inside of the school as well. Anya and her friends were long gone before the police arrived. As far as the school was concerned, they were more worried about silver nitrate spillage outside of the labs.

Anya looked at her surroundings. Every house was well decorated for Halloween. Children were laughing. She wished everything would remain normal but she knew it never would. She remembered how the man had smiled at her and Eric when he ran away. She knew he would be back. There were no reports about the police finding a woman's body either. It meant that Luna had escaped as well.

"Come on, Anya," said Susan. She was already in the car with the rest of the girls. "Tabitha is saying that the boys just texted her. They are on their way to the party too."

Anya nodded at her. "Coming!" and she went to join her friends in the car, looking forward to enjoying the Halloween party just like any normal teenager.

This print book is available in ebook form from the following

Amazon Kindle Stores
Barnes & Noble
Apple iBookstores
Kobo ebooks
Google Play
Sony Reader Store
All Romance ebooks
Bookstrand
Coffeetime Romance

www.ingramcontent.com/pod-product-compliance
Lightning Source LLC
LaVergne TN
LVHW020528100826
845148LV00010B/1379

* 9 7 8 1 6 1 8 4 5 2 4 5 0 *